The Shadow Idol

A.C. Boler

Published by Clink Street Publishing 2023

Copyright © 2023

First edition.

ISBN:
978-1-915785-09-1 - paperback
978-1-915785-10-7 - ebook

This above all, to thine own self be true

Hamlet, William Shakespeare

PROLOGUE

Rue Saint-Paul, Paris – June 20th, 1970, 2 a.m.

The road to freedom is a path well-travelled by rogues, poets and painters who once sought solace and safety in this great city.

An exotic scent of Moroccan sandalwood spiralled up from a burning incense stick and drifted through the cloying summer heat of the Marais apartment. White muslin drapes blew in and out of the open French windows with a gentle ease as if the city were taking sultry nocturnal breaths. Notebooks, filled with scrawled lines of erratic poetry, were scattered across the parquet floor and an old leather-bound journal lay open on the coffee table.

Standing at the Baroque fireplace was a twenty-seven-year-old man, his weight resting on his left hip. Closing his eyes, he dragged his fingers down his bearded face which had aged him beyond his years. Gone was the classical beauty of Michelangelo's David; the carved jawline and curling flaxen hair of his youth had long since faded. All that remained was the lost image of a man who, for a few wild years, had held the world in his hands like a firecracker.

'Joe, honey,' the languid voice of a young woman floated across the living room from where she reclined on a velvet chaise longue. 'Put some music on, it's as quiet as death in here tonight.'

Wandering over to the record player, Joe placed the needle into the groove of a vinyl LP. An expectant crackle sprang from the speakers as "Into The Night" by The Gracious Dawn filled the apartment with the counter-culture soundtrack of the 1960s. He traced his thumb across the album sleeve, emblazoned with the image of four young men advancing out of the shadows of anonymity into the spotlight of the world, and took a sharp intake of breath.

With a trembling hand, he raised a bottle of whiskey to his lips and drank hard, only pausing when his eyes fell to a small bag of white powder on the coffee table. Snatching the bag, he drew out two elongated lines and, without hesitation, inhaled them both in quick succession.

'Take it easy, Joe,' Angela said, slurring her words. 'You know what happened last time.'

The burning high slithered through his veins, a demonic serpent writhing through the wreckage of his frame. He staggered back across the room, collapsed onto an armchair and was unconscious before his head hit the cushion. Two hours later, the sound of his suffocating breaths shook Angela Jackson from her turbulent dreams.

'Help me … help me get to bed,' he gasped, clutching his chest as the pain tightened its grip.

Angela, dressed in an Indian silk robe which billowed over her fragile body, helped her soulmate out of the armchair and into the bedroom where she crawled under the sheets and passed out beside him.

As night paled into a new dawn, sun streamed into the apartment and Paris awoke to a fresh summer's morning.

Joe Hawkins, America's most infamous rock star, lay dead in his bed.

CHAPTER ONE

San Francisco, California – March 16th, 1987

Time waits for no one. And time, this morning, was impatient.

William Kendrick strained his neck muscles to lift his head from the sterile white pillow, his ears pricking at the sound of his captor unlocking the security doors one by one. Scratching his calloused fingertips through his beard, he listened closer to a muffled hum of voices that moved at a systematic pace along the corridor.

They were late.

He hauled his legs over the side of the bed frame, pulling at the sweat-soaked sheet that clung to his leathered skin. Grappling for a cup of tepid water on the bedside cabinet, he pressed it to his lips, washing down the tinge of disinfectant gripping to the stale air. Slowly he turned his head towards the locked door, sharpening his stare at five young faces that appeared at the observation window.

His jailers had arrived at last.

'Mr Kendrick, good morning,' the voice reverberated around the hospital room. Doctor Wesley Marshall released his finger from the intercom button and turned to his students. 'This is William Kendrick, forty-four years old, admitted with advanced liver cancer. He has six months left at most. No family.'

One of the students peered through the observation window to look at the patient sitting on the edge of the bed, his hands clasped together on his lap to disguise their persistent shaking.

'If he's a cancer patient, then what's he doing up here on the psych ward?' the student asked.

'Ah,' the doctor said, 'I think we should let Mr Kendrick explain that.'

He unlocked the door to room 127.

William Kendrick pushed himself up off the bed into some semblance of a standing position. A loose hospital gown hung down to his knees, his arms presented as stiff as rifles at his sides. His eyes widened to meet the curious gaze of each of his guests as they entered the room.

'My name is Joe Hawkins,' he said, lowering his voice to a whisper, '*and I'm a dead man.*'

*

Tyler Rafferty sped his car north through lush Californian countryside, where blossoming almond trees and budding grapevines sweetened the air beyond the highway.

The previous night he stood alone at the window of his student apartment, watching in silence while his friends packed up and left for spring break. His grades this semester had been, *"Somewhat disappointing again, Mr Rafferty,"* his tutor, Professor Edward Kessler had said. *"You will not graduate if you continue with this attitude and these unfounded ideas. Your final case study is due at the end of May, and you have not secured a patient or deigned to submit a proposal. Do I need to remind you of your father's generosity towards this college?"* Tyler wiped his dampening palm down the seam of his jeans and turned up The Beastie Boys playing on the car radio. *How could I forget?* he thought.

A letter peeked out from his bag on the passenger seat. From the dozens of case study requests that Tyler had mailed to every psychiatric unit in California, suggesting an alternative therapeutic way to treat schizophrenia patients, this had been the only reply. Checking his digital watch, he pressed his foot hard on the gas pedal.

The sun had begun its late-afternoon descent across the sky when he drove through the suburbs of San Francisco, following the deepening amber light that rose and fell towards the bay. Arriving at the underground parking lot of Saint Cecilia's Hospital, Tyler switched off the overheated engine of his flame-red Ford Mustang: the obligatory ostentatious gift sent from his father on his twenty-first birthday.

'Twelfth floor,' a formidable receptionist said, not looking up as she waved her pencil in the general direction of the elevators.

Nurse Cynthia Wallace heaved open the security door onto the psychiatric ward.

A wave of nausea, the like of which Tyler had prayed would not come back to haunt him, lurched up from his stomach. The antiseptic air swam into the back of his mouth, flooding his mind with the last memory of his dying mother. She lay in the deep shadows of a hospital room, a blanket resting across her paper-thin shoulders, a ghost of the vibrant young woman who Tyler wished he still knew. His leg muscles weakened as he collapsed onto a chair outside the doctor's office.

'Mr Rafferty, please come in,' Doctor Wesley Marshall said with a broad smile as he opened his door. 'I am so pleased you could come to visit us so soon.'

The office held a sanitary cleanliness and pristine order. Stacks of medical journals, overflowing with the latest ground-breaking theories, took pride of place on the bookshelves. Doctor Marshall poured Tyler a cup of strong coffee from the percolator and offered him a seat in front of his desk.

'You mentioned in your letter that you have a patient here who I could study,' Tyler said, gulping his coffee and drawing his attention from a segmented model of the human brain that lay intricately deconstructed on top of a filing cabinet.

'Yes.' Doctor Marshall sat down at his desk. 'Two weeks ago, we transferred a patient called William Kendrick from a medical centre in Boulder Creek after he fell ill at his home. It was our oncology team who discovered his liver cancer which, I'm afraid to say, has remained untreated for some time.'

Tyler made no effort to conceal a weary sigh, running a hand through his sun-streaked hair that skimmed down the back of his neck. 'He's a cancer patient?'

'When William was told his cancer was terminal, he became distressed and claimed that he wasn't William Kendrick at all. This behaviour persisted, so he was brought up here to my unit for further assessment. William is suffering from a specific grandiose delusion, which makes him believe he is living someone else's life and memories.'

Putting down his coffee cup on the desk, Tyler leaned in closer. 'So, who does William think that he is?'

Doctor Marshall opened a patient file, tracing a typed name with the tip of his pen. 'William Kendrick believes that he is a dead Sixties rock star called ... Joseph Hawkins.'

'Joseph Hawkins,' Tyler said, trying to suppress the glimmer of a smile. 'You mean *Wild Joe* Hawkins, the lead singer of The Gracious Dawn? But William must know that Joe Hawkins died in 1970.'

'William's deep fear is that he will die before his perceived identity is believed.' He stood and picked out three other patient files from the filing cabinet, handing them to Tyler. 'As you know, a patient will emulate the identity of the person whose lifestyle, attitude and actions match their own subconscious needs and unfulfilled desires in life. However, delusions of grandeur as extreme as William's are not so common. He has created an entire lifetime filled with the perceived memories of this Joe Hawkins character.'

Tyler flicked through the pages of medical notes and clinical observations. Tortured faces captured in Polaroid photographs were stapled to the inside sleeve of each file, the patients' eyes were wide and fixed down the camera lens. 'Is William dangerous?'

The doctor shook his head and sat back down at his desk. 'He pushes my staff's patience to cause a reaction and then backs off again just as quickly. It seems to entertain him.' He hesitated and cupped his hands together on top of William Kendrick's file. 'William is an exceptionally clever man, Tyler. Our tests show he has an intelligence which borders on the level of genius.' He checked his watch, seeming restless. 'Now, I imagine that your college professor has told you to follow the standard routine of taking two formal interviews with your case study patient, followed by further observations?'

'Yeah, that's pretty much it.' Tyler said with a shrug.

'I see. Then I think it would be wise to come up with another strategy. Your professor ...?'

'Kessler.'

'Yes, Kessler, well he's not living in the 1980s. The study of psychology and psychiatry has moved on in recent years. You cannot hope to take an outdated text-book approach if you want to truly understand a man as complex as William Kendrick.'

Doctor Marshall opened his desk drawer, extracted a piece of paper and held it up: *The Positive and Negative Syndrome Scale.* Tyler was aware that this was the revolutionary new way to evaluate the behaviours and thought processes of schizophrenia patients. He reached across the desk, feeling the paper tighten in the doctor's grasp before he released it.

'William Kendrick is a master manipulator,' Doctor Marshall said. 'He will want to trick you, he will want to lie to you and he will want you to believe his truth at any cost. He will want to play mind games with you, and he will want to win. You will need to think outside of the box that Professor Kessler has deemed fit to put you in.'

Tyler scanned the list of schizophrenic symptoms and behavioural disorders erupting off the page in his hand: delusions, hallucinations, hostility, suspicion, emotional withdrawal, anxiety, tension, depression. Folding the paper, he slotted it into the back of his notebook. 'Do you think William will mind me studying him?'

'He's quite adamant that it's you he wants to talk to,' Marshall said, leaning back in his chair. 'Last week William broke into my office and not for the first time. I discovered him sitting at my desk, with your letter in his hands, and since then he's been insistent that you should come here to meet him.'

'Why is he so interested in meeting me?'

'Mr Rafferty, the only truths within William Kendrick's own mind are these: that he is Joe Hawkins and that he wants to talk to you, and you alone.'

The two men walked side by side through the ward.

Placid cream walls tunnelled fading fragments of sunlight towards a common room. Tyler paused at the door, watching rows of lost souls who sat in the quiet contentment of their late-afternoon medication. He tried to shake off Professor Kessler's monotone voice droning through his mind. *"I warned you last year that you cannot help people with recklessness and naïve ideas about alternative treatments. Proven psychological research and medication are what cure the sick. One more step out of line and I will remove you from this college."* As Tyler followed the doctor, he feared that William Kendrick could now be his only hope to graduate and avoid a career of his father's orchestration.

They stopped at a room at the end of the corridor.

'There's a panic button on the wall if William gets too agitated,' Doctor Marshall said and unlocked the door.

Tyler crept into the room, his white Converse shoes squeaking against the grey laminate floor with each tentative step. His eyes darted towards a hospital bed, its leather restraints hanging like limp arms from each side of the guard frame. A nurse had positioned an armchair by the window, the occupant of which did not move, nor seem to notice that his guest had entered the room. Dragging a plastic chair from beside the bed, Tyler placed it in front of the patient and sat down. The only sound, in the otherwise silent room, was the ticking of a caged clock above the door.

'Hi, Mr Kendrick, sir. My name's Tyler. I'm a psychology student from Los Angeles.' He cleared his throat as its dryness worsened. 'Doctor Marshall suggested that I should talk to you.'

A timid smile broke across William's mouth and a glint sparked through his sapphire eyes, splintered with shards of grey, which had seemed lifeless moments before. 'Tyler Rafferty,' he said, his voice rising and falling with each delicate syllable that passed his bitten lips. 'I was interested to read your letter, but it was, in fact, me who wanted to talk to you. Doctor Marshall is quite suggestible to any idea which might, uh … ease his life.'

'You're interested in my case study, Mr Kendrick?'

With a little effort William pushed himself up from his armchair. 'There will be no answers yet. The answers will come, as will the questions, but for now I need your help.' As he bent down, the bristles of his beard threatened to scratch Tyler's cheek. '*I am not crazy*,' he whispered deep into his visitor's ear.

William Kendrick grimaced as he straightened himself up, rubbing the skin on his arms which held a tint of jaundice. He ambled over to the bedside cabinet, holding his weight on his left hip and moving with a lethargic stiffness.

'No, kid, I am not crazy,' he said, filling a paper cup with water. He shuffled his bare feet back across the room, handing the cup to Tyler. Wincing in pain, he slumped into the armchair and wrapped his arms tight around his body. 'For the past seventeen years, I have lived in this cruel existence of a world as William Kendrick, the man who was my saviour, the man who gave me my freedom – at a terrible price. The doctors say I have a psychosis, but they know nothing about my torment, about having to live a life of lies and deceit. They know nothing about living in this world as a captive soul.'

Tyler sipped the stale water and placed the cup on a low table, bolted into the floor by the window. As he leaned back, he took the opportunity to steal a closer look at William's face. In the dim afternoon light, he thought he saw a fleeting similarity to the notorious Joe Hawkins of old; the rock legend whose wild life story had featured in the music magazines that Tyler devoured as a teenager. His stare traced along William's bearded jaw, then up to a pair of piercing eyes which bored straight back at him. 'Mr Kendrick, when I spoke to Doctor Marshall, he explained to me that you're experiencing a specific condition–'

'I don't have a *condition*, man,' William turned his head away as his light, mocking laugh rattled around the room.

'Are you finding something funny, sir?' Tyler asked, leaning down to his bag and rummaging for his notebook and pen.

'Y'know, the doctors in this place are so intent on trying to cure the sick that they never stop to consider whether it's even necessary.'

'What do you mean?'

'The people held captive here aren't doing anyone any harm.' William's laughter faded, wiping his mouth with the back of his trembling hand. 'They're quite content to live in the safety of the worlds that exist within their minds, but the men in white coats keep telling them they're wrong ... always wrong. The doctors want to expose the patient's souls, plunge needles into their arms, force drugs down their throats and then hurl them out through the revolving doors to become someone else's problem.'

'I think places like this are only trying to help people.'

'I bet you do,' William said through a snorting chuckle. 'Do you have any idea what it's like to be forced to spend seventeen years of your life as someone else, huh? Oh yeah, I can imagine your perfect life, Tyler: Daddy paying your way through college, Mom at home worrying about her precious boy. You choose to sit in a concrete box all day with your head buried in irrelevant theory books, believing that everything you are being told is the truth. That is your life, Tyler, that is your ... *condition*.'

Tyler hesitated. Respect, curiosity and enquiry: the three golden rules of psychology that his tutors had drummed into his head on his first day of college, beat back through his mind. 'I don't think my life is relevant to our conversation,' he said. *I have worked damn hard without the help of my father, and as for my mother* ... but he knew better than to reveal any personal information about himself to a patient. 'I've come here to talk to you, Mr Kendrick. I'd like to make some preliminary notes if that's alright?'

Arching his body forward, William narrowed his eyes. 'You must be *real* desperate to drive all the way to San Francisco to meet me. What's in it for you, I wonder?'

'I think you'd make an interesting case study patient, that's all.' Tyler closed his notebook before he had written a word. 'Doctor Marshall said that you wanted to speak to me. Is there anything particular you'd like to talk about today?'

'I want you to help me – you scratch my back and, uh, I'll scratch yours.' William's head fell back into the comfort of his armchair. 'You'll get to study the *supposed* psychiatric patient in all his glory, and I'll get to cleanse my soul before I die. I need to tell you the truth about Joe Hawkins' life and death, which has been hidden from the world for all these years.'

Tyler's attention wavered as Doctor Marshall's face appeared at the observation window. William turned his head with a rapier stealth towards the door, his body tensing with such friction that in one swift movement he erupted out of the armchair.

'You've got to get me out of here,' he hissed, digging his fingernails deep into Tyler's shoulders, his face flushed. 'I promise I'll tell you everything, but only if you get me the hell out of here.'

'I can't help you like that, Mr Kendrick. You're in the best place to be looked after, in your present condition.'

'I don't have a condition!'

William lunged down and tore the notebook from Tyler's hands, throwing it hard against the window. He turned and began to pace around the room, his bare feet sticking to the sanitised floor with each unsteady step. Tyler, sensing his chance to escape, grabbed his bag and retreated towards the opening door.

'I'm sorry, man, really … I'm sorry!' William's head hung like a helpless child, his greying hair, peppering a once youthful shade of wild honey, clung to his sweating face. 'Please don't leave me here, you've got to help me.'

Tyler caught his breath as Doctor Marshall locked the door behind him. He peered back through the observation window at William Kendrick, who stood alone in his hospital room with the sole company of a gently ticking clock.

'I screwed up,' Tyler said, watching the doctor press four digits into the keypad outside his office, as a green light flashed, and the door unlocked. 'I swear, that's never happened with a patient before.'

Doctor Marshall raised his eyebrows and sat down at his desk. 'You have never met William Kendrick before.'

With a curt rap on the door, Nurse Wallace entered the office. Tyler dipped his eyes to swerve the disapproval in her glare, as she handed him his notebook which she had carefully retrieved from William's room. 'Is there any hope for him?' Tyler asked, watching the nurse leave.

'A patient with such an extreme and unique psychosis is a gift for my students, but William cannot stay here indefinitely. If this behaviour persists, then he will be moved to a more secure facility upstate. Although, he does have one option left open to him.' Doctor Marshall pointed to a stack of folders on the bookshelf. 'There is a new antipsychotic drug which is being tested by the FDA and I think William could be a suitable candidate for a trial, under my guidance. We need to see how it affects patients with an existing long-term illness.'

'Experiment on him?' Tyler asked, folding his arms. 'Surely there must be another way.'

'All my patients here have a part to play in the decision-making process of their treatment. Even as a test case, I wouldn't force William to do anything that he doesn't want to do.' Marshall hesitated. 'Tyler, what exactly are your plans for studying my patient?'

Tyler traced his fingers over a sharp crease that now slashed across the cover of his notebook. 'As I mentioned in my letter, Doctor, I want to study the new developments in the cognitive treatment of schizophrenia patients. If I can observe and question William's behaviour and thought processes, I might be able to get to the root cause of his psychosis. I need to look all the way back to his childhood, because there must have been specific events in William's past that activated his present condition. If those root causes can then be treated with cognitive therapy to challenge his negative thought patterns, rather than mask them with medication, then I'm sure I could persuade William that the Joe Hawkins delusion isn't viable, enough for it to be reduced as a controlling influence in his life.'

Doctor Marshall's brow hardened, resting his elbows on the desk. 'I want it made clear that you are only here as an unqualified student. You are an observer, nothing more than that. You will not attempt to influence or treat William in any way. Is that understood?'

'Sure, of course,' Tyler said with a petulant smile. 'That's understood.'

The doctor relaxed his body into the chair. 'Not long after I graduated, I did an internship at a psychiatric unit in Sacramento run by a French doctor called Fabien Gerard. For the first two weeks, Doctor Gerard only allowed me to sit and talk to his patients because he wanted me to learn how to *listen*. Well, I learned more in those two weeks about the mysteries of the human mind than in all my years at college.' He checked his watch; the evening rounds were now late. 'Perhaps you should try to talk to William again tomorrow.'

Tyler flung his body into the driver's seat of his car, revving the engine to a guttural roar that resonated through the parking lot and onto the twilit streets of San Francisco.

A cheap hotel opposite the hospital would suffice for an inevitable sleepless night. Sitting on the edge of the bed, Tyler took out his notebook from his bag and watched a stream of blank pages flowing between his fingers. *I have got to make this work*, he thought. As he closed the notebook and threw it onto the floor, the bedside telephone rang. Picking up the receiver, Tyler rubbed the knotted muscles in the back of his neck. 'Hello.'

'Don't hang up on me, man, I don't have much time,' a light voice said down the line.

'Who is this?'

'Listen carefully: go to 1896 Big Basin Highway and ask for Adeline. Tell her that William sent you. Get her to take you to my house, look in my basement—'

A violent click on the end of the line struck into Tyler's ear. 'Mr Kendrick …?'

CHAPTER TWO

The undulating residential streets of San Francisco dispersed into rural homesteads and open farmland. Tyler stifled a yawn and turned the car onto the Big Basin Highway, which snaked fifty miles south through the Redwoods State Park, down to Boulder Creek. As the road curved deeper into the forest, a wall of colossal redwoods and firs veiled the early morning light.

At the boundary of the State Park, the trees unravelled enough to accommodate a scattering of houses along the road. Tyler eased his foot off the gas pedal and stopped outside a dilapidated bungalow, struggling to defend itself against the invading woodland. Getting out of the car he checked his watch; eight o'clock seemed a reasonable enough hour of the morning to interrupt the life of a stranger.

The fragrant forest air thickened with the scent of pine. Tyler took a deep breath as he walked up the path and knocked on the front door, brushing off specks of red paint that had freckled onto his knuckle.

The door opened an inch.

'Hello, Adeline?'

'Who's there?' an elderly voice asked.

'I'm sorry to bother you so early in the morning, ma'am. My name's Tyler. William Kendrick told me to come and see you.'

The door creaked open and a woman in her late seventies stepped forward, her ashen hair straggling over the shoulders of her faded floral dress. 'Billy sent you, did he?' she asked, squinting at the young man standing on her doorstep who was trying to flatten out the creases on his Motörhead T-shirt.

'William, yes. He wanted you to show me his house if it's not too much trouble.'

'Hmm, did he now?' Adeline stepped back into her hallway to retrieve a key from a carved wooden sideboard and placed it in her skirt pocket. 'Well, if he wants me to show you his house, then I suppose I'll have to show you.'

Walking together along the forest road, the distant hum of a generator jostled with the chiming of birdsong floating down from the trees. Along the verge, a line of spring saplings vied for daylight beneath the dominant shade of the old firs.

'How long have you known William?' Tyler asked.

'Six years now,' Adeline glanced across at the stranger walking beside her. 'I've lived here all my life you see. It seems like only yesterday when I first saw him standing outside my house.' She stopped and rested her frail hand on Tyler's arm. 'He seemed so lost; he had that look on his face ... they all have that same look.'

'Who?'

'Oh, the poor souls, those folk who have lost all hope in life. You see them, only if you want to see them, of course.' She released her hand from his arm and continued their slow walk. 'They come to me, those poor lost souls. I couldn't have children of my own, so I've taken care of anyone who crossed my path.'

'I'm sorry.'

'Don't be sorry, son,' Adeline said, guiding Tyler onto a rough stone driveway. 'Billy helps me around the house, and we sit and talk. I never quite understand some of the stories he tells me, but he likes to make me laugh. I suppose we protect each other from this strange world we find ourselves living in.'

A white-timbered house stood alone on an overgrown plot of land. Tyler felt the morning dew seep through his shoes, as he walked across the once fertile lawn now ensnared with weeds. Splinters of sunlight struck through the trees, warming damp patches of moss that adhered to the rotting veranda. From the side of the house appeared a dog, of dubious breeding, who erupted into a tirade of barking aimed solely at Tyler.

'Quiet down, Francis, there's a good boy,' Adeline hollered and took the key from her pocket, steadying herself while she unlocked the door. 'I think I'll rest out here,' she said, easing herself onto a bench on the veranda while the dog settled at her feet. 'You take your time.'

Tyler pushed open the front door and took a cautious step inside.

A heady stench of cigarettes and stale beer had saturated the very bones of the house. Dust particles clung to broken beams of daylight that struggled to infiltrate the dirty living room windows. An overflowing ashtray balanced on the edge of a coffee table, the burnt-down remnants of a joint still tingeing the air with a honeyed pang that caught in the back of Tyler's throat.

Turning around on a frayed Moroccan rug, he surveyed a room that provided only the simplest of comforts for its owner. A pair of binoculars rested on the windowsill, seeming to afford the slightest voyeuristic view through the trees to the neighbouring bungalow. Scratch marks on the floorboards dug a trail from where a writing desk had been dragged around the room, following the progress of the sun as it crawled around the house.

Tyler wandered over to the desk and leafed through a collection of handwritten notebooks, buried beneath lurid drawings of naked bodies and reptiles entangled in a Hieronymus Bosch vision of hell. 'You're quite an artist, William,' he said under his breath. Biting the skin around his fingernail, he felt like an intruder in another man's home and unsure why he was even there.

A narrow corridor led to the back of the house.

Hanging aslant above a low door was a painting of a fishing boat, a Greek flag billowing from its stern while it sailed on aquamarine waters. Tyler straightened the painting and turned the door handle. The memory of a horror movie whirred to life in his mind, as he tugged a cord above his head, illuminating a set of stairs that descended into the basement. Putting a hesitant foot on the top step, he knew that whatever was hiding down there, William Kendrick intended for him to find it.

Taking each slim stair in turn, Tyler's hand grappled onto the brick wall, its coarse surface grating against his fingertips. As he searched in the gloom for another light cord, he found an oil lamp and a box of matches on the bottom step.

He struck a match and ignited the wick.

The mellow light melted over piles of books, from Jack Kerouac to Hermann Hesse and Arthur Rimbaud to Friedrich Nietzsche, a stagnant library of the great and notorious rose from floor to ceiling. Creeping forward Tyler lifted the lamp higher. Light swept over the back wall of the basement, revealing hundreds of newspaper clippings and photographs of Joe Hawkins on stage in his Sixties heyday. The idol's body was clad in black leather, a silk scarf draped around his neck, golden hair curling around his penetrating eyes which struck through the darkness at the prowler in his private realm.

'I guess this goes to prove that you're one obsessive fan,' Tyler said.

Taking a shallow breath of the stale air, he walked over to where a stack of home-movie reels were leaning against the side of a wooden chair. When he looked closer, he saw a leather-bound journal perched on the armrest. Putting the lamp on the floor, he sat down and opened it, releasing the scent of ageing musk from its yellowing pages.

THE JOURNAL OF JOSEPH HAWKINS

My name is Joseph Thomas Hawkins.
I was born on October 3rd, 1942.
This is my life. These are my words. This is my truth.

May 13th, 1953 (Petersburg, Virginia)

How many nights have I spent with my eyes drawn to the heavens, wondering if there is another boy trapped on a lonely planet, trying to escape the terrifying universe within his own mind?

This is the fourth time we have moved in my short life. As I start to settle into a new town and make friends, then we must pack up again and follow my father's military career across the country. I do not fit in with the other kids at my new school and I do not want to. They are not the same as me. They are not as clever as me. They do not see things in the same way as me.

I do not know who Joey Hawkins is supposed to be.

My nightmares came back last night. I am trapped at the bottom of a well, the black water is up to my mouth. I can hear my sister screaming. I cannot breathe and her screams are like wolves howling in my ears. Then another nightmare begins: futuristic visions of war and death, storms and strife. When I wake, I feel traumatised, it makes me want to withdraw into myself.

It is all just a bad dream, Joey, my mother says ...

A creak at the top of the basement stairs made Tyler's heart jolt.

'Are you alright down there, son?' Adeline's voice echoed into the darkness. 'Did you find what you were looking for?'

Tyler closed the journal, tapping his fingers on its supple cover and making the decision to slip it into his bag. 'Yeah, I think I did.'

Adeline struggled to lock the front door and secreted the key in her skirt pocket, giving it a reassuring tap at her hip. 'The stories that William tells you, what are they about?' Tyler asked, offering his arm to aid her down the steps and across the damp grass.

'I suppose he talks about his past when he was a younger man. He tells me stories about how he felt trapped in his old life, and how he escaped.'

'Did he ever mention any family?'

'No, never. I did ask him once, but he said that his parents died when he was young.'

Walking back along the road, Tyler clutched the strap of his bag tight over his shoulder, enjoying the relief of the fresh forest air in his lungs. 'Have you always known him as William Kendrick, or has he ever referred to himself by any other name?'

'No, son, he's always been William, or Billy, for as long as I've known him,' Adeline said, looking away into the depths of the forest.

Arriving back at the car, Tyler shook the old woman's hand. 'Thank you. I'll give William your regards.' He waited for Adeline to reach her front door, before starting the engine and driving as fast as he could back to San Francisco.

Keeping close by Doctor Marshall's side, Tyler walked through the hospital ward and along the patient corridor. 'William has been insistent that you would come back,' the doctor said, as he unlocked the door.

'I'm sure he has.'

Striding into the room, Tyler took the journal from his bag and placed it on the table. William bent his body forward in the armchair, extending his nicotine-stained fingers to draw them across the leather cover. He closed his eyes. 'You found it,' he said, flashing one eye open. 'Bet you had a good look inside.'

Dropping his bag to the floor, Tyler sat down on a chair already positioned in front of the window in anticipation of an expected visitor. 'I found some interesting things in your basement.'

A smile stretched at the corner of William's mouth. 'I need to tell you everything before it's too late, but I will not speak one word of my truth while I'm held captive here.' Heaving himself up, he rambled around the room, pausing to point a trembling finger straight at Tyler. 'I have never surrendered my freedom and I have no intention of starting now. I know what they're doing with those pills they keep trying to force down my throat. I will not be their experiment, man. I will not let them destroy what's left of my mind.'

Tyler stood, folding his arms. 'Everything in your basement, Mr Kendrick, everything in that journal …'

William eased his weight onto his left hip and tilted his head towards his shoulder. 'Get me out of here, and uh, I'll tell you.'

Tyler walked back through the ward and stopped at the common room door. An assortment of patients sat in neat rows, waiting for Nurse Wallace to greet them with a plastic pot of pills. A stocky male nurse followed close behind her, carrying a water jug to help ease the medicine down their willing throats. Remembering his conversation with Doctor Marshall from the previous day, Tyler would have to take a different approach to studying this patient.

'I need to take William Kendrick out of here,' Tyler said, entering the doctor's office and sitting in front of the desk. 'For one day.'

Doctor Marshall looked up from an open patient file. 'Mr Rafferty, you're not taking him anywhere.'

'William has made it clear that he won't talk to me while he's here. The only way I can attempt to understand what has caused his present condition is if I can talk to him in an environment where he feels comfortable. Please give me permission to talk to him away from here for one day to carry out my primary questioning.' Tyler paused, watching the doctor's frowning face. 'Then I'm sure I could persuade William to comply with your drug trial.' He surprised himself at the effortlessness of his lie.

Doctor Marshall shook his head. 'Mr Rafferty–'

'William doesn't just believe that he is Joe Hawkins, I think he has spent his entire adult life being pathologically obsessed with him. I want to understand what has caused him to become the person he is today.' Tyler exhaled a heavy sigh. 'To be honest, Doctor, I don't have any other choice but to make this case study work. This is my last chance. If I don't graduate then my life is over.' *I will not be consigned to the mail room of my father's law firm*, he thought. *I will not be his errand boy.*

'Tyler, you are not taking my patient out of this hospital, is that understood?' Doctor Marshall closed the file on his desk. 'You must be in control of your case study, and you must be in control of William Kendrick.'

The two men walked along the corridor towards the nurses' station. Tyler raised a timid smile, hoping it would temper Nurse Wallace's fractious scowl. 'You need to establish a relationship of trust with William,' the doctor said, 'then he'll open up and talk to you.' He placed a hand on Tyler's shoulder. 'Take all the time you need.'

Doctor Marshall began his morning rounds with Nurse Wallace in tow. When they had disappeared around the corner,

Tyler entered the common room. William sat alone at the back of the room, away from the other patients and with the journal open on his lap.

'Mr Kendrick, sir, I really would like to talk to you some more.'

'I've told you, kid, the only way I'll talk to you and tell you my truth is away from this place. I don't care how you do it, but you need to get me out of here.'

'I can't do that.'

'I get the feeling you really don't have any other choice right now, do you? Get me out of here, for one day, and I promise I'll be honest with you. I'll answer all your questions and tell you everything you need to know to write your precious case study.' William leaned back in his seat and folded his arms, pursing his lips tight shut.

'Shit.' Tyler circled William's chair and lowered his voice. 'I'll be breaking the law if I take you out of here without consent, even for one day. Do you understand that?'

William slowly nodded back.

Tyler glanced towards the other patients who sat motionless in mis-matched armchairs, seeming lost in the wilderness of their sedated minds. As his watch bleeped, his heart sank into his tightening chest; there was no time left to secure another patient as intriguing as the man sitting in front of him. William Kendrick was his last chance to write his case study.

William parted his mouth into a mischievous grin. 'Get me out of here, *now*.'

A reckless heat spiked through Tyler's veins as he motioned for William to stay sitting. At the common room door, he checked the corridor was clear before approaching Doctor Marshall's office. With a trembling finger, he tried to remember the correct order of four digits he had seen the doctor press into the keypad. Holding his breath, he waited until a green light flashed and the door unlocked.

Tyler rifled through papers and files then opened the desk drawer. Reaching his hand inside, he pulled out a set of keys and a bottle of antipsychotic medication. With no time to process his thoughts, or consider the consequences of his actions, he stuffed the drug bottle and keys into his jacket pocket. Pausing at the door, he listened to Nurse Wallace's strident voice ringing through the ward, before running into the common room to help William out of his chair and into the corridor.

'Wait,' William said, pointing towards a storeroom. 'My clothes.'

Cardboard boxes were stacked inside the cramped storeroom, each with a patient's name written across the front. Tyler found William's box of possessions and tore off the lid. With some effort William had soon dressed himself, and, despite the creeping warmth of the morning, he draped his body in a short sheepskin coat.

William clutched the journal under his arm and kept close behind Tyler as they approached the security door. Taking the keys from his pocket, Tyler slipped one in the lock and gave it a sharp turn. The dull thud of the closing door seemed to chase the two men along the hall towards the elevator. Descending to the ground floor in silence, William's sour breath whipped across Tyler's cheek as he leaned in closer and said, 'This is going to be one hell of a ride, Tyler Rafferty.'

CHAPTER THREE

**The Journal of Joseph Hawkins – November 17th, 1955
(Grayling, Michigan)**

My mother believes our lives will be roses and sunshine every time my father receives another posting with the army, and we have to move again. We are living the American dream, or so my parents want to think.

I have been on my own for as long as I can remember, and I want it that way. I make it easy for my family to keep me at a distance. I cause teenage hell, scream at the top of my lungs, embarrass them in public so they leave me at home as often as possible. I spend hours sitting outside on the steps of our veranda, writing down the ideas that have been tumbling around my mind.

Most afternoons after school, I get lost in my imagination reading history books about the ancient world, wishing I could visit those glorious cities of the past. My haven of escape is the movie theatre, I am captivated by the hypnotic fantasy worlds. When I sit in the darkness, where no one knows who I am, the films seem to speak into my soul.

These feelings of being different from everyone else started from as young as I can remember. I can sense a change inside me, as if I am withdrawing from myself. I cannot talk to anyone about how I am feeling, and I cannot tell anyone about some of the things that have happened to me during my life. I fear that if I confide my secrets to my family then I will not be believed. 'This is another one of your games, Joey Hawkins,' they will say.

I feel trapped between being a child and a man.

My mind is cracking open, so another world is being revealed. When I close my eyes and enter the dark void between consciousness and sleep, I see a shaman emerge through a pillar of light. He is a Native American Indian with a wolf at his side. As he walks towards me, I see him raise his right hand and beckon me to follow him into the night.

In recent months my nightmares have returned, this futuristic vision of a metropolis engulfed in flames on the shore of a tempestuous ocean. There is a terrible storm, a warship is sinking, and I watch in horror as the sailors drown in the churning seas. Then another, more tender, dream begins like a lighthouse penetrating the black shadows in my mind. A beach illuminated by a swollen moon, an ancient forest and a mystical lake. I can hear soft music and gentle laughter all around me. I am a child – vulnerable, a pure soul – and a beautiful couple, with wildflowers in their hair, pick me up and play with me.

They are so beautiful.

In my dreams I want them to be my parents.

CHAPTER FOUR

The growl of Tyler's car resonated out of the hospital's underground parking lot and into the depths of San Francisco's morning traffic. While Tyler drove, William crooked his head out of the open passenger window, closing his eyes and allowing a brisk wind to blow away the last traces of the hospital's antiseptic stench embedded in his tangled hair.

'I need a drink,' William said. 'I need to flush out all the drugs they forced into my body. I need to uhm ... clear my mind.' His voice trembled, running his fingers across his mouth. 'Can we get some beer?'

'I don't think beer is going to help you right now,' Tyler said, pressing his foot on the gas pedal while trying to ignore the frown from the man sitting beside him. 'So, where do you want to go?'

William reached into his coat pocket and took out a blunted pencil. He turned to the back pages of the journal, shielding his words with his hand, and began to write. 'South,' he murmured, 'take me south.'

William Kendrick remained quiet, tuning the radio until he found a station playing languorous blues of a bygone era. The cloying dampness of sweat stuck Tyler's T-shirt to his back, while his patient's silence and mere presence in the car began to consume him with a claustrophobic unease.

'The doctors think I'm crazy, don't they?' William eventually asked.

'Crazy isn't a word we're encouraged to use,' Tyler said, keeping his strained concentration on the highway that took them further south. 'Alright, they don't think you're crazy, but there is evidence to suggest that you're suffering from a specific type of psychosis, which seems to be affecting your thoughts and behaviour.'

'Hmm, we'll see about that.'

Tyler took one hand off the steering wheel and bit his finger-nail, before pointing to the journal that lay open on William's lap. 'What's in that book of yours?'

'This is the true account of the childhood of Joey Hawkins, the turbulent life and *supposed* death of Joe Hawkins and the creation of William Kendrick.' He closed the journal and tapered his stare on Tyler. 'And you, my new friend, are going to read every word of it, then you might understand why we've both ended up here.'

Checking the car's clock, Tyler tried to calm the rolling in his stomach before resuming his attention on the highway. 'Mr Kendrick, we don't have a lot of time and I do need to ask you some questions.'

'There will be plenty of time for your questions, Tyler,' William said, closing his eyes.

'Are you going to tell me where we're going?'

'Interstate 5 … and keep on drivin'.'

In San Francisco, Doctor Wesley Marshall, now sallow faced, ran into his office and picked up the telephone receiver, pressing three buttons in quick succession.

'911, what's your emergency?'

'Get me the police. Now.'

The day fell into endlessness.

The sun trailed across the sky towards the mid-afternoon and the fertile green landscape of northern California withered into wide desert plains. While William slept, the only company for Tyler was the radio beating to the melancholic tones of Muddy Waters and Bo Diddley. However, he began to think that William was not asleep at all, that he had one eye half-open, keeping a watchful check on their progress south.

On the outskirts of Bakersfield, Tyler pulled into a gas station. He rested his aching body against the side of the car and filled the tank, enjoying the brief respite from spending the past five hours in the muted company of William Kendrick, but now fearing what trouble he was in. Tyler looked at the man sitting slouched on the passenger seat, wrapped in the deep folds of his sheepskin coat. He was going to have to examine an alien world, a world solely populated by a man convinced of his own false existence.

'We'll drive for a couple more miles, and then will you talk to me?' Tyler asked, getting back in the car, concerned that most of the day had already been lost to William's guarded silence.

William kept his eyes down on the journal and drew his fingers through his grizzled beard. 'Uhm, sure, kid, sure.'

The sun dipped lower into the horizon, grazing the sky with shards of blood-red light. A languid smile rose across William's mouth as the car passed a road sign welcoming them to the Mojave National Preserve. Following his patient's mumbled instructions, Tyler turned the car off the freeway and onto a remote strip of cracked asphalt that stretched between undulating mountain ranges and widening plains, drawing them deep into the heart of the desert. Tyler took a quick glance in the rear-view mirror, watching light clouds start to muster and blacken into a brewing storm.

'There!' William flung his arm in front of Tyler's face, pointing to a high sandstone bluff, an ancient megalith born out of the valley floor. 'There, man, there it is.'

Tyler veered the car off the road and onto a desert track. Sand pinged off the overheated bodywork until the harsh terrain forced him to slam on the brakes. While the engine ticked and cooled, he sat in the driver's seat and watched William trudge away from the car, stumbling around a thick patch of barrel cactus.

'Are you coming?' William shouted over his shoulder.

Tyler checked his watch, grabbed his bag from the back seat and got out of the car. A low growl of thunder rumbled around the valley and echoed off the distant hills. Gripping the strap of his bag a little tighter, he followed William's slow progress up a steepening trail. Tyler had allowed a stranger, an obsessive schizophrenic whom he knew nothing about, to lure him to this barren wilderness, a willing participant in what he now feared was a well-planned game. Winding around the top of the trail, he found William standing on the edge of a ridge, motionless and with his body drenched in the dying sun.

'Are you ready to talk to me, Mr Kendrick?' Tyler asked, letting his bag fall to the ground.

William tilted back his head and inhaled a lungful of the parched desert air. He turned and riveted his moistening eyes straight at Tyler. 'My name is Joe Hawkins. I was America's greatest rock star, the circus master who wielded the destruction and decadence of Dionysus, but with the gentle soul of a poet.' He stepped forward until the two men's faces were almost touching. 'You want to know my truth, kid?' he asked in a delicate voice. 'Then I'll tell you my truth.'

William brushed past Tyler and collapsed onto the edge of a smooth rock. With a quivering hand, he took a pack of cigarettes from his coat pocket and stuck one between his dry lips. Kicking the sand from his shoes, Tyler looked out across the desert plain at the storm-laden clouds threatening to draw in. 'Why have we come all the way out here?'

'This wilderness was my sanctuary,' William said, cupping a lighter around his mouth and stretching out his legs in front of him. 'This corner of the universe was my experimental playground. I needed to come back here one last time … before the end.'

Tyler bent down, fumbling for his notebook and pen in his bag. 'Mr Kendrick, I really do need to ask you some questions.' Sitting down on the rock he took a deep breath, feeling it pull into his taught shoulders. 'Why don't we start with some background. Can we talk about your early childhood?'

'Well, I was born Joseph Thomas Hawkins on October 3rd, 1942, in San Diego near the military base where the army had posted my father. Every fall, the Santa Ana winds would wreak their havoc from Baja to Los Angeles. On the morning of my birth, the maternity nurse looked out at the storm and told my mother that her child had been born under the omen of the *devil winds*. Sure enough, on each birthday when those Santa Ana winds blew, it stimulated the depression that would haunt my life.'

'Do you have any siblings?'

'I was born first, my parents' golden child,' William said through a brittle smile. 'I have a brother, Mike, and a little sister, Patty. I loved those guys, although I tormented them from as young as I can remember. They must have thought that my games and tricks were kinda cruel. I liked to push them, test their limits. But uhm, in my mind we were just having a good time.'

'I'd like to talk about your relationship with your parents if that's alright?'

'Ha! Yeah, I'm sure you would, *Professor* Rafferty.' William giggled and sucked on the cigarette, holding it between his thumb and middle finger. 'I don't have parents anymore.'

Tyler drew in a breath that sank through his lungs to the pit of his stomach. 'I'm sorry.'

'Don't be sorry, man. They're not dead, it was easier not to acknowledge their existence in my life, not to involve them.' William shrugged. 'My father was working his way up the army ranks, so I was trapped in an insular military family, a wandering childhood moving from one town to another and never staying more than a couple of years in one place. I guess my life was normal until the age of six. Up until that point, I could have had a regular life like every other dead-behind-the-eyes kid on this planet. At that age, my soul changed, it became irrevocably damaged.'

Tyler wrote hurried notes across a new page of his notebook, the pen scratching against flecks of sand blowing across the paper. *I need to find evidence of childhood experiences and behaviours, a specific stimulus that could have been a trigger for William's schizophrenia and the formation of the Joe Hawkins delusion. He had strict parents, a military family. He tormented his siblings, was this to assert control over them or was it for his own childish entertainment? He does not want to acknowledge that his parents exist – I need to find out the reason why.* 'What happened to you at that age?' Tyler asked, as he continued to write his notes.

'My father had been promoted to Captain, so we drove from our home in Sierra Vista, Arizona to Tucson to celebrate with my paternal grandparents.' William took a harsh draw on the cigarette. 'It was a warm September morning; clear blue skies rose to eternity and the sunlight across the desert seemed to set the world on fire. As a treat, my father allowed us to have the radio on in the car, and I can still hear Patty sitting beside me, quietly singing along to "It's Magic" by Doris Day. When we arrived, I ran away to explore the field at the back of my grand-parents' house.' William's voice faltered. 'That was when I found the disused well, overgrown with weeds, which my father had repeatedly told me to stay away from. The next thing I knew, I was falling into the dirty water, my tiny hands were trying to grab at the wet bricks …'

Tyler gripped his pen as it came to an abrupt stop on the page of his notebook.

He had heard this story before, the infamous childhood memory of young Joey Hawkins which had been retold by music journalists over the years. A patch of thick cloud drifted across the sky, swathing his face in a grey shadow while he stared at William Kendrick.

'That was the first time I experienced fear, Tyler.' William continued with a light voice. 'My head was barely above the water. I was trapped, struggling to breathe and it was only a miracle that my sister had been following me and saw what had happened. After all these years I can still hear Patty's screams coming from the depths of her stomach. Y'know, I don't think I ever got over that feeling of being trapped,' he gasped, clutching his chest. 'I couldn't escape, I couldn't escape …'

'Take a deep breath, Mr Kendrick,' Tyler said to the man sitting beside him, his pen still poised where he had stopped writing moments before.

'Just a bad dream, Joey,' William said, closing his eyes and smoking the cigarette.

'What was a dream?'

'For months afterwards, I would wake at night screaming. I guess uh, looking back at it now, I must have been psychologi-cally traumatised. My mother would tell me that it didn't really happen, it was all a bad dream, nothing more than that. From then on, the relationship with my parents started to break down. I learned what shame felt like.'

'Shame? That's a very strong emotion for a young child to feel.'

'Well, I started to wet the bed.' William lowered his head to shield a slight redness drawing across his face. 'I crept down the hall to my mother's room and dreaded having to turn the cold door handle and tell her I'd done it again. Night after night, the shame of what I'd done burned inside me as I went back to sleep in the wet sheets. That was when my childhood died, killed in an instant. The woman who I loved made me feel ashamed.' He lowered his head as his voice sank. 'And I hated her for it.'

Trawling his memory of the lectures he had endured from Professor Kessler for the past four years; Tyler began to wish he had paid better attention. Time was striding away from him, and he needed to find a way to persuade William to recall his own childhood and not that of Joe Hawkins. 'What did you feel was so bad about your relationship with your father?'

William rolled his eyes and flicked the dead cigarette onto the ground. 'My father would always remind me that you could only achieve success in life through good behaviour and obedience of the rules. One summer I discovered a fascination for petty theft, nothing serious, but I was caught leaving a store without paying for a copy of *Mad* magazine. My father was back home, and he stood in front of me with his hands behind his back, like he was taking a military inspection. Well, I cast down my head until he finished telling me that I had done wrong, I had always done wrong. I held back every one of those tears burning behind my eyes, I wouldn't let him see it. I just lifted my head and smiled straight back at him.'

Tyler brushed away the sand that had settled on his jeans, trying to ignore a louder rumble of thunder that loomed closer. 'I think you're still sounding bitter towards your parents.'

'No, man, I'm not bitter, just resigned to the fact that I'll never see them again. They haven't played any part in my life for the past twenty years. They were the ones who never encouraged my creative development as a child, because they wanted me to live a life that was so far away from where my dreams were taking me.' William shook his head, lifting his hand to shield his face from the smouldering cinders of the sun, his fingers rippling the ruby light across his eyelids. 'If it had been up to them, I would be living in suburbia behind a white picket fence, as some dick in the diplomatic service with a perfect wife at home, having unachievable dreams that only belong to other people. I guess I should be grateful to my parents because, without them knowing it, they pushed me so far away that I only had one choice left: to pursue the life I was destined to live.'

Tyler began to write but sensed that William was craning his head towards the notebook. *Having a distant relationship from his parents may have been William's <u>activating event</u> – this could be the original trigger for his mental illness. Look at Attachment Theory and the role of the absent military father. William appears to be weaving a fabrication of Joe Hawkins' childhood through the tapestry of his own memories. How much of what he is telling me is the truth?*

'What are you writing there?' William asked, a muscle at the corner of his eye twitching.

'I'm making a few notes about something called Attachment Theory.'

'What about it?'

'Well, it suggests that children can suffer with detachment from an absent parent. They can find it hard to cultivate friendships and often go on to live a nomadic lifestyle. As an adult they can have problems managing their emotions and some resort to drug and alcohol abuse and …' closing his notebook, he lowered his voice as if he were speaking to a frightened child '… some people are prone to fantasies, to creating an alternative and exaggerated reality in which to live.'

'Hee hee hee, are you finished?' William asked, snorting with laughter. 'Oh, you're something else aren't you, man, a real fuckin' Freud in the making. Yeah, I can see that you've read all the textbooks and are going to try to fit me into an old theory.

Well, let me ask you something, *Doctor Freud*: do you think I've spent my life allowing people to force me into their neat little boxes, huh? No, kid, it won't be that easy for you.' Leaning forward, he prodded his fingers deep into Tyler's chest. 'I will not come to you, my friend, I will only guide you to the entrance of my labyrinth and then you're on your own. Come inside my mind, Tyler, take a good look around, try to find me in there and only when you've found me will I let you judge me.'

William struggled to stand, throwing up a plume of sand that danced into the air from the back of his coat. He ripped Tyler's notebook from his hand, tossing it as high as his weakened arm could manage. 'Sure, you read your theory books and see if you can make me conform, you carry on doing that for the rest of your life and I'll tell you this, Tyler Rafferty, you'll be just like all the other tedious people in this world. You'll be *nothing*.'

Clambering off the rock, Tyler bent down to retrieve his notebook from the edge of the escarpment, brushing the sand from its cover. 'You need to calm down.'

'I'm an individual soul,' William said, craning his face until his acetone breath stung Tyler's eyes. 'Don't try to screw me into one of your pre-ordained theories. If you want to be someone in this world then do something different, throw away all those old ideologies and judge me as a person who's lived a more exciting and cruel life than you'll ever understand.'

Tyler took a step back. 'I want you to do something for me.' If he had any chance of uncovering his patient's real memories and understanding his sudden volatility, then he would have to discover what was affecting his behaviour. 'I want you to empty your coat pockets.'

William wiped his hand across his mouth. 'You want me to do what?'

'I need to know if you've taken anything, other than the medication the hospital gave you. Now, Mr Kendrick, please empty your pockets.'

Thrusting his hands deep into the pockets of his sheepskin coat, William pulled out a pack of cigarettes, a lighter and a wad of folded dollar bills. As he clutched the insignificant items, his widening eyes sparked, dipping his head towards Tyler's bag lying on the ground. 'Now, kid, I think it's your turn.'

Tyler hesitated before walking over to his bag, sensing that William was pushing him into a tightening corner. In one swift movement, he tipped his bag upside down, letting his wallet, car keys and yellow Walkman tumble out. However, it was none of these items that seemed to make William's face blanch; the drug bottle which Tyler had taken from Doctor Marshall's office had fallen out and landed with a soft thud on the ground. William reached to pick it up, holding it to the fading light that shone through the orange plastic and illuminated the white pills inside.

'What's this?' he asked. 'An insurance policy if I got too psychotic for you to control? What were you going to do, man, slip them in my food?' He leaned forward and pressed his mouth to Tyler's ear. 'Don't play games with me.'

William turned and threw the drug bottle out over the edge of the ridge, watching it land in the valley below. As Tyler buttoned up his stonewashed denim jacket, an unspoken sense gripped the storm-fuelled air that two very different people had collided, and those two people were going to be at war.

CHAPTER FIVE

The Journal of Joseph Hawkins – October 8th, 1957
(Oakland, California)

Riding the bus home from school, I am sitting on my favourite seat at the back where I can watch everything and everyone, and where no one can see me. It is an enjoyable anonymity, until I decide to make myself the centre of attention, for a little fun.

I feel like I am moving down a long tunnel. The teachers are processing us through school, year after year, filling our impressionable souls with truths only they believe in. You can get a lot out of school, if you keep an open mind, but it can do a lot of harm too.

School is a dangerous place to spend your childhood.

I will not be bound by the teachers' rules, they will not tell me what to do, what person to be. I will stay loyal to what I believe in, honest to the person who I am and true to my own spirit. There is a distinct line forming in my mind, a barrier: on one side is good and on the other side is bad. I am both the smartest kid in school and the class clown and that gives me the power because no one knows which Joey Hawkins they are going to get.

It is just as easy to scare people as it is to make them laugh. It is simple to break down authority when you smile in its face.

The teachers know I am trouble, that I like to act the fool and play games. It fascinates me to see how much they can take, how far I can push them before they break. I am the oldest in class, a wild beast they need to tame to protect the other kids, a wolf they must cage. Some days I sit at the back of the classroom, observing what is going on. I can see the fear in the teachers' eyes when they watch me, knowing that in my secretiveness and silence I am plotting my next move. I am more intelligent than all the staff and it scares them to death. When the bell rings at the end of the day, I raise a charming smile and wish the teacher, 'A very pleasant afternoon, ma'am'. Her uneasy smile in return rewards my victory.

For the past six months, while my father is overseas, we have been living at my aunt Irene's house in the suburbs of Oakland. I persuaded her to let me set up a bedroom in the attic so I can have my own space, some privacy away from the rest of my family. Uncle Tony has been away on business all this time, but I am not fooled by my aunt's lies. I am convinced he is in jail: a travelling salesman who murdered bored housewives in their homes, or a truck-driving killer, prowling the highways for his prey.

Aunt Irene thinks I do not know about the bottles of liquor she keeps hidden in the cupboard under the kitchen sink, or that I can see the sadness in the depths of her eyes. I can see everything. I can see straight through the mask of lies to the truth underneath.

My parents have no idea what is going on inside my head and they have no idea how to deal with me. I am desperate to learn and expand my consciousness, to push the boundaries of knowledge. While all the other teenagers are wasting their lives drinking milkshakes in the local diners, I go to the library. I study Plutarch's biographies, devour Sophocles, Jung, Nietzsche, Rimbaud and all the existentialist poets. When I read these magnificent books, it is as if I am switching on the lights inside my mind. I want to be like the great writers and philosophers, be remembered for all eternity and create meaning to my life.

Every weekend, I go to the bookstores and cafés in San Francisco, where the Beat Poets hang out and perform. Hiding amongst the crowd, I study these literary men who look like they truly understand the world. I like how it makes me feel when I see my idols ... excited ... maybe a little scared. I want people to have that same reaction towards me. I want to make people FEEL something for me.

Last week I sat alone up here in my room, my hands shaking with anticipation as I read a new book by Jack Kerouac called

On the Road, fascinated by a world beyond my reach. I read it cover to cover and the next morning I picked it up and read it all over again, copying down sections of the magical text in my notebook.

Kerouac's beautiful vision is so clear in my mind: a dark poetic man existing on the fringes of society, with no limits, no expectations, just a dream to go up like a rocket and blaze across the stars. I have seen a glimpse of a flagrant and incessant world of hard drugs, hot sex and cool jazz … and you have to hitch-hike to get there.

That has become interesting to me – very interesting indeed.

Nietzsche planted a seed in my mind that if I push existential thought right to the edge of oblivion then I can have the power to be my own god, the commander of my own destiny. Kerouac has now tempted me with a world in which I can push those boundaries and explode that seed.

Kerouac's words have ignited a fire inside me, and it will burn, burn, BURN!

CHAPTER SIX

William Kendrick stood on the edge of the escarpment with his hands clasped behind his back, his gaze transfixed on the mountains straddling the western horizon, their scuffed peaks radiating with a deep crimson light. Tyler kept a cautious distance and sat down on the rock. *No one knows I'm out here*, he thought, feeling the first drops of rain spatter onto his face as the storm drew nearer.

'Look, I'm sorry if I upset you,' Tyler said, knowing he had little time to get the conversation back on track and was desperate to placate his patient. 'Why don't you tell me more about your school days. Did you make any friends?'

'I guess I was popular. I was a fun guy to be around.' William turned and settled himself onto the rock beside Tyler. 'I knew how to make people laugh, tell wild stories, keeping everyone entertained. Although deep down I was shy and most of the time I preferred my own company. I did things that all the other kids were too scared to do themselves, so there was always a small group of disciples who liked the way I thought and behaved. Some people were drawn to me, maybe, uh ... like a magnetic attraction, in the way that you're drawn to the most interesting and dangerous wild beast. Fear and attraction always go together. Fear and attraction always become power.'

Tyler cleared his throat, trying to calm the tightness that refused to release its grasp around his chest. 'Did you trust anyone to get close to you?'

'I had a small circle of friends who allowed me to learn how to draw attention to myself, how to test people and see how far I could push them.'

'What about girls?' Tyler asked, making quick notes. 'Did you start to form any personal relationships?'

'In the fall of '59 we moved to Colorado Springs. On my first day at Thomas Jefferson High School, I sat beside Miss Betty Carlton, and I adored her from the moment she said, "Hello". She was real pretty, man, real pretty. I remember she always wore her auburn hair tied with a green ribbon.' William tilted his face to the sky and smiled. 'We were seventeen years old and for a year she made me happy. I cared for her, even though I would always act crazy, making her play along with my childish pranks, like sneaking into drive-in movies before getting caught, testing her to see how far I could take situations. She'd end up crying, but it was the first time I discovered that I could be in total control of a relationship.'

A lightning flash cracked like a lion tamer's whip across the darkening desert sky. Tyler stood and stuffed his notebook into his bag. 'I think we should get back to the car, this storm looks bad.' He extended his hand down to William, who grabbed hold of it and heaved himself off the rock. 'Why was it important to you, at that age, to feel like you needed to control people?'

'Early on in my life, I knew that if you're the one in control, then you're the master of your own destiny. People are like animals, they demand to be controlled, herded and led. It's always easier to let someone else show you the way, to tempt and guide you along the unsafe path.' William stumbled as his leather boots slipped on the loose stones and sand along the trail. 'I had to keep moving schools, so I soon discovered that being quiet and settling in was never going to be an option. I could feel an ever-increasing unease inside my mind. I began isolating myself more and I became fascinated with what the teachers wouldn't tell you … the dark side of what really went on in the world that they didn't want you to see.'

'Like what?'

'Sex, death, drugs. All of those taboos fascinated me.' William stopped walking and turned to face Tyler. 'There was a masked underworld of hidden knowledge, far more useful to me than the pointless information the teachers tried to force down our throats. Around that time, I became obsessed with Friedrich Nietzsche. I read *Twilight of the Idols* and *The Birth of Tragedy*, studying the promise of a new way of thinking. His words pricked my imagination, tore open my mind to a darker ideology and a new possibility for human existence.'

The red Ford Mustang came into view like a beacon across the sand. Delving his hand into his bag for the car keys, Tyler sensed they would not be returning to San Francisco tonight. William leaned his unsteady weight against the side of the car, tipping back his head to let heavier drops of rain splash onto his face. 'Do you have anything to drink?' he asked, licking his lips and scratching his beard. 'I really need something to drink: a beer, anything. It would help me to remember things more, uhm … clearly.'

'How often do you drink alcohol, Mr Kendrick?'

'Every damn day, Tyler, but only when I'm *real* thirsty,' William said through a long grin, sinking his body into the passenger seat and slamming the door. 'The bottle in my hand never let me down. It never judged me or told me what to do. It was my only constant friend.'

Tyler battled to control the car as it clawed through the churning sand and skidded back onto the Kelbaker Road. The rain rolled and drummed to a ritualistic beat, swelling the desert air with a metallic scent. 'These fluctuating behaviour patterns that you had as a child, were you ever depressed, what we call manic depressive?'

William slumped lower into the seat and stroked his forehead with his fingers. 'If that's what you want to call it, then yeah, I guess that's what I had back then, these mood swings. All through high school there was a black mist inside my mind. I, uh, suppose I had it since the day I was born, but it all changed soon after my eighteenth birthday.'

'Your behaviour changed at that exact point do you mean?'

'Right, right,' William said, looking out at the eclipsing savannah sweeping past the car. 'It was like something snapped inside me, and it made my behaviour worse than ever. I went from these extremes of being charming and shy, to being irrational and angry, real angry, man. In my mind, back then, I guess I was just feeling … trapped.'

Checking the rear-view mirror, Tyler could not outrun the storm that was pursuing the car back towards the Mojave Freeway. 'Did you ever have suicidal thoughts or want to harm yourself in any way, even as a boy or a teenager?' he asked, glancing across at William as his head sank to his chest. 'It's alright, it's nothing to feel ashamed about.'

'I don't feel ashamed about it, but you're right, those thoughts did occur to me back then.' William's voice faltered, appearing to be captured in deep thought. 'Y'see, Tyler, I didn't want to die, I wanted to feel … alive, to push life a little further, see how far it could go. Nietzsche's words began to haunt me, "What doesn't kill you makes you stronger". I became obsessed with it. I wanted to test it, to take it on, roll the dice and win. Yeah, I dug that idea a lot back then.'

Tyler shifted his restless body in the driver's seat, still unsure whose memories William was recalling – his own or Joe Hawkins' – and knowing that he was on borrowed time to find out. Turning the car off the drenched freeway and into a gas station, the hunger in Tyler's empty stomach seized him so hard that a wave of dizziness ripped up into his head. Wandering around the store, he picked up a couple of stale-looking chicken sandwiches, but as he went to pay, he saw William go to the refrigerator, take out a six-pack of chilled beer and draw his mouth into a broad grin.

'You know that beer really isn't going to help your present situation.'

'I'm dying, kid, it can't make my situation any fuckin' worse.' William smiled and guzzled down a can of beer until his breath ran out.

'Where did your interest in poetry come from?' Tyler asked, throwing the grocery bag onto the back seat of the car and starting the engine, trying not to give William any margin to hamper their conversation. 'I saw all the books in your house.'

'I guess, seeing poetry for the first time as a live performance at the cafés and bookstores in San Francisco changed it for me. Words became alive, they had meaning, and they could cause a reaction.' William took an elongated pause before speaking again. 'I became fascinated with how words could flow, there was magic to their progress and sequence, which could give them an alluring beauty and a dangerous power. I knew that to be a great poet you had to experience everything you were writing about. The greatest poets knew pain, man, real physical pain.' He jabbed his fingers into his chest. 'Suffering would carry the greatest reward. Experiencing the greatest loss would be the risk you'd have to take to be a great poet, for your name to live on forever. That idea opened my young mind to an entire world full of possibilities for poetic writing, existential thought and who Joey Hawkins could become.'

Without saying a word, Tyler pressed his foot hard on the gas pedal, speeding them further along the freeway, where opaque clouds lingered low over the desert. A dark shadow infiltrated the car through the windshield, sheathing the contours of William's bearded face. 'You don't believe me, do you?' he asked, turning to Tyler and keeping his voice soft. 'You don't believe that I'm Joe Hawkins.'

'Joe Hawkins died in Paris in 1970. I think your current thought processes and perceptions about Joe are something we can look at, something we can work together on.'

'My name's Joe.' The lines on William's forehead deepened, but his voice remained as light as a whisper. 'Why don't you call me Joe?'

'Mr Kendrick,' Tyler said, watching the dimmed headlights of an oncoming truck loom towards them. 'I've got to stay neutral in this situation. I have to call you by your own name.'

William flung his body towards the driver's seat, grabbing the steering wheel with both hands, and forcing the car onto the opposite side of the road.

'Stop!' Tyler tried to force William's clenched hands off the steering wheel as the truck bore down on them.

'Hee hee hee!' William screeched with a manic laugh, his eyes flaring wide. The sound of blaring horns seemed to funnel into Tyler's ears as he fought to control the car on the wet road. At the very last moment, before the truck hit them or had to swerve, William jolted the steering wheel, forcing the car over to the safety of the other lane. He collapsed back onto the passenger seat and cradled his arms around his body like a sulking child. 'Why don't you believe me?'

'You could have killed us!' Tyler yelled as he regained control of the car. 'Have you got a death wish?'

A furtive smile lifted at the corners of William's mouth as his attention returned out to the desert plains. 'No, I don't have a death wish, merely a certain indifference for the future, nothing more than that.'

Tyler's leg muscles cramped while he drove. He was walking with bare feet across broken glass, a lone driver on a remote highway under the control of an unstable psychiatric patient. He could only listen to William Kendrick's waspish breaths, as the burnt sienna sky surrendered to a veil of darkness and the storm closed in around the car.

CHAPTER SEVEN

**The Journal of Joseph Hawkins – July 5th, 1961
(San Antonio, Texas)**

I am finally done with school.

The army have given my father a six-month posting to West Germany, so my parents decided it would be best if they sent me to live in Texas with my maternal grandparents, that I can cause less trouble being with them. My brother and sister have been sent back to Aunt Irene's in California to spend the summer there. Even though my grandparents are straight and strict, I love them with a tender affection. It gives me a great deal of amusement to let them find banned literature in my bedroom and see their disapproval when my hair grows longer. It keeps me entertained.

Of course, I made a scene about leaving Colorado Springs. I vented all my anger and frustration at Betty until she cried. I did not mean to hurt her, but I learned a long time ago that when your life is a constant torment of moving around, you must leave precious things behind, even the people who you care about most.

I liked Betty and maybe that was the problem. I could not deal with the fact that my father's career was tearing my life apart again, so I shouted at her until I made her cry because I could not cry myself. When the day came for me to leave, I could not bear to say goodbye. I just got in my parents' car, and we drove away. It is now dawning on me that perhaps I was responsible for how I treated her, that I was the one who screwed it up. The angel child with ribbons in her hair will never know how much I cared.

I have no control mechanism over my behaviour, it is all or nothing, and I wonder how destructive that will prove to be.

Every night, I lie on my bed and write more extreme ideas and poetry about the human condition, as if my words are mirroring the chaos that I can feel developing inside my mind. I have been studying the great poets – Byron, Wordsworth, Whitman – honing and rewriting lines in my notebooks to perfect my craft. I think I was born at the wrong time. I should have lived in the nineteenth century and been one of the celebrated poets of the day, living a short and tragic life, but leaving behind a great legacy of revered literary works to be remembered by.

I want to create a name for myself which will become legend.

For now, and for the first time in my life, I am free from my parents' constraints. I have cut the leash. I am free-falling, uninhibited and loose into an existence of pure freedom.

There do not seem to be any consequences to my actions in the brave new world I find myself living in.

CHAPTER EIGHT

The magenta neon sign of the Mojave Desert Motel glowed into view across the highway. The tension in Tyler's shoulders began to loosen, as the fear of being stuck out in the wilderness with William Kendrick, was replaced in his mind by the reassurance of a lockable motel room door.

Driving rain had given way to a light drizzle when Tyler parked the car in front of the motel office. A teenage girl sat behind the reception desk, coiling a strand of bleached perm between her fingers, enthralled by the latest Madonna video playing on MTV. Tyler turned to William, who sat curled up like a gnarled beast on the passenger seat, and made the decision to go alone to get them a room for the night. Heading into the office, he tried to suppress the creeping sensation that it was William's intention to guide him to this isolated corner of Joe Hawkins' world. He attempted a weary flirtation with the bored reception girl who rolled her eyes, took his cash and handed him a room key.

The two men walked in silence around a neglected swimming pool that sank into the dirty depths of the motel complex; an overturned sun lounger lay drowned in what was once the shallow end. Tyler unlocked a room at the end of the corridor and stepped inside, leaving William leaning against the doorframe.

'All I'm saying, Mr Kendrick, is that we can work together to explore what's causing you these problems,' Tyler said, trying to clear the tension that hung between them. 'I'm trying to help you here.'

William slammed the door shut. 'So, you're playing the game, humouring me, huh? You think I'm some crazed freak who you can write about in your case study.' He dragged his hands through his hair. 'This is real life for me, Tyler, real fuckin' life.'

Tyler stood motionless in the middle of the room while William opened the window, lifting his face to an opalescent moon rising high above the desert. 'I learned a long time ago that there's no one to hear the screams of a lost man in a solitary world. That is what my life has become, that is my … *condition*.'

'I'm sorry,' Tyler said, sitting down on the edge of one of the two single beds.

William collapsed onto a shabby velvet armchair which attempted to complement the Seventies floral kitsch of the room. 'It's not about being sorry, man, I don't need anyone's sympathy. The world out there has made me into the person who I am today.'

Tyler decided to remain quiet, in their brief acquaintance this was the most unguarded his patient had been. Whatever truth was hiding in the crevices of William's imagination, his wrecked soul appeared to wholly believe it.

'Our fragile human lives are like transient reflections of the great planets and stars looming above us,' William said. 'The simple truth that prevents man's utter dismay at his own mortality is that he doesn't know in advance when the end will come. That's not my fate, Tyler. I'm a dying star, watching helpless as a black hole draws me into its tight, unyielding grasp. But whatever lies before me, I will make damn sure I tell you my truth, whether you want to believe me or not.' He took his cigarettes from his coat pocket, but realising the packet was empty, he threw it across the room. 'I will leave this world with a cleansed soul. I'm owed that much.'

Tyler reached over to the grocery bag and took out a fresh pack of cigarettes, handing them to William, as he walked past the armchair and went into the bathroom. Ice-cold water stung Tyler's skin as he pressed his hands to his face. While the water dripped into the dirty sink, the television evening news penetrated the tissue-thin bathroom walls. He peered around the door. William was perched on the edge of the armchair, studying the battling images of President Reagan and Mikhail Gorbachev flashing across the screen. Shaking his head and muttering to himself, he stood and switched off the television set.

When Tyler left the bathroom, he found William sitting with his right ankle resting across his left knee creating a platform on which to write. His head was slanting to one side, moving his pencil with a careful concentration across the page of his journal.

'Rafferty, Rafferty,' William said, not looking up at Tyler who walked across the room. 'What is that ... Irish?'

'Yeah, my great grandfather came over from Ireland, moved to California looking for a new life.'

The last wisps of cigarette smoke escaped out of the window into an infinite night sky that had transformed into a ploughed field of stars above the motel. Tyler took one last lungful of the chilled evening air, freshening his clouded mind, before settling himself back onto the edge of the bed. 'Alright,' he said, taking out his notebook from his bag, 'you were going to tell me about your college years.'

William's voice softened, shifting his body in the armchair. 'My parents made me enrol at the University of Houston on their political science course. But my new creative desires weren't being satisfied, so I went to this arts club that held poetry readings, showed independent movies and debated Eastern philosophy. I was shy and unsure of myself, but after a few weeks, I became confident enough to share the words and ideas developing inside my mind.'

Tyler wrote some notes, trying to ignore the muffled sound of a girl's laughter seeping through the wall from the adjoining room. 'Did you feel that you fitted in with the people you were meeting there, that you had a sense of belonging?'

'I did,' William said and stroked the cover of his journal. 'For the first time in my life I felt like I was part of something important, there was meaning and relevance to what we were discovering and discussing. The club owner, Gene Minetti, became somewhat of a mentor to me, and I was thrilled when he picked me out for special attention. Y'see, he had this natural power to allure men, women, anybody, as if he could draw you out of your comfort zone and into his own. It blew my mind, man.' Hesitating, his face paled. 'It was around that time I had my first, uh … experiences …'

Tyler looked across at William's dilating eyes. 'With drugs?'

'Not with drugs, Tyler, no, nothing like that,' he said with a gentle voice. 'One night, Gene invited me into his office at the club. We sat for hours listening to Elvis on the record player, talking about the poetry of Arthur Rimbaud and drinking bourbon. Then, as I went to leave, he stood in front of the door and pulled me by my belt buckle towards him. Adrenaline seared through my veins, my body succumbing to the touch of his fingers, as I let him unzip my pants and go down on me. As I closed my eyes, I experienced the greatest thrill I'd ever felt.'

Tyler twisted his pen between his fingers. 'You erm, like men in that way?'

'No, no, it wasn't like that. Y'know, looking back now I can see that I was young, perhaps a little naïve about life. I wanted to be like my heroes from the ancient world, who could achieve gratification in any way they pleased. I always loved women, but I enjoyed the thrill of a good time too, no matter who it was with. After that night, I would sneak into the underground clubs and bars on the darkest fringes of Houston, where there was a whole new world of different and interesting people who behaved as if there were no consequences or remorse to their actions. You could drink, let go and see where the night took you, not knowing what would happen or who you could end up with. My eyes were being opened to the real world at last, that it was alright to experience every pleasure on offer. I suppose, uh, it was all part of my experiment into unexplored taboos, and it thrilled me. It was something to tweak my curiosity … curiosity to see what would happen.'

Tyler watched William's focus draw around the motel room to where a collection of framed black and white photographs, from the golden era of Las Vegas, hung on the wall above the beds. William offered a weak smile to Frank Sinatra and Dean Martin, who laughed back at him through their raised whiskey glasses.

The hunger in Tyler's grumbling stomach burned. He passed a sandwich to William who shook his head in a silent reply, fixing his eyes instead on a can of beer lying beside the grocery bag. With a fleeting hesitation, Tyler handed him the can and sat back on the bed. 'Were you involved with any women at this time?'

'There was a girl called Lori,' William said through a long gulp of beer, nodding his thanks to Tyler. 'We dated for a while when I was in San Antonio, and I think she was the first girl who I was ever in love with, she was precious to me. She was intelligent and that's what attracted me to her. Y'know, I even think she brought out the best in me too, my charm and ability to be loving and kind. I kept going back to San Antonio at weekends to be with her. Part of me was excited to see her, although I was more eager to indulge in my new-found passion for hitch-hiking.'

Tyler crammed a chunk of dry chicken into his mouth while keeping a watchful check on the can of beer in William's hand. 'Wasn't hitch-hiking dangerous even in those days? Why did you like it?'

'Maybe that's what attracted me to it; standing on those endless dusty roads, stretching out your thumb with the calm knowledge that it was a calculated risk. It was like you were rolling the dice down the highway. Who was going to pull over? A lonely truck driver, a killer on the run, or an older woman who wanted to seduce you on the back seat of her car. It was the thrill of not knowing what sort of trouble you could get into that turned it into my obsession.'

Tyler took another bite of his sandwich. 'What about your studies, what were you interested in?'

'I was reading books on the human condition, a lot of Sándor Ferenczi and Freud.' William took a long drink of beer. 'I wanted to find out how people worked, and I liked the idea that everyone is suggestible.'

'Suggestible to what?'

'Well, people will conform because their thoughts and behaviour can be manipulated, and that's the key to getting them to do whatever you want them to do. All the most powerful leaders in history – Nero, Hitler – they knew that the people they wanted to influence were suggestible.' Finishing his beer, he threw the can towards a trash basket in the corner of the room.

'Nero and Hitler were some of the worst dictators in history,' Tyler said, swallowing his last mouthful of food. 'I mean, they only got their power through fear, intimidation and some misguided belief that what they were saying was the truth. They brain-washed the innocent masses into believing an ideology that didn't exist, an idea fabricated in their own minds to suit their own causes.'

'Very good, Tyler, you know history,' William said with a warm smile. 'I was never interested in dictatorship, though. I was only ever interested in creating a *reaction*, so people could learn something about themselves from their own responses to me: fear, repulsion, admiration, love. I guess I wanted to shape the individual soul to enable their development as a member of humanity.' He stopped talking and watched a frown deepen across Tyler's forehead. 'Why are you looking at me like that?'

'It's just …' Tyler brushed the crumbs from his jeans and looked back down at his notes '… I thought you said that you were feeling shy.'

The lights from a lone car driving into the parking lot of the motel struck into the room and lit up William's rigid body in the armchair. 'Mmm, I was shy. At first, maybe I was afraid of people's reaction. When I performed my poetry at the arts club, it took a long time to get used to people watching me, but the exhibitionist inside me was really starting to emerge. The good and bad sides within my mind were forming two very distinct personalities. Part of me was kind, shy, charming, intellectual: the *nice* Joe.' William's eyes enlarged, revealing a momentary manic flash which vanished in an instant. His voice plunged to a deep rasp. 'And then there was the beautiful monster, the wolf, the *other* Joe, the exhibitionist drunken disciple of Bacchus, the Joe who would ultimately destroy me: good ol' JoJo.'

'Are you saying that the shy boy inside you was being influenced by another, stronger side of your personality?'

William pushed himself up from the armchair and stood in front of the open window. 'Right, it was clear to me that it was time for young Joey Hawkins to die.' He took a deep breath of the cold night air. 'I needed to find a place where my new emerging existence could thrive. There was a whisper on the wind from the west. Los Angeles was murmuring my name, and my soul decided to answer its call. I could sense it all the way across America, Tyler, California was a burnishing Elysium, and I was the young moth drawn to its beautiful flame. It would be my place in the world where, at last, Joey would be free to grow and become … Joe.'

William's face drained of colour, and without any warning he lurched towards the door.

'What are you doing?' Tyler leapt to his feet and grabbed William's arm, stopping him dead in his tracks.

'We need to get out of here, right now.'

'If I upset you with something I said, William, then I'm sorry, I really am.'

'My name is not William.' He flung himself onto one of the beds, wrapping his coat tight around his body and turning his back on Tyler. 'My name is Joe Hawkins, and if you want proof, then tomorrow I'll give you proof.'

'And where are we going tomorrow?' Tyler asked, reaching behind his back to lock the motel room door. 'Because I'm getting the impression that you've got no intention of going back to San Francisco any time soon, do you?'

William rolled his head across the depths of a relatively clean pillow and closed his eyes. 'We're going to Los Angeles.'

CHAPTER NINE

The Journal of Joseph Hawkins – March 15th, 1963 (Houston, Texas)

Texas is becoming tiresome.

There is a world beyond the confines of my current life, a world existing on the perimeter of society … a dangerous place that I can feel drawing me towards it.

I have grown from a boy, buried in books and movies, to a young man who wants to put all that he has learned into practice. I have become interested in people, how they think and how they behave.

My college room-mates do not appreciate my new-found fondness for drinking, nor how loud I like to play my Frank Sinatra and Chuck Berry records at night. Finding their weaknesses and pushing their boundaries of tolerance seems to cause a reaction. People dare to judge me when I get drunk and cause a scene, but you cannot question others' actions until you truly understand your own.

Last week, I was messing around with my friends on our way back from a party, and I thought it would be funny to try to break into a sorority house by climbing onto the roof. I was caught, of course. When the cops arrested me, I experienced an overwhelming sense of anger, with an underlying thrill beating through my body. I was charged with being drunk, causing a disturbance. You know, it was a joke … a little fun. The cops were pushing me around, wanting me to break down and submit to their authority, but I refused to give them that satisfaction.

I want to explore a path less-travelled and see how many other people I can persuade to come along for the ride. I want to get a response from people, an emotional and physical reaction. I want them to learn something about what their souls are yearning for, yearning to be. You need to travel undisturbed in silence, free of limitations and physical boundaries, raze your thoughts to the ground before planting a new seed of divine creation.

There is an ever-increasing urge inside me that I want to be a performer of some kind. Rock 'n' roll music has seeped into my soul. When I listen to music, it creates an unconscious awareness that performing is something I want to do, that I need to do. Although, I am struggling to believe I can ever achieve it, trapped inside this insular Houston life.

I cannot contain my other desire to move back to California to study literature and poetry, it consumes all my thoughts. I have applied to transfer to UCLA in September to enrol on their English Literature course. My parents are furious.

This is an era of a new awakening. These are fertile times! I shall seek out all the world's gratifications and pleasures, with no restraints, no limitations, simply a pure joy in life. Perhaps it is my destiny to join in a great experience, a revolution to explore a new reality.

I want people to understand that you should never take anything in life for granted.

Things are never as they seem.

You should always question everything you are told.

CHAPTER TEN

A fat bunch of keys clung to the sturdy, uniformed thigh of Nurse Cynthia Wallace. She stood like an embattled guardian at the entrance to the psychiatric ward: no one in and no one out. She had wedged a clipboard deep into her hip, her attention secured on the closed door of Doctor Wesley Marshall's office.

The doctor was already buttoning up his pristine white coat and pouring himself a steaming cup of coffee. He felt wholly responsible for the constricting headache he was nursing; sleep had not come easily last night, and William Kendrick was the sole cause of his deepening discomfort.

The telephone on his desk rang.

'Hi, Doctor, it's Tyler. I know I'm in trouble, but I can assure you that William is safe. I'm going to bring him back, but I need more time.'

Doctor Marshall put down his coffee cup before he had taken his first precious sip. 'Do you have any idea what you've done? You must know I had to call the police.'

'Please, we don't need to get the police involved. William wants me to help him, he wants to be here. He's starting to open up to me and–'

'Tyler, this is for your own safety and protection. We have no idea what William is capable of. You need to come back to the hospital right now.'

'Doctor, I know I've broken the rules, but this was the only way that William was going to talk to me, to trust me. I swear I only have his best interests at heart. I'm going to bring him back, but I don't have much time and there are some things I don't understand. Right now, Doctor, I need your help.'

Doctor Marshall checked his watch. He tried to ignore the persistent squeaking of Nurse Wallace's leather shoes as she paced outside his office, waiting for the morning rounds to start. 'Alright,' he said, lowering his voice.

'I've got no idea if William is telling me his own memories or what he thinks are Joe Hawkins' memories.'

'It's his perceived idea of Joe's memories that he's telling you, no doubt confused with the experiences and emotional reactions of the young William Kendrick.'

'That's what else is bothering me; his neighbour, Adeline, made no reference to Joe Hawkins at all. I think William must be able to control the Joe delusion, using it as and when it suits him, changing his personality depending on whose company he's in. Everything he's telling me seems to be logical in its construction and chronological detail, he's demonstrating absolute coherence and conviction in his thought processes. It doesn't make sense.'

Doctor Marshall opened William's patient file, with a photograph pinned to the inside cover. William's head dipped towards his left shoulder, his blue eyes looming straight down the camera lens and his mouth drawn into a wide smirk. 'He wants you to believe that he's Joe Hawkins and doesn't want you to know who William Kendrick really is. You need to find out the reason why.'

'Do you think I should engage with what he's telling me when he's speaking as Joe? Play along with what he thinks are his own memories?'

'If listening to his perceived memories of Joe Hawkins allows him to open up and trust you, then yes, engage with what he's telling you, show him interest and empathy. However, you must remain objective in your own mind. Allow him to talk freely to verbalise his anxieties and emotions, question what he's telling you, but don't challenge his identity or you'll lose his trust. You must be careful though; the more you indulge William in Joe's life, the more the lines between reality and fantasy will become blurred, and the more dangerous his behaviour could become. Until William is back at this hospital, you must remain in control of the situation.' The clock in the office struck eight o'clock.

'Tyler, you have a choice: either you return William here today, or I leave the police to find you. Is that understood?'

Wesley Marshall put down the telephone receiver and took his first long-awaited sip of steaming arabica.

CHAPTER ELEVEN

The Journal of Joseph Hawkins – November 22nd, 1963 (Westwood, Los Angeles)

My new college friends and I crowded into the television room on the UCLA campus to watch the news report of JFK being assassinated before our young, impressionable eyes.

The horror of it haunts me.

The sniper's bullets blasted the President away, like an eternal morbidity caught on camera. I am trying to process what I saw but I'm struggling to make sense of it. I cannot stop thinking about it, playing those images over in my mind. It has had a powerful impact on me, an abiding knowledge that even the greatest people can be destroyed in an instant. Perhaps through the tragedy and violence of their premature death, their names will live on forever and they will be immortal.

I need to make myself a better poet. No, I need to make myself a GREAT poet. I must search my soul, test its limits, experience and feel everything, then make everyone else feel it too. There needs to be a systematic disordering of all my senses, shake things up to see what could happen, see how far I can push a situation before it breaks.

I will become a visionary by challenging the very meaning of existence. If I can stare into the void and dare it to look back at me, then I can reach a state of pure oblivion, the promised land of absolute zero. Only those people who are brave enough to destroy themselves in the process of becoming a visionary will be able to break through the veil of the unknown to reach the celestial splendour on the other side. It is a calculated risk, a gamble, a roll of the dice.

I have been studying a library book on the psychology of crowds, how they think and their collective behaviour. You see, one person could tell a crowd to be anything or do anything, they could cure that crowd of all their pre-conceived neurosis and beliefs. An audience will react to the idol bathed in a spotlight on stage through their own expectations, emotions and fears. They will react to everything the idol says ... especially if it is something they were not expecting to hear. The person who is in control of the crowd will become a threat, but an interesting threat.

These days though, I think I am opening my eyes at last. I am beginning to see the world as it really is ... a voyeur on the brink of a new reality.

There are a thousand ideas and dreams burning beyond the reaches of my soul, and I need to act upon them.

CHAPTER TWELVE

The sun spilled over the horizon, throwing its clear light across the highway and beaming through the windshield of the car onto the anxious face of Tyler Rafferty. While he drove, Doctor Marshall's words of warning replayed on a loop through his tense thoughts. *"For your own safety and protection … the more dangerous William's behaviour could become."*

There was no morning rush hour out here, only the occasional heavy-loader, and a slow stream of red-eyed drivers on their westward return from Las Vegas. The bitter stench of stale beer smothered the air in the car, a constant reminder to Tyler of what was the overpowering influence in William Kendrick's life.

'Did you read my journal last night, kid?' William asked.

'Yeah, I did.' Tyler had spent a restless night reading the journal, while keeping one eye on his patient who slept in the adjoining bed. 'What made you feel that you couldn't stay in Texas, even though you were in love with a girl, and were fitting in, getting attention?'

'I knew I had to get away from Texas once and for all. Y'see, all the while I was there, my parents could try to control my life through my grandparents.' William extended his arm out of the car window, watching the wind blow away the last dusting of desert sand into the suburbs of Barstow. 'Los Angeles and the west coast of America is the dream, man. It gives you the freedom to be whoever you want to be, and that was something I could never have hoped to achieve if I stayed in Houston.'

Railroad trains were parked up for mile after abandoned mile through the industrial outskirts of the city. The stifling memory of suburban America filtered back into Tyler's thoughts; the forced kindness and sympathetic smiles from neighbours who did not know what to say to a ten-year-old boy who had just lost his mother and whose father was shutting out the world. 'Why did you choose to transfer to an English Literature course at UCLA?' Tyler asked, burying the unwelcome memories back into the depths of his mind. 'From what you said last night, I thought you would have preferred to study philosophy or psychology, something like that.'

'Just like you, huh?' William asked, drawing his mouth into a wide smile. 'Why did you choose to study psychology, Tyler?'

'I suppose I wanted to learn how to help people.'

'Bullshit!' William roared with laughter. 'C'mon, don't lie to me, man, tell me the truth.'

'Alright, that's partly true,' Tyler said, trying to ignore William's eyes drooping into a half-closed gape towards him. *I think he's testing me. Is he starting to trust me?* 'I didn't want to be a corporate lawyer like my dad, jobs like that don't achieve anything worthwhile. I've always wanted to understand people, understand what makes them behave in the way they do. I suppose I was always curious to know what was possible within the human mind, what people are really capable of.' Tyler stopped talking, desperate to change the subject away from himself. 'Go on then, tell me why you decided to study literature.'

'As a teenager I became fascinated with poetry and literature. The great creative minds of Rimbaud, Kerouac and Nietzsche had the biggest impact on me, it made me want to live and experience what they felt and thought.' William closed his eyes, allowing the low sunlight rippling through the windshield to sweep over his face. 'Life is so transitory, Tyler. When you die, all that you'll leave behind are the words you wrote, or the music you recorded, or the movie you slaved to create. My words, my poetry and my music will remain forever ... my soul is etched onto paper and vinyl to create a great sense of timelessness. Literature is one of the purest art forms, there is a flow of consciousness to it, giving you the power of a god to control life, fantasy and reality. I suppose, uh, I saw the chance to study literature and poetry and allow it to shape me into the man who I truly wanted to be.'

William had fallen asleep when Tyler parked at a roadside diner, its retro chrome lines burnishing in the morning light. His curiosity had been growing towards the journal that lay closed on his patient's lap. Switching off the engine, he lifted William's limp hand, took the journal, and opened it.

'What are you doing?' William was awake and bleary-eyed.

'I was curious to read some more.'

'Were you now? All in good time, Tyler, all in good time.'

He closed the journal and handed it back as the comforting warm aroma of bacon and melting maple syrup wafted into the car. 'I think we should get some breakfast.'

Tyler held open the door for William, who lowered his head and wrapped his coat collar high around his neck, not looking up again until he sat down at a vacant booth in the farthest corner of the diner.

'Are you alright?' Tyler asked, sitting at the table and watching William skim his eyes around at the other diners.

'Sure, kid, I'm fine.'

Waitresses in pastel-blue dresses skirted around the booths, juggling coffee pots and plates of food. Tyler glanced at the Fifties rock 'n' roll memorabilia hanging from the grease-stained walls, before drawing his attention back to William who was perusing the laminated menu. Studying the loose waves of greying blonde hair that framed William's face, Tyler could not deny that he bore a physical similarity to Joe Hawkins. He took his notebook from his bag and began to write. *Was William's physical resemblance to Joe Hawkins what triggered his obsession? Two similar-looking men, born at the same time, but destined to live very different lives. He appears to be wary around strangers, there is a deep mistrust of people. He seems to be starting to trust me, so I must placate him and keep him talking. I must remain in control of William Kendrick.*

Tyler ordered breakfast and waited for the waitress to fill their coffee cups, before attempting to resume the conversation. 'Did you enjoy studying in California?'

The deep lines on William's forehead eased as he blew across the steaming surface of his coffee. 'Y'know, I loved it. For the first time in my life, I was contented, even happy. UCLA was another world that I could never allow myself to believe existed. I could study all of the literary heroes who I had worshipped since I was a boy. But I was crucified in class by my peers when we had to write our own plays and poetry collections, *group feedback* it was called … boy, they wouldn't know great literature if it kicked them hard in the ass.' He shook his head and took another sip of coffee. 'I was challenging the artistic and literary boundaries, and all they wanted to do was slam the door in my face. That hurt me, man, really hurt me.'

Tyler gulped his coffee. 'Why do you think your peers didn't like what you were writing?'

'Well, I had an excess of creative vision, but no advanced technical ability to form pieces of work that had real power to them. It frustrated me that I couldn't yet fulfil what I wanted to create, to turn the beautiful, chaotic vision in my mind into a reality.'

Two plates of food arrived at the table, accompanied by a cursory smile from the bottle-blonde waitress. Tyler ate and watched William pick at the limp pile of ochre eggs on his plate. 'Were there any friends or other strong influences in your life by then?'

'I made friends with fellow students who understood me, who enjoyed my company unconditionally: Lenny Michaelson, Joel Arden and Bud Goshen. We loved debating Nietzsche and Jungian philosophy, spent hours hanging out discussing the lives of the great nineteenth century poets or the future of American politics. Most of my friends from that time would remain close to me until the end of my life.' William's voice dropped. 'Then there was Sonny Nelson. He was older, wilder and was a bad influence on me from the day we met. He made me feel like it was alright to push situations further, let down your barriers, get loose and see the possibility of what could happen. When I arrived in California in the fall of '63, I was withdrawn, still a little naïve about life. It was Sonny who really got me started on the drink and drugs, and I followed wide-eyed his every word and reckless action.'

'Didn't any of your other friends try to stop you?' Tyler asked through an open mouthful of eggs.

William glared across the table until Tyler closed his mouth and swallowed his food. 'I didn't listen when my other friends told me that Sonny was a bad influence. We'd ride out into the desert, to the Joshua Tree National Park and the Santa Ana Mountains, spend bountiful lost days experimenting with LSD, peyote and mescaline.'

A teenage waitress refilled their coffee cups and slipped a flir-tatious smile at Tyler, but one voracious grin from William sent her scurrying away from the table. Peering over his shoulder, he observed the waitress with an intense interest as she retreated behind a row of morose truck drivers perched along the length of the counter. William's hand quivered as he turned back around and lifted the cup to his lips. 'Y'know, it wasn't so long ago that girls would have done anything for me, would have sold their souls to be near me, to sleep with me.'

Tyler dipped his head until the flash of colour receded on his cheeks. He finished a last mouthful of food and pushed away his plate, drawing his eyes to a clock on the wall. Across the crowded diner, he thought he could hear a dull *tick, tick, tick* hammering in his ears as he watched the hands reach nine o'clock. In one hour, he was due in Professor Kessler's office to present a case study proposal which was still a jumble of disconnected ideas churning around his mind. Gulping another mouthful of coffee, he feared that he would not be seeing the Professor, or Doctor Marshall, any time soon.

'You seem to remember everything with a very clear percep-tion, William,' Tyler said, returning his coffee cup to the table. 'Even though you were experimenting with drugs at the time.'

'I have a very acute memory, Tyler.'

'People only have an acute memory for things they're inter-ested in remembering.'

William slowly put down his cup as a broad grin slithered across his lips. 'I think you're still playing the game with me, aren't you? You're waiting for the moment when I get something wrong, testing me and trying to catch me out.'

'I'm not playing games with you,' Tyler said, trying to keep an appeasing tone while sensing a discomforting silence pass between them. He leaned across the table until he was inches away from William's face. 'The truth is that Joe Hawkins died in Paris in 1970. It's 1987 and William Kendrick is very much alive and sitting in front of me. It's you, William, who I'm here to study.' He stood, putting on his denim jacket.

William eased his body into the booth and tilted his head towards his right shoulder. 'You haven't asked me why I chose you. Why I chose to tell my story to a student, when I could have spoken to a professional. Yeah, there would be plenty of doctors in white coats wanting to get inside my head to find out what's going on in there. Have you wondered why I chose to talk to you, kid?'

Tyler was about to walk away from the table but stopped and looked back at his patient. 'I have no idea. Why did you choose me?'

'I chose you because of who you are, and yes, what you are.' William drained the dregs of his coffee and tucked a couple of dollars under the cup. 'I knew that I didn't need a psychoanalyst to misinterpret everything I said and how I said it. I had to choose someone intelligent, but with an uncorrupted mind. Someone still young enough to have some spirit left in them to challenge what they're being told.'

'I'm flattered, I think,' Tyler said, folding his arms. 'What made you so sure I'd listen?'

William pushed himself up, swaying his weight across both hips until he found his balance. 'I think you like a risk, and you couldn't miss out on analysing someone *real* interesting. I knew from your letter to Doctor Marshall that you'd be curious, and I knew your curiosity would come knockin' on my door. Besides, an adventure is always more interesting when someone's got something to lose.'

Tyler stayed a few paces behind William, who walked with a slow gait across the diner towards the door. He buried his hands deep inside his coat pockets, only lifting his head to give a playful smile to the young waitress at the counter.

Every thought in Tyler's mind told him to turn the car north, back to San Francisco, to return William to the care of Doctor Marshall. But the constant reminder of his unwritten case study kept his hands locked on the steering wheel and his eyes on the road ahead that took them further west. The only feeling of relief pulsing through his exhausted body was that he was returning to a place he knew, the City of Angels, where he called home.

'By the summer of '64, I was indulging my darkest Kerouac fantasies in one long road trip across America,' William said as Tyler drove. 'I was twenty-one years old, hitch-hiking from town to town with the freedom of the open road but enjoying the threat and thrill of trouble too. When I explored New Orleans, I found the bars in the worst parts of town, where sailors and hookers hung out. There was always the excitement of pushing a situation as far as it would go, and then running away before a fight broke out.'

Tyler took his attention off the road for a split second to glance across at his patient. 'What do you mean; the threat and thrill of trouble?'

'I was craving the sensation that prowls in the pit of your stomach, the thrill of living on the edge, not knowing if you'd survive the night or die. On one road trip out to Arizona, Sonny and I got a ride from this guy in his beat-up truck. He went on talking about all the bad things he'd done, all the bad things he wanted to do, his voice was getting in my head, man. Then he turned off the highway, pulled out a knife and demanded all our money. There was a terrible fight, Sonny kicked the knife out of his hand and beat the guy until he stopped moving. We jumped out of the truck and carried on hitching back to Los Angeles, bloodied and bruised.'

'Was he dead?'

'Perhaps. He, uhm, didn't look too good when we left him.' William lifted his hand to his mouth to conceal a mischievous giggle, unseen by Tyler. 'These have always been dangerous roads to travel. You never know what sort of trouble you're going to get into or who could lead you astray.'

The desert hills on either side of the highway began to flatten out when the car entered the neighbourhoods of eastern Los Angeles.

'This was my home, my place in the world,' William said, staring out at the wide residential streets framed with bungalows. 'Back then, there was a constant sense that we were part of a generation who could make a difference. We had a chance at breaking down all the political boundaries that our parents had inflicted on this country. There was something stirring in that warm Californian air, and I breathed it in until my soul burned. Los Angeles would be my stage, the city that would allow me to become the man who I truly wanted to be. It would provide me with an arena so great and so powerful, where I could act out all the beautiful, creative ideas I'd had since I was a boy. That lethal combination of Apollo's beautiful poetry, and the dark rock music of Dionysus, were about to wage a war on each other under the bright Californian sun, and all it needed was one man to stand at its beating heart and orchestrate the wonderful creation.'

Another perfect spring day broke through a layer of smog which had started its daily descent over the polluted metropolis to the west. William shifted his frail body in the passenger seat, watching the silhouette of Los Angeles rise like a phoenix from the concrete ashes on the horizon.

He closed his eyes.

'*I'm home,*' he whispered.

CHAPTER THIRTEEN

The Journal of Joseph Hawkins – June 5th, 1965
(Santa Monica, Los Angeles)

LA in the summer is a paradise on Earth, it is warming my soul.

I spend every day walking shirtless along Santa Monica Beach all the way to Venice, with only my notebooks for company, enjoying the simple delight of having no particular place to be. It feels like, as my college years have come to an end, my future is taunting me to reach out and touch it.

Anything seems possible.

I first met Clark Rivers last semester at UCLA when he stood up for a short story I had written, a re-telling of *Oedipus Rex* set in present-day Los Angeles. 'Bravo! That is art right there, Hawkins,' he shouted across the lecture hall, loud enough for all the students and the professor to hear. Clark was someone who I wanted to know and needed to know. He looked like he truly understood the world, as if he had just walked out of a film noir club in Paris. From the moment Clark and I first shook hands, I could sense the universe had tied our destinies together. When he looked at me through his black-framed glasses, he saw straight into my soul, and I think we both knew that we were going to be brothers in arms.

Clark plays keyboards in a band with some of his college friends, and they performed at a graduation party in Westwood. Standing there with a beer in my hand, listening to the band play "Johnny B. Goode", I felt the reaction from the students all around me who were going crazy. There was a tangible energy in the air. I want to know what it feels like to be on a stage, to look out and see hundreds of people reacting to me perform. I think it would make me feel alive.

Since that party, every night in my dreams, I can see a concert.

I am standing centre stage in a vast auditorium, enveloped in a blinding white spotlight. I hold my breath, the audience are all getting loose, dancing around in a state of eternal bliss as if they are experiencing the best night of their lives. Songs, music and poetry are playing, and the vast imaginary crowd are going wild. In a distant corner of my mind, I can hear every member of that audience chanting my name, 'Hawkins! Hawkins! Hawkins!' When I wake, I can sense an overwhelming urge to make this vision into a reality, this dream is my future beckoning me towards it.

The streams of poetry I have written since I was a boy will become songs … songs of great power and importance. I wonder if a song could actually change society, change the way people think and feel, that it could go beyond a mere collection of words into something magical.

To expand my mind to the limits of existence, I must experiment more with drugs. Taking drugs is a complete sensory and metaphysical experience, but at the same time there is a danger, a risk, a gamble. Each time you take drugs you are rolling the dice. Everything you think you know is flipped inside out. You drag your soul, kicking and screaming to the edges of oblivion, cracking open your mind like an egg; delicate and splintered.

The trips out to the desert with Sonny have triggered something within me. I feel like the drugs have activated the spirit of the shaman, the Native American Indian with a wolf at his side, who has resided inside my mind since I was a boy. The drugs have fed him, stimulated and fertilised him, so his spirit has grown, spiralling up from my solar plexus and into my mind.

A satyr now walks beside me, he is the essence of my soul's liberty, a fawn of Dionysus to guide me on this new journey of discovery. I want to step through the door from the known into the unknown, then I will have the power to change society's preconceived ideas and beliefs. Anything is possible if you have the bravery to step through that door without any fear.

My generation shall be the overseers of a new creation beyond humanity, a new humanity on the brink of existence. We shall have clear eyes to see things as they are: limitless.

I will make my perceptive vision into a reality ... or die trying.

The time has come for me to follow fortune's star and be engulfed in its burning train of fire!

It will be a gracious new dawn.

CHAPTER FOURTEEN

The car struggled through dense traffic that choked downtown Los Angeles and dissipated into the back streets of Santa Monica. Tyler parked in a bay behind a basketball court and switched off the engine, but William Kendrick made no effort to get out.

'We're here,' Tyler said to his silent passenger. 'Venice Beach, like you asked. You wanted to see the ocean.'

William grappled at the door handle and hauled himself out of the car. He stood, cradling his arms around his body, seeming fascinated by the low moaning of the ocean in the distance. By the time Tyler locked the car and reached the boardwalk, William had lowered his head and walked away.

Venice Beach still clung to the Sixties revolution that exploded along this length of the Californian coast. Hippie clothes stalls and tarot readers' booths jostled for trade in front of mural-daubed buildings, the air rippling with the sound of applause from a group of tourists huddled around a street magician.

'I liked it here,' William said, stopping to watch a fire breather shoot a dragon's breath high into the sky, the stringent aroma of paraffin sticking in the back of Tyler's throat. 'I liked that it drew all the strangers, all the drifters who didn't seem to fit in anywhere else. The beach over there was crammed with young people smoking weed, dancing around with flowers in their hair, all having a good time. There was a hot, endless sense of pure joy that we enjoyed that summer of '65.'

'Where were you living then?' Tyler asked, slipping on his Ray-Ban sunglasses while they walked.

'After I graduated college, I had no plans about what I was going to do with my life, so I decided to stay in LA and enjoy the summer. I spent every day writing endless streams of poetry and songs in my notebooks. I never knew where I'd sleep each night and I loved it. My college buddy, Joel Arden, had taken a summer job in a bookstore and was given the keys to a book repository behind Santa Monica Beach. A couple of nights a week he'd let me sleep in there, undisturbed. When darkness fell, I'd go out and lie on the sand, listening to the crashing waves and staring up at the moon for hours, meditating on its mesmeric power which seemed to be fuelling my creativity. You could see a lot at night around there, man, hiding in the shadows watching people when they thought no one could see them.'

'You liked spying on people?' Tyler asked. 'Do you know it's wrong to do that?'

'Ah, there's nothing wrong with a little voyeurism,' William said through a wide smile. 'I liked it since I was a boy, watching people from a distance knowing they couldn't see me, but I could see them. Yeah, it gave me a great deal of pleasure.' He rested his arm across Tyler's shoulder. 'Did you ever watch a movie, or a play, or go see a band?'

Tyler's muscles tensed under William's touch. 'Yeah, of course. Why?'

'Then you are a voyeur too, my friend.' Drawing his face close to Tyler's ear, he lowered his voice. 'The voyeur sits in the shadows and watches a peep show, a movie, a concert, or a stranger getting ready for bed – there's no difference. They don't know who is sitting there watching in anonymity, enjoying a violation of their private world, getting off on the silent power you exert over them.'

Tyler pulled away, trying to get a more comfortable distance between them. 'Were you finding some direction in your life, do you think?' he asked, navigating around the clusters of tourists and locals meandering up and down the length of the Ocean Front Walk.

'I think I was starting to,' William said, keeping his head low. 'I was going through a physical and mental metamorphosis at the time, changing from a college kid into what I perceived a Beat Poet should be like. Back then, I believed that, uh, from a generational perspective, it was important for any human development to make a clean break from the past. I was experiencing a powerful change. I burned a lot of the old notebooks from my youth, destroying all the childish ideas, forcing me to create new ideologies and words that were more powerful than I could ever imagine. It cleared my mind to give me a more dangerous creative freedom.'

Towering palm trees protected the golden sands from an encroaching procession of tattoo parlours and Mexican food counters. While they walked, William's voice kept falling, forcing Tyler to move closer beside him. 'Why were you so determined to remove any trace of your old life, of your childhood?'

'I wanted to destroy Joey Hawkins' past, giving me the freedom to create a new future,' William said. 'That summer I had time … a rare gift. I'd felt trapped in school for all those years, and after I graduated college, I enjoyed coming here to write and think with no pressure or expectations put on me.'

'Could you see a new persona evolving in your mind by then, Mr Kendrick?'

'Yeah, Professor Rafferty, you could say that. Joe was starting to evolve in my mind; an unknown butterfly was trying to rip out of young Joey's shell, kicking and screaming into the world. For weeks that summer I'd been pondering the idea of starting a band. It would be an all-encompassing musical, theatrical and metaphysical experience.'

The boardwalk curved around a wide stretch of beach. Tyler looked out across the panoramic view of the Pacific Ocean, knowing he was about to broach the subject he had been dreading. Attempting to choose his words with care, he took a long breath of the saline air and turned to face William.

'I once read an article in *Rolling Stone* magazine, which said that Clark Rivers and Joe Hawkins saw each other on Santa Monica Pier in 1965 and started The Gracious Dawn. Wasn't that how the story went?' He realised too late that his tone had changed, as an unintended pang of cynicism had crept into his voice.

'It was Clark and *me* on the pier that day.' William prodded his fingers deep into his chest. 'Clark and *me*.' He hurled himself onto a bench under the shade of a palm tree, turning his body away.

'Alright, take it easy will you,' Tyler said and sat down beside him. 'You and Clark were on Santa Monica Pier …'

William's voice mellowed as he turned to Tyler, waiting for a group of tourists to pass by before he spoke. 'So, uhm, it was a sweltering afternoon and, as I walked along the shoreline, I heard someone calling to me, "Hey! Joe Hawkins!" I looked up and there was Clark leaning over the pier wall, smoking a joint. I hadn't seen him for a while, and he was looking down at me like he didn't recognise the person who I'd become over that summer.'

'How had you changed?'

'I'd lost weight, my hair was to my shoulders, and my body was tanned and hard. Clark said I reminded him of Michelangelo's statue of David, that I was the ancient warrior of Santa Monica Beach.' William lifted a gentle smile. 'I joined Clark on the pier, and, as we walked past the fairground rides and rows of fishermen, we started catching up. He asked me what I'd been doing all summer.'

The pungent scent of burning incense permeated from an open-fronted jewellery store and swirled around the two men sitting on the bench. William's head fell back, sniffing the musky air with an open mouth.

'And what had you been doing?' Tyler asked, trying to retain his patient's concentration.

'I told him that I'd been writing some poetry and songs. "Sing one to me, Joe," Clark said. I was still shy though, and I didn't think I had much of a voice, but he encouraged me, so I sang a few lines.' William inhaled a deep breath and parted his lips, letting a stream of light singing slip from his mouth. '*Ride into the night, break the walls that held you tight, free the soul you search to find, start the revolution inside your mind* … When I finished, Clark had a bemused look on his face, as if he were staring straight at his destiny. As we stood at the end of the pier, looking out across the ocean, Clark turned to me and said, "You and me, Hawkins, should start a band." I smiled back at him and said, "We shall be called The Gracious Dawn." On a perfect summer's day, I began to see that music could be the vehicle for my words to become powerful, to become living poetry.'

The hum of guitar music flowed along the length of the Ocean Front Walk, swelling the air with the smoother sounds from the Sixties. When the melody reached William, his face crumpled. 'I need a drink, man,' he said, pointing in the direction of a liquor store nestled along a side street. Tyler shook his head, watching William reach into his coat pocket and draw out a couple of folded dollar bills. 'Don't give me that disapproving look, kid, I'm going to die anyway.'

'Alright,' Tyler said with a resigned sigh. 'Sit there and don't move.'

While he perused the dusty shelves, stacked with cheap wine and imported spirits, Tyler sensed the rigorous scrutiny of the store owner observing his every move. As he opened a refrigerator and took out a six-pack of beer, he tried to ignore the disappointed voice of Professor Kessler in his mind, telling him that he had failed to submit his case study proposal in time. Clutching a brown paper bag, Tyler stepped back outside and looked to where he had left William five minutes before.

The bench was now empty.

Tyler spun around, scanning the faces of strangers swarming along the length of the Ocean Front Walk. A shimmer of sweat was about to prickle across his upper lip, when he spied a man in the distance standing alone on the shoreline. He had rolled his jeans above his ankles and dark splashes of seawater had mottled the bottom of his sheepskin coat.

'Mr Kendrick!' Tyler shouted, running across the beach and dropping the bag. 'What are you doing?'

William turned and met Tyler's glare for an instant, before flashing his eyes at the paper bag nestled in the sand. Falling to his knees, he took out a can of beer and gulped it down his throat until the air in his lungs ran out. 'Is everything alright?' he asked, grinning up at Tyler.

'Please can you not wander off like that. I do have some screwed-up semblance of responsibility for you.'

William chuckled, took another long drink of beer, and looked away towards the ocean's horizon. 'Clark and I knew we had something special. We were going to be a diamond, a big bright shining diamond. When he invited me to move into his apartment on Rialto Avenue, it was the first time in my life that someone had offered to take care of me. But I wasn't stupid, I knew Clark wanted to keep an eye on me, keep me out of trouble.' He put down the empty beer can and wove his hands through the sand, making wide circular patterns. 'That made me feel good, y'know. For the first time in my life it made me feel wanted.'

A dusting of delicate clouds eased their way across the infinite powder-blue sky. William rested his body flat onto the warm sand and placed his hands behind his head, letting the sunlight dapple across his face. Tyler sat down, pulling out his notebook from his bag. 'What drugs you were taking by then?'

'Oh boy, it was more a case of what I *wasn't* taking.' William laughed, pushing himself up into a sitting position. 'LSD, grass, mescaline, uppers, downers and whatever pills, powders and liquids I could get my hands on. I tried anything and everything for the experience of seeing what would happen. Y'see, blowing my mind and trying to reach nirvana, allowed me to take a step back, to create distance between my mind, body and spirit so I could discover the meaning of being alive. I suppose I was experimenting, testing my limits.'

'William, what you saw as experimentation was the behaviour of someone becoming a drug addict.' Tyler took off his sunglasses and tucked them in the top pocket of his denim jacket. 'Do you see that?'

'You need to understand what those times were like back then. This was the Sixties.'

'I don't know, it sounds like you purposefully pursued the drugs and not just because it was the culture of the time.'

William pursed his lips. 'Mmm, alright,' he said. 'I had to learn what my limits were. I wanted to test my personal boundaries, shake things up a little and, yeah, I had fun while I was doing it. I went off for days at a time, swallowing handfuls of pills and vials of liquid not knowing what would happen, what mind trip you would go on. I was starting to see that the drugs were becoming kinda essential to my development.'

'Essential, how?'

'They break through your personality, disorganise your perception of reason and annihilate your inhibitions ... they nourish your mind, man.'

Tyler turned to a fresh page of his notebook and started to write. *Look at the long-term psychological effects of LSD on his pre-existing schizophrenia. William has not had any medication for two days and it does not seem to have any impact on his mental state or his negative thoughts. He is only showing physical symptoms: headaches, vomiting and stomach pains and those are consistent with his cancer. Alcohol does not have any effect on his ability to recall his perceived idea of Joe's memories. Doctor Marshall was right; William trusts me if he thinks I believe he is Joe. But I must remain objective. I must catch him out, prove to him that he cannot be Joe Hawkins. Can I cure his delusion with reason?*

William grasped fistfuls of sand, letting it flow between his fingers. 'For the rest of that summer, I was writing songs with Clark who left the band he had been playing with. We needed a drummer and a guitarist, so Clark invited a couple of guys called Dean Harley and Frank Sanders, who he knew from his new age philosophy group, to join our rehearsals in the garage behind Clark's apartment. When I shook Dean's hand, I could sense he wasn't sure about me as a lead singer, but I think he could see that my poetry and lyrics were something special. I was blown away when I heard Frank play his guitar for the first time. He closed his eyes, as if he were in a trance, and filled the garage with these raw, rasping blues. Clark and I looked across at each other, knowing without speaking a word that, at last, we had found our unique sound. That day though, Tyler, I was scared to even raise my voice. I sat twisting the microphone cable in my hands, feeling too shy to sing. I felt uncomfortable, all of a sudden there were a thousand eyes watching me … *expecting* something from me.' William looked away across the ocean. 'That afternoon, The Gracious Dawn were being born. My past, present and future had collided. The beautiful and destructive dream had begun.'

CHAPTER FIFTEEN

The Journal of Joseph Hawkins – August 28th, 1965
(Rialto Avenue, Los Angeles)

I am on the verge of a life that is bigger and more important than even I can understand. It feels magnetic, as if I am being drawn towards my destiny.

There is an electric anticipation in the air.

I have discovered what happiness can feel like. The hot, endless summer days have been the perfect conditions for making music, consuming my mind with a calm sense of contentment. Clark has been teaching me how to sing properly, to strengthen my voice. 'It's a matter of confidence and practice, Joe,' he keeps telling me. We spend hours working on ideas, imagining how we will make our band the biggest in America. Then we head down to the backstreet cafés at Venice Beach, scraping together enough loose change between us for a home-cooked meal, listening to The Kinks and The Beatles on the jukebox and hanging out on the beach in the afternoon.

Every morning, I look at my reflection in the bathroom mirror, my hair still wet, never combed, tilting my head to see how the curls fall around my face. I stand naked, moving my weight from hip to hip, studying the slightest muscle movements under my lithe skin with a new, clearer awareness. I want to see what other people see, and I want to be in complete command of how one day I will show myself to the world. Although, when I look at myself, I still see Joey – the shy, slightly chubby boy – who is now hidden within the body of a warrior.

This is a strange new reality.

Last night, I telephoned my brother. Once more I appear to be a disappointment to the Hawkins name. Mike told me that our father is upset because I am now wasting my life with a rock 'n' roll band. He says I will never amount to anything unless I chose a proper career. He wants me to follow in his footsteps, to serve with the United States Army and climb the military ladder. It is an absurd idea.

My father's words have ignited a bonfire inside me.

I will prove him wrong.

I will never see my father again.

CHAPTER SIXTEEN

At a Los Angeles law firm, residing behind a gleaming glass-fronted façade, Daniel Rafferty was in his executive office suite, engrossed in the due diligence of another faceless corporate takeover. The persistent ringing of the telephone on his desk cut through his concentration.

'Yes, what is it, Grace?'

'Mr Rafferty, I have Professor Kessler on line one for you.'

Daniel massaged the pulse at his temple as he pressed the flashing button on the telephone. 'Edward. How are you?'

'I'm good thank you, Daniel. It was great to see you at the clinical research fundraiser last month.' The Professor cleared his throat. 'I wanted to bring something to your attention, I think we both want to avoid any further embarrassment.'

Daniel Rafferty loosened the grasp of his imported silk tie from around his collar. 'What has he done this time?'

'As you know, our college remains deeply appreciative of your support and generosity.'

'What has he done, Edward?'

There was a hesitant silence on the end of the line. 'I'm presuming that your son has not been in touch with you this week?'

'No, when I last spoke to Tyler, he said he was going away for spring break; a party weekend on the coast, then a few days with his grandparents in Carmel.'

'I see. Well, I have just had a call from a Doctor Wesley Marshall in San Francisco. Yesterday morning your son took a psychiatric patient out of hospital without consent, and they are nowhere to be found. I'm afraid the police have been informed.'

'He's done what?'

'I'm sorry, Daniel, but there's little option left but Tyler's failure to graduate,' the Professor said. 'We have been more than accommodating to your son's unfathomable ideas and attitude. I warned him last year that our processes and regulations are in place for a reason, for his own protection. He cannot hope to have a successful career by being reckless and ignoring years of proven psychological and psychiatric practice. I've tried to help him, but I'm afraid he's gone too far this time.'

Daniel looked at a framed photograph on his desk. His young wife cradled their new-born baby boy, her eyes brimming over with maternal pride, while her devoted husband stroked the face of his first and only child.

'Leave this to me, Edward.'

He hung up the telephone, grabbed the photograph and, in one quick movement, slammed it facedown onto his desk.

CHAPTER SEVENTEEN

**The Journal of Joseph Hawkins – October 31st, 1965
(Venice Canals, Los Angeles)**

A placid lament of lapping water is soothing my spirit as I sit on the canal path, hanging my legs over the stone edge, while I try to process the changes happening in my life.

Dean Harley's father lent us some money to record three demo tracks in a studio on Santa Monica Boulevard. I gave the session everything I had, singing as if my life depended on it. After we had finished recording, we sat huddled in the engineer's booth and listened to what we had created. That was the first time I heard my voice playing back on a record and it blew my mind, it thrilled me. Is that what I sound like? Is that how other people will perceive my voice? It seemed like another part of my personality that was disconnected from my true self.

We hauled the demo to every record label in town with an eager anticipation. You see, I worked out that if you charm the receptionist, then you have a better chance of getting your music into the hands of the A&R guys. At one of the labels, I saw a beautiful auburn-haired girl sitting at the reception desk wearing a paisley silk scarf over her dress. As I leaned over and told her all about our band, I slipped my telephone number into her hand and pulled the scarf from her neck, wrapping it over my shoulders as I smiled at her and walked away.

I could feel the Santa Ana winds blowing into my life, my mood sinking into the dirty depths of depression as every record label in town rejected us. When the security guards at some of the major record company offices saw the four of us standing there – my hair curling to my shoulders, Clark with love beads around his neck, Dean's new handlebar moustache and Frank wearing his favourite striped pants – they would not even let us through the front door.

They are blind to our vision.

Frank has found us a new rehearsal space. His friends rent a magnificent old beachfront house, and while they are at work in the day, we are free to be there and perfect our craft. We are living in a beautiful simplicity, working together to form melodies around my words. It feels like we are creating something special, music to last for an eternity. As a band we sound different. Dean can hold these tight jazz beats, Frank plays both rhythm and lead guitar and then Clark's electronic keyboard unites us. We sound unusual and that will make us stand out from the crowd. We are now a group, connected through one communal, creative mind.

These days, I am drinking more until I can feel the monster stir inside me. JoJo is growling and wicked. There is no control mechanism over my behaviour, the demon within me is nourished by booze, coming to life at the worst possible moments and ruining everything. I am pushing situations further, for the thrill of seeing what would happen. There is no harm in wanting to enjoy life and have a good time while I am still young, is there?

I can sense a tangible change happening within me. My voice is beginning to strengthen, to deepen. Alcohol and drugs will be essential to calm my insecurities and fuel my transformation into a new incarnation of my personality. The small gigs we are now playing have not only given our band the chance to start to develop into The Gracious Dawn but have given Joey the spark to transform into a rock star.

Alone in dreams I can start to see the future man I long to be.

Joe Hawkins is being born.

CHAPTER EIGHTEEN

The Venice Canals resided in a peaceful tranquillity.

A patchwork of pastel-fronted houses hugged the edges of waterfront paths, where rowing boats swayed to an unheard rhythm beneath the water. Tyler and William stepped onto one of the white timber bridges straddling the canal.

'Even in those early days, I was adamant we were going to be as big as The Rolling Stones,' William said, resting his elbows on the railings, and watching the bottle-green water flowing underneath. 'We had been playing at some local college parties, but we needed a break and a late-night billing at a dive bar on Sunset Strip, called The Honey Trap, was it. Man, it was the worst bar in LA: hookers, pimps, dealers, drifters who came in off the street, bored businessmen in town for one night who had no idea where they'd walked into. But, for three nights a week, it gave us a small platform to perfect our sound and learn the art of performance, even if only fifteen people were watching.'

'How were you feeling, with people paying you some attention?' Tyler asked, leaning against the railings.

'I was excited … and I was nervous.' William gave Tyler's arm a nudge as they resumed a languid walk across the bridge and onto the canal path. 'I was a mess when we did our first gigs. I turned up still high and drunk, in the same clothes I'd been partying in all week. But, uh, during those few months, I think I was the most scared I've ever been.'

'What were you scared of, William?'

'It scared me that other people were holding my destiny in their hands. Our future as a band was dependent on us getting a record deal, but every day we were being told by the labels that our sound wasn't working, that our songs, with rock and blues at their core, weren't commercial enough to be played on the radio. That hurt me, man. I tried not to show it, but the rejection hurt. It felt like, once again, something good in my life was being taken away from me. Then I would have to go on stage, feeling the anxiety rise because I was an artist showing off his unfinished canvas. Everyone was watching the performance … judging it and expecting to be given something from it, like exposing your naked and vulnerable soul to the devil. I was constantly self-critical, feeling like I didn't belong or deserve to be there. I wasn't comfortable on stage, so I stayed close to the other guys, twisting the microphone cord in my hand like it was a security blanket.'

'Why did you feel so uncomfortable and self-critical?'

William raised his head to glance at Tyler while they walked side by side along the canal path. 'Well, I was on stage with everyone looking at me, and all I could feel were those old insecurities. I wasn't comfortable with the new slim, beautiful way I looked, so at most of our early gigs I sang with my eyes clamped shut. It took me a long time before I found the confidence to open my eyes and show myself to the crowd.'

Tyler stopped outside a weatherboard bungalow at the end of the path, sniffing the air which had become drenched with the heady perfume of blooming hyacinths. William bent down and picked off one of the indigo florets, cupping it around his nose, and inhaling the intoxicating aroma.

'Were you alone at that time, did you have a girlfriend?'

'No, I wasn't alone,' William said. '*She* was with me.'

'Who?'

'Angela.' He opened his eyes. 'Angela Jackson.'

'Angela Jackson was Joe Hawkins' long-term girlfriend, wasn't she?'

'Right, right.' William's face softened, breathing in the sweet scent of the hyacinth floret once more. 'I had seen her around LA a couple of times, then one night she came with some girlfriends to watch us at The Honey Trap.'

'Can you tell me what she was like?'

William smiled as he slipped the flower into his coat pocket. 'Her hair shone like a chestnut in the fall, emerald eyes, delicate pale skin and an infectious laugh. She transfixed me. I had retained some of the southern-gentleman's manners, which my grandparents had taught me, so I insisted that Clark, who had met her before, should introduce us. We clicked as two souls collided in the universe. The next night, she took me home and I discovered what it really meant to make love.'

William lit a cigarette and rested his body against the jagged bark of a palm tree at the end of the canal path. Tyler gripped the strap of his bag over his shoulder, still uneasy about playing along with William's perceived memories of Joe Hawkins. *He has constructed a fictional relationship with Joe's girlfriend too*, he thought. *An imagined relationship that he could control through his obsession with Joe.* 'What was it that drew you to her?'

'Ah, she was real pretty but had a vulnerability which made me feel like I wanted to please her and take care of her.' William winced as he dragged hard on the cigarette. 'Even though she was only nineteen, she had a hidden strength behind that vulnerability. She was wonderful … but uhm, I knew from her first smile that she would always be the most beautiful woman in the room, and that could only lead to one thing … trouble. Angela knew what I was like even in those early days, that there would always be others.'

'Why would she stay with a man who'd cheat on her?'

'Oh, that was the easy part,' William said, sucking on the cigarette, and blowing the smoke away. 'We had, what would now be called, an open relationship. Her door was ajar, and mine was swingin' off its hinges. She had other lovers, but she made me feel like she needed me to take care of her, and we always came back to each other.' William inhaled a sharp breath as his voice cracked. 'Angela Jackson would be dependent on Joe Hawkins to survive.'

Venice Beach was now teeming with tourists enjoying a temperate LA afternoon. When the two men reached the Ocean Front Walk, William's body began to shake. He pulled out his hand from his pocket and drew it down the length of his coat.

'What's wrong?' Tyler asked, stopping alongside.

William pointed a quivering finger at a makeshift clothes stall. 'That.'

T-shirts were stacked in a myriad of lurid neon colours, all bearing the same iconic image: Joe Hawkins, the legendary pose. A white linen shirt billowed back to reveal a lithe naked torso, a paisley silk scarf lightly gripping to the idol's chest. It was the image of a man capable of selling a million records. A young god stripped to the waist, hair the shade of autumn wheat curling around his face, his eyes brooding straight down the camera lens to lure the impressionable disciples deep into his soul.

'I don't want to see it.' William staggered back, his arms flailing at his sides. 'Get me away from here.'

'It's alright, take it easy.'

'Twenty years, Tyler,' he said, ripping his hands through his hair. 'Twenty years since that photograph was taken and still it haunts me.' Scratching his fingers down his face, he paced around the boardwalk. 'I'm still for sale, they still own me.'

'Why are you so upset?' Tyler asked, wary not to aggravate William any further. 'I mean, it's Joe Hawkins' most famous photograph, the same image I saw all over your basement.'

'It wasn't real, man, it wasn't me,' William said, his face now sullen. 'It was one moment in time and it's on sale for all eternity. Every click, every stammer of the camera's shutter would end up being a nail banged into my coffin. I didn't realise it at the time of course, I was a young wolf, howling and clawing at my destiny. By that time, I saw myself going through this process of becoming a new person. The existentialist's dream was at last coming true for me, and I was blinded by it.'

William sank his head, pushed past Tyler and began a laboured walk back to the car. An unexpected pity rose in Tyler's chest as he stopped walking and watched a lonely man struggle to weave through the crowds, a stranger in a world where he no longer seemed to belong.

Arriving back at the car, Tyler found William perched on the hood. 'We need to leave now if we're going to get back to San Francisco tonight,' he said, taking out his car keys from his bag. 'And you'd better hope I can clear up this mess with Doctor Marshall.'

'Yeah, you're right,' William said through a slow smile. 'We can't let Doctor Marshall down now, can we?'

'For the past two days you've done everything in your power to avoid going back to the hospital and now you're more than happy to go back?'

'Who said anything about going back to the hospital? You said we needed to go to San Francisco and that's exactly where we'll go, but first we need to make a couple more stops here in Los Angeles.' Tyler's body stiffened as William slid off the car and inched towards him. 'We're so close, my friend, so close to the end of one life and the birth of another.'

'I have to take you to San Francisco. Doctor Marshall has called the police; they're out looking for us right now.'

William snatched the car keys from Tyler's hand and unlocked the passenger door. 'I can't go back there, not yet, not until I've done what I came here to do. I'll tell you my story, you'll get to write your case study, then I promise I'll go back.'

'Don't you understand that I've got responsibilities here? I've got a bar job, if I don't turn up again tonight, I'll get fired. I'm probably going to get arrested now too, even before I get kicked out of college. I've already had one formal warning.'

'Ah, now we're getting to the truth,' William said, dropping the keys into his coat pocket and leaning his arms across the roof of the car. 'What sort of trouble must you be in if you had no option but to drive all the way to San Francisco to meet me? What sort of trouble must you be in at that college of yours if William Kendrick was your only hope?'

'It wasn't my fault if that's what you mean,' Tyler said, folding his arms.

William's mouth peeled into a wide grin. 'Go on.'

'Alright. I had a small disagreement with my professor last year. A patient I was studying had no quality of life, she was being poisoned by the drugs the doctors were giving her when they weren't necessary in the first place. She was depressed because she was lonely after her husband died, when all she needed was someone to talk to her, to listen to her. I suggested she could stop taking the drugs, that a more cognitive treatment approach might help, then she tried to take an overdose of pain killers. I swear, though, it wasn't my fault, but I was blamed and given a formal warning for endangering a patient. I only wanted to do the right thing, to help ease her pain, that was all.' His head sank to his untied shoelaces. 'I wanted to help her.'

'Very admirable,' William said, taking the keys from his pocket and hurling them at Tyler. 'Then what are you waiting for? The sooner we get going, the sooner you'll do the right thing for me too, right?'

Tyler picked up his bag and threw it onto the back seat. 'Fine, we'll carry on for a couple more hours and then we're going back to San Francisco.' He slammed the driver's door and tightened the seatbelt across his chest. *Who the hell are you?* he thought, sweeping the car out of the parking lot and onto Santa Monica Boulevard, back towards what was once the epicentre of Joe Hawkins' world.

'That's when it all changed,' William said with a quiet voice. 'As the flames of Joe's fire were ignited, the veil of darkness in my soul began to fall.'

CHAPTER NINETEEN

The Journal of Joseph Hawkins – April 23rd, 1966
(Santa Monica, Los Angeles)

A new sensation is stirring inside me. There is a brewing of ideas in my mind as I spend every day walking the streets of LA … walking and thinking. I need to be a conduit, a vehicle to allow my words to permeate through. I need to become the man who will allow Joseph Hawkins' poetry to explode onto the world, become the man who people will remember forever.

The gigs we are now playing, night after night, in the bars and clubs all over LA are showing me what a crowd can do, how it behaves. You see, an audience has a mass psychosis and a group psychology that is ripe for the circus master to manipulate from the centre of the stage. There is a dangerous possibility to feed off each other's energy. A rock 'n' roll show can be an experimental theatrical performance where the audience feels something. I want people to be free, to move, jump, dig how the music makes them feel in that moment and react to it with no inhibitions.

I want people to see our band perform and experience a change within themselves, within their minds. I want them to listen to my words, songs and poetry and challenge their thought processes, then there will be the possibility that we can change this world for the better.

When I am on stage, I look out and see an audience who have paid their hard-earned money to be entertained. Every night, I feel the pressure that I cannot disappoint them, even when we are playing to a handful of people at midnight. We are giving each show everything we have because you never know when it could be your last performance.

Clark was right, with practice and confidence, my voice is getting stronger and deeper. With each show we perform I am learning what my voice can do. There is now range, tone, softness and strength through which my words and lyrics can radiate into the audience.

A voice can be a powerful weapon to control, manipulate, shock and entertain ...

Tonight, The Gracious Dawn open at the Whisky A Go Go.

CHAPTER TWENTY

Sunset Strip. The road of broken dreams stretches from east to west past nightclubs, music bars and topless joints. As the car inched its way bumper-to-bumper through heavy traffic, William rested his fingers to his lips, concealing a giggle. 'The band were getting talked about all over town,' he said. 'We were gaining a reputation of sorts, and yeah, I heard what was being said about the wild lead singer of The Gracious Dawn.'

Tyler turned down INXS playing on the radio. 'What were people saying?'

'Girls would telephone all the clubs asking when that horny motherfucker in the tight velvet pants was coming back to perform, hee hee hee,' William chuckled. 'Y'see, uh, even in those early days, once my confidence grew, I wasn't afraid to use sexuality in my performances. I possessed a lethal combination of attraction and danger which the other singers on the scene didn't quite achieve. I was twenty-three and looked like Adonis, the Greek god of beauty and desire who had fallen from heaven and landed on Sunset Strip. I guess it would now be called star quality; a natural, youthful energy as if I didn't have a care in the world. I knew that my behaviour both on and off stage was really giving people something to talk about. I worked very hard on my reputation, Tyler, and I wasn't going to disappoint anyone who came to see us perform.'

The wide lanes of Sunset Boulevard hauled streams of traffic past an endless succession of low-rise tattoo parlours, clubs and liquor stores. 'This place, man, it never changes,' William said, watching a group of men loitering outside a music bar, clad in ripped jeans and with long permed hair straggling down their backs. 'In the Sixties, you couldn't move for all the pimps and pushers, the swathes of young people crowding outside the nightclubs which still clung to a distant era of Hollywood glamour. People gravitated here, they came to Sunset Strip to live or to die, there was nothing in between. It was a den of decadent debauchery.' William pointed towards the steep incline of Larrabee Street. 'Pull up, we'll walk from here.'

Before Tyler could switch off the engine, William had heaved himself out of the car and was making slow progress down the hill. Turning onto Sunset Boulevard, William's boots became rooted to the sidewalk, his head falling back to inhale a lungful of the thick, polluted air. 'Yeah, that smell, man, that raw Sunset Strip smell,' he said, as Tyler reached his side. 'Nothing else quite like it. It's still the same after all these years, I swear you can taste the seediness in the back of your throat.'

As a police car screamed past with its sirens blaring, Tyler turned his head away and raised the collar of his jacket high around his neck, hoping they were not looking for him.

'Do you come to these places, kid?' William asked, waving his arm around at the music bars clustered along the street. 'Tell me what the bands are like that play here nowadays.'

'It's still all about rock music around here. I come to see bands with my friends like Poison and Mötley Crüe – they're incredible. When I see them perform, it makes me forget my life, makes me feel like I can let go, have no pressure or expectations put on me for a few hours at least.' Tyler looked across to see William's face break into a contented smile as they walked side by side in a slow parade along the Strip.

'Now,' William said, 'Edie Harrison, the booking agent for the Whisky A Go Go, was looking for a new house band and she came to see us play one night at The Honey Trap. Sure enough she saw something special in us and saw something *very* special in me. The Gracious Dawn were on their way.'

The iconic scarlet exterior walls of the Whisky A Go Go sculpted around the corner of Sunset Boulevard and North Clark Street. William stood with his hands resting on his hips, studying the flyers stuck to the front of the building that hailed LA's latest rising band, Guns N' Roses.

'Ha! When we played here it was The Turtles and Jefferson Airplane.' William turned around and pointed down the length of the Strip. 'The crowds flocked from one club to the next, from The Galaxy, Pandora's Box and Bido Lito's all the way here to the Whisky. You had to walk in the street because there were so many people thronging around here every Friday and Saturday night, it drove the cops crazy. Everyone waited in expectant fervour for their next entertainment to commence, listening for their rallying call, waiting for someone to step forward and lead them into battle. You should have been here back then, kid, it was like, uh, everyone knew each other's business and we wanted to put this place on the map. LA was at the centre of an exploding universe, and we were the fire-starters at its core.'

'You want to go inside I suppose,' Tyler said, watching William dip his head into a low nod. 'Alright, stay here and don't wander off.'

Tyler disappeared inside the club through an open side door. When he re-emerged five minutes later, he found William standing with his hands clasped behind his back, his bemused face pressed up to the images of long-haired rockers plastered to the walls.

'I spoke to the manager,' Tyler said. 'I told him that you used to work here back in the Sixties, and you wanted to look around for old times' sake.'

'Yeah man, *the good ol' times*,' William said in a sarcastic drawl before heading inside.

Tyler ran his hand along the corridor wall, snagging his fingernails on the edges of frayed posters showcasing the evolution of rock music from Velvet Underground to Van Halen. Sitting down in a booth, he left William standing in the middle of the empty club.

'Right where you're sitting, Tyler, that's where Steve McQueen and Brian Jones once sat ... right there.' William pointed towards the booths along the wall. 'This place was packed, there were dancers in cages above the dance floor, people standing on the tables demanding to have a good time. By the spring of '66, we were opening for Buffalo Springfield and Captain Beefheart. Y'know, even in those early days we wanted to blow those guys off the stage. I started to see that my poetry and words weren't going to be enough for us to break through as one of this country's biggest bands, we would need to give the audience something more.'

Tyler observed his patient, who moved with shallow steps around the club as the soles of his boots stuck to the un-mopped floor. *Did William come here to watch The Gracious Dawn play?* he wondered. *Was that the trigger for William to start emulating Joe?* 'I imagine that coming here to see The Gracious Dawn perform in the Sixties must have been exciting,' he said, watching William for any reaction.

'I didn't see it back then, Tyler, how special those nights here were,' William replied with a deepening warmth in his eyes. 'It was the only time in the band's career when our songs were so new, so raw, that we could watch them evolving right there on stage. Y'know, we worked hard; we didn't just play gigs, we *worked*. We'd start playing and not know, night after night, where each song was going to take us. Then we settled into a hypnotic rhythm that left me free to do whatever I wanted with it.'

'You make it sound like you wanted to control the music.'

'Control it, manipulate it, make love to it. It was as if I could connect with the vibrations from the audience, the words and music fed off them. It had an almost mesmeric quality, giving your mind permission to let your subconscious go wild.'

Tyler stood and roamed around the club, peering over the bar stocked with bottles of hard liquor. 'Do you think there was a definite point in your life when your perceptions about Joe Hawkins began to control your thoughts and behaviour?'

William flinched, causing a vein in his forehead to buckle. 'Control?' He slowly rubbed his hand down the length of his left arm, swathed in his sheepskin coat. 'You think Joe *controlled* me?'

'I think there must have been a certain point when he engulfed your life and influenced your thoughts and behaviour.'

William turned and released a heavy sigh. 'Listen, Joe Hawkins was only one aspect of my triumvirate: there was Joey, Joe and Joseph,' he said, flicking each of his fingers in turn. 'So, if you want to put it that way, I'm sure there was a moment when Joe would take over Joey's life and thoughts. Y'see, Joe was too powerful for young Joey to control anymore.'

'You could clearly see Joe Hawkins evolving as a personality in your mind by then, Mr Kendrick?'

'Joe was now a fully developed butterfly, screaming into the world and luring anybody who was drawn towards his beautiful and dangerous flame.' He stepped nearer to Tyler and widened his eyes. 'And they loved him for it.'

Walking towards a shallow set of steps, William mounted them one by one. Taking his place front and centre on the stage, he rested his right foot on the base of a microphone stand abandoned from the previous night's performance. He pressed the shaft of the stand all the way up his thigh to his crotch and cocked his head to the left, lifting his eyes out into the heart of the vacant club.

'Get it on!' William's voice screamed out of the crackling speakers. Stretching out his arm, he extended every joint and tendon in his hand until the tip of his trembling finger pointed straight at Tyler. 'The young, expectant audience looked up to us, searching for someone to guide a lost generation towards the possibility of a revolution. I can still smell the slender spiral of incense coiling up from the top of Clark's keyboards, signalling to me that my time had come. I hung my eyes to my black-heeled boots, my body clinging to my purple velvet pants – no underwear – guaranteed to tantalise the young disciples. The girls at the front of the stage wouldn't look above my groin for the entire set.' William licked his lips, letting the glow of a spotlight fill his face, as he rolled his hips from side to side with slow serpentine movements. 'Clark was hunched over his keyboards, his white shoes tapping, as Dean lifted his drumsticks and started a quick beat.' Caressing his mouth against the microphone, William cupped his hand behind his ear and began to sing. '*Wake me from the sea of screams, ease my soul that lives to breathe, call my name, come to me, be the one, my freedom's dream.* The words flowed from my mouth and hit the crowd between their eyes. They were interested, this was new. I had them under my spell as Clark's head dipped into a keyboard solo and the blonde go-go dancers moved in time to our music. The energy changed as our set neared its end, the mass consciousness thought as one. Gently the crowd rose and gently they swayed as my voice reverberated into their souls. *Pictures of apricot sunsets, and gold diamond rings, she captures me. Memories of Eden, of sweet wine and violets, she comforts me.* The last chords led into a stunned silence that broke into a roar from the heaving mob.' William closed his eyes and his head fell back. 'The tamed beasts hung from every word pouring from the poet's mouth ... hypnotised.'

'Mr Kendrick,' Tyler said, hearing his own voice crack like a rifle shot through the empty club.

William snapped open his eyes. 'I need to get out of here.' He reeled backwards, knocking over the microphone stand. 'Get me out of here, now.'

Tyler opened the fire exit door and stood aside as William staggered past, falling against the exterior wall. 'What happened in there?'

'It's my memories,' he said, gasping for breath. 'They feel so real, whether you want them to be or not, like wicked ghosts haunting your soul.' Pushing past Tyler, William began a laboured walk along Sunset Boulevard with his head low and his hands buried in his coat pockets.

Tyler's troubled concentration dragged along the length of the sidewalk, following William back to the car from a safe distance. *If he was a fan of The Gracious Dawn, then he would have gone to watch them play,* he thought. *That is how he knows the details, because he came to Los Angeles and saw Joe Hawkins perform. William saw what he thought was himself on stage and that's what triggered his obsession. He is determined to hide the real William Kendrick from me, there must be a reason why. One way or another I need to break through to the real man buried in the depths of his mind.*

William leaned against the side of the car with his arms wrapped around his body, humming an old Sinatra tune to himself. Tyler helped him into the passenger seat and drove in silence through the deepening afternoon light, sensing his case study and future career slipping further away.

CHAPTER TWENTY-ONE

The Journal of Joseph Hawkins – August 30th, 1966
(West Hollywood, Los Angeles)

Jesse Winters, the president of Hudson Beat Records in New York, came to California to check out the latest bands on the LA scene. When Jesse saw our late-night set at the Whisky A Go Go, he really did not think much about us, but Edie Harrison persuaded him to come back on the Friday night to watch our first headline billing show. That was when Jesse finally saw how special we were. He even got his LA producer, Pete Adler, to come and watch us the next night to make sure that he was not crazy to sign The Gracious Dawn.

That Saturday night at the Whisky, in front of both Jesse and Pete, was one of the best gigs we have ever played. I had a new fire burning inside me. We did not just show them what we could do, we made them feel it … feel the possibility of what we could become, and it blew them away.

The air in the club was stifling hot, drinks were flowing and girls in minidresses were dancing up against well-dressed young men in their best suits. I let the tension build, immersed in the spotlight I closed my eyes, my hair falling over my face, my body rolling and caressing the microphone stand as if it was a girl I wanted to seduce. Enticing the audience along with me, I goaded them to let go, until we exploded into a crescendo performing "Into The Night". You see, every show is an opportunity to entertain, but more importantly it is an opportunity to gain experience of how to be a better performer.

When I walked back into the dressing room after that set, our lives changed in an instant. Jesse Winters offered The Gracious Dawn a record deal right there and then.

Last night, I was lost in a beautiful LSD wilderness and was late for our set at the Whisky, opening for The Byrds. When I finally walked on stage, still high and drunk, something triggered inside me as we started playing our new song, "Farewell, Fragile Child". There was a voice in my head telling me to say out loud the thoughts that have been fermenting in my mind for months. I was about to unleash the pent-up anger towards my mother and father, which I had suppressed since I was a boy …

Standing on stage, looking out at the young audience, I realised that you must destroy all the stifling lies and false ideologies instilled inside your mind by your parents. Only when you have cut those toxic parental chains can you have the clarity of thought to give birth to your own essence of existence.

As the song reached its climax, I gripped the microphone and at the top of my lungs I screamed, 'Fuck you mother! Fuck you!'

A shiver swept through the club.

One by one the dancers froze in their cages.

A communal intake of breath.

I stunned the audience into silence and while my 'profanity' has just got our band fired from the Whisky A Go Go, I suspect it will not be for the last time.

CHAPTER TWENTY-TWO

A rock band, lingering from their afternoon sound check, sat along the length of a scratched mahogany bar. Their dyed hair straggled over the padded shoulders of their black leather jackets, sleeves rolled to their elbows, heads nodding along to the throbbing beats of AC/DC echoing from the stereo.

'Yeah, this was it,' William said, entering the Troubadour bar with Tyler beside him. The West Hollywood venue had changed little over the decades. Music fans still jostled around a low stage and leaned over the edge of a wood-panelled balcony, ready to get the best view of the latest bands. 'This was the place where good ol' JoJo came to raise hell from the bottom of a brandy bottle.'

William heaved himself up onto a stool, while Tyler thanked the bartender who placed a glass of orange juice and a bottle of chilled Mexican beer in front of them. William snatched the beer bottle and poured half of it down his throat, before slamming it back down onto the bar. He delved his hand into his coat pocket for his cigarettes and lit one, drawing an ashtray towards him and blowing the plume of smoke away.

'If the band accepted Jesse Winters' offer of a record deal,' Tyler said, taking out his notebook and pen from his bag, 'Joe would have responsibilities and expectations put on him.'

'Right, right,' William said, before downing the other half of his beer. 'Well, after what happened with the rejection from all the labels in LA, we had no choice but to make this record deal with Jesse work. We were in the studio recording our first album with Pete Adler and the legendary sound engineer, Bob Blake, the only two men who could shape our sound into something marketable, which could be played on national radio. We were excited that this was our chance to get our music out to the American public, for people to appreciate and accept our work. Recording in a professional studio was a strange reality for all of us, it was a different way to hear our music evolve, different from when we were playing in the clubs.'

'How was it different?'

William picked at the label on his beer bottle, flecking damp specks of paper onto his jeans. 'There's a sterility to recording in a studio. There's no audience, no reaction, no symbiosis of energy. We had to record sections of a song over and over again and that side of it frustrated me. After we finished recording the first songs though, we had a sense that what we had created was special and it would last for years, not just a few weeks.'

Tyler tried to ignore the hissing laughter emanating from the band sitting at the other end of the bar, as he watched the tattooed drummer raise a bottle of Jack Daniels to his mouth. 'How was your drinking by then?'

'Pretty bad, I guess,' William said, shifting his flustered face away from the drummer, who laughed and swigged another mouthful of whiskey. 'I had been entirely seduced by the bottle in my hand. I was drunk and high when we recorded "Farewell, Fragile Child", which would be the final track on the album. It was one of those beautiful, serendipitous moments; the lights in the recording booth were dimmed, candles flickering in front of my closed eyes, so I could get loose and create the magic. What we recorded that evening was musical perfection, then sure enough Pete told me to do another take. Man, that was it, I lost it. I could feel JoJo lurching up from my stomach and he was angry as hell. I grabbed a full bottle of red wine and smashed it over the mixing desk. Watching that wine flow over the controls and onto the floor, it was as if my words and poetry were disintegrating before my eyes, extinguishing the fire of our beautiful creation.'

'Why do you think your behaviour was becoming more physically destructive?'

William stubbed out his cigarette in the ashtray, shifting his weight on the edge of the barstool. 'It was a little fun, nothing more than that. It was a way for me to, uhm … maintain the balance of control.'

'So even though Joe's behaviour irritated people, the band and the label knew they would be dependent on him to get success,' Tyler said, raising his voice so he could be heard above the screeching guitars of a heavy metal band starting their sound check.

'Right, and that would prove to be the start of our problems. Jesse took us to New York to play some gigs. Those shows were getting us great reviews and it was a big deal for an unknown band from California to break through onto the New York scene. We carried on working on the album during the day, but when we had some free time, I hunted down all the movie theatres and bookstores in the city. There was one place, however, where I knew I had to visit.'

Tyler looked up from his notes and sipped his juice. Making no effort to ease the hint of sarcasm in his voice, he said, 'Let me guess, a bar?'

'No, man, not this time. I wanted to go to an exhibition at The Met about the treasures of the ancient world.' William tapped his yellowed fingertips on his cigarette packet. 'Do you know what the greatest lost treasure of the ancient world is?'

Tyler put down his glass of juice, his skin bristling at the thought of being caught out by one of his patient's games. 'I have no idea … gold, silver?'

'The general assumption and misconception of your Eighties capitalised generation is that all treasure in life is material.' He leaned in closer. 'The greatest lost treasure of the ancient world is a person: Alexander the Great.'

'You were interested in Alexander the Great?' Tyler asked, before realising the answer to his own question. 'You liked him because he ruled the ancient world, the great controller of mankind.'

William erupted into a peal of laughter and slammed his hand onto Tyler's back. 'Right, that was true. Alexander was so clear to me, like the images in a hundred history books I devoured as a boy. A resolute vision of a warrior, sculpted with youth etched onto his face. His head tilted to one side with an effortless ease, his weight resting on his left hip, hair curling around his ears and determination burning in his eyes.' William shifted his weight on the stool, dipping his head towards his left shoulder. 'When my image as a rock star emerged, it wasn't my own image that I showed to the world, it was Alexander's.'

Tyler lowered his voice and closed his notebook. 'So, have you believed in the past that you are other people, William, other than Joe Hawkins?' His heartbeat quickened as he teetered on the brink of his patient's truth. 'You thought you were Alexander the Great too?'

'Yeah, Professor Rafferty, I'm Alexander the Great! I'm Joe Hawkins! I'm Jesus Christ too!' William thrust his face towards Tyler's ear. 'I've told you before, kid, I'm not crazy.'

William slammed down a couple of dollar bills and attempted to find his balance getting off the stool. He paused to drawl his mouth into a broad grin at the ginger-haired lead singer of the rock band. 'Good luck, man,' he said, as his smile faded and he sidled out of the bar.

Grabbing his notebook, Tyler followed William out onto Santa Monica Boulevard. 'You can sit here if you like,' William said, sitting down on a low wall and curving his body away, 'but I'm not talking to you anymore. I'm not in the mood.'

Tyler sat beside him, keeping a careful distance. 'I'm sorry, but I had to ask.' He dropped his bag on the ground and rubbed his watch strap around his wrist; he had little time to get the conversation back on course. 'You were telling me about the exhibition at The Met. I'd like to hear about that.'

The tension around William's eyes relaxed as he slowly turned his head to Tyler. 'Y'know, the promise of an eternity of art and culture all under one roof was thrilling. My hands brushed along the sealed glass cases in each gallery, containing objects last held thousands of years ago, maybe by Alexander himself. I had an overpowering sense of my own reality, my own place in existence, in history and in time – perspective, I guess you could call it.

I went from one gallery to the next and that's when I saw it … a painting hanging on the wall in front of me.'

Tyler stood and took out his car keys from his bag. 'What was so special about this painting?'

'It was a depiction of Alexander the Great's death in 323 BC. He was lying dead in bed, his body draped in a sheet and with mourners worshipping at his feet. As a boy, I'd read Plutarch's account of how Alexander's body didn't decompose, it remained lifelike and pure for days after his physician had pronounced him dead.' A coy smile broke at the corner of William's mouth. 'It got me thinking; what if Alexander wasn't dead? What if he was still alive in a coma and his lifelike state at the time of his embalming was mistakenly attributed by his followers to him being a god?'

'That's crazy,' Tyler said, folding his arms.

William pushed himself up from the wall and rested his elbows across the roof of the car. 'For the briefest moment, as I studied that painting, an insurmountable spark of an idea was unwittingly instilled in my mind, where it would reside until I needed it once more. The most famous man in the world could appear to have died, when in fact he was still alive.'

CHAPTER TWENTY-THREE

**The Journal of Joseph Hawkins – February 23rd, 1967
(West Hollywood, Los Angeles)**

Last night Angela and I were driving along Sunset Boulevard. Erupting into the night sky was a billboard for our eponymous debut album, bathed in spotlights a hundred feet high:

> THE GRACIOUS DAWN – WAKE UP TO
> A NEW SOUND!

No other band has ever had a billboard in LA to advertise their music. A strange sensation struck through my body ... excitement, a thrill ... and at the same time the blood ran cold in my veins. There was my face on a billboard which the previous week had been used to sell cigarettes. I saw a young idol, a beautiful god and I knew he was not real, he was not me. How am I ever meant to live up to the perfect image the record label have created? We are now on show for the world to purchase at any price.

My life has changed forever.

The poet is for sale.

All I want is for my words to reach far inside people's souls, to touch the frightened, fragile child which still exists within them. As a band, we must always put on a good show and that must be our driving force. I will create a rock concert that is so cool, so explosive, that an audience can feel it, experience a raw energy that sweeps them off their feet. People will remember how it made them feel for the rest of their lives. When I write a song,

I do not see it as a collection of words, but an entire performance in my head, so when it is performed it becomes a consensual dramatic conversation between us and the audience.

Some days, I think about how our songs and my words could have personal consequences for anyone who listens to our records or reads about us in magazines. It scares me that what I am saying could be misinterpreted. The media is something I must retain complete control over, I will manipulate them to my advantage, say only what I want them to hear.

We are all changing since the band signed our record deal, there is an increasing pressure on our young shoulders that this album must achieve high record sales and radio plays. As the weeks and months pass, I feel like no one understands me. My mind is fighting a constant battle. I neither know what side I am fighting on, nor for whom I am meant to be fighting.

Solitude has become a vital part of my new existence. I need to get away, I need a sanctuary, somewhere I will be left alone to contemplate my life.

Solitude is the only way I can attempt to change crisis into clarity.

CHAPTER TWENTY-FOUR

A burgeoning twilight cast long shadows that drew across the Los Angeles skyline and came to rest against the walls of the Sunset Vista Motel on La Cienega Boulevard. Tyler swung the car into the parking lot, finding a secluded bay where prying eyes could not see his car from the street. William struggled out of the passenger seat and staggered back as if someone had punched the air out of his lungs.

'This was my refuge, all those years ago,' he said to Tyler, who surveyed the decaying motel building, its exterior still painted in the pale mint and pink hues of its fashionable Fifties prime. William kept his eyes drawn to the upper corridor and tucked some cash into Tyler's hand. 'Ask them if room 23 is free, I'd very much like to see that old place one last time.'

Tyler went into the office and returned five minutes later clutching a room key. 'Room 23.'

The stale air in the humid motel room was soured with the residual scent of casual love affairs. Running his hand along the discoloured cream walls, William stopped to draw his fingertips down cracks where olive green paint peeled underneath. The previous residents of the room had covered every surface with scrawled graffiti; for seventeen years, Joe Hawkins' disciples had flocked here with the desire to spend the night in their idol's bed.

Tyler watched William walk around the room, wavering by the bathroom door where some fresh red ink read: *Ride into the night, RIP Joe.* Closing his eyes, he slid his fingers down the wall.

'Are you OK?' Tyler asked.

William nodded back and stood by the window, peering out across the darkening streets of West Hollywood. 'Y'know, these few blocks were my universe. You wouldn't think that a couple of streets could be the making and breaking of one man, but it happened, and it all happened down there.'

Tyler looked around at the dingy room. 'Why did you want to stay here?'

'This was my favourite place to live, my sanctuary. For a few dollars a night it allowed me to live at the centre of Joe Hawkins' world.' He paused to sniff the sultry air emanating into the room from the street below. 'This was my private space at the centre of my realms of both business and pleasure. I had The Gracious Dawn's office and rehearsal space, while on the periphery were all the topless bars in which to spend many pleasurable evenings, uh … degenerating my mind.'

Tyler sat on the edge of the bed and tried to ignore the odour of cigarette smoke leaching through the wall from next door. 'You actually enjoyed staying here?'

'This place became somewhat of a hideaway for me, somewhere to stay when Angela and I had fought. I still enjoyed not knowing where I was going to sleep each night and I liked to have a selection of secret bolt holes around LA for when I needed to, uhm, get away.'

'Somewhere for you to bring other women?'

'Something like that, yeah,' William said, slipping a grin over his shoulder before resuming his attention on the cars piling up at the intersection of La Cienega and Melrose Avenue. The repetitive glow from the changing traffic lights penetrated the dusk creeping into the room. 'I'll tell you something, kid, LA had a pulse back in the Sixties, like it was alive. These streets survived on a beat of music and revolution pumping through its veins. Those days were special, they hit a moment in time, grabbed at the underbelly of the nation's unease.'

'And I suppose Joe Hawkins came along at the precise time to manipulate that unease,' Tyler said, as he stood and joined William by the window.

'Y'see, it was Vietnam. The time was ripe to grasp at the sense of disquiet and make The Gracious Dawn into a band who wouldn't be afraid to act as a mirror to how the nation was feeling.'

'I thought you said Joe's father was in the army. Was he involved in the Vietnam War?'

Deep lines furrowed into William's forehead as he drew his hand along the wall, flecking the floor with cracked cream paint. 'The war had a deep impact on me at that time, watching the horror unfold on the television set. I was having nightmares of children being burned by napalm, blindfolded soldiers tied up in front of firing squads. Every morning, when I woke, I knew my father was right in the middle of it, helping to orchestrate that terrible destruction of humanity.'

Tyler kneaded the strained muscles in his shoulder and went to the bathroom, leaving the door ajar so he could keep one eye on his patient. While he washed his hands, he glanced around the bathroom door. Now alone, William pressed his face against the windowpane, tracing his fingertips along the outline of the liquor stores and bars on the street below.

'So, it was going to be a political statement the band wanted to make?' Tyler asked, wiping his hands down the back of his jeans and sitting at a small table.

William bent down and took out a warm can of beer from the grocery bag, struggling to pull the tab with his quivering fingers. 'We weren't a political band, that was never on our agenda. I think we mirrored society, not politics – politics is only ever a private and personal search for power.' He took a long gulp of beer and meandered around the room, keeping one arm clasped around his body and craning his head to read the graffiti on the walls. 'I guess we were telling people that it was alright to start their own journeys of discovery, to challenge what their parents had forced them to believe about the world. I wanted to give people a sudden understanding that they could be whoever they wanted to be, to have complete freedom of thought.'

Tyler opened his bag and took out his notebook, flicking to the back pages where he had secreted *The Positive and Negative Syndrome Scale*. He scanned the list of symptoms and behaviours:

anxiety, depression, suspicion, thought-withdrawal, manipulation, and made a brief note and rating beside each one. 'That could be dangerous though.'

'Perhaps.' William straightened his head and took another mouthful of beer. 'I really didn't care if people loved or hated us, I just wanted to make people think, encourage an audience to change their ideas and thought processes. That doesn't make their reaction and behaviour my fault.'

'Should one man's words or ideas wield that sort of power?'

'Sure, why not? It only takes one well-placed word to start a revolution.'

Tyler raised his eyebrows. 'Or a riot.'

William grinned, lifted the beer can to his mouth and, in one long gulp, emptied the contents down his throat. Tyler tried to swallow the persistent guilt that he was feeding his patient's addiction, while knowing only the promise of alcohol would keep him talking. 'Do you think Joe Hawkins was entitled to have that kind of influence on young people?'

'Yeah, sure. If it wasn't me, then who would?' William asked, running the back of his hand across his mouth. 'Freedom of thought is within everyone's grasp if you open your mind to it. But the only way to open your mind is through knowledge and the best way to gain knowledge is through experience. Y'see, ideas aren't conceived in a vacuum by great philosophers. You have to do something with an idea, develop it, transmit it and then allow others to transform it into something special.'

Tyler put the end of his pen into his mouth and chewed it. He kept his concentration secured on William who continued to roam around the motel room, stopping to read the scribbles of Joe Hawkins' poetry on the walls. 'Some people fear freedom though,' Tyler said. 'I mean, not every person going to a Gracious Dawn gig would have wanted those ideas pushed onto them.'

'Right, right. I wanted people who were too afraid to experience freedom to at least try to reach out to it, to feel that fear and act upon it. Standing on stage, I could hold the door to enlightenment open for people, but I could never force them through to the other side. Y'see, you must always allow for the free will of the individual.' William took a long breath and pointed his index finger at Tyler. 'People, at a basic psychological level, feel safe with routine and structure. The world is out there to be enjoyed and explored, but they prefer to hide away in their living rooms watching life being acted out on their televisions. People like being told by DJs what songs to listen to on the radio, allowing themselves to be manipulated by the advertising giants who tell them what products to consume. Life and freedom of thought are the great unknowns, and it scares people to death, man.' Stepping over to the table, he pressed his rough fingertip onto the centre of Tyler's forehead. 'If you can change what's in here, free your thoughts and face your fears, only then can you change the world.'

William disappeared into the bathroom and slammed the door. Now alone, Tyler listened to the constant rumble of traffic, accompanied by the sporadic sound of his patient vomiting into the toilet. He cleared his throat against the cloying air and flicked through his notes, trying to find any evidence or coherence of William's true memories. *How do I make this work?* he thought, throwing his pen onto the table. *How do I find out who this man really is?*

Leaving the bathroom, rubbing his bloodshot eyes, William sat down on the edge of the dilapidated bed, its old wooden frame creaking under even his slight weight.

'You had chosen to be more isolated as a boy,' Tyler said. 'And now Joe was part of a close group, surrounded by people.'

'Right, that was true.' William paused to light a cigarette. 'I think in those early days I enjoyed the cocoon, I felt safe within the group of people around me. I enjoyed being on the road, we had a great time. Don't forget, Tyler, we were a bunch of long-haired kids let loose into the big wide world, even though my behaviour went further than the rest of the band. I was running wild. Night after night, gig after gig, city after city, slamming down shot after shot until I had drowned the demons incubating in my soul. I didn't give a damn when a girl jerked me off as

I stood at the bar, in front of anyone sorry enough to be nearby. God help anyone who got in my way on nights like that. Then, after months of shows, we got our first big headline billing at the Avalon Ballroom in San Francisco … and it scared me to death.'

'That's what you wanted all along, wasn't it? You were getting the attention that you craved.'

'I guess so, although I was still nervous because it was our largest audience yet,' William said, sucking hard on his cigarette. 'Backstage, I drank a bottle of wine and swallowed a lump of hash to deal with how that gig made me feel. Standing on stage at the Avalon Ballroom, I realised that I had complete power to make thousands of young people, most of whom were no older than me, do anything I said. Then the adrenaline kicked in and boiled over into my performance. I goaded the audience to see what would happen, and sure enough with each tease and taunt that surged from my mouth, I began to see the spark of a revolution in their eyes.'

The screech of a speeding police car tore into the motel room from the street below, stalling Tyler's troubled concentration. Taking a moment to re-focus, he chose his words with care. 'Do you think the Joe Hawkins persona was now fully developed in your mind by this point?'

William gently rocked his body back and forth on the edge of the bed, gripping his cigarette between his thumb and middle finger. 'I think, uh … the more shows we did allowed Joe to really develop, yeah. The world was seeing me become the exhibition-ist and circus master, *Wild Joe*, but I could still feel young Joey Hawkins clinging onto life inside me, cowering in the back of my mind like a frightened child trapped at the bottom of a well.'

'You kept saying that Joey wanted to change his life, that he wanted to become Joe Hawkins, the famous rock star,' Tyler said, watching William's eyes sharpen across the room to where he sat at the table.

'No, kid, no, I never said that I intended to be the *famous* rock star, I just wanted to achieve recognition. Fame was merely an accidental consequence of my new existence; it is only ever a ruinous by-product of success. I'll tell you the truth; I wanted us as a group to be successful and quickly. I wanted to perform and gain recognition as a poet and musician, for my words to change society. More than that though, I wanted my poetry to make me immortal, so my name and words would live on forever. Y'see, by May '67, our single "Into The Night" was climbing up the charts, being played every minute on national radio, so one day we woke up and we were no longer an unknown band from LA … we were famous.'

'Can we talk more about your family? When was the last time you had any contact with them?'

William's body stiffened forward, extinguishing the cigarette in a glass ashtray balanced on his thigh. 'My brother telephoned me here and said he'd bought a copy of our debut album and listened to it with his friends. He was proud of what I'd achieved, y'know. Then he played the LP to my parents who sat in their living room in silence. My mother wanted to try to understand what I was doing with my life, but my father would never accept my career choice. When my sister and mother came to our show in San Diego, I walked straight past them in the hotel lobby and didn't even look at my mother when she called my name.' He took a harsh breath. 'I never saw her again.'

Tyler stood and stretched as he walked around the motel room. 'Can I ask you something, Mr Kendrick?' Resting his back against the door, he folded his arms. 'Do you believe in fate and destiny?'

'I don't know. Perhaps, maybe,' William said. 'Why do you ask?'

'I was just wondering if you felt somehow destined to take on Joe Hawkins' persona.'

'Mmm,' William murmured, stroking his fingers through his beard and tilting his head towards his shoulder. 'Destiny, I always thought, was something that everyone was in control of. So, from that perspective, it was my destiny to become Joe Hawkins because I made it happen. As for fate … no, fate is something different.'

'What do you mean?'

William straightened his head and pierced his eyes at Tyler. 'It was destiny that created Joe Hawkins and fate would decree he had to die.'

CHAPTER TWENTY-FIVE

**The Journal of Joseph Hawkins – June 18th, 1967
(Monterey, California)**

The Gracious Dawn are here at the Monterey International Pop Music Festival to play alongside The Mamas & The Papas, Grateful Dead and Jimi Hendrix. This afternoon, as we walked on stage, we have the biggest selling single in America. "Into The Night" has reached number one in the Billboard Hot 100. At last we have earned our rightful place on this vast stage alongside the great bands and artists.

We have been playing countless gigs.

The more shows we play, the more the crowds come along with an eager look on their faces. It feels like they do not just want to see a band, they want to be entertained with a performance that is new and somehow dangerous. The word has got out that we are a group to see, and the audiences are growing before our eyes. We have gone from playing to fifty people at midnight, to having twenty thousand faces at a festival watching us, expecting something from us and expecting something from me. They are demanding to be entertained and I will not disappoint them.

At each show I am learning how to be a better performer. I close my eyes, drawing in the raw energy from the audience until it consumes my mind and body. Straddling the microphone stand, I rock it from side to side, mirroring its sway with my hips in time to the music. Then, in one smooth movement, I fall to one knee, stretching out my arm towards a girl in the front row, her eyes widening as she takes my penetrating voice deep inside her soul.

We have spent months travelling in a beat-up old VW van. I sit in the back with my feet hanging out of the open window, watching the world breeze past and writing poetry in my note-books. Standing on stage at the festival grounds, I look at those young music fans in the crowd, all having a good time with flowers in their hair and the promise of a revolution beating in their hearts. The look on their faces will always stay with me. There is a longing need in their eyes for something to change, that they deserve change, this new dawn is their time.

I am having some leather pants made for me to wear on stage, to be slung low around my nimble hips. I am naked underneath black leather, teasing people with what lies beneath. I am alive inside the body of the beast, wearing its skin. I am the T-Rex from a million years ago and other people are lower down the food chain. I have always had a fascination with reptiles and snakes, their primeval quality, the colours and facets of their skin and their peristaltic motion. They are my totems ... everybody fears them.

I am a snake. I am a lion. I am a wolf.

You cannot tame a wolf.

I have created a vision of the beast that some days I can feel prowling inside me. Standing front and centre on stage, I am sultry, brooding and dangerous. Perhaps Joe Hawkins is a care-fully contrived satire after all.

California is changing overnight – it is a powder keg and Joe Hawkins will be the spark to make it explode. I am balancing on the brink of an absurd situation as the audiences are expecting me to lead them into battle every night in every endless city. There seems to be a counter-revolution and we are being drawn into it, whether we want to be or not.

I am beginning to wonder if what I give people is ever going to be enough.

The fight for freedom has always been an ancient war fuelled by man's original temptation to destroy order and structure. If I can shake the foundations, disorientate society and knock it back to its core, then people will experience something new, discover what it is to be human. I want to participate in the creation of a storm and stand at its heart, while all around me people are forcing themselves to open their eyes. William Blake wrote, 'The road of excess leads to the palace of wisdom', and he was right.

I always believed that you had to retain a constant state of revolution, if you did not, then you would be dead. America was conceived in violence; it is inbred in its nature. Destruction and annihilation strips everything back to a more primal way of life. It is like ploughing a field, you must first churn it up before you can plant the new seeds of creation.

There is someone over my shoulder, a shadow lurking at the corner of my vision. I can see him watching me, following me, he is studying everything I do. At every gig, every bar, every place I stay he is there.

He is waiting to get me.

I can see him.

He is a faceless stranger.

CHAPTER TWENTY-SIX

The evening traffic thronged past Tyler and William who stood on the corner of La Cienega and Santa Monica Boulevard. William's hunched shoulders loosened as he surveyed a converted warehouse on the opposite side of the street.

'That was The Gracious Dawn's office back then,' he said, waving his hand at the red-brick building. 'We developed our music in a makeshift rehearsal room in the basement, constructing these primeval sounds that reverberated off the walls, raw and unformed. By then, all that mattered to me was the music we were creating, it had become my sole focus. Yeah, that old place gave me the reassurance that my life had a purpose and I belonged somewhere.'

William took a lasting look across at the building, before turning and following Tyler with a pained gait down the darkening street. Deep electronic beats pumped from the music bars clustered along Santa Monica Boulevard, as groups of young women wearing gold spandex mini-skirts and teetering in white stiletto heels, handed out flyers in front of neon-fronted strip clubs.

'We were back in LA recording our second album *Venice Beach Blues*,' William said. 'Y'know, those times were the start of my real Jekyll and Hyde days.'

'What do you think was making your behaviour worse?'

'Man, there was so much pressure put on us to create music even better than our first album, to create hit singles greater than "Into The Night", "Freedom's Dream" and "Memories of Eden" which had topped the charts all over Europe, Australia, South America … it was too much for any of us to deal with. Sometimes I would show up at the studio as a poet: stoned, calm and wanting to engage in the recording process. The next day though it all changed, and I would stay in a bar all day not giving a damn that I was meant to be in the studio. I knew the guys would always forgive me when I walked in rollin' drunk, flash Joey Hawkins' mischievous smile and all was forgiven. I guess it was all part of the game, no one knew which Joe they were going to get, just like when I was a boy.'

William stood under the green and white striped awning of Barney's Beanery. He dipped his head towards the entrance, motioning for Tyler to open the door so he could creep in behind him. A stream of customers lined up against the bar and packed into multi-coloured booths, ready to get a strong drink and a hearty meal. The early evening buzz intensified as the two men wove through the crowded restaurant and sat at a vacant table, William raising his head only high enough to watch a group of men playing pool at the back.

Tyler ordered the beef chilli while William considered the menu. 'I'll have those three please, *muh dear*,' he said, stabbing his finger at the menu while keeping his eyes, and his wolfish grin, fixed on the waitress standing beside their table.

'Hungry?' Tyler asked.

'No, just curious to see if the food here still tastes the same.'

Tyler checked his watch, keen to keep William engaged in conversation while his mood was stable. 'I want to talk some more about your interest in control if that's alright?'

William turned his stare away from the waitress at the bar who was loading a tray with drinks. 'Yeah sure, what do you want to know?'

'How do you think one person is capable of controlling thousands of people, say in an audience?'

William rested his hands on the table, taking a long breath before he spoke. 'Because, my friend, I had studied how a crowd works. An audience is a witness to the event taking place on stage, but it can also take on a mass belief, so the individual starts to lose a small piece of their own identity. The crowd thinks together, it acts and speaks as one collective morality, which can only lead to one thing.'

'It can be controlled as one, by one person.'

'Very good, Tyler, very good,' William said through a glinting smile. 'A crowd is a mass of emotional responses and sexual impulses which can be manipulated at a subversive level. A crowd will behave in a way that an individual could only ever dream about, all at the orchestration of the idol standing on the stage.'

'Like some sort of subconscious communication, a group thought insertion?'

'I guess it was an attempt to communicate, an experiment where you try to strike a balance between the object and the receiver. Playing to an audience there is a beautiful tension, there is an opportunity for a reaction, but uh, at the same time there is an obligation for the artist to perform well.'

'People have to retain their individuality within a crowd, though,' Tyler said, taking out his notebook from his bag and making some brief notes. 'I mean, it would be a disaster if twenty thousand people at a concert all became one unruly mob.'

'That's right, it would be a disaster.' William erupted into a crackling laugh. 'It would all be over, the end of the game.'

The waitress placed a double scotch on the rocks and a bottle of Mexican beer on the table. While William drank, Tyler looked around at the photographs of celebrities who had enjoyed Barney's hospitality through the years. On the wall behind the bar was a framed photograph of Joe Hawkins taken in the late Sixties. He sat on a wooden stool wearing a short sheepskin coat, an easy smile breaking across his face as he clasped a beer bottle in his hand.

'You said that you had a triumvirate of personalities,' Tyler said, slowly drawing his stare away from the photograph and onto his patient who sat twisting a button on his coat. 'Who do you think was really performing on stage: Joey, Joe or Joseph?'

William gulped a mouthful of scotch and relaxed his body into the seat. 'It was Joe, the born circus master, who performed. I wasn't playing a contrived rock star role though, no, it was always important that it was *me* on stage.' He poked his fingers into his chest and took another long drink. 'When I was in the band's dressing room before each show, I sat in the corner in silent contemplation ... preparing, listening, observing. Y'see, it's never the snarling wolf that's the most dangerous, Tyler, it's the wolf silently watching you from the shadows. Then, as soon as my foot touched the stage, I allowed the music to take me over, giving me the freedom to be whoever I wanted to be. Some nights I was the simple singer and poet, and some nights I became Dionysus, the god of chaos with a satyr on my shoulder, pushing the audience as hard and as far as they dared go. Then, after the show was over and the party moved to the nearest bar, I became JoJo, drunk and high ... and then Joseph ... well, Joseph was left to pick up the pieces the next day.'

The waitress arranged four plates of food on the table, receiving a wide smile from William in return.

'You were interested in Dionysus,' Tyler said, picking at his chilli. 'Was that in the same way you were interested in Alexander the Great?'

'The innermost nature of Dionysus was excess, so yeah, he interested me,' William said, smothering a chicken enchilada in salt and pepper before taking a small bite. 'He was the god of the mask, living a dangerous life and knowing the importance of dying at precisely the right time. Dionysus was the great liberator, who allowed your intellectual and creative thoughts to run wild. He orchestrated the churning-up of the essence of life, whilst being surrounded by the storms of death. It was a cult of all-encompassing intoxication, attempting to reach the divine. So yeah, you could say that he interested me *very* much.'

Tyler picked at his food, his appetite lessening at the thought of his father finding out that he was about to be kicked out of college and arrested by the police for kidnapping a psychiatric patient. 'Do you think Joe's character and behaviour were becoming a disguise for Joseph?'

William chewed his food with a slow and considered ease, not taking his focus from Tyler. 'I've always maintained that everyone has more than one personality, like everyone has two souls: good and evil. I saw these personalities with a perceptive clarity so that, like Dionysus, I could assimilate the circus master, the wolf, the shaman and metamorphose into them when I was on stage.'

As more diners came into the restaurant, the noise level continued to rise, forcing Tyler to lean closer across the table so he could hear William's soft voice. 'Isn't that dangerous?'

'It was a necessity of the time,' William said, easing a morsel of chicken down his throat. 'I was a warrior, waging a battle against American capitalist values, crushing the lethargic spirit out of people and awakening the idea of a new existence in them. I thought I could show people a surreal alternate reality existing beneath the surface, a hidden underworld tempting you to step through the door ... only if you are brave enough. I knew I could never do that with only one facet of my personality.'

'You wanted to create enlightenment in people through some sort of impulsive destruction?'

William put down his fork and drank the last of his whiskey, pushing away the glass of melting ice and drawing the bottle of beer towards him. 'Destruction is merely a process of re-order, of thoughts and ideas.'

'But what gave Joe Hawkins the right to wage some existential war on the world?'

'My intention wasn't to cause a war, Tyler. I went on stage with the intention of, y'know, playing good music, giving the crowd and the cops a little playful fun, to have a good time. I wanted to get my kicks while I was still young enough to get away with doing whatever the hell I liked.'

'It didn't always turn out to be playful fun though, did it? Joe Hawkins wanted to cause chaos that could have put all those young people in the audience in real danger, there were serious consequences to Joe's actions. I think he wanted to influence and change society to suit his own fantasies about living in some hippie Age of Aquarius world that could never really exist.'

William's eyes bored into Tyler across the table, hesitating for a moment too long before he spoke. 'It is true that I did things because other people were too scared to do it themselves. I wanted to test the boundaries of reality, see how far it would go and now I had a stage on which to do it. I was simply watching the crowd's action and reaction playing out. Besides, uh, I always maintained that the police presence at our concerts caused more of a negative reaction than anything I ever did.'

Tyler gave up on his food and pushed away his half-eaten plate of chilli. 'Can we talk some more about your addictions?' He checked his watch again, conscious that his bar shift was due to start in an hour. 'Was it the alcohol or the drugs that were now dominant in your life?'

'Drinking had overtaken my experiments with drugs, it was the only way for me to deal with my life. I still craved to go out at night and roll the dice, play the game. What sort of trouble was I going to get into? Would I live or would I die? I suppose I was still curious to see what would happen.'

'That would annoy the rest of the band, wouldn't it?'

'I guess you could say that the person I became annoyed them. Y'see, the more success the band had, the worse my behaviour would get and the more I sank into depression, worse than anything I had felt before.' William gulped his beer and wiped his mouth with the back of his hand. 'The voices in my mind were getting louder every day … goading me … telling me to do more dangerous things, pushing life even further.'

'Voices?' Tyler asked. 'Have you heard voices before?'

'Yeah, kid, I've heard voices before. I've always heard them. They're like lions roaring in my mind, but I had to decide whether to ignore what they said or let their words manipulate me.'

'Was it Joe Hawkins' voice you were hearing, Mr Kendrick, telling you to think a certain way or to do things?'

'*It was the shaman,*' William whispered, drawing his eyes to meet Tyler's stare. 'It was the lost voice of the Native American Indian who I used to see in my dreams as a boy, with a wolf at his side, calling me towards him into the night.'

'And you felt that the drugs and alcohol would help you to silence the voices?'

'Right, very good, Professor Rafferty.' William lowered his head into the depths of his coat collar. 'Very good indeed.'

Tyler clicked his pen and wrote in his notebook. *Thought insertion is a classic symptom of psychosis. The voices have put ideas and beliefs into William's mind, making him think there was a strong external force influencing his behaviour since childhood. William appears to have filtered out his own thoughts and memories and replaced them with Joe's. He seems to be able to control this filter. His neighbour, Adeline, said that she only knows him as William or Billy, but he only wants to show me Joe Hawkins. Is this a contrived deception for my benefit?*

Turning to a fresh page of his notebook, Tyler thanked the waitress while she cleared the table. 'There must have been people at the time who only wanted to be around Joe for his money, his fame.'

William raised his head to look across the restaurant as a loud cheer erupted from the pool table. 'Man, you don't know the half of it. I had many fruitful nights at the strip joints and topless bars around here, they were my dark haven of escape. I drank myself into oblivion with whoever I was entertaining, whoever wanted good ol' JoJo to keep them drunk all night and surrounded by beautiful women. Although, I think my behaviour reflected the company that I kept.'

'What do you mean?'

'I liked to keep my circles of friends separate from each other. If I went out for a quiet dinner with my old college friends, who enjoyed a good debate, then I would mirror them, be a restrained, intelligent conversationalist. When I went out with the Hollywood hangers-on, oh boy, I ran wild, pushing life all the way to the limits. I would stagger into the street and pretend to be a matador with cars speeding towards me like raging bulls, or balance on the ledge of a hotel balcony thirty floors up, enjoying the danger of dicing with death. Then the next day, I spent hours walking the streets of LA, or whatever city I was in, still drunk, high and trying to find my way back from whoever's bed I'd ended up in.'

'That's not the image of Joe portrayed by the teen magazines at the time, was it?' Tyler asked, closing his notebook.

William snorted out a laugh and shook his head. 'Oh man, our record company was trying to paint this image of Joe Hawkins as some sort of available sex idol for your virgin teenage daughter to fantasise about behind her bedroom door. The reality was that Joe Hawkins, at twenty-five years old, was a lost poet, an alcoholic, a drug addict, sleeping in his own vomit and screwing anyone with a pulse.' Flicking a handful of dollar bills onto the table, he heaved himself up, trudging away towards the door to leave Tyler sitting alone at an empty table.

Tyler Rafferty creaked open the door to room 23 of the Sunset Vista Motel.

He reached his hand into the darkness and flicked on the light switch, listening to the sound of dripping water coming from the bathroom, and the heavy rasping breaths from the only other occupant of the room. 'Mr Kendrick,' he said, approaching the man who sat on the floor beside the bed with his legs splayed out in front of him.

William pulled out his cigarettes from his coat pocket and lit one. 'I'm fine, kid, just fine.' He exhaled a plume of silver smoke that escaped through the open window.

Pacing around the cramped room, Tyler's digital watch bleeped; failure to turn up again to his late shift at a Santa Monica music bar would mean instant dismissal. His stomach retched at the thought of telling his father that he could not even hold down a bar job.

'Please don't leave me alone tonight, Doctor Marshall wouldn't like it,' William said, flicking a slanting glance across at Tyler as he rocked his body against the bed frame. 'I … I really need to talk to you, there's so much more you need to know.'

Tyler dragged his hands down his face, knowing he had no choice but to remain with the patient in his care and risk losing his job. Sitting at the table, he snatched his notebook towards him. 'Alright.' He picked up his pen, tapping the tip on a clean page. 'You thought that the only way to deal with your life and fame was to push the limits, searching for a constant sense of oblivion. Is that right?'

William stubbed out his cigarette in the ashtray on the floor. 'Drinking was the only way I could handle the pressure being put on me by the label, the press and the band. It was the only way I could cope with the fame following me around. My face was becoming one of the most recognised in the world.' He took a sharp breath. 'I'd meet my friends for breakfast, but I'd still be out from the previous night, watching them eat their pancakes while I carried on drinking beer.'

'Did you feel let down by the people around you, that no one offered you any help or stepped in when it got that bad?' Tyler asked, making no effort to ease his hardening tone of voice.

'Some of my closer friends tried, but it was a different time, not like today where you get sent off into a rehabilitation clinic for two weeks and come out the other end cured. This was the Sixties and problems like that weren't spoken about. Not just because it was the culture back then, but because no one would dare to say a fuckin' word to me that I had a problem, or that I was becoming an embarrassment. It remained unspoken.'

'Did you go see a doctor?'

'Only to get another prescription of sedatives. I chased those pills down my throat with a bottle of brandy, trying to dampen the fire raging inside me.'

William struggled to stand and pulled out a can of beer from the grocery bag. Taking a long drink, he stood by the window looking out at the streets of West Hollywood.

'Have you ever felt that you lost control?' Tyler asked, turning his pen between his fingers. 'I mean, Joe thought he had power over everyone who came to see The Gracious Dawn play.'

'I always thought I was in control of people's reaction to me.' William poured the rest of the beer down his throat and threw the empty can into a trash basket. Cradling his arms around his body, he walked across the room and perched on the edge of the bed. 'Y'see, I had gained enough live performance experience to understand how the audiences had changed from when we worked the clubs. We had been playing vast festival grounds through the summer of '67, so I really had to exaggerate my performances to make an impact.' Leaning down, he tugged off his boots and slid under the bed sheet, nestling his head on the pillow. 'During a song, I'd stop singing and wait for every member of the audience to give into the silence before I released an animalistic scream from the depths of my stomach. I wanted to see how long I could hold them before the pressure snapped. Yeah, it was important that I retained control, even in those chaotic situations.' His eyes closed and he succumbed to sleep.

Tyler took out his Walkman from his bag, pressed the headphones to his ears and let Aerosmith drown the city sounds outside the motel. He turned up the volume and wrote in his notebook. *William's delusion is a carefully contrived fantasy. I think he is trying to control me too and manipulate what information he is telling me. His real memories are so hidden within his perceived memories of Joe, that I have no idea how to reach his truth. All I can do is keep William talking. Sooner or later, he will let his guard down and I will discover who this man really is. There is something un-nerving about the way William looks at me, as if he can look straight into my soul, he can see straight through me. DO NOT TRUST HIM.*

Tyler removed the headphones and pulled off his shoes. He got into bed beside his snoring patient, trying to balance his body on the farthest edge of the stale mattress. The motel room yielded to darkness, mellowed by a luminous neon glow infiltrating the thinning drapes. Clamping his eyes shut, Tyler prayed that tomorrow would bring him closer to discovering William Kendrick's true identity.

CHAPTER TWENTY-SEVEN

**The Journal of Joseph Hawkins – February 10th, 1968
(Cleveland, Ohio)**

I am getting sick and tired of people telling me what I can and cannot do. This country was born on free speech. I have something to say and a stage on which to say it, but the cops are determined to silence me.

They arrested me on stage last night at the Cleveland Public Auditorium, like I was the devil incarnate and they were God's angels trying to protect their innocent young flock. I could sense the authorities were on edge even before we arrived here in Ohio, police brutality has been making headline news all over the country and then our circus troupe rolls into town.

I was still cranky from the bad shows we endured this week, so I was looking for a way to release some tension. I was backstage in a quiet corner with a pretty college girl, getting to know each other a little better. Just as I had slipped my hand under her blouse, an altercation started across the room. The girl's boyfriend had been looking for her and was not too happy when he saw how comfortable we had been getting. I tried to calm things down, when a police officer came over and beat me in the ribs with his baton. So, with my usual appreciation for authority, I told the cop to go screw himself. Oh boy, that was it, he was raining down blows, until I heard our road manager, Kurt, yelling and trying to pull him away from me. Realising his mistake, the officer apologised, but I refused to shake his hand. I just smiled back and asked him if he wanted my autograph.

The police eventually let me go on stage, only because there would be a riot if we did not perform. I wanted to exact some revenge, provoke the cops to re-balance the control. I worked up the audience, telling them what had happened backstage, how I had been attacked. Then, when the pressure reached its peak, I screamed, 'I want to start the revolution and I want to start it NOW!' The audience swelled like a raging torrent towards the wall of cops. An officer walked onto the stage, tapped me on the shoulder and told me that I had gone too far. So I goaded him, 'Say your piece, little man, say your piece.' Frank came over, still playing his guitar, and whispered in my ear, 'Cool it, Joe.' But I was not done yet.

I wanted to push the situation as far as it would go, to see what would happen ... action and reaction in perfect harmony. The cop tried to take the microphone out of my hand and that was all the provocation I needed. I screamed at the top of my lungs, 'Say your goddamn piece, little man!' The police dragged me off stage, beat me up outside and threw me in a jail cell for good measure. I did not even fight back when they were beating me, I will not give them that satisfaction. You must never yield to authority.

I was just having a little fun.

I cannot trust anyone, even the people around me. Our so-called manager Leonard is a joke, telling me what I can and cannot do, he has no idea how to manage a rock 'n' roll band. He will have to go. We would be better off being managed by Tommy Seagram, who has been helping us out on the road since last year. He is the only person with the balls to tell me how it is and not what lies I want to hear to keep me happy. Perhaps it is better to have someone younger and less experienced running our team, that way I can still pull the strings and be in complete control of my destiny.

We are in a constant flux of travelling around America to promote our new album *Venice Beach Blues*. We get on an airplane to another concert or television show, and I am trapped in a confined space, so of course I am going to unwind and have some fun with the stewardess in first class. It gives me time to think, and maybe that is the problem, because it gives me time to drink too.

Our lives have become a constant routine of cars, hotels, airplanes – be here at this time, stand there, sing this song, pose for a photograph, sign this contract and smile for the cameras, Joe, smile! The fans come from miles around to see us play bigger and bigger venues. When I am in the dressing room, I can hear them chanting my name, calling me to the stage to perform. Then for the next hour they carry on screaming for us to play "Into The Night". It is always the same wherever we go. I am starting to wonder if these people are actually listening to anything of meaning that I have to say.

Angela and I are still together insofar as our souls are connected, but that does not stop both of us playing around. When she finds out about another girl, she will get her sweet revenge with one of my friends, making sure I hear about it. We fight like cat and dog, but she keeps coming back to me because she needs me, no matter what sort of monster I become.

I must get away as often as possible. No one knows where I go, and I intend to keep it that way … I must always keep people guessing. I drive all over California from one town to another, staying in motels or sleeping on the back seat of my car out in the desert. Sometimes a girl I know will take me home to her parents' house. They have no idea who I am, I am simply introduced as, 'My friend Joe, the poet'. I enjoy living the life of a normal man, where I can spend a few days sitting outside, writing in my notebooks and finding some peace in my life.

Once I return to LA, I am Wild Joe Hawkins again and the quiet, restrained poet must be hidden beneath the mask once more.

I fear that my life is becoming a charade.

Dark clouds linger over once gentle dreams.

CHAPTER TWENTY-EIGHT

Los Angeles awoke to a deep auburn haze that burned through the Hollywood Hills to the ocean in the west and permeated the windows of the motel room. Tyler woke and was lost in his drowsy thoughts when he became aware of a weight on the bed beside him. William was sitting perfectly still, wrapped in his coat and with his hands resting on his lap.

'What are you doing?' Tyler asked, sitting up and pulling the blanket over his torso.

'I was watching you sleep,' William said with a light voice. 'You cry in your dreams, Tyler, as if you are trapped in a maze that you can't escape.' He stood and headed to the bathroom, pausing to glance back over his shoulder. 'You called out for your mother.'

William dragged the heels of his leather boots as he lumbered across the parking lot of the Sunset Vista Motel. Tyler unlocked the car and flung his bag onto the back seat, slamming the door and turning his back to his patient.

'Why are you angry with me, man?' William asked, approaching the car. 'What have I done now?'

'Nothing,' Tyler said, knowing that when midnight had dragged into the early hours he had lost his bar job. 'Nothing at all.'

The car coasted along Santa Monica Boulevard, under vast billboards advertising the latest season of *Dynasty* and the forthcoming summer movie release of *The Lost Boys*. William remained silent, waving his hand at each intersection to instruct Tyler to keep heading northeast, away from the centre of Los Angeles.

Gripping the steering wheel, Tyler tried to supress a yawn while he drove. His sleep had been a fractured string of naps, lying in a motel bed with William gasping for breath beside him.

'Do you think living in LA was allowing your negative behaviour to get worse?' he asked.

William sank his shoulders into a deep shrug. 'I realise now that this city of dreams was probably the worst place on Earth for Joe Hawkins to live, a drug-addled alcoholic rock star who had endless people to indulge him in his own self-destruction. Y'see, LA fed all my darkest desires. It has this anonymity, like uh, I was living in an anonymous city, and I wasn't accountable to it or anyone else. LA can kill you with misplaced kindness, it is a fake and fickle friend. I guess people thought that keeping me happy was easier than having to deal with the monster who would emerge if I didn't get what I wanted. I just needed someone … anyone, to say no to me, but nobody would fuckin' dare.'

Tyler followed William's pointed directions, steering the car into a winding climb through the Hollywood Hills. The steep verges of the Western Canyon Road fell to the valley below. Trees thickened across either side of the road, tingeing the air with a dry scent of sycamores that disguised the pervading city fumes. William's mouth parted into a wide grin, flashing his broad front teeth.

'What's so funny?' Tyler asked.

'Did you ever see *American Bandstand*?'

'Sure, I've seen a couple of the classic re-runs.'

'What about The Gracious Dawn, did you ever see our episode?' William asked, not waiting for a reply. 'Back then, *American Bandstand* was broadcast straight into the homes of every all-American family. Then, calling out from the censored safety of their television screens was Joe Hawkins, riled in black leather and ready to storm the world through the wide-eyed youth of the nation. I don't think the producers had any comprehension of what I was capable of, but they knew there was something about "Into The Night" that they didn't want to broadcast.'

'Why, what was wrong with it?'

William ran his thumb over his bottom lip. 'The line, *Start the revolution inside your mind* – yeah, they didn't want that anti-establishment ideology invading the homes of middle-class America.'

Tyler tried to keep his concentration on the contours of the narrow road that wound up the hill. 'The band had no intention of changing it?'

'We were angry as hell that they dared to try to censor us, so I decided to perform the song as I wanted the audience to hear it. When the moment came, and the cameras were rolling, I looked straight down the lens and let, *Start the revolution* slide out of my mouth as smooth as silk. Boy, the producer was furious. "You goddamn long-hairs were told not to say those words! Do you want us taken off air? If you think we're letting you back out there to perform your new song then you've got another thing coming!" I thought the guy was going to have a heart attack, hee hee.'

'And I suppose the kids watching at home loved it?'

William winked across at Tyler. 'Yeah.'

Griffith Park sprawled onto the southern slopes of Mount Hollywood.

The copper domes of the observatory came into Tyler's view from behind a line of oak trees, as he turned the car into a vacant parking bay and switched off the engine. William reached to the back seat, grabbed a can of beer from the grocery bag and drank hard. He tumbled out of the car, tripping over his feet as he erupted into a ferocious cough that forced him to spit bloodied phlegm onto the ground.

'You need to ease up on that stuff,' Tyler said, watching his patient stagger back against the side of the car, clutching his stomach and still clinging to the can of beer in his hand.

'You need to mind your own business.' William grinned and took another long swig of beer.

If I can keep him talking as Joe then maybe I can catch him out and uncover who William Kendrick really is, Tyler thought, tucking his hands in the pockets of his jeans. *It is only a matter of time before he slips up and gets something wrong. It is a dangerous game to play, but the sooner I can get to William's truth, the sooner I can return him to San Francisco before the police find us.* 'I once read an article about how Joe Hawkins used to get arrested on stage while the band were still playing,' he said. 'Was that really true or was it all part of the act?'

'Right, that was true,' William replied, easing up his body and catching his breath. 'I, uh, think it depended on where we played and how chaotic I decided each show needed to be. Some nights the cops were great, they did a good job of protecting both the band and the fans, although most nights they hated us. When I was on stage, the cops would all be watching me, their hands fixed to their hips ... waiting. And I swear I could see my father's face peeking out from under their caps.'

'Waiting for what?'

William took another long swig of beer and leaned against the car. 'Anything would get them irritated, especially when I let a profane word fall from my mouth.' He tossed away the empty beer can and walked with a languorous gait across the parking lot with Tyler beside him. 'Y'know, I always maintained that the police presence at our shows triggered most of the trouble. If they weren't there, then the audience wouldn't have anything to fight against.'

The Griffith Observatory stood like a temple to a long-forgotten ancient god, presiding over the City of Angels lying prostrate at its feet. Clipped lawns spilled over the edge of the hill, down into the chequerboard pattern of city streets below. William stood at the top of one of the symmetrical paths, squinting up at the building's bulbous domes which burnished with a muted luminosity in the mid-day sun. 'Around that time,' he said, 'I started to think that I was in more serious trouble with the authorities.'

'The police, you mean?'

'No.' Checking over his shoulder, William lowered his voice. 'The FBI.'

While they walked along an observation point, jutting out from the path and daring any visitors to peer over the steep drop, Tyler thought back to *The Positive and Negative Syndrome Scale: Delusions of Persecution.* 'Why do you think the FBI would be interested in you?'

William shook his head, reaching the end of the observation point. 'The FBI had me on their watch-list. The band's provocative anti-war message, the way I could entice a reaction from thousands of young people, encouraging them to start a revolution within their minds. I knew the authorities were keeping an eye on me, but after the riot at our show in Cleveland, I noticed it getting worse. I was being watched, strange clicking noises on telephone lines, someone looking at me a little too long in a bar. I was convinced someone was following me, and Angela noticed it too. There was a guy who was always there in the background watching everything I did, hiding in the shadows. I even began to think that he looked like me, it was messing with my head. That's why I kept moving around places, using my bolt holes so no one knew where I was.'

'That could have been paranoia though,' Tyler said, letting his bag drop to the ground and leaning against the wall. 'I mean, all the drugs you were taking at the time and the alcohol abuse could make you have feelings of persecution, paranoid tendencies. You were probably seeing things that weren't as they seemed.'

'No, kid, this wasn't some drug-related-hallucination-chickenshit,' William said, inching closer to Tyler. 'The FBI opened files on me which would stay open until my *supposed* death. Man, they're probably still active today. J. Edgar Hoover wanted me scraped off the bottom of his shoe. Y'see, back then the police and the FBI had waged a war on the demon rock 'n' roll music that was leading the youth of America into revolt and student protests. All they had to do was follow the burning trail of destruction to find the ringmaster standing at the centre of the stage: Joe Hawkins.'

Tyler looked towards the glinting peaks of the skyscrapers huddled together in the business district. 'My dad first brought me up here to the observatory when I was eight years old. I think I had a dream that week about being an astronaut. I wanted to jump on a space shuttle and whoosh, I'd be gone.' He lowered his head and kicked a stone beside his foot.

William rested his elbow on a pivoted telescope that provided a view through the smog into the heart of the city. 'When

I moved out to LA, this was one of the first places I came to. I stood up here looking out, imagining other people's lives and not my own. This was where *Rebel Without A Cause* was filmed. James Dean stood right where you are standing, Tyler, captured for all eternity on celluloid as Jim Stark. Coming here made me feel close to it, close to that part of Hollywood that I had been fascinated with since I was a boy. It made me feel like I could reach out and touch it, as if the city down there was promising me that I could be part of its world.' He dropped his voice. 'But at night this was a dangerous place to be, a place to spend some private time, enjoying certain, uh, *shadier* pleasures the city had to offer.'

He drew out his pack of cigarettes and lit one, cupping his hand around the lighter. Tyler checked his watch. As each hour slipped through his fingers, he sensed William drawing him further into the disorientating labyrinth of Joe Hawkins' tumultuous life, luring him away from discovering his real identity. Tyler raised his frowning face to meet his patient's temperate smile and realised that was exactly what William intended.

'Why didn't Joe go solo?' he asked. 'I always thought he should have been a lone star.'

William shook his head, sucking on the cigarette. 'Oh, that was easy, it was all about us as a band; it was how we were meant to be. I was always the accidental rock star, but I was only ever meant to do it with those three guys, a band of brothers showing the world a different way to listen to music.'

Tyler arched his torso over the edge of the observation point, his mind lurching with dizziness into the valley below. 'The manic-depressive episodes you were having, were they turning into something stronger, something beyond your perception of control, do you think?'

'I guess so,' William said. 'Angela kept trying to get me to see a psychiatrist because by then I was having these manic episodes which would last for days. My behaviour was beyond anyone's control by then. Anything would trigger it, a bad review or a bad gig. I was torn between enjoying some of our best performances to enduring some of our worst. Sometimes we were booked into the wrong place, the wrong city, where the audience didn't appreciate what we were trying to do, that we were trying to create art through our music.'

Tyler pulled up his body and rested his elbows on the wall. 'This was self-inflicted pressure though, wasn't it?'

'I suppose it was,' William replied through a deep sigh. 'Being on stage and being the performer was keeping me alive. We were touring pretty heavily through '68. When I walked on stage, I could pick up from the vibe when it was going to be a great show – there was an electric tension, a beautiful friction. I rested my boot on the base of the microphone stand and held my breath, drawing in the erotic pressure that stung the air until I could feel the stand pressing into my groin and making me hard. Nights like that did a lot to remind me what the hell we had wanted to achieve all along. It made me feel like I was in the game. When we played down there at the LA Memorial Sports Arena that summer …' he raised his chin towards the stadium in the distance '… we got rave reviews, although I didn't feel like it was a great show.'

'Why?'

'Because there was too much pressure put on me, man,' William said, as he tugged his hand through his hair. 'The fifteen thousand strong audience came expecting the usual crazy Gracious Dawn gig, but I had to give a pitch-perfect, artistic and creative performance because it was being filmed for a TV show. I felt the expectation from everyone that we had to produce a show that reflected us as the greatest live band in America. The tension was unbearable, and I could feel the pressure building as I walked on stage. I looked out into the audience and there in the front row was Miss Angela Jackson with her latest lover, a notorious Hollywood actor with a reputation worse than my own, taunting me with it.'

'Do you think this pressure you'd put on your life had gone beyond what you could cope with?'

'I was just feeling … lost. I didn't know which way was up anymore. The audiences were getting crazier each time we played.

They came for trouble and not for the music or my words. It happened all over the place and who gets the blame when the crowd goes wild?'

'Joe,' Tyler said.

William dipped his head into a low nod. 'Every sublime line of poetry, every beautiful piece of music that we had strived to create was dissolving into a fairground freak show. I had commitments and conditions put on my life, contracts to sign and deadlines to meet, and somehow everyone involved in the band was dependent on Joe Hawkins … and they hated me for it. I was not equipped on any emotional level to deal with the realities of being a rock star, and I had no idea the devastating consequences that would cause.'

CHAPTER TWENTY-NINE

The Journal of Joseph Hawkins – May 18th, 1968
(San Jose, California)

In a backstage corner of the Santa Clara County Fairgrounds, I am drinking a bottle of warm red wine, listening to The Steve Miller Band play their set, while I wait to be called to the stage for The Gracious Dawn to headline at the Northern California Folk-Rock Festival.

The audience of thirty thousand music fans are wired, the psychedelic drugs are flowing and the sweet scent of marijuana is intoxicating the air. The sun has just come out and clothes are flying off. Girls are dancing with garlands of flowers in their hair, love beads around their necks and peace symbols drawn on their bare chests. By the time we walk on stage, I am hoping the tension will be at its peak, ripe to be manipulated for a performance to be remembered.

I do not know what is wrong with me these days. One minute I am revelling in my life: the sold-out shows, being on the front cover of international magazines, the fans' adoration and the musical creativity. This is everything Clark and I dreamed about that day on Santa Monica Pier when we conceived The Gracious Dawn ... then a dark cloud infiltrates my thoughts. I can sense a disquiet, an unease as if the powder keg is about to explode. Martin Luther King has been assassinated, there are race riots on the streets in every city and a pointless war is still raging in Vietnam. It feels like we are in the middle of an annihilation that will destroy everything; the final obliteration has arrived. Now everyone is looking to me, expecting me to create a whole album of new songs to reflect the ominous mood hanging over the country.

The fans have trapped The Gracious Dawn in a constant battle to stay relevant. At every gig and festival, the audiences are getting younger and wilder while the venues get bigger. In the band's early days, there was a beautiful and powerful reaction from the audiences, a natural, reciprocal exchange of energy. Now I must force a reaction from them, scream at the top of my lungs until something … anything … happens.

We have lost the ability to let songs evolve like they used to when we played in the clubs. Our songs have become frozen, static entities that cannot breathe anymore. I am still upset that everyone rejected my idea for a live show featuring my new poetry collection. It is an injustice, but what is the point in me being angry? I am getting tired of trying to please everyone.

Even the mechanics of the band has changed, we now have publicists, business managers, accountants, secretaries and lawyers. The Gracious Dawn has gone from being a simple creative exercise into a capitalist machine that is falling out of our control.

Sitting here, I am watching Clark, Frank and Dean standing together beside the stage talking in whispers. No doubt they are talking about me, 'What are we going to do about Joe's drinking?' You see, they are true sons of Apollo, their lives are all about harmony, reason and order. They have moved onto higher meditation and a purer existence, but I am still hurtling along life's highway, a true disciple of Dionysus drowning myself in beer and wine. Their way of life is not on my agenda. I know Tommy Seagram is paying people to keep an eye on me, hiring nursemaids and babysitters to keep me out of trouble. I can see straight through it. I do not like this game, although I will play along with it … for now.

Last week, an LA newspaper printed a photograph of me and a young British model leaving a nightclub together in West Hollywood. I had taken off my favourite aquamarine silk scarf and tied it around her swan-like neck. It was an innocent situation, but the headline screamed: *JOE HAWKINS IN LOVE, SUM-*

MER WEDDING PLANNED! The news spread like wildfire across America, teenage girls lost their minds. These media lies are on the front page of every cheap magazine in the country to be consumed for people's entertainment.

Angela will be furious.

Everything I do, everything I say is scrutinised and criticised. Will I ever be a normal man again? I cannot even get into a car at whatever auditorium we are playing at, without a hundred girls screaming in my face. I am a poet, but I am having my clothes torn off by teenagers, these bubble-gummers who worship me with their soul's idle eyes. They all want a piece of Joe Hawkins as if they deserve to have a piece of me ... they think that they own me. What do they want from me?

Then there is another part of me who thrives on the fans' adoration. They follow me day in day out, stalking me around LA. I can hear them whispering behind my back, but I always stop and talk kindly to every one of them. Before our shows I like to spend half an hour chatting to fans outside the back of the arena, slip them a couple of dollars so they can get home. I always prefer to talk to a kid going through a hard time at school, or a homeless guy who has been on the streets for twenty years – that is real life, and it interests me. You see, I must always give something back to the screwed-up society that I find myself existing in.

The magazines and newspapers will never report this quiet, compassionate side of me. They want to focus on my bad behaviour and ignore the truth that I am a man who has feelings, who can be generous, funny, gentle and kind. That is Joseph, the real man, the shadow idol trapped behind the rock star, who the world will never see.

I have easy friends to indulge me in my own self-destruction every night. I can feel their sharpened claws stabbing me in the back, pulling me down. The hangers-on cling to me, sucking the life out of me ... but I do not care. Angela warns me that they only want to spend my money and exploit my connections. I know they are using me, but I am using them. It is all too easy.

I am drinking more than ever before, trying to numb the weight of fame that I can feel crushing me. I am already drunk when I arrive at parties, and I carry on drinking until I pass out in the corner of the room, while everyone else has a good time around me.

I do not sleep anymore. I have become a rolling drunk, falling down in the street, kicked out of every bar in LA and having sex with any girl who knocks on my hotel room door.

The line in my head separating good from bad has blurred out of all recognition.

I always knew, since I was a boy, that you balance on a hair's breadth between genius and insanity. All the great thinkers knew it was the gamble … the price you would have to pay. The time will come when your mind slips through your fingers and you lose your grip, only to fall from the heights of genius into the numb void of madness.

It is a sad and lonely fate.

That is why I was so impatient for the band to get success quickly, for us to go up like a rocket and blaze across the stars, and why I know Joe Hawkins is not destined to live for very long. I fear that I will not live to see thirty.

I am losing my way.

Someone help me.

CHAPTER THIRTY

The winding hills above Los Angeles yielded to a clear cerulean sky.

Tyler turned down the car radio when the one o'clock news started, dreading that he would hear his own name reported instead of the gun violence and race riots consuming the city. As he glanced across at his patient, curled up in the passenger seat, he could sense the last strands of hope snapping that he would be returning to Saint Cecilia's Hospital before nightfall. *Doctor Marshall has probably called Professor Kessler,* he thought. He tried to muffle his father's voice that began to resonate between his ears, *"Don't let your mother down again."* Tyler turned his head away, hoping William would not notice him swallowing down the first prickle of tears behind his pale blue eyes, but knowing he would see everything.

'Oh man, you should come up here at night,' William said, narrowing his stare away from Tyler while the car coasted along Mulholland Drive. 'Some nights I drove up here in my new black Porsche, a gift from the label for our record sales. The moon would hang so low in the sky it was like you could reach up and touch it.' He extended his arm out of the car's open window, caressing the undulating silhouette of the hills with his fingertips as if he were conducting an imaginary orchestra.

'What about your behaviour, was that still deteriorating?' Tyler quietly asked.

William grunted with laughter. 'My behaviour, yeah man, it was always *my* behaviour, *my* fault. I was only having a good time, Tyler, that was all. I was making the most of what short time Joe had. I knew the band hated it when I turned up at the studio, drunk and dragging along a girl I was entertaining that day, or the Hollywood leeches who I'd been drinking with since the night before. I knew it riled them, so I'd do it again and again.'

'Do you think Joe's depression was starting to be reflected in the live shows?'

'Y'know, I always tried to be professional when I was on stage, to try to rise above how I was feeling inside and give a good performance. The fans came demanding to be entertained, show after perpetual show and I had nothing to lose; I had to give them the best of me. When we played at the Long Island Arena, it was like holding a firecracker in your hands. It was a sweltering New York summer, the air crackling with tension and anticipation, like on a tropical night before the thunderstorm breaks. Backstage we could all sense it was going to be one of those shows where you *knew* what would happen. I can still hear the audience chanting my name, "Hawkins! Hawkins! Hawkins!" We came on an hour late, after The Who had performed. As the friction mounted, I became the shaman, dancing and swirling my body in a ritualistic trance. I pulled the silk scarf from my neck and tied it around the low-slung waistband of my leather pants like a matador. I fed off the pressure, moaning and writhing my hips from side to side, then taunting the audience until I got what I wanted: the beautiful explosion. The audience crashed up against a barricade of cops in front of the stage, chairs got hurled as they ripped the auditorium apart, destroying all of our equipment.'

'You now thought you were a shaman and not Joe Hawkins?' Tyler asked, changing the radio station until the wailing guitars of Bon Jovi reverberated through the car.

The canyon road deepened into the valley as William seemed to consider his words with care before he spoke. 'Well uh, a concert is a mass healing ritual, a group cleansing, orchestrated by the shaman. The crowd was my tribe onto which I could impart my metaphysical knowledge. The shaman could alter his consciousness, open himself up to the spiritual world and awaken his guides through music, dancing, hypnotic rhythm, sleep deprivation and drugs.'

'Becoming the shaman was another metamorphosis, another mask to hide behind?'

'The shaman was an incarnation I suppose, the most serious side of my personality. He was the real reason for my existence. Y'see, when I was a boy and the spirit of the Native American Indian entered my dreams, he conceived the shaman within me. He showed me the importance of evolution, of your life evolving into your death, then your spirit evolving again into a higher state of consciousness.' William faltered and his face paled. 'When I emulated the shaman that night at the Long Island Arena, I was pushing the audience harder and harder until I broke them. But I didn't realise that I was breaking Joe, and the band, too.'

A tranquil wind wound up through the canyon. William's hand quivered, scribbling his pencil across the back pages of the journal. His forehead remained hardened with an engrossed concentration, his mouth parting and closing in a silent commentary.

'What are you writing?' Tyler asked, stopping the car at a set of traffic lights.

William cupped his hand around the words on the page. 'Oh, just some observations,' he said through a lethargic smile. 'Nothing for you to concern yourself with … yet.'

Tyler accelerated the car away, resuming his focus on the snaking canyon road. 'If Joe was so disaffected being in the band, why didn't he quit, walk away once and for all?'

William closed the journal and rested it on his lap. 'Angela kept trying to persuade me to leave the band and focus on being a poet and a writer. I walked into The Gracious Dawn's office and told our manager, Tommy, that I thought I was having a nervous breakdown from which I would never recover. When I said I was going to quit the band, he persuaded me to stick it out a while longer, until the new album was finished. Maybe he thought it was attention-seeking and maybe it was a cry for help, but as I walked out of the office that day, I wanted to give up on myself.' His voice cracked. Slowly he wrapped his arms around his body encased in his sheepskin coat. 'I wanted to give up on Joe Hawkins.'

A floral-painted road sign welcomed Tyler and William to Laurel Canyon.

A dull ache rose through Tyler's chest while he drove through the small residential community where the hippie music scene had once spread its message of peace and love. The Country Store resided at the heart of the area's serene seclusion. Bright-coloured murals covered its crumbling redbrick façade, harking back to its Summer of Love heyday. Tyler pulled the car into a parking space behind the store, remaining silent while he switched off the engine.

'Are you alright, kid?' William asked. 'You're very quiet.'

'My mom shared a house up here with a couple of friends in the Sixties. She left Michigan when she was eighteen, came out to California looking for a more exciting life. I think she felt drawn to LA, that it would give her the opportunity to be the free spirit she dreamed of being. When my dad was at work, she told me stories of how she met Joe Hawkins, and all the other famous people who lived around here, the wild parties that used to happen.' He took a deep breath as his head fell. 'I've not come back here, not since …'

William struggled out of the car and slammed the door. 'What was her name, your mother?'

'Barbara Emmett,' Tyler said. 'That was her name before she married my dad. She took a job as a typist at the same law firm as him, that's how they met.'

'*Barbara*.' William purred the name and licked his lips. 'Yeah, there were a lot of real beautiful women living around here back then. I'm pretty sure I slept with most of them.'

'Don't.'

'Hee hee hee.' William giggled and brushed past Tyler.

A sprinkling of houses were secreted along narrow trails and steep hills, allowing its residents to enjoy the semi-rural privacy the community offered. Across the road from the Country Store, a timber-framed house burrowed into the wooded serenity of Kirkwood Drive, its exterior walls disguised behind a luxuriant blanket of ivy.

'That was Angela's apartment,' William said, pointing up at the top floor of the house. 'Which, of course, I paid for. I used to lean over the balcony with a beer in my hand, watching everyone coming and going: Frank Zappa, David Crosby and Joni Mitchell strollin' around, minding their own business, living their perceived idea of what normality was – normal in the insanity that our lives had become. Yeah, this place had a gentle heart to it. I think this was the closest I ever got to living as part of a community, which was something I never thought I could have.'

Tyler folded his arms and looked up at the house. 'The relationship with Angela, tell me how it changed from those early days living here.'

'We were happy and in love back then, before the height of my fame ruined our young lives. Angela and I still fought like cat and dog though, because I was always entertaining a girl next door or disappearing for days on end with my friends. Then there would be another ferocious fight, and I would have to stay in one of my other bolt holes in LA. Over a few short years, I watched her change from the muse of a penniless poet into the girlfriend of America's biggest rock star. Y'know, when we first started dating I had no money and nothing to give her. We celebrated every one of those early pay checks coming in, thinking we had made it in life. As my fame rose, I think Angela thought she had to act like the girlfriend of a rock star, wearing fur coats and driving a new sports car every year.'

'It sounds like the destructive nature of the relationship seemed to suit you both.'

William faltered, struggling to catch his breath before he spoke. 'Angela and I both had the same dark fantasies and we fed off each other, we liked to push each other, scare each other.' While they walked back down Kirkwood Drive, William waved his arm around at the roads that zigzagged away into the hills. 'I raced my car all around here, up onto Mulholland, both of us high, drunk and playing a game of chicken. I was good ol' Jim Stark in *Rebel Without A Cause*, slamming his foot on the gas pedal towards the cliff edge, rolling the dice, knowing all the best games contain a risk of death, because death was daring you to outwit it.'

Tyler helped William to sit at a picnic table at the front of the Country Store. 'You didn't care if you lived or died driving around like that?' he asked. 'Or that you might kill someone else?'

'It was all part of the game, man. There has to be a certain risk of death in the game for you to live, it's the great gamble. It's all over if you lose, but if you win ... boy, then you'll know what it's like to really live on the other side.' William brushed his hand across the splintered wooden surface of the table. 'I wanted to roll the dice and see what would happen, challenge death and then spit in its face when I rolled and beat it again and again. That was my darkest macabre fantasy; to see how far you could push life before you reached the perimeter of death.'

Entering the store, Tyler checked over his shoulder to see William sitting hunched under the shade of a large sun umbrella, his arms were wrapped around his torso while he quietly talked to himself.

'Have you got a telephone?' he asked the girl behind the counter, who pointed towards the back of the store. Tyler riffled through his jacket pocket and pulled out a crumpled piece of paper, dialling the number written on it.

'Good afternoon, West California State College, Psychology Department. This is Tammy.'

'Hey, Tammy, it's Tyler. Can I speak to Professor Kessler?'

He listened to the static crackle, followed by a foreboding click.

'Mr Rafferty,' came the disappointed voice on the other end of the line. 'I believe you were due in my office at ten o'clock yesterday morning. Are you going to amaze me with an excuse?'

'Professor, I need a couple more days. My patient–'

'Yes, I'm aware of your patient. I've spoken with Doctor Marshall.'

'Shit,' Tyler said, covering the mouthpiece of the telephone with his hand.

'Do you have any comprehension about what you have done? Once again, you have put the reputation of this college in jeopardy.'

'I know I've taken a slightly unorthodox approach to this case study, but–'

'Tyler,' Professor Kessler interrupted, 'if you are not back in my office by Friday morning, then I'll have no choice but to remove you with immediate effect and the police can deal with you. I expect your father has spoken to you?'

Tyler's chest muscles baulked. 'No, I've not spoken to him for a while.'

'I see. Well, I'm sorry but for your own wellbeing I had to let him know what you have done, and he's very disappointed. I will hold you personally responsible if your father withdraws the charitable donations which my research team relies on. Now, I expect you back here by Friday, this is your final warn–'

Tyler slammed down the telephone receiver, ending Professor Kessler's threat before he had finished making it. He tried to disguise the shaking in his legs as he walked back across the store, raising a weak smile of thanks to the girl at the counter. His thoughts were swarming around his head like flies; he was running out of time to infiltrate William's true memories, before returning him to the care of Doctor Marshall, to save his now uncertain future.

'What about the drugs and alcohol, was your dependency worsening?' he quietly asked, sitting down at the picnic table opposite William.

'Yeah, it was really deteriorating by the international tour in the fall of '68. But we were having a good time and were excited to play in Europe. The gigs in London, Copenhagen and Paris thrilled me, I think they were our career-defining shows. It felt good being in the smaller venues again. It was a blessed relief from the large concert halls and sport arenas we had been playing back home. Y'know, the crowds came to listen, not to expect anything, simply to listen to great music and to beautiful poetic lyrics, and I loved them for it. It reminded me what the hell we wanted to do all along. As the tour progressed, the drugs and booze got harder … and the women, oh man, it was an all-consuming Bacchanalian decadence. In Amsterdam, the fans pressed pills into my obliging hands.'

'You could have said no.'

'I don't think the word *no* was in my vocabulary back then, kid.' William laughed. 'I never thought about the consequences of my reckless actions, especially for other people. There was no compromise, it was all or nothing. When we arrived at our hotel in Cologne, Germany, I decided to ease the pressure by taking some of the pills that I'd hidden in my boot when we flew in from Amsterdam. Later that day, when my absence was noticed, our tour manager, Kurt, found me in the bathtub of my suite; unconscious, naked and still inside a member of the hotel's house-keeping staff. Kurt made excuses to the journalists gathered downstairs for a press conference, told them I had exhaustion, the usual bullshit that no one actually believed. So the band did the press conference and a national TV show that night without me, with Clark taking over my vocals. By the end of the tour there was a crippling tension. I was devastated that the others had received rave reviews for the TV show without me.'

'You were jealous that the rest of the band got all the attention?'

William peered back over at the house nestled into the hill on Kirkwood Drive. 'No, I wasn't jealous, I was angry as hell. I'd always relied on the guys to keep me alive on stage, that's how the band worked. After Germany, I saw that The Gracious Dawn could survive without Joe Hawkins after all. That upset me … really upset me. I'm only human and, like the next man, things like that bothered me.'

Tyler stood, resting his hand on his patient's back. 'We should get going.'

William kept close by Tyler's side with his hands buried in his coat pockets. 'While we were on tour, we were trying to rehearse tracks for our third album. I'd run out of ideas, my poetry was drying up, so Frank ended up writing most of that album. I didn't feel like I had anything more to give, Tyler,

I'd been bled dry. Our record label was steering us to create music that sounded commercial, passive songs to be consumed through the radio waves, and it sent my mood tumbling again. We'd gone from a debut album that crashed through musical conventions, with rock and blues at its core, to churning out popular hits that would guarantee television show appearances and high chart positions.'

Arriving back at the car, William ran his hand across the over-heated bodywork, its flame-red paint was now dusted with sand and tree pollen. 'Can I drive?' he asked. 'Just back down the hill.'

Tyler clasped the car keys in his hand. 'Are you kidding me? After your death wish stunt out in the Mojave Desert, there's no way you're driving this car. Besides, my father would kill me if anything happened to it.'

Keeping a wary check on his now sulking passenger, Tyler started the engine and turned onto Laurel Canyon Boulevard. A bitter sadness jarred in the back of his throat, as he looked out at the place where his mother once lived and knew true happiness. He pressed a cassette tape into the car's radio and turned up the volume, sinking his body into the driver's seat as Metallica's *Master of Puppets* album surged through the car.

'Who's this?' William asked, tilting his ear towards the radio speaker.

'It's my favourite band.' Tyler wavered before he spoke again. 'Sometimes, when I listen to their music, it's like I can escape into the songs … like finding a place that drowns out the thoughts in my head. Their music makes me feel better about things.'

'That's good,' William said through a soft smile.

The winding hillside lanes coursed into wide highways and boulevards pumping towards the heart of Los Angeles. Tyler's leg muscles hung like lead weights, keeping his foot clamped on the gas pedal, still unsure where his patient was taking him. A sudden chill slithered through his body. William had not only guided him to the entrance of his labyrinth, but had followed him inside, and was moving the walls as Tyler searched in the darkness for the truth at its core. He took a long breath. 'Do you have any intention of going back to the hospital?'

William shrugged with a cool indifference. 'I may go back … and I may not.'

'And how am I meant to explain that to Doctor Marshall and the police? You don't get it do you? I've risked everything to help you.'

'Hee hee hee … you need to relax a little.' William chuckled. 'I was just messing with you. Of course I'm going back to the hospital, and I'll clear everything up with the police. I promise I'll sort it all out.' The lines around William's eyes tensed as he watched a blanket of smog smother the city into the western horizon. 'By 1969 my career as a rock star would start its final destructive course. Joe Hawkins was about to cause a storm that would cost him his life.'

CHAPTER THIRTY-ONE

**The Journal of Joseph Hawkins – November 14th, 1968
(Topanga Canyon, California)**

I am haunted by my nightmares, the same wretched visions I had as a boy …

A storm rages at sea. A ship is breaking apart as it sinks, and I watch from the shore as the desperate sailors cajole each other overboard. From the depths of my soul, I can hear those sailors screaming as they clamber through the swirling debris. I can see their eyes, wild with fear, their tiring arms and legs fighting against the foaming black water. All I can do is stand on the shore and watch, helpless, as they drown. Then I turn and see my satyr dancing on the sand beside me, revelling in the torment and horror.

I cannot focus on anything good in my life. Depression is like a disease that eats you alive, it feeds upon your wretched soul. I do not feel anything as I walk into the darkness, my restless mind is trapped inside the hollow shell of a man.

Joey Hawkins is cowering at the bottom of a well, staring up towards the light wishing someone could hear his screams. He is a vulnerable, broken child who needs someone to comfort him, to stroke his head and tell him that everything will be alright. Then, in the swift beat of my heart and the flash of a camera bulb, Wild Joe – the young wolf bathed in a spotlight – rips back into my consciousness and takes over again, tearing my life apart. I am trapped in a world that I do not understand and cannot escape. I am lost at sea, drowning and there is no one to rescue me.

The people around me cannot hide the fact that my behaviour is really becoming a problem. As we came out of the airport in Miami,

I overheard Kurt say the flight was like being trapped on an airplane with a lunatic. I had spent the whole journey screaming at the top of my lungs then drinking until I passed out. As soon as I go out of town, everyone will sit in the LA office and talk about me, 'We have to do something about Joe!' You know, when all you ever hear are people saying you are crazy, you start to believe that it is true.

Now, when we go on tour, I have a bodyguard shadowing my every move. He is there for my protection, but he is my jailor. In the early days, I was free to go wherever I pleased and with whom I pleased. I dread the moment when the post-show party is over, and I return to my hotel room in whatever city we are in. All night long, I can hear hundreds of fans outside the hotel calling my name. As I pass out with a bottle in my hand, I am alone. I do not know where I am or who I am. You can be the most worshipped man in the world but lie in bed feeling empty and lost. On the road, it is easier to drink myself into oblivion rather than deal with this torment.

My drinking has gone from being a pleasure, to being a dependency, to being a disguise.

Joe Hawkins is turning from a matinee idol into a Greek tragedy. I am hiding the real man behind an invisible mask, a hero with a thousand faces. My spirit is slipping away, my soul is cracking, splitting into two halves. I am fighting to retain the balance over both sides of my personality, but I am powerless, and it scares me more than I can say.

Last month it was my birthday, and Angela held a party for me and my friends in a room at the Chateau Marmont. As I stood there, I had a deep-rooted sensation that I had reached twenty-six, but I would not live to see thirty. When Joel Arden and Bud Goshen presented me with a bottle of champagne, I saw the look on everyone's faces, that look of trepidation whenever I have a bottle of booze in my hand, as if they are a witness to a slow and deliberate suicide. There is sadness in their eyes for my looming fate.

I can sense the tide is turning against me.

The whole world wants a piece of me, to take advantage of me. Someone from my past has rung the band's office, threatening to tell stories to the newspapers, to reveal dirty little secrets about things I have done, indiscretions in my college years which I do not want the world finding out about now. My lawyer, Walt Wilson, says I should not worry, he can sort it out. Once we have paid off this guy, all I can do is hope to never hear from him again. However, I know only too well that hope is a false friend you cannot trust.

I do not know who Joe Hawkins is supposed to be anymore. I have imprisoned myself in a constant state of pretending to be an ideal rock star for the world to purchase at any price. I do not care what the fans think about me, what the fans expect from me … but I am addicted to them, I get high from their love and adoration. I need their obsession flowing through my veins because when they are gone, I am alone again.

The crowds are getting more powerful, they are starting to call the shots. I am seeing the audience's reaction at our shows from a whole new perspective. I have always been at the forefront on stage, looking out at the chaos unfolding in front of me. Now I watch our concerts descend into chaos through the audience's young, impressionable eyes. All this time I thought I was the puppet-master pulling the strings, with the power to manipulate thousands of people, but it is the fans who have the power over me, demanding that I perform like a circus clown for them.

I am losing control.

There is now a tangible distance within the band. I arrive at gigs in my own limo with my own people, hang out in separate dressing rooms, come together for the show and then leave after that night's battle is over.

Last week, Angela and I took a few days away to visit her younger brother, Rick and his girlfriend Linda in San Jose. When we came back to LA, Tommy Seagram told me that everyone had agreed a deal for "Into The Night" to be used in a television commercial for an airline.

FLY INTO THE NIGHT WITH
SOUTH AMERICAN AIRLINES!

It is a violation.

They are selling our souls to the devil, prostituting our music to the highest bidder. I do not want our work bastardised like that. We have always worked as a four-piece, we make decisions together and we share writing credits and royalties equally.

This is the death of my relationship with The Gracious Dawn.

Our innocent, creative dream is lost.

CHAPTER THIRTY-TWO

At a deserted student apartment block in Westwood, two men took a cramped elevator to the fifth floor. The abandoned calm, of the usually bustling corridors, teased Tyler's nerves while he unlocked his front door and held it open for William, who shuffled into the living room and sank into an armchair.

'Why do you want to see where I live?' Tyler asked, slamming the door and throwing his bag to the floor.

'Curiosity,' William said. 'Simple curiosity.'

Tyler picked up a pile of dirty laundry from the couch and threw it into his bedroom. 'We'll stay here tonight and then first thing in the morning we're going back to San Francisco,' he said over his shoulder as he headed towards the kitchen. 'Just sit there and don't touch anything.'

William waited for the kitchen door to swing shut, before his eyes darted to a red flashing light on the telephone answering machine. He lifted himself out of the chair and skulked across the room, pressing the message button and turning down the volume so that only a faint voice came out of the speaker.

'*Tyler, this is your father. I've had a call from Professor Kessler. Is it true that you have taken a psych patient out of the hospital without consent? The police are trying to find you. What did you think you were doing? I'm up to my neck at work right now, I don't have the time to come over there and—*'

The threat of a smirk crumpled across William's mouth. 'Thank you for your concern, Mr Rafferty,' he said, pressing the delete button.

By the time Tyler returned to the living room, clutching a pizza delivery menu, William had eased himself back into the armchair. 'Do you live alone, Tyler?' he asked, raising his eyebrows into a look of complete innocence.

'No, I share with two other guys. Everyone who submitted their case study proposals in time has gone away for spring break, but not me.'

'Are they your friends?' William asked, pointing at a photograph of four students lying on the grass in front of an imposing Palladian concert hall on the college campus, Tyler hugging an elfin girl who lay beside him.

'They're in my class.' He took the photograph from the wall, brushing flecks of dust from the glass. 'That's Carla, we dated for a while.'

'Interesting,' William said, half-closing his eyes. 'Very interesting.'

Tyler hung the photograph back on the wall and straightened it, before picking up the telephone and placing a pizza order. 'Do you want to talk some more?' he asked, as he finished the telephone call and sat down.

'Yes. Why do you hate your father?'

'That's not what I meant.'

'A frightened little boy who's still scared of his father, I see that in you.' William leaned forward in the chair. 'What is it you are so scared of, I wonder?'

'I'm not scared.' Tyler glared back across the room, folding his arms. 'And I'm not scared of *him* if that's what you think.'

'He can't look at you, can he? Let me guess; you have your mother's eyes, is that it?'

'Don't.'

'I'm only curious to know about you, man, that's all.' William tapered his gaze at Tyler, his head dipping to his left shoulder. 'I'm right though, aren't I? He cannot bear to see his dead wife still alive in your eyes.'

Tyler tried to temper the heat that rose up his neck as he pulled out his wallet and extracted a small photograph of his mother. A white daisy was nestled behind her ear and her sparkling eyes brimmed into the camera lens with the innocent vitality of youth. He stood and handed the photograph to William.

'When my mom got ill, it wasn't the cancer that destroyed her, that tore our lives apart,' Tyler said, meeting William's fixed interest, 'it was the endless treatment and the drugs the doctors forced her to endure, and she still had to die. It wasn't fair. I was powerless to help her, to save her. As a ten-year-old boy I stood in silence at her bedside feeling numb inside as I watched her fade. My world fell apart when I heard the last gasp of air slip from her lungs. Afterwards, Dad sent me away for months to live with my grandparents in Carmel while he grieved, but when I moved back, I couldn't do anything right. He spent all day and night at work, so I rebelled at school, seeking out trouble at every opportunity. I guess I wanted him to notice me again, that was all.'

'There's something about her, I ...' William hesitated as he studied the photograph in his hands, caressing his thumb over the young woman's face. 'She was beautiful.'

Tyler tucked the photograph back into his wallet. Picking up his bag from the floor, he took out his notebook. 'Now, Mr Kendrick, we had reached 1969, I think.'

William leaned back in the armchair, wrapping his body into the deep folds of his coat. 'That was the beginning of the end,' he said, keeping his eyes planted on Tyler. 'Y'know, we weren't like every other band who put on the same show every night, I wanted to create a unique experience each time and it was really becoming hard. When we performed "Into The Night" in these enormous auditoriums, Frank used to play a ten-minute guitar solo, so twenty thousand people are then staring at me, demanding to be entertained. What the hell was I meant to do, man, dance like a performing dog for them? I started to really loathe that song. I liked being unpredictable at every show, I liked the chaos, and now people were expecting that from me every night. Joe Hawkins was becoming predictable; it was becoming a routine and I resented it. I always believed that I was an honest person, Tyler, but I felt like I was being dishonest to my own spirit to play this Joe Hawkins character. At that time there was a distinct change from feeling the creative release of being on stage, to me becoming angry.'

'Who were you angry at?'

William placed his journal on the armrest of the chair and ran his fingers across its cover. 'I was angry with JoJo, the out-of-control alcoholic, for allowing me to become the person I was turning into. I was frustrated that society had distorted my plans to create enlightenment. The audiences were mocking it, demanding something more out of me than I was prepared to give. They didn't want Joe the poet anymore.' He paused to catch his breath. 'They wanted the circus clown.'

Tyler stood and opened the living room windows. He looked down at his car which he had hastily parked behind a wall, trying not to draw any unwanted attention to their campus visit. 'Joe Hawkins was responsible for what he had become,' he said. 'There was no one else to blame for his drinking and drug addiction and that's what caused his frustration. Do you see that?'

'You're blaming me for it?' William asked with a baffled expression. 'You think I was to blame for Joe turning from a shaman into a circus freak?'

'I think Joe was responsible from the start for his own creation, yeah,' Tyler said as he sat down. 'It was Joe Hawkins himself who decided to take on the persona of a rock star, to create the image of a sex symbol, and then he becomes angry and frustrated when the tide turned against him. That's what I think anyway.'

William's eyes fell to a half-closed scowl, his head lowering into the folds of his coat collar. 'I fell into a trap of my own creation, you're right. I knew that being Joe Hawkins would crush me, and yet I still rolled the dice and took the risk as I willingly walked into the limelight. I, uhm, always maintained that you had to be honest about who you are as a person, be true to your own spirit. I thought I'd achieved that in myself, but in reality I'd lost all perspective of who I was. The freedom I'd fought for since I was born, fighting against my parents, school and authority was now a losing battle.'

The front doorbell rang, causing William's body to tense forward. Tyler opened the door only a crack to pay the delivery man, before placing an open pizza box on the table, filling the apartment with a comforting aroma of hot dough and spicy pepperoni.

'Your generation,' William said, trying to swallow a small mouthful of food, 'I guess all they know about Joe Hawkins is what the press wanted them to know.'

'What do you mean?' Tyler said, before taking a large bite of pizza.

'Like the T-shirt stall on Venice Beach, selling an image that the world still demands. People don't want to remember me how I was before I died, they don't want to remember me when I was a washed-up alcoholic and twenty pounds heavier. It's the same for my memories. The world only remembers what it wants to, it only remembers the fantasy of the dangerous and shocking things I did; being arrested on stage, getting hurled out of bars night after night, the parties, sex and drugs. The world doesn't know about the rest of my life back then … Joe Hawkins' real life.'

'Joe's personal life, you mean?'

William threw the half-eaten slice of pizza back in the box and sank his body into the comfort of the armchair. 'I mean the life I lived day in day out that people know nothing about. The normal times I spent doing what other regular people do. No, the good days were never reported to the world.'

'So, Joe did have good days back then?' Tyler asked, reaching down to pull off his shoes.

William's head lolled across the back of the chair, his tired eyes succumbing to the warmth of the room. 'When Angela and I were having a good phase, we spent precious time together. We drove away from the stifling world that my life had become, finding a remote place with hills to climb, grass to lie on with the woman I loved. One day, during the softness of summer, we drove through the Los Padres National Forest and found a lake surrounded with high rocks. I watched Angela slide her freckled body into the water as her dog, Skye, lay on our warm clothes. The trees around the water's edge provided us with our only protection from the outside world. When night fell, the crescent moon danced across the water, as we swam around each other in an ethereal courtship, our naked bodies tangled around the reeds in the opaque water. I watched Angela pull herself out of the lake with a pale tranquillity. She sat on the edge of a rock, the moon illuminating her skin like a beacon in the darkness to show me the way home. The sharp scent of burning pine from our fire washed across the water and engulfed our souls. Y'know, that smell will always take me back to that night, Tyler, the night when we were the only two people alive. The world doesn't know about times like that, it only wants to remember the rock star who cannot even be destroyed seventeen years after my death. The world never understood that I was a real person, a mortal man who breathed the same suffocating air as everyone else. My life is still one that I cannot live up to.'

'I guess I'm guilty of that too,' Tyler said, reaching across for another slice of pizza.

'There were things I did that no one knew about, and no one ever will,' William said, stroking his fingers through his beard. 'Quiet days when I attended a play or a poetry reading, sitting minding my own business, listening as a mere face in the crowd. Days I spent living what I perceived to be a normal life away from the band, drinking beers with my friends, playing football, kidding around. I, uh, always knew how to laugh and be funny, keeping everyone entertained. I drove all around LA, hanging out at friends' houses, having a good time. Those were the real Joe Hawkins days, the lost days I'll never find again.' William stood and ambled over to where Tyler sat, placing a hand on his shoulder. 'It was my choice to take the unsafe path, it was my actions that would cause my life to change.' Steadying himself, he turned and headed into the bathroom. 'It was all my fault.'

When William returned five minutes later, wiping a trace of vomit from his beard, Tyler reached to grab the last slice of pizza. 'How much of that self-destruction was real though?' he asked. 'I mean, do you think Joe was playing up to the hype, acting out a living myth he had created around himself?'

William rubbed his eyes and sat down in the armchair, curving his torso forward over his knees. 'Oh, my self-destruction was real, man, but the memory of my worst behaviour is a void, there's nothing there. I have no connections to those memories.'

'You don't remember any of it?'

'Only what people told me the next day, what trouble I had gotten into the night before. I heard things back all the time, things I had done that I have no memory of. My friends would watch as I balanced like a tightrope walker along the balcony ledge of my penthouse suite, stark naked, before they dragged me back into the bedroom, left me to piss on the carpet before passing out on the floor. Nights when I was blind drunk, racing my Porsche the wrong way along Sunset Strip, not giving a damn if I lived or died. Those times, Tyler, when my life got that bad, are a dark tapestry of other people's perception of my behaviour.'

Tyler picked up his pen and wrote some quick observations across a new page of his notebook. *William has experienced episodes where he has lost track of time, not knowing what he has done. Does he believe that another, more dangerous aspect of his personality carried out his destructive behaviour? Is that why he cannot remember parts of it? Jekyll and Hyde.*

'Did you feel there were no boundaries in your mind, nothing to tell you when you were going too far, or you could hurt yourself?' Tyler asked, glancing up from his notes. 'I just don't get why, when you had the world at your feet, you would let your behaviour become that bad.'

'Why?' William asked. 'Because I could and because no one else had the balls to try. I wanted to *feel* life. I sought out extremes of danger for the experience. It was a reckless and incessant pursuit of pleasure, naïvely thinking it would bring me happiness and rid me from the torment that my life had become. It was thrill-taking, not thrill-seeking. I suppose I was curious to see what would happen, that's all it was ... curiosity. I was proving to anyone watching that, even as one of the world's most famous rock stars, all the trappings of a celebrity life really meant nothing to me.' A yawn drew across William's face. 'Around that time, I rang my lawyer and told him I wanted to write my will.'

'At twenty-six years old you were planning for your death?' Tyler took a long drink from a can of Coke before resuming his notes.

'Yeah, I was thinking about my own mortality every damn day. I wanted to make sure, if anything happened to me, that Angela would get everything and, in the event of her death, my estate would revert to my brother and sister. When I signed my name at the bottom of the page, I knew I was signing Joe Hawkins' death warrant.'

Tyler closed his notebook and watched as William gave in to sleep. He lay crumpled in the armchair, his breathing a succession of grating rasps. Tyler covered his patient with a blanket, took the journal and switched off the living room lights. *I have no idea who you are, William Kendrick*, he thought, heading into his bedroom and slamming the door. *No idea at all.*

CHAPTER THIRTY-THREE

**The Journal of Joseph Hawkins – February 6th, 1969
(Hollywood, California)**

We are in the studio recording tracks for our third album, which I am trying to persuade the band to call *Wolf At My Side*. The label want it released by April, so we are all feeling an unimaginable pressure.

As a band, you will never be as good as your first album because you put your heart and soul into it, your life depends on its success, so you give it everything. Each successive album, year on year, is pandering to the record label's financial demands and to the fans' expectations. Rock 'n' roll should be wild, loose and raw. Once you force the creative process in a sterile studio you start to lose the spirit of the group, its vision and its soul. You risk becoming predictable.

Last month, when we were in New York to perform at Madison Square Garden, I met a journalist called Dianne Rollins from *Music Hits* magazine who came to review our show. She walked into my dressing room to interview me, and when we shook hands I experienced an instant connection, a meeting of minds. There is something about her nature and her spirit that intrigued me, she has a mystical soul and I sense that I will be drawn back to her again.

There are still plenty of other women embroiled in my life, friends who become lovers and lovers who become friends. Then there are the groupies ... although sleeping with them feels like nothing more than a soulless masturbation for me. It is all too easy.

Angela is trying to keep up with me all the time, keep up with my chaotic life. It was my money that changed her, so I suppose I am responsible for what she has become. Part of me feels that as a man … as her man … I must provide for her, I want to spoil her and make her happy, but it is papering over the dark cracks appearing in our relationship. When she catches me with someone else, she cuts up my clothes, screams at me that I am a monster. She gets angry about my sexual preferences, certain things I enjoy doing with her that she only tolerates to make me happy. Or when I cannot get it up for weeks on end, she will taunt me with it, knowing I will react to it and another fierce fight will ensue. When I see the wildfires blazing in her eyes, I know I must get out of town to let things cool off. It is a destructive relationship, but I love her and want to make her happy. That is all I can do.

I am floundering from these extremes. Some days I live in a simplistic blissful happiness, enjoying life, playing a great gig, sharing a beer with friends and feeling positive about my future, like having a complete delight in life. Then we endure a bad gig, where there is no reaction from the audience, and it pushes me towards a nervous breakdown from which I am never going to escape. I wake in the night and feel like my spirit is possessed by wicked demons. In my nightmares I am falling into a well … my hands are grappling at the wet bricks as I spiral into the murky water to drown.

Angela keeps telling me to quit The Gracious Dawn and, if I were not tied into this contract with Jesse Winters and Hudson Beat Records, I would walk away for good, go and live in a distant part of the world and be left alone. I yearn to spend quiet days reading books and writing poetry with a calm mind, but I cannot see through the static disturbance in my thoughts. I need peace and clarity, but I have no idea where to find it.

Ever since my childhood, I have tried so hard to reach the perimeter of life and existence, that I have trapped myself in its destructive embrace. The world keeps ripping me back, kicking and screaming, dragging me back from the edge of oblivion by my fingernails, demanding more of me, demanding more of Joe Hawkins.

Every morning I wake and fear that my life is building up to something so destructive that it will seal my fate, perhaps seal all our fates. I am beginning to wonder what would happen if you really pushed an audience as far as it would go, imagine it was your last ever show and there were no consequences to your actions. Maybe that is how we can all, as a communal group, reach absolute zero … we can all look into the void, the point of no return.

I am convinced the authorities want to stamp me out, shut me down and have me killed. They see me as the ringleader, provoking America's young, impressionable minds into riot and revolt. A scapegoat is needed to blame for this dysfunctional society, and I am their man.

Sometimes life scares me, more than anyone will ever know.

My only choice now is to destroy the circus freak to save the life of the poet. It is more compassionate to slit the throat of the wounded young wolf, rather than watch it rile and suffer in pain. It is better to wash away the spider trapped in the bath, than leave it to suffer its fate.

The time has come to leave behind the wolf in black leather. I must change once more, rip off the broken mask that has disguised the true man existing in Joe's shadow.

You see, it was rock 'n' roll that created Joe Hawkins and perhaps it is only right that it will destroy him too. I need to shed the protective skin which I have relied on for the past few years, flay the beast until it bleeds to death. I will take off the costume of the clown, wipe the paint from my tired face and show the world the real man underneath, strip myself back to what society once deemed to be 'normal'.

For years, I have straddled the fence between life and death and I somehow managed to keep that balance, now I can feel the pendulum pulling me towards death. I muse on it day in, day out. My star is collapsing in on itself, pulling me into a black hole from which I will never escape. I have descended to hell where rats and snakes and wild dogs roam. I close my eyes and see the ghost children, they are faceless, playing in the darkness with the broken bones of lost souls.

The sweet intoxicating wine from Bacchus' cup now tastes bitter in my mouth.

The tragedy is that Joseph Hawkins is in love with life, he is desperate to live. Joseph Hawkins loves to joke around, be the life and soul of the party, making everyone laugh and keeping everyone entertained. Joseph Hawkins loves to watch movies, read books, write poetry, draw and paint, finding comfort in life's simple pleasures. I must find a way to save him before it is too late.

In my dreams I am surrounded by a terrible storm.

When I wake, I pray that storm will come along to blow away the nightmare my life has become.

CHAPTER THIRTY-FOUR

Tyler woke late, sullying his plans to leave Los Angeles before the worst of the morning rush hour had suffocated the highways and before their overnight stay at his student apartment was noticed. Lying in bed, he could hear that his patient was already awake and pacing around the living room. Coming out of his bedroom, yawning and scratching his head, Tyler thought he saw William slipping something into the back pocket of his jeans.

'Is everything alright?' he asked, throwing a change of clothes into his bag.

William's hand fell back at his side. 'Everything's just fine.'

The meandering curves of the Pacific Coast Highway would lead the two men back to San Francisco and to an overdue appointment with both Doctor Wesley Marshall and the police. Saline winds lingered over cliff tops and mingled with the lament of soft-rock guitars playing on the car's radio.

William sat with the journal open on his lap, scribbling notes while he whispered lines of Arthur Rimbaud's "Ophelia" under his breath. 'Tell me something, Tyler; why did your relationship with the Carla girl end?' he asked, keeping his eyes drawn to the journal.

'I don't think she really understood me,' Tyler said. 'I guess we grew apart after a while. She dated one of the football team after me though.'

'Yeah?' William lifted his head and grinned across at Tyler. 'Did she now?'

The deepening scent of damp vegetation, still glistening from the previous night's rain, tumbled down from the hills and freshened the stale air in the car through the open windows. Tyler kept his concentration on the winding road, relieved to be returning to San Francisco, but aware that he only had a few hours left to discover William's truth, and he needed to keep him talking. 'I read Joe's journal again last night. Why was getting recognition as a poet so important?'

'Growing up, uhm, I never had anyone make me feel like I was good enough or tell me what I did was right. I wanted someone to recognise the person who I really was, because recognition is simply proof of your existence and that's all I ever needed.'

'You felt like everything was building up to something destructive. What did you mean?'

'Y'know, The Gracious Dawn worked in a strange perfection of three Apollos balancing one Dionysus, but once that balance began to swing out of control, then the band would break down. We could all sense something was coming, like an unstoppable omen.' William's voice cracked, turning his eyes away from Tyler. 'It was Texas. One night in Houston would destroy both Joe Hawkins and The Gracious Dawn ... for good.'

By the early afternoon, the car was roaming through the dense forest roads of the Big Sur State Park.

The wheels growled as Tyler turned the car onto a rocky trail that led to a café, housed in a renovated old ranch building. Grabbing two coffees, he headed back outside to find William sitting at a table on a patch of grass overlooking the ocean. 'Tell me about what happened in Texas.'

William whispered his thanks and wrapped his trembling hands around the coffee cup. 'Houston was the first date on our biggest tour yet, and it was a disaster before I even left LA. Angela and I had another ferocious fight, which left my mood spiralling.'

'What was the fight with her about?'

'She'd come over to the Sunset Vista Motel and caught me uh ...'

Tyler swallowed hard. 'Caught you doing what?'

'She caught me with some acquaintances. Y'know, we were having a little *adult* fun.' A furtive grin undulated across William's mouth as he slowly ran his tongue along his bottom lip. 'I knew Angela was coming over that afternoon, so I purposefully left the motel room door unlocked for her to walk straight into an orgiastic scene from the debauched depths of the ancient world. A writhing, moaning, serpentine pile of naked bodies on the bed indulging in every pleasure your wildest, wettest dreams could imagine. As the door opened, and Angela walked in, I sank my teeth into the nearest curve of warm flesh and grinned up at her. I knew it would cause a reaction and boy she was furious with me, more than I'd ever seen her. "You pig, Joe Hawkins!" she yelled, throwing the bedside lamp at my head. "I'll go to the press, honey, tell them what you're *really* like."'

Tyler shifted his body on the wooden seat and took out his notebook from his bag. 'Wouldn't going back to Houston be Joe Hawkins' big homecoming gig?'

'It would, you're right.' William grimaced, taking a sip of coffee. 'The show was in the University of Houston Sports Arena on April 8th, 1969, and ten thousand college kids kept swarming in like bees. The air was stifling and backstage you could sense the same electric friction that had been at our other shows. That night, though, there was a very different atmosphere, as if the audience wanted something more. I was backstage in the dressing room drinking from a whiskey bottle to temper my mood, which only added to the deathly tension. I could tell everyone was upset at me for being drunk again. When I emerged on stage into the spotlight, I held my breath and listened to every voice in the arena chant my name, "Hawkins! Hawkins! Hawkins!"' William's head fell, struggling to breathe as he pulled out his cigarettes and lit one.

'Take your time.'

'We opened the show with a couple of new songs which Frank had written,' William said, as he regained his composure through a long stream of smoke. 'The audience were getting real over-excited, then the atmosphere changed. I was getting angrier as they kept shouting for us to play "Into The Night", so I screamed into the microphone, "What are you all here for? Do you want to be entertained?"'

'Joe had done worse than heckle an audience before.'

'Perhaps,' William said, keeping his voice soft. 'I had become fascinated with the idea of pushing an audience as far as they'd go, to see what could really happen if you removed all barriers to human behaviour. I decided to perform as if it was Joe Hawkins' last ever show. I guess I really didn't care anymore about what could happen, or there might be consequences to my behaviour. That night there were no limits, just action and reaction in perfect harmony.'

'You wanted to start another riot?'

'No, kid, that night I wanted to start a war. It was the final straw for Joe Hawkins being the performing circus dog for people to consume at any price for their ... entertainment. I was going to give them a show they'd never forget. We carried on playing "Venice Beach Blues", "Alone In Dreams" and "Angel of LA" and, as the tension mounted, I pulled off my shirt and threw it into the baying mob who tore it to shreds. Standing in a single spotlight, stripped to my flesh, I teased down the waistband of my leather pants to my hip bones – no underwear – the temptation of a glimpse of hair sending the girls in the front row wild. I kept taunting the fans, goaded them to stand up for themselves, to stand up against authority, venting my tirade at the wall of cops in front of the stage. I yelled, "Get it on! Get angry! Stand up and fight against these cops telling you what to do! They're trying to stop us having a good time here!"'

William's mouth turned up at the corner into a mischievous smile. 'I saw Clark's face from behind his keyboards, a look telling me that I'd once again stepped over the line, but this time I'd gone too far. I carried on shouting at the audience, "We're here to start the revolution and we're gonna start it NOW! Do it! Do it!" Then, as the heat intensified, the pent-up frustration of the audience erupted out of them like caged beasts. Surging forward, they ripped up chairs and engulfed the stage so that

Clark, Dean and Frank had to abandon their instruments and retreat to the dressing room. I leapt off the stage into a heaving mass of bodies who were stripping off their clothes right down to their underwear. I became the shaman, leading all my young disciples around in a beautiful ritualistic dance. Later, after the carnage had ended, I stood bare chested on the balcony, looking out at the desolate scene in the empty arena, knowing in that moment of bewilderment and wonderment, I had destroyed The Gracious Dawn. The police, of course, blamed me for instigating another riot, like I had deliberately encouraged the audience to tear up the place like a bunch of fuckin' animals.'

Tyler drained the last of his coffee and looked out across the ocean. 'But that's exactly what Joe did, William. He wasn't going to take any responsibility for his actions or understand that his behaviour was putting all those young people in danger. You just can't see it or don't want to see it.'

'It's true that I wanted a reaction. I wanted people to stop being passive members of an audience and become something greater than themselves, let go and see what would happen. Although, I didn't want to take all the blame for causing another riot.' A spark in William's eyes seemed to wither as he drew in a deep breath. 'But you're right, this was meant to be Joe's big homecoming performance. It was my declaration of independence, but it was the final straw for the police and the authorities. I was now a condemned man.'

A humid wind blew up from the ocean. William let out an involuntary shiver, even though the temperature was already creeping towards the low seventies. He edged himself forward on the wooden seat, cradling his arms around his body, as Tyler kept his tense concentration on his notebook. 'Joe had finally achieved the destruction he was seeking all along.'

'Perhaps I had,' William said, flicking the cigarette end to the ground and crushing it under the heel of his boot, 'but destruction of the present is the only way to create a new beginning and a new future. People strive to live in an unrealistic utopia of a world without struggle, a world of no pain or destruction, but that would be a terrible world. There would be no tragic poetry written about a futile war, or beautiful songs performed about suffering a broken heart. No, that utopian idea died a long time ago. I saw that, in the dark dystopia of my mind, struggle and destruction were my driving forces and without them I would be like all the bored, tedious people in this world.'

'What about the fans, hadn't Joe's actions ruined it for them too?'

'Well uh, looking back at it, after Houston maybe the fans did feel I'd ruined everything. They were the ones who wanted it though, demanded it, they enjoyed it. No matter what I did it was never enough, they always wanted something weirder and wilder. Two days after the Texas show, a newspaper reported on the concert and condemned my anarchic behaviour, they even said I'd flashed my cock in front of all those sweet southern college girls, which I swear, man, I never did. It was music to the ears of the FBI and my arrest warrant was issued that same day. Even though I knew I was innocent, there was no way out. So, Walt Wilson and I walked into an LA police station, and I was arrested for battery against the police, criminal incitement to riot and lewd behaviour. The authorities had caught me at last, Tyler, and they were going to make a real good example out of me. Day after day, The Gracious Dawn were blacklisted on radio stations, our records were removed from music stores and promoters cancelled concerts. People didn't want us coming to their town to corrupt their kids. I became both the shaman and the scapegoat, a threat to the moral decency of the United States.'

William fumbled his hand into his coat pocket and drew out his cigarette lighter. Picking up a discarded napkin from the table, he rolled it into a tight stick and held the flame underneath the tip until it burned. His clouded gaze became enthralled by the flame, watching it crawl towards his trembling fingers.

'I had started to believe in the myth of Joe Hawkins,' William said, turning his head from side to side, mirroring the burning paper that he twisted in his hand. 'I was a lost shaman who'd become disinterested in defining his own role in society; I was only interested in pursuing my own macabre fantasies.'

His eyes narrowed as he dropped the last inch of burning paper onto the table. 'In a few short years I'd gone from being a man asking the questions – and daring to suggest the answers about freedom, about existence – to being a man on his knees at their mercy. I thought Joe Hawkins was a sorcerer, a shaman whose mind could stretch to the farthest reaches of the universe, who could penetrate space and time in order to create enlightenment. Now my deepest fear had come to pass: Joe Hawkins was a mere mortal man on a fool's errand.'

The smell of burnt paper hung in the air between the two men, acrid and bitter.

'Do you like fire, Mr Kendrick?' Tyler asked.

William picked up his lighter from the table and flicked the ignition wheel in front of Tyler's face. 'Ha! Professor Rafferty thinks I have some sort of Icarus complex, right? That I flew too close to the sun, and I got burned. Man, I know what you're thinking, my craving for Joe Hawkins' immortality. Oh yeah, baby, in my dreams I can fly!' He stood and let out a snorting chuckle, clamping his arms around his body as he walked back to the car.

Tyler headed over to a payphone and dialled a San Francisco number, scribbled on a slip of paper he had been keeping in his jacket pocket. Listening to the crackling ringtone, he watched William pull out a small bag from inside his boot, of what looked like tobacco, and roll it into a long, perfectly formed, cigarette.

'Hi, Doctor Marshall, it's Tyler,' he said into the dirty telephone receiver.

'Mr Rafferty, this has gone on for long enough. Where are you?'

'William is safe and willing to come back to the hospital. I just need more time to try to persuade him to tell me his real memories before it's too late.'

'He's still only speaking as Joe Hawkins?'

'William hasn't strayed from his perceived idea of Joe's memories, not once. It's like he's in an intensive, perpetual state of psychosis.' Tyler glanced across to his patient who remained seated on the hood of the car, smoking the cigarette through a broad smirk. 'I'm humouring him by playing along with his stories, but he's built a brick wall around his true memories that he doesn't want me to break down. It doesn't make any sense that he lives and speaks to Adeline as William Kendrick but will only show me Joe Hawkins.'

'I have a feeling William is playing a very intricate game. You need to listen carefully to what he's telling you, then read between the lines, because that's where the truth of his real memories and negative thought patterns will lie. Now, I will not tell you again; bring him back here before the police find you.' The doctor paused on the other end of the line. 'Tyler, has William had any alcohol or un-prescribed drugs since he left the hospital?'

The sweet scent of marijuana wafted on the breeze from the car towards Tyler. 'No, Doctor, I promise he's not had anything.' Hanging up the telephone, he looked across at William, who winked and exhaled a long stream of fragrant smoke.

Tyler navigated the car along the rugged coastline north, through the white weather-board idyll of Carmel, where his beloved grandparents lived; the only place since his mother's death where he had known what a real home could feel like. As a ten-year-old boy, every Saturday morning he would sit on the steps of the veranda with a child's naïve hope that he would see his father's car pull up outside the house. By Sunday night he would lie in bed, silently punching his fist into the pillow. 'After Texas, what happened with the band?' he asked, forcing the memory away.

'The tension was at breaking point,' William said. 'Everyone was angry at me for ruining the creative dream we'd worked so hard for. I needed to get away, get the hell out of LA and be left alone. So, I took my car and drove, not stopping until exhaustion led me to Sedona, Arizona. Y'know, I think those were the worst days of my entire life. I stayed in a motel on the edge of town, and it made me feel uncomfortable, an intruder in a place where I didn't belong or even want to be. I spent every day walking in the canyons and climbing the red rock buttes like a lost, aimless nomad. I'd sit on the edge of an outcrop, watching the dying embers of daylight drawing any last trace of hope and energy from my body. When night fell, I began drinking again, smoking weed, taking pills and cocaine until it triggered an aggressive paranoia. I was having a panic attack, like I was trapped at the bottom of a glass bottle. Man, I had never felt so low and so alone, not only physically but a sense of complete detachment from my own life, feeling so dead inside that I swear I couldn't feel my heart beating anymore. I, uh, always believed that to feel is to think, if I could feel something then it was real, but I couldn't *feel* anything … and it scared me to death.'

'What were you so scared of, William?' Tyler asked as he drove, looking across at the man beside him who was tightening his arms around his body, swathed in the comfort of his coat.

'I guess it was the fear of being trapped inside my life with no way to get out alive. In the stillness of those nights, I lay in my motel bed, praying the bottle in my hand would rid me from the sad comedy my life had become.'

'Eventually you'd have to go back to LA.'

William turned his attention out of the passenger window to the picturesque lives of suburban America residing behind the protection of white picket fences. 'Yeah, I knew I had to go back, we had to play some gigs because we had the expensive *Wolf At My Side* album to pay for. During those erratic shows through the summer of '69, when I walked on stage I was disconnected from it all. I was lost, washed up and crackin' up. I went to The Village Studios in LA to record my new poetry collection, *Essays On Existence*. A voice in my mind was telling me I had to get those poems recorded so they'd be preserved forever, my words presented to the world on my own creative terms, as I wanted them to be heard. I could feel my heart beating again and maybe, with the rest of my life in ruins, Joseph Hawkins would be taken seriously as a poet …' William's voice trailed off and he seemed to withdraw into his thoughts once more.

'Go on,' Tyler encouraged him as he drove.

After a long hiatus, William cleared his throat and spoke again. 'I, uh, threw myself into a movie project I had written called *The Faceless Stranger*. I'd been working on the script for months with the help of my old college pal, Lenny Michaelson. We rented a small office on Santa Monica Boulevard so we could work all day like professional screen writers. Lenny asked some of his friends from the UCLA Film Department to help make the movie, and we filmed sequences all over Southern California and the Mojave Desert ... y'know, I was happy again.'

'Were you acting in this movie?'

'I was playing the lead role of the faceless stranger, a hitch-hiking nomad and a dangerous lone wolf.' William turned his head towards Tyler, widening his eyes. 'The killer on the highway.'

Tyler gripped the steering wheel tighter as another day slipped through his fingers, and he was no closer to discovering his patient's truth. William had trapped himself in an impenetrable vacuum between two worlds: the lonely realm of William Kendrick and the destructive fantasy of Joe Hawkins.

While the sun lowered across the clement waters of Monterey Bay, Tyler was running on lost time to unravel the threads that bound those two worlds together. Tomorrow morning he would return William to a locked hospital room and never see him again.

CHAPTER THIRTY-FIVE

**The Journal of Joseph Hawkins – August 22nd, 1969
(Chicago, Illinois)**

My soul is troubled.

Sitting here at the writing desk in my opulent hotel suite, I feel like my life is no longer my own. I do not understand this reality, this false friend. I cannot relax, every day I am just going through the expected motions of being a rock star.

Our short American tour has begun, and we are playing some shows in Chicago. There are now undercover cops in the audience ... waiting ... watching ... one derogatory or inflammatory word out of my mouth and I will be arrested, again. I had to sign a bond which forces me not to swear or entice an audience reaction in any way, it has been hung around my neck in shame.

America has changed.

Those wide-eyed teenagers with flowers in their hair who came to our early festival performances are gone, replaced with dope-heads who only want a good time or a riot. Music fans are looking to the darker rock of the British bands and those innocent summer days of peace and free love seems to be a paradise lost forever. The musical soundtrack to our great revolution is becoming outdated and irrelevant, even the journalists who first applauded The Gracious Dawn are now turning against us.

Last weekend we played a set at the Woodstock Music and Art Fair. Tommy Seagram had originally turned down our invitation to perform, but when we heard that Janis, Jimi and Ravi would all be there, we persuaded him to change his mind. Something told us that this would be a festival not to be missed. I had been drinking all day, watching Santana and Canned Heat, when The Gracious Dawn eventually walked out on stage at two a.m. after Creedence Clearwater Revival had performed. We were greeted by the odour of half a million unwashed bodies, stale wine and weed hanging in that farm air. Standing in awe at the front of the stage, I looked out into the darkness at people lying in every direction, some asleep, most unconscious, but everyone covered in mud. Amid the occasional flicker and glow of cigarette lighters, and a lone cheer miles away in the distance, I serenaded them all with "Memories of Eden", "A Poet's Lament" and "Distant Shores".

I fear I will never persuade enough people to change the way they think, to change society, change the world. My failure is all-consuming. The only way for me to deal with it is to spend all day drinking until I pass out. I am incapable of working to a normal touring schedule, I can just about manage a weekend of shows before I collapse.

I spent another blissful night with Dianne Rollins who had flown here from New York. I cannot seem to keep away from her. We are passionate lovers, only when my exhausted, broken body can manage it, but when I wake in the morning, at the forefront of my mind is Miss Angela Jackson. No matter what I do, no matter who I am with, I will love Angela to death.

My reasons for drinking and drug taking have somehow changed. JoJo, the satyr's puppet, fuelled with beer and brandy, has diminished in my mind. I am now a quieter, calmer poet, using booze to retain the numb sense of emotion inside me. A few years ago, I was experimenting to learn what my limits were, now I have no choice but to drink every day to try to escape a prison of my own making. It dampens the fear inside me that I will be incarcerated by the courts. I cannot live in a cage. I will not survive. After Houston, I promised the rest of the band I would try to quit drinking. When I spoke those words, I knew it was a lie. A whiskey bottle will be in my hand until the day I die.

At night I wake and sense my fate looming like a dark shadow.

For months I have walked the streets of LA, trying to work out what the hell I was meant to be doing with my life … is this it? There is a bench on Santa Monica Boulevard where I sit writing in my notebooks, hoping no one will notice me. I am gripped by both relief and sadness that Joe is gone, the young, beautiful Adonis with fire burning in his eyes is lost. I have shunned leather pants in favour of jeans and loose shirts, which help to hide my expanding waistline. I eat too much, and I drink too much and it is reverting my body into the sturdy mammal of my youth.

Joe Hawkins' early homage to the image of Alexander the Great is now obsolete, it has served its usefulness. When I look at my picture in magazines, all I can see is the painful reality that I have metamorphosed into the wreck of a man. My rounded face is hidden behind a thick beard, bouts of venereal disease leave me limp and useless for weeks on end, my stomach hangs over my pants and all I can feel is shame … shame and embarrassment that this is what I have allowed myself to become.

My life is a joke, but no one is laughing anymore. The joke is on me.

I was invited to audition for a couple of movie roles. When I walked into the room, I saw the look on the producer's face, he wanted the beautiful iconic rock star, not the man I am now. The embarrassment of that rejection haunts me. I can hear everyone laughing at me behind my back and it is triggering these brutal panic attacks.

I spend endless nights sitting in my car in the Hollywood Hills overlooking the city that was my creator and now has destroyed me. Closing my eyes, I am Jim Stark, the rebel without a cause. One squeeze on the gas pedal and I will speed towards the cliff edge with only a split second's chance to jump out of the car before the fall.

Sitting here in my solitary reflections, I have extinguished the flames that have burned inside me all these years. There is a quietness in my mind that I have not experienced since I was a boy.

It is time to roll the dice again.

I am being drawn towards the end.

The void is finally pulling me in.

CHAPTER THIRTY-SIX

The late-afternoon sun fractured through soaring redwoods, casting claw-like silhouettes over the ferns and wild berry bushes that carpeted the forest floor. Mellow lamplight shone out from Adeline Parker's home like a beacon on the shore of a turbulent sea. Tyler slowed the car and navigated along the narrow driveway leading to William's darkened house.

'There's my boy, Francis!' William shouted, as he got out of the car and walked towards the veranda where his dog had been sleeping. 'Has Adeline been taking good care of you?' Stroking the dog's head, he glanced over his shoulder and dropped his voice. 'And I think you've already met my friend, Tyler Rafferty.'

At the side of the house, a Triumph Speed Twin motorbike languished against its footrest. The amaranth red paintwork was dented, and its once-gleaming chrome lines were scuffed to a tarnished opacity.

'Beautiful, isn't she?' William asked, pointing at the bike. 'I don't get to take her out much these days, though.'

'It looks like it's seen the world,' Tyler said as William smiled back, extracted a key from behind a pile of logs and unlocked the front door.

The house remained exactly how it had been left, a stifling stale scent welcoming the owner back home. Tyler sat at the writing desk in the living room, moving the pile of lurid drawings to one side and taking out his notebook from his bag. *I must read between the lines of what William is telling me*, he wrote. *He likes the idea of being dead while you are alive. Did he want to kill William Kendrick's life and memories so he could feel Joe Hawkins alive inside his mind?*

'I wanted to spend one last night in my home, Tyler,' William said, sinking into the comfort of his tattered armchair. 'Then first thing in the morning, I promise you can take me back to Doctor Marshall, and you'll be free of me for good.' He drew his thumb across his bottom lip and his eyes sparked across the room. 'There's some beer in the fridge, man.'

Once Tyler was in the kitchen, William lurched out of the armchair and prowled across the room towards the writing desk. He tore into Tyler's notebook, rifling his calloused fingers through the pages of scribbled notes. *William is suffering from a severe delusional psychosis ... false perception of Joe's memories ... altered sense of reality ... paranoia ... depression ... I must question William from an objective position of curiosity ... play along with his story to keep him talking ... speak to him as Joe to gain his trust ... find evidence that he cannot be Joe ...* <u>*DO NOT TRUST HIM – WILLIAM KENDRICK IS A MASTER MANIPULATOR.*</u>

William flicked to the back of the notebook, where Tyler had tucked *The Positive and Negative Syndrome Scale* between the pages. A mischievous grin rose across his mouth, as he ran a trembling finger down the list of schizophrenic behaviours, with scrawled ratings and notes that Tyler had written beside each one.

'Very good, Professor Rafferty,' William said under a soft giggle, folding the paper, and slipping it into his coat pocket. 'But you have got me all wrong.'

The slam of the refrigerator door was William's cue to place the notebook back on the desk and retreat across the living room. He settled himself into the armchair, mumbling his thanks to Tyler who handed him a bottle of ice-cold Mexican beer.

'Did writing poetry and creative work give you some stability back in your life, do you think?' Tyler asked, sitting down and trying to get comfortable on the wooden chair.

William took a long drink of beer and wiped his mouth with his hand. 'I had more free time as the band still weren't able to play as many shows after what happened in Texas. Writing became my safe place, an escape from the threat of the court case. My poetry collection *Essays On Existence* was published, and I was thrilled that my work would get a national audience. When the box of books arrived from the publishers, I, uh, allowed myself to cry.'

'Why?'

'Because it was the only thing in my life that someone hadn't tried to screw me over for or take away from me. I had a long fight with the publishers who were insistent my infamous younger face was on the cover. I told them I'd refuse publication if they didn't use my real image, Joe Hawkins with a rounded, bearded face. That poetry collection was the first, and only, time I presented my true self to the world.' William's voice faltered. 'Y'know, I think the fans appreciated what I'd written, but there were no ripples of recognition across the artistic world that a great piece of poetic work had been published. I was kidding myself that a rock star would ever be taken seriously by the literary establishment as a poet … but perhaps after my death that would change. I was drinking harder than ever before, a death-wish alcoholism to numb the pain of rejection.'

A deepening gloom consumed the house.

Tyler reached towards a lamp on top of an overflowing bookshelf, illuminating the room with a muted light. 'What about the court case in Texas, how were you going to deal with that, knowing Joe could end up in jail, that he'd be taken away?'

William released a guttural chuckle. 'Oh boy, I was in serious trouble and not even good ol' Walt Wilson could get me out of that fix.' He took another drink, before resting his beer bottle on the threadbare Moroccan rug. 'The trial had been fast-tracked to take place in September '69. I guess they wanted to deal with me as quickly as possible to avoid any further unrest. Once the trial started, I knew the judge had to find Joe Hawkins guilty, hold me up as an example to the disaffected youth of America: this is what happens, kids, when you dare to break the rules. There were ten witnesses, all of whom were cops or the relatives of cops. One sixteen-year-old girl lied under oath and said I'd dropped my pants and flagrantly masturbated on stage. Well now, she was the niece of the Houston police chief! It was a joke, man. I stood in the courtroom and told the truth; I was exercising my First Amendment right to freedom of speech and artistic expression without the fear of prosecution, nothing more than that. I had committed no crime.'

Subdued lamplight drew around the room, lingering over the writing desk and settling on the threads of a dreamcatcher nailed to the wall. 'What about your emotional state at the time?' Tyler asked, looking up from his notes. 'How were you feeling?'

'I guess I was giving the impression that I wasn't focusing on the outcome of the case, but young Joey was in the forefront of my mind, and he was terrified. I was a condemned man walking.' William reached to grab his beer bottle and drained the last of it down his throat. 'By the end of the trial Clark, Frank and Dean came to defend me, and I was grateful to them for that. Of course, it didn't take the judge long to find me guilty of criminal incitement to riot, guilty of battery against police officers, guilty of lewd behaviour … guilty of being Joe Hawkins. I knew he was going to crucify me. When I walked out of the courtroom, with camera bulbs flashing in my face, I realised that Joe wasn't invincible, he was a mere mortal after all: stupid, immature and fucked-up.'

Tyler watched as William stood and walked over to the window, pressing his hands against the cold pane of glass. The world outside was now drenched in moonlight and stars, their ancient luminosity glimmering through the canopy of trees surrounding the house.

'We put in an immediate appeal, and I was let out on a seventy thousand dollar bond before sentencing. I decided to drive back to California on one last great road trip with Joel Arden, who had come over for the trial. We stopped off at San Antonio, Tucson and San Diego, and I guess I was curious to see those old places of my youth. Part of me felt like I was finally exorcising the demons in my past.' William kept his back to Tyler, tracing his fingertips around his distorted reflection in the dirty glass. 'When I returned to LA, and while I still had my freedom, we started work on *Shadows And Silence*, which would be the band's fourth and final studio album.'

'Do you think the old, familiar structure of Joe's life gave you some sense of comfort?'

'Y'know, it was the same recording routine again and maybe it did give me some comfort. I think it was my favourite of all our albums because I was happier with the raw blues sound. That album felt like it was the end of the bullshit, this was us and we were pleasing ourselves and not pandering to the pressure of record sales or commercial radio playlists anymore. We had already agreed with our record label that our fifth album would be a live recording from one of our LA shows, so this was the end. Once the studio album was done, I could finally walk away from it all.'

'I think *Shadows And Silence* was my favourite Gracious Dawn album,' Tyler said. 'My grandpa bought me the LP for my sixteenth birthday.'

'Yeah?' William slid his fingers down the glass. 'We were playing as we did when we first met, lettin' it roll and trying to prove to everyone that The Gracious Dawn still had it.' He paused, closing his eyes. 'But that album was Joe Hawkins' suicide note, a requiem and self-penned obituary to his lost life as a rock star.'

Tyler stopped writing. 'His suicide note?'

'Oh, all the clues are there, man.' William turned his head, looking at Tyler over his shoulder. 'You have to listen to my words very carefully. Songs like, "Give Me Peace", "Return To The End" and "Times Are Changing", I was telling the world I'd had enough, that I needed a clean slate. I was telling the world that my life needed to change and there was no way back for Joe. You listen to that album again and you'll hear what I mean.'

Tyler's focus remained on William who began to walk around the room. 'In October '69 I turned twenty-seven years old, it would be the last birthday Joe Hawkins would see. I knew in my heart that Joe's time was up. That Christmas, the band played a weekend of concerts in San Francisco and, by the time we hit the stage on the second night, I was exhausted. I only managed a couple of songs before I could feel my spirit drain from my body and I collapsed. As I staggered back up, my frustration exploded and I kicked over Frank's guitar amplifier, then hurled my microphone stand off the stage into the audience. I don't remember much else about that show, other than the anger and embarrassment about what my life had become.' William blinked his eyes away from Tyler and drew his fingertips hard across his forehead. 'The Gracious Dawn were over, man. Joe Hawkins would never appear on stage again.'

'What about the legal appeal?' Tyler asked. 'Surely that must have given you some hope.'

William sat down and pulled off his boots, releasing an acerbic stench that permeated the living room. 'In January 1970, Walt Wilson telephoned and said he'd heard my sentence was likely to be fifteen months' hard labour at the Texas State Penitentiary, to make a real good example out of me. Then he warned me I could be attacked or even killed in jail. Boy, what a way to welcome in the new decade.' William shook his head and his voice faltered. 'I … I couldn't live behind bars; I couldn't survive as a caged butterfly. I knew I had to escape America before I could be sent to jail, then Walt told me that France had little power to extradite a US citizen for the *offences* of which I had been found guilty.'

'Joe had jeopardised his own freedom by his own actions, William,' Tyler said, resting his pen down and rubbing his strained eyes.

'I know that now. I was beginning to see that Joe Hawkins wasn't indestructible.' William picked at an unravelling thread on the armrest of his chair. 'Y'see, before the trial started, I had an accident on Sunset Boulevard. I had been at the Whisky A Go Go drinking it dry, and when I was eventually kicked out, I staggered into the street. I was playing my favourite game of cat and mouse with speeding cars, dodging in and out of the traffic. That night though I got clipped, but this time I didn't bounce back like I'd always done. I cracked some ribs and hurt my leg – the cat had extinguished its last life. It was a sign that the next fall would be my last. Y'know, a man could walk on the moon, yet I couldn't seem to cope with walking through my daily life on Earth.' William drew his eyes down to his trembling hands resting in his lap. 'Yeah, man, that proved to me what I needed to do.'

Tyler watched William's head sink lower, sensing his defences were starting to weaken. He softened his voice as he closed in on his patient's truth at last. 'What did you need to do, Mr Kendrick?'

'I, uh, looked at the ruins of my life and I made a decision. If Joe Hawkins, the great rock star, wanted to be free from turmoil then he was going to have to die.' He lifted himself out of the armchair and pointed towards the couch where Tyler would no doubt spend a restless night. 'Sleep well, kid. Tomorrow's going to be a long day.'

Tyler lay down, pulled a moth-holed blanket over his body and opened Joe Hawkins' journal. Once again, he had been tantalised through a crack in the door, only to have it slammed in his face. The stringent headache that now seared from temple to temple seemed to warn him that returning William to the hospital in the morning would not go smoothly.

CHAPTER THIRTY-SEVEN

The Journal of Joseph Hawkins – January 13th, 1970
(Santa Monica, Los Angeles)

'You appear to be a talented individual, Mr Hawkins, admired and adored by the young people of this nation. But you have taken advantage of the position you hold, bringing out the worst, and not the best, in those young people who looked up to you. You have achieved a privileged platform which afforded you the ear of the nation, and you have chosen to abuse that privilege. Your forthcoming sentence must reflect the severity of your crimes.'

– Judge Nicholas Bernstein

These words have haunted my mind for months. It is a sad truth, but there appear to be consequences to my actions after all. Like always in my life, I have discovered the truth too late.

I have turned into a lone ghost, resorting to going through my telephone book, trying to find any one of my old girlfriends willing to have sex with me. Joe Hawkins has become the washed-up-sympathy-fuck of Sunset Strip. Everyone wants to worship at your feet when you are the toast of the town, but when you fall from grace you fall alone.

I am a social pariah.

Last month an earthquake shook Los Angeles to its core. It reverberated into the recesses of my soul, as if this great city has given me its final warning. There is no other choice left for me now, I will not allow the courts to imprison me for crimes which I feel I did not commit.

I will never surrender my freedom.

My decision is made. I am going to Paris.

Today I woke feeling like I have lifted a weight from my shoulders. I am happy that I honoured my recording contract, I kept my side of the deal. I suppose I seem happier. I have cleaned up my act and I am relieved that my old life – Joe's old life – is ending at last.

I intend to spend the next week saying goodbye to my beloved Los Angeles. There will be unrestrained abandon. I will race my car through these suffocating hills, close my eyes and roll the dice one last time. I will bid adieu to every topless bar and strip joint in this town, pay my last respects to those dear young ladies.

Angela and I drove to Santa Barbara to say goodbye to her parents, who will take care of her dog while we are away. On the journey home, as each mile passed, I reflected on my short, young life and lamented what I had lost. I have drunk away my best years.

During the last weeks of recording *Shadows And Silence*, I think the rest of the band believe that I have turned a corner. I suppose I seem engaged in the recording process. I appear to be quieter, happier and optimistic, but you must always keep up appearances … in this, at least, my mother taught me well.

What no one knows is that this will be my last act as a rock star.

Yesterday, I went to The Gracious Dawn's office and cleared out my desk. Our junior assistant, Dylan Elliot, sat on the floor sorting through piles of fan mail from all over the world. When I sat down beside him, he showed me a scrapbook that he has been keeping for the last four years. The rise and fall of Joe Hawkins laid out in black and white in front of me. I told Dylan the rumours were true; I was leaving for Paris. The kid had this look on his face, like he really did not want me to go. I saw that a teenage boy had sacrificed his formative years to work for the band, looking up to me, a false prophet, to guide him. All I could do was tell Dylan that I would see him again soon. But I knew, as I spoke those words, it was a lie.

When dawn's light fades, all that remains are shadows and silence.

It is time to bring the curtain down.

CHAPTER THIRTY-EIGHT

A crash from a garbage truck woke Tyler with a jolt from his troubled dreams. Tugging his fingers through his tangled hair, he got up from the couch and wandered into the bathroom, feeling his muscles and joints clicking back into place with each stiff step. The rhythmic dripping of tepid water from his chin pooled into the sink. *Today is going to be a very long day*, he thought.

There was not a sound emanating from William Kendrick's bedroom.

Walking into the kitchen, Tyler hoped to find something to satisfy his rumbling stomach, other than the beer stacked in the refrigerator. All he found was a scrap of paper propped up against an empty wine bottle on the kitchen table.

> *Tyler,*
> *I cannot go back to the hospital yet. I must tell you the rest of my story and we do not have much time left. I need to tell you about the events that led to the death of Joe Hawkins and the birth of William Kendrick.*
> *Meet me at the airport ...*
> *Joe*

'William!' Tyler shouted into the silence that sank through the empty house. He flung open the bedroom door and, when his eyes adjusted to the gloom, he saw an electric blanket lay pulled back across an unmade bed. Tyler ran into the living room and grabbed his notebook from the writing desk, stuffing it into his bag. He was still rummaging for his car keys in his jacket pockets when he came to a stumbling halt on the driveway.

His keys – and his car – were gone.

'Shit,' Tyler said, punching his fists against the front door. He darted into the kitchen and thumbed through an outdated telephone directory, trying to find the number of a cab company in Boulder Creek. All he could do was sit and wait on the veranda, with William's dog asleep at his feet, listening to the hammering of his heart in his ears, muffled by the rustling of insects in the trees.

The mid-day sun journeyed through a cloudless spring sky, while Tyler sat hunched on the back seat of a taxi. If he could find William before he reached the airport security area, then he would have to find a way to persuade him to return to the hospital. *I must stop him*, he thought. *What game is he playing with me now?*

The taxi veered into a parking bay at the entrance of San Francisco International Airport.

Tyler slung his bag over his shoulder and ran into the glass-encased building. A sign pointed to the check-in desks for domestic flights, but it was the sign at the opposite end of the terminal that pricked his attention: *International Departures*. Breaking into a run, he dodged suitcases and crowds gawking up at flight information boards. His leg muscles tightened as he came to a skidding stop. Standing motionless at the centre of the terminal was William Kendrick. His head was dipped towards his left shoulder, arms hanging rigid at his sides and an old canvas bag resting by his feet.

William's stare struck through Tyler like a shard of light piercing through the glass terminal building. 'Good to see you, kid,' he said as Tyler strode forward.

'What the hell were you thinking!' Tyler shouted, hurling his bag onto the floor. 'Do you have any idea how much trouble I'm already in without you disappearing? And if there's one scratch on my car–'

William slanted his head towards the other shoulder. 'Y'know, I'm so glad you decided to join me.'

'Are you kidding me, what was I supposed to do? You vanished leaving that note, stealing my car, of course I had to come and find you. This stupid game you're playing has gone on for long enough. I'm taking you back to the hospital right now.'

'I've told you before, I'm not going back to the hospital until I've finished telling you my story.' His face hardened into a deep-set grimace. 'You don't get it do you? The world has waited all these years to hear Joe Hawkins' truth, and now you want to stop me. You want me to die with my soul in turmoil. I can't let you do that to me, man. I've waited too long.'

'My life is falling apart. Why can't you see that?' Tyler took a step back. 'And what the hell are you even doing at the airport?'

'Well now, that's the fun part.' William bent down and picked up his bag. 'We're going to Paris.' He winked at Tyler, before walking away across the terminal towards the security checks.

'William!' Tyler pushed through the passengers joining the end of a snaking line. 'You can't go to Paris. I have to take you back to Doctor Marshall.'

'*We*, Tyler,' he said over his shoulder.

'What do you mean, *we*?'

'I mean that we're going to Paris, you and me.' William took out a passport from the back pocket of his jeans, handing it to Tyler.

'My passport … what the hell … you stole it when we stayed over at my apartment, didn't you? I knew I saw you put something into your pocket that morning.' He snatched the passport from his patient's outstretched hand. 'No, I've had enough. We're going to get the car and I'm taking you to Doctor Marshall.'

'Now where would the fun be in that?' William reached into his bag and extracted two paper tickets, handing one of them to Tyler. 'I'm getting on the one o'clock flight and you're coming with me.'

'Why don't you understand? I'm trying to help you. Why can't you see that?' Crimson waves swept up Tyler's neck and onto his face. 'Please, I have to take you back to the hospital.'

'The only way for this ride to end is for you to come with me.' William let the other passengers shuffle past him towards the security check. 'Don't you want to know how I did it?' His stale breath struck Tyler's face. 'Aren't you curious?'

'Did what, William?' Tyler slammed his hands onto his head, crumpling the paper ticket between his fingers.

'Don't you want to know how Joe Hawkins faked his death, how he fooled the world?'

'Can't you tell me, without going all the way to France?'

'No, I need to show you. I need to go back there and lay some ghosts to rest. I want to see where they buried Joe all those years ago.' He leaned in closer and lowered his voice. 'You only have one choice left to make: either I get on the airplane alone and you never see me again, or you come with me and we play this adventure through to the end.' His eyes narrowed towards two police officers who were striding through the airport towards the boarding gates. 'C'mon, kid, we need to go.'

Tyler inhaled a sharp breath as he turned and saw the police officers scanning the faces of travellers packing into the terminal building. He followed William through the departure lounge towards the boarding gate. A flight attendant at the fuselage door offered them both a complimentary smile and directed them towards the smoking section at the back of the jet.

Taking his seat, Tyler tightened the safety belt across his lap, hoping the churning in his stomach would ease. Reaching into his bag, he pulled out his notebook and turned to the back where he expected to find *The Positive and Negative Syndrome Scale*, his only guide through the blinding maze of William's perceived memories.

There was nothing but blank pages in the back of his notebook.

William turned to the now pallid-faced young man sitting beside him and drew his mouth into a sheepish grin. As the plane tore down the runway, Tyler put on his headphones, closed his eyes and let the propulsion thrust his body into the back of the seat.

He was now entirely alone.

CHAPTER THIRTY-NINE

The Journal of Joseph Hawkins – February 18th, 1970 (Rue Saint-Paul, Paris)

My name is Joseph Hawkins, poet.

I am a fugitive living in Paris: unstructured, free and loose … there are no rules. For now, I am safe from incarceration, and I can begin to enjoy being Joseph for the first time in my life.

It is strange being here in France, my mind feels so remote from Joe Hawkins' claustrophobic world that I have left behind. I had not anticipated how hard the adjustment would be – not to have the daily kick of being a performer, doing the shows, having the adoration from the fans. I never understood that fame was yet another one of my addictions. I was so desperate to escape from it, now I wake feeling withdrawal symptoms. It makes no sense, but I need to relish the change in my life, being so far away from the toxic existence I once knew.

I have spent blissful afternoons at my good friend Josephine Laurent's apartment on the banks of the Seine, drinking beer on her balcony and enjoying the peace and time to think without distractions. She leaves me be and I love her for that. I first met Josephine at UCLA, when she came over from the Sorbonne as a guest lecturer on the nineteenth century French literary movement, an expert on the genius minds of Proust, Baudelaire and Flaubert. There was an instant connection, a meeting of minds, and she has remained a loyal and true friend. She is one of the few people in my life who appreciates who I really am, not Wild Joe the rock star, simply Joseph, the poet.

Exploring Paris takes up most of my days, sometimes in the company of René Moreau, who Josephine has introduced me to. He is a freelance journalist for the national newspapers, and I enjoy hearing his opinions on the recent wave of student protests. We have spent many relaxed lunches in street-side bistros, debating the state of French and American politics over plentiful bottles of wine.

Walking along the slender roads that weave through the Marais to the Seine, I stop to listen to every street musician who I pass. I am enjoying simple pleasures, having time to spend browsing in the bookstores on the Left Bank, or sitting outside a café, drinking beer and watching life go by.

There is a battle of confusion raging in my mind. I am on the other side of the world, but I do not know what I am supposed to be doing. For years, other people tried to structure and organise my life whether I wanted them to or not. When I lived in America, I was constantly surrounded by people, now I am only surrounded by the lonely world of Joe.

I have always written what I saw in my dreams. Now, when I try to sleep, there is only darkness behind my eyes. Most days I spend hours staring at my reflection in our bedroom mirror, trying to see myself there ... somewhere ... but I see nothing at all. Writing has always been an easy escape for me and now I must force it to come. I am trying to work on another movie script idea, but my words are left flailing around in my mind as vague thoughts because I cannot hold onto them. There are no connections.

Boredom is fuelling my drinking. Angela spends all day with her new friends, and I have nothing to fight against anymore. I feel alone, unable to even speak the language, trapped in the solitary torment of my own imagination.

I never thought freedom would feel like this ... it is a tainted liberty.

CHAPTER FORTY

A hotel on the Rue de la Bastille resided in ageing Parisian comfort. The cramped third-floor room was now empty, the sheets on two single beds lay dishevelled and the remnants of a bottle of cheap red wine dripped onto a threadbare burgundy carpet.

Tyler Rafferty and William Kendrick sat at a table on a café terrace, both nursing strong black coffees.

'Y'know, I'll never get bored of seeing this,' William said, waving his hand across at the traffic circling the vast Bastille intersection. 'I guess back then I liked the idea that the hardest, most fortified structures can be broken down and razed clean off the map. It made me wonder if it could be that easy to destroy Joe Hawkins, raze him off the face of the Earth too.'

'That's great, William,' Tyler said, making no effort to temper his hardening tone. Taking a sip of his bitter French-roast coffee, he tried to placate both his infuriation and the jetlag that riddled his exhausted body.

'Feels good doesn't it, man?' William asked, widening his eyes across the table. 'Going with the flow, seeing what life throws at you and runnin' with it.'

Tyler slammed down his coffee cup. 'What the hell are we doing here, William? Because I get the feeling we haven't been going with the flow at all. I think you knew exactly what you were doing and have planned this stupid stunt from the start. Am I right?'

'Does it scare you that I'm the one with the plan and you're the one in the dark?'

'I'm not scared, if that's what you think.'

William took a small bite of croissant, chewing it with a slow ease. 'I think you've been scared for your entire life, but you just can't see it.'

'Can we not talk about me right now?' Tyler slumped in the chair and folded his arms. 'All I want to know is why you've dragged me halfway around the world and managed to get me into more trouble than I ever thought possible. Shit, my dad is going to kill me. Professor Kessler has probably already kicked me out—'

'Relax, take it easy.' A mischievous grin undulated around the rim of William's coffee cup as he pressed it to his mouth. 'You could always telephone Doctor Marshall.'

'Oh, I would telephone him, but for some strange reason his number wasn't in my jacket pocket when I looked for it this morning.'

William's grin mutated into a crackling laugh. 'Oh, you knew it wouldn't be straightforward when you decided to meet me. This is important, Tyler, we had to come here. I need to show you the place where Joe came to die all those years ago.' His voice trailed off into the depths of his coffee cup. 'I need to put Paris and all of its ghosts to rest.' Reaching into his coat pocket he placed a handful of coins on a metal dish, leaving the garçon a generous tip.

Tyler stood and waited for William to haul himself out of his seat through a loud groan. 'When you fled LA in 1970 to avoid going to jail, wouldn't people have noticed that all your possessions were gone?'

'Well uh, I didn't have many possessions. There were a couple of essential items I took, things that meant something to me.'

'Like what?'

'I pretty much had the clothes I stood up in, my favourite suede jacket and leather boots. I packed some photographs of me and Angela, my Super 8 camera and of course my poetry and notebooks. I had my copy of *On the Road* by Jack Kerouac, a book about Hieronymus Bosch, Plutarch's *Life of Alexander the Great* and a collection of poems and letters by Arthur Rimbaud.' He glanced over his shoulder. 'Like I said, essential things only.'

Tyler walked beside William around the wide curve of the Bastille intersection. Delivery trucks were double-parked, unloading their supplies of vegetables and cheeses into the food stores along the Rue Saint-Antoine. Narrow side streets concealed an array of boutique art galleries and quiet cafés, only frequented by the local residents of the area. William gave Tyler's jacket sleeve a tug to draw him away from the bustle of the Rue Saint-Antoine and onto the calm of the Rue Saint-Paul. The slender road lay dappled in a delicate shade that crept over the walls of an apartment building, dulling its Beaux Arts façade.

'This is where it all happened,' William said. He snatched a pained breath and staggered against a wall, grey dust flecking the back of his coat. 'Angela had been getting ensconced with the Paris in-crowd, going to classical concerts and the ballet, making a new circle of fashionable friends. She thought I was too drunk to notice when she would stay out all night at the most expensive hotels so she could be with ...'

'With who?'

'Later, uh, we'll talk about *him* ... later.' William straightened himself up and pointed across the street at the apartment block. 'This is where Angela and I stayed in the spring of 1970 and where Joe Hawkins died.' His breath cut out and his body began to shake. 'This will be harder than I ever imagined.'

'It's alright, we don't have to stay.'

'No, kid.' William stepped out across the street. 'I have to go inside there one last time.'

A young woman, wrapped in a chic Chanel coat, was approaching the apartment block, delving her hand into her pocket to retrieve her keys. Tyler felt a violent shove in his back from William, forcing him towards the building. While she unlocked the dark green front door, Tyler raised a timid smile, hoping it would be enough to convince her that he lived there too. She returned him a polite nod and held open the door, leaving him standing by the entrance while she disappeared up a staircase. Releasing a tight breath, Tyler stuck his head out onto the street and motioned to William that it was safe for him to come inside.

William stepped into the entrance, his eyes focusing on an exterior courtyard beyond two glass-panelled doors. He moved with uneasy steps through pools of amber light gleaming from the polished brass lamps. At the end of the stone-paved hall, his hand quivered as he twisted a bronze door handle.

'Yeah man, this was it,' he said, walking into the courtyard beside Tyler and pointing up at the third-floor apartment. 'I liked how the daylight danced across the pages of my notebook as I sat up there, and when the sun moved around in the afternoon, I dragged my writing desk to the next window.' He turned around and looked up at the windows on the opposite wall, running his thumb over his bottom lip. 'There was a classical pianist living here, and all day her stream of music floated into our apartment. It must have annoyed the other residents, but it provided me with a soothing soundtrack as I tried to write.'

William took tentative steps back through the doors and into the entrance hall. Stroking the staircase wall with his calloused fingers, he lifted his left foot and rested it on the bottom stair. 'I went up and down here every day ...' His voice trailed away as he turned his bloodshot eyes to Tyler.

'What's wrong?'

'I can't do it. I can't go back up there,' William said, gripping his hand to his chest. 'I suppose I thought that if I went up there now, Angela would be waiting to welcome me home. But she's not up there, is she?' Stumbling back, he pushed past Tyler and retreated towards the front door. 'This place is full of ghosts.'

Tyler watched William walk away with his head down and his hands buried in the depths of his coat pockets. He knew well enough by now when to give his patient some space, but he also knew better than to let William Kendrick out of his sight.

An abundance of fresh fruit was stacked on a stall on the Rue Saint-Antoine. William bought a paper bag of Spanish strawberries, offering one to Tyler as they crossed the road. The crumbling buildings and constricting streets of the Marais district drew the two men under an imposing redbrick archway at the entrance to the Place des Vosges. Tyler slipped on his sunglasses, as the afternoon sun warmed the Baroque porticos of palatial houses that encased the grand garden square.

'This became a sanctuary to me,' William said, between small bites of a succulent strawberry. His boots crunched over the immaculate gravel pathways, before he sank onto a wooden bench nestling under a row of linden trees. 'I sat here every day, making notes and thinking.'

Tyler sat beside him, trying to ignore the creeping sense of isolation that had disturbed his thoughts since they arrived in Paris. William had lured him to the other side of the world to a place where he felt no connections and where there was no one to help him. *He wants me to feel isolated,* Tyler thought, *a fugitive like Joe Hawkins when he came to Paris in 1970. William thinks he can control me by isolating me. I must not let my guard down.* 'Did you still feel trapped by Joe's life, even when you were on the other side of the world?' he asked.

William ate another strawberry, pausing to catch his breath. 'I still felt trapped inside Joe's life even here. It took me a long time to shake off LA and adjust to being a simple writer living in Paris. I knew, like all the greatest writers before me, that Paris was now my safe haven, a place of solace where the American authorities had little power to send me back to a jail cell. I began to feel like I was in recovery, that Paris was going to heal me. I even began to think about my family, more than I ever had. I asked Angela to telephone my brother and sister to let them know I was doing alright.'

'How come your feelings towards your family had changed?'

'Being here in Paris, y'know, it gave me a sense of perspective that for my entire adult life my past had been responsible for the destruction of my present. I knew if I didn't deal with my past now, it would jeopardise my future and I couldn't let that happen.' William tipped back his head and took an elongated breath. 'I cleaned up my act, cut down on the booze and lost some weight. Angela and I even talked about maybe having children, starting to imagine a future together, like normal people.'

'That was good, William,' Tyler said, leaning back on the bench. 'That was a positive step to make.'

'It didn't last of course, that was a fantasy which could never be a reality with the constant threat of Joe's old life hanging over us. I was soon back on the booze, smoking every second of the day and I was starting to get real sick. I had acquired a vicious cough, so Angela insisted I go to a doctor who Josephine recommended. The doctor told me to stop smoking and suggested I should spend a couple of weeks away from the city, perhaps in Italy or Spain.'

'I thought you'd have to stay in France, considering your trouble with the law back home?'

'Well, if it appeared that we were a young couple on vacation, then we thought it would be alright, that we would go unnoticed. So, we rented a car and drove through France to Italy. Oh man, those were good days ... the last good days Angela and I would spend together. By then our relationship felt like she was a fragile child for whom I was somehow responsible. We drove all around the Italian Lakes, finding cottages to rent and living simple quiet days. I spent blissful hours exploring local villages, then climbing the wild hills, looking out across the water to the promised land that lay beyond my reach.'

Tyler yawned, trying to battle the jetlag dragging through his body. He raised his head to the spring sunlight that marbled through the trees, enveloping the garden square under their secretive canopy. William's body jerked forward on the bench beside him, a tirade of fierce coughing forcing him to double over.

'Are you OK?'

William turned away, attempting to conceal droplets of congealed blood that he had caught in his hands. 'Everything's fine.' Cleaning the blood with a tissue, he heaved himself up off the bench, groaning in pain.

'Did you contact anyone back in LA?' Tyler asked, as they left the garden and walked under a shaded brick cloister enclosing the square.

'I rang Walt Wilson to ask how my legal appeal was progressing and it was not good news. My sentence was due to begin at the end of March, so the courts had not yet noticed that I'd fled the country. I spoke to Clark and asked how the *Shadows*

And Silence album was doing, and I was thrilled it had received critical acclaim.' William lifted a smile which soon sank. 'I hinted to him that perhaps I'd come back to America someday to clear my name and we'd record music again. But I never wanted to stay on the telephone too long, I was always aware the FBI had connections overseas and I didn't want to let my guard down.'

'Do you think the issues with your identity were made better or worse by being here in Paris?'

William glanced across at Tyler walking beside him. 'Issues with my identity ... yeah, kid, you could say I had fuckin' issues with my identity back then. Being here, on the other side of the planet, JoJo could always manage to come out and cause hell. There was a constant war by then between Joe and Joseph. Joseph felt like a fugitive, his only means of escape was to sit and write in his notebooks all day, trying to find some purpose in his life. Whereas Joe couldn't cope with feeling trapped here with nothing to fight against, no platform or audience for his words and ideas, unable to return to America. His only escape was to become JoJo and prop up a bar, drinking until he was paralytic.' William appeared to withdraw into his thoughts before he spoke again. 'But those spring days in Paris began to show me that there could be another way for Joseph Hawkins to live his life in peace, without the fears and pressures of Joe's old life.'

Tyler lowered his voice. 'Faking your death?'

'Exactly,' William said, stopping under the triumphal red-brick archway that connected the peaceful garden haven to the thunderous streets of central Paris. 'While Joe Hawkins' life very publicly crashed off a cliff into a thousand burning pieces, maybe no one would notice another man jumping out of the speeding car before the fall and quietly walking away to start a new life of freedom in a distant corner of the world.'

A faint hint of colour on William's face vanished in an instant. Grasping his stomach, he released an anguished cry of pain as his legs buckled and he collapsed to the ground. Motionless, he lay with his eyes closed, his chest barely rising. Tyler fell to his knees, taking off his jacket and laying it underneath William's head.

'Mr Kendrick,' he said, shaking his shoulder until he finally saw a flicker of one eye opening.

After a moment, William began to come around. He grabbed hold of Tyler's arm, his eyes now wide. 'Please don't let me die yet, please … I need to tell you everything, I need to tell you …'

'We have time. I promise we have time.'

William moaned and straightened himself up, craning his head toward Tyler's blanching face. 'Now, my friend, we're getting to the good part. I need to tell you about the events which led to the death of Joe Hawkins.'

CHAPTER FORTY-ONE

The Journal of Joseph Hawkins – March 29th, 1970
(Place des Vosges, Paris)

A tender spring breeze is sighing through the trees above me, as I while away a few hours on my favourite bench in this grand old square.

I have been trying to write some ideas for a novel, but I am scribbling disconnected words in my notebook which have no meaning. I cannot think. I cannot breathe. There is numbness inside my mind, an opaque fog prevents me from drawing on my creative past or imagining any possible future for Joe Hawkins.

The walls are closing in.

One evening last week, I went out for dinner with Josephine to talk about an idea for a lecture series she was thinking of making. When I came back to the apartment, I found what I thought was a bag of cocaine on the kitchen table. I snorted a line, feeling it hit the red wine in my bloodstream and blowing my brains away. I realised too late that it was heroin. As I passed in and out of lucidness, Angela helped me into a hot bath to recover. While I came around, it gave me time to think. I thought about what my life, what Joe's life, had become. You see, everyone falls under Joe's destructive spell in the end, all of them, Angela included.

I heard her bare feet creeping across the parquet floor in the hallway and into the bathroom, so I decided to freak her out. I held my breath under the water, my eyes wide and pitched to the heavens. She said, 'Come on, cut it out, Joe, you're scaring me.' She reached into the water, grabbed my shoulders and shook me as hard as she could, but I did not move. Thinking I was dead, she made a noise like an animal whose throat had been cut. She kept screaming my name as she collapsed, her body seeming to shatter into a thousand pieces as she hit the bathroom floor.

I held a long … painful … silence … then, as the tension was about to snap, I erupted out of the water and laughed in Angela's face. 'What were you trying to do scaring me like that?' she screamed at me. 'I thought you were dead.'

I stopped laughing as I looked down at her shivering body and said, 'Honey, Joe Hawkins is already dead.'

I have always maintained the future is uncertain.

The past, like the future, is a place taunting you with its dreams and hopes, but you can never go there. You will never reach tomorrow; it will always be beyond your grasp. All these years, I thought the future would take care of itself, but now I cannot take that risk. I must protect my future. Joe has been holding Joseph Hawkins' precious life in his volatile hands for too long.

I must save Joseph from Joe and be the hunter of my own destiny.

My body is finally punishing me for my reckless behaviour. The drugs I have been prescribed for my cough have left me feeling dead inside. I am drowning, unable to breathe. For so many years I was not living, I was not even existing. I was teetering on the brink of an existential nightmare; I was always trying so hard to 'become' when my soul simply wanted to 'be'. I must be prepared to let go of all of it, detach myself from Joe Hawkins and revert to a more primitive way of being and thinking, cut the chains and discard everything of my old life.

Only then will I find the true freedom my soul has been yearning for.

CHAPTER FORTY-TWO

Tyler waved down a taxi on the Rue Saint-Antoine and helped William onto the back seat. Their progress across the city slowed and jerked through the traffic sitting in solid defiance along the Rue de Rivoli. The taxi driver cursed and swung the car into a side street, taking them onto the embankment road hugging the length of the Seine.

Clutching his bag on his lap, Tyler looked across at the man sitting beside him. 'Why couldn't Joe just stay out in France for a couple of years, until the legal appeal was sorted back home, and the authorities had backed off?'

'It was too much of a risk,' William said. 'The American authorities would never give me my freedom. I was convinced the CIA were keeping an eye on me too. I was a dangerous free spirit they wanted to destroy. All I knew when I left America was that I couldn't go back there any time soon. I didn't know what I was going to do or how I was going to do it, but I only had two options left: fight or run and I had become tired of the fight. Over that previous year, I had a couple of conversations, nothing serious, just passing comments with Jesse Winters.'

'What sort of passing comments?'

William drew his hand across the greasy taxi window, tracing his fingertips over the outline of slate rooftops huddled on the Rive Gauche. 'Y'know, what would happen to the band's record sales if Joe died. Jesse said our record sales would probably go through the roof.'

'Are you saying that Joe was going to fake his own death for the good of the band?'

'Hell yeah, good ol' Joe saves the day!' William released a guttural laugh. 'No, man, I knew my death would be the final nail in the coffin for The Gracious Dawn. My actions had already killed what we'd all worked so hard to achieve. I had no idea that when I died my fame and notoriety would elevate to an unimaginable new level. I figured the death of Joe would be the end of all of it, but the fame didn't die, did it? It was only the beginning. To be more famous in death than you are in life, Tyler … well, that's a hard truth for a man to live with.'

The taxi pulled up at the imposing gates of the Louvre Museum.

The majestic palace hemmed in hordes of tourists, willing them to experience a millennium of art and treasures protected behind its neoclassical walls. William paid the driver and kept his head low, shuffling away from the crowds towards the entrance of the Jardin des Tuileries, where the tip of the Eiffel Tower peeked above a line of immaculately clipped hedges. A delicate scent of early-blooming roses vied against car fumes and a carbolic odour radiating from the entrances to the ageing métro stations beneath the city's streets.

'Earlier,' Tyler said, 'you mentioned that Angela would stay at expensive hotels so she could be with … *him*. Who did you mean?'

William turned to face Tyler, lowering his voice. 'It was the man who would play an unwitting role in the charade of Joe Hawkins' death: Angela's young lover, Julien Gaston.' He dripped each syllable of the name from his lips with a seemingly deliberate precision.

Tyler extracted his notebook and pen from his bag and scribbled down Julien Gaston's name. 'Who was he?'

'He was a young playboy who'd set himself up as a celebrity drug dealer.' William's shoulders sank into a nonchalant shrug and continued his slow walk. 'If there was anything you wanted, Julien could supply it. He was obsessed with fame and the big celebrities of the time, like uh …'

'Joe Hawkins.'

'Right, right. Joe Hawkins, man.' William nodded. 'If there were celebrities around, then Julien would never be too far behind.'

'Angela was having an affair with him?'

'They were sleeping together on and off. I met Julien during the band's '68 tour of Europe, which was when he and Angela first got together after our Paris show. She adored the fact that her part-time lover could provide her with anything she wanted.'

Crimson skies above Paris warmed the white marble faces of classical statues posed on plinths along the broad gravel pathways. The pangs in Tyler's stomach burned at the aroma of seared steak radiating from the street-side cafés beside the Jardin des Tuileries. He hoped that his patient would eventually notice, or care, that they had not eaten properly since breakfast.

'I saw Julien one evening in a notorious club on the Left Bank called the Jazz Palais,' William said, 'surrounded by a harem of models. He waved me over to his table and said, "It is a pleasure to see you, Joe. I hoped you would visit this great city again and enjoy all of its *hospitality*." Later that night, I was in the toilets of the club, when Julien walked in and handed me a wrap of white powder. "A small gift, my appreciation of your creative work, Monsieur Hawkins."'

'He gave you cocaine?'

'Yeah, the purest quality coke. You'd get so high you thought you were going to die.'

Children screamed in delight while they raced wooden boats across the rippling surface of a fountain at the heart of the gardens. William eased his body onto the stone edging and dipped his hand into the cold water, raising his head only high enough to keep a watchful eye on the tourists and families strolling past.

'This Julien guy must have wanted something in return.' Tyler sat beside William on the edge of the fountain. 'You don't get anything for free.'

'Sure, he wanted Joe Hawkins' trade, even though the thought of scoring repelled me. I began to hear that Julien had certain, uhm, shadier connections which could prove useful to me. Back then Paris had been infiltrated with Chinese dealers who were flooding the market with cheap junk. One night, Julien introduced me to Eric Chang, an unpleasant businessman who could get you anything you wanted, no questions asked. If there was a tricky situation you needed to be fixed, he was the guy to help.' William rested his elbows on his thighs, smiling at the children who ran past clutching their toy boats. 'Y'know, it was only a matter of time before the American authorities discovered I'd fled the States and had no intention of returning. If I wanted to start a new life then I figured I needed a new passport, and a new identity, so I could move around as I pleased. I needed to be more careful if I wanted to remain undetected.'

'And this Chinese businessman was going to help you?'

'I saw Eric Chang again at the Jazz Palais, sitting alone in a private booth. Over a bottle of cognac, I asked him if he could arrange a new passport and birth certificate, with no questions asked. I also asked him, if I wanted to disappear for good, what he could do to help me. I, uh, never cared about money. I liked to live day to day, but after what happened in Texas, I knew I had to protect myself. I had to have the means to disappear and fund my new life when the time came. My accountant had made some investments for me, and I'd drawn hundreds of thousands of dollars against Gracious Dawn advances. Most of it paid for Angela's lavish lifestyle, but it was easy for me to syphon off fifty thousand dollars into a private account which no one, especially Angela Jackson, would ever find out about.'

'And you trusted this guy to help you?' Tyler asked, as he stood and threw his notebook into his bag. 'Wasn't that a risk?'

'Yeah, man, it was a risk, but what choice did I have at that point? It seemed Eric had a reputation that he could fix anything, but if you crossed him you'd pay for it. It was in both our interests for any illegal arrangement between us to remain private.' William struggled to stand, catching his balance on Tyler's arm and peering over his shoulder at the darkening gardens. 'I took out some money and set the wheels in motion. In early May 1970, a message was left at our apartment instructing me to come here. One of Eric's men arrived and handed me an envelope containing a birth certificate and a fake American passport, as easy as that. I opened the passport and there was Joe's photograph with a new name printed underneath: William Stanley Kendrick. That afternoon, I held a new life in my hands. I had given Joe Hawkins the means to die and William Kendrick the chance to live.'

Tyler and William wound around the side of the Louvre and crossed over the Pont du Carrousel, easing them over the smooth waters of the Seine to the Left Bank.

A warren of darkened streets soon obscured the soft silhouette of the river. Tyler's pulse beat a little faster, as he allowed William to lead him through a maze of disorientating alleyways, where sinister-looking figures loitered in the doorways of underground bars and private adult stores. Soon the cobbled backstreets unravelled onto the tree-lined breadth of the Boulevard Saint-Germain. In the distance, the welcoming green sign of the Café de Flore seemed to quicken William's stiff pace.

A waiter seated Tyler and William on the café terrace, where a collection of polished wooden tables sheltered under an elegant white canopy. Tyler devoured a charred steak, licking the seasoned butter that slithered down his fork onto his fingers. 'At some point you were going to have to tell Angela about the plan to fake your death.'

William cut a morsel of rare meat and slipped it into his mouth, washing it down with a glass of mellow red wine. 'Angela got back to the apartment late one night, and I was sitting at the kitchen table waiting to destroy her world. I told her I was left with no other choice; for me to live in peace and free from imprisonment then Joe would have to die. She looked at me not knowing if this was one of my games. "Angela, listen to me, honey, and listen good, it's very important," I said to her. "You love me, don't you? You'd do anything for me, wouldn't you?" She didn't reply. I then reminded her that it was her lover's heroin I had overdosed on.'

'So, you did want to emotionally control and manipulate Angela, the woman who you said was your one true love?' Tyler ate another mouthful of steak, keeping a wary eye on William who refilled both of their wine glasses.

'It was the only way to deal with her, Tyler, her soul was lost to drugs by then,' William said, his eyes flaring wide across the table. 'Man, I wish I'd kissed her and told her I loved her, but I was like a focused bird of prey. It was all about me and my search for freedom and I couldn't let anyone stand in my way, not even Angela Jackson, the woman I adored. Y'know, I thought that after a couple of years away on my own we'd be back together in some private corner of the world, without Joe and his problems in our lives, that it would be freedom for us both. All I needed was for her to trust me and to be there when we could be back together again.'

The early evening on the Left Bank had sprung to life as streetlights flickered on, and conversations flowed around the café tables. Tyler finished the last of his salted fries and pushed away his plate, not noticing William refill both of their wine glasses once more. Picking up his pen, he scribbled a note. *William must have followed Joe Hawkins to Paris in 1970, that is the only way he could know all these details. His obsession was out of his perception of control by this point. How far was he prepared to go to satisfy his obsession with Joe? What was he hoping to achieve by stalking him all the way to France? Did William want to harm Joe to satisfy a perverse control over him? I need to be careful. William Kendrick is a dangerous man.*

Tyler let a last mouthful of wine slide down his throat, enjoying the warming sensation of his tense muscles loosening their grip on his bones. His tired body acquiesced to the comfort of the leather chair, leaning back he watched the other diners leave their tables and disappear into the depths of the Paris night.

William's head fell and he began to rock his body in his seat. 'It wouldn't be until years later that I had to grieve for the death of Joe Hawkins, and I had no idea that I'd spend the rest of my life grieving for him. Yeah, Tyler, that part I didn't see coming. Maybe I should have gone to jail and served time for my crimes in Houston. If I had known what my life would become, then the events of one night in June 1970 would never have happened.'

CHAPTER FORTY-THREE

The Journal of Joseph Hawkins – May 20th, 1970 (Montmartre, Paris)

From your emergence into existence on the day of your birth, you are granted a simple choice to make: to live or to die. At twenty-seven years old I choose to be on the side of LIFE. However, there is only one way for Joseph Hawkins to live as a free man.

As I looked out at the expansive view from the heights of Sacré Coeur towards Père Lachaise Cemetery in the distance, I made the decision to kill Joe Hawkins in one month's time. It will be my long-awaited Independence Day. William Kendrick will be born from Joe's death as a free man. The door is creaking open, tempting me to step through to the other side. You see, your old life can be disposed of just that easily.

I have pushed my mind and body to the brink of death, solely for the experience of satisfying my perverse curiosity to see what would happen. It made me feel alive, to run wild and not give a damn about the consequences to my actions. Now I am tired, lost in the wilderness with the soul of Joey, the broken child, still cowering inside me.

The last years of my life have made me see that you must stand at the gates of hell before you can enter heaven. There is a certain inevitability to death … but not if you are its master. It only takes one small step through the door to reach the other side.

The time has come for Joseph to emerge from Joe's shadow.

It will break my heart to leave Angela behind, but all that lives must die.

My love once gleamed bright in the emeralds of her eyes.

CHAPTER FORTY-FOUR

A sultry blanket of cloud settled over Paris and a chill swept across the city from the north.

The bells of Notre Dame struck ten o'clock, and William was tolerating a late breakfast at a Bastille café. The memory of last night's red wine dragged through Tyler's head and scoured his parched throat. A second strong coffee provided him slight relief and only seemed to worsen the persistent rapping of hardened fingertips on the table from the man sitting opposite him. While Tyler drained the last drop of his coffee, William paid the waiter and trudged away from the café.

The two men sat in silence in the back of a taxi that rambled northeast along the Rue de la Roquette. A police car raced past with its sirens blaring causing Tyler to sink into his seat. 'Relax, they're not looking for us,' William said. 'You're safe here with me, man, I promise I won't let anything happen to you.'

An imposing stone wall opened like a welcoming lotus flower at the grand gated entrance of Père Lachaise Cemetery, the infamous final resting place of Joe Hawkins. 'Oh, you've got to be kidding me,' Tyler said under his breath as the taxi came to a stop.

The tree-lined Avenue Principale drew William and Tyler into the most illustrious cemetery in the world. A crisp morning mist hung over the intricate tombs, a Gothic masterpiece to the timeless remembrance of death. Tyler stood, half-closing his eyes, listening to the eternal echo of a horse-drawn hearse weaving along the cobbled paths. After a moment, he felt William brush past, hauling his imagination back into the twentieth century.

Along the path, two Japanese girls were studying a map of the cemetery, each clasping a single red rose. 'Mmm,' William muttered under his breath as he watched the two girls disappear around the corner of the Avenue du Puits. 'C'mon, kid,' he said, as Tyler reached his side. 'This way.'

A light chatter of birdsong drifted through the acid-green trees and muffled the low rumble of city traffic encircling the cemetery. Tyler paused to watch slivers of morning light dissipate the mist and pierce an elaborate stained-glass image of a saint emblazoned on the wall of a family mausoleum.

'It was early June 1970 when I last came here,' William said, as Tyler re-joined him, and they continued their walk around the perimeter of the cemetery. 'I spent all day thinking and planning.' He stepped off the path and wove between the graves. 'Ah, here it is.'

'Honoré de Balzac,' Tyler said, reading out the inscription.

'One of the great minds.' William stroked the spine of a marble book that formed part of the headstone. 'Victor Hugo came to Balzac's funeral. Giving the eulogy he said, "Alas, this powerful worker, never fatigued, this philosopher, this thinker, this genius has lived among us that life of storm, of strife, of quarrels and combats, common in all times to all great men."'

'How come you remember that quote so well?'

'I remember it, because those are the words I would have liked to be said at my funeral, about me. My own funeral, from what I've read, would prove to be somewhat more, uh, impromptu.' A frail grimace broke across William's lips as he moved away from the grave and stepped back onto the path. 'I knew from my first visit here that all the greatest creative minds in history were rotting a few inches below my feet: Wilde, Molière, Proust.'

'Joe Hawkins,' Tyler said, with a hint of sarcasm in his voice.

'Yeah, man, good ol' Joe too. It was only right that Joe was buried here, where poets are revered and respected, but that was Joe's destiny, not Joseph's. When my time comes, I want to be scattered on the wind from Los Angeles to San Francisco at a place where there are no shrines or memorials.' Tyler watched William's penetrating stare linger on him for a moment too long before he turned and walked away.

William sat down on a bench under the shaded protection of a gnarled oak tree, lit a cigarette and tipped back his head to exhale a long stream of smoke. 'I suppose you'd like to know how I did it, how I fooled the world that Joe Hawkins had died.'

Tyler gripped his notebook on his lap, remembering his conversation with Doctor Marshall. *"You must listen very carefully, read between the lines because that's where William Kendrick's truth will lie."* He drew in a deep breath. 'Yeah, that's something I'd very much like to know.'

William pointed two cigarette-clasping fingers at Tyler. 'A wave of heat had blown up from the south and settled over Paris for a week. On Friday June 19th, 1970, I spent a normal day with René Moreau. We strolled all around the Left Bank, stopping off in bookstores and talking about an article René was working on for a Paris newspaper about the European heroin epidemic.'

'Did he suspect you were up to anything?'

'Y'know, Tyler, I'd spent so long trying to keep up the pretence with my friends that I was happy, but René saw straight through to the truth that I was a broken man. He kept asking me if I was feeling alright, because two nights before I'd overdosed again, this time in the toilets of the Jazz Palais. I was still in a bad way. I was having trouble breathing, so René took me back to the apartment. I made any excuse for him not to leave me alone. "Don't go," I begged him. "Stay a while for a drink, don't leave me, do it for a good friend."'

'Why didn't you want him to leave?'

'I suppose the reality of knowing I wouldn't see him again triggered a frantic fear inside me. He agreed to stay for a drink but left soon after, saying he had a meeting with a newspaper editor. I watched from the front door as he walked away down the Rue Saint-Paul, pausing to wave back at me, before he turned the corner and was gone … I never saw him again.' William took a pained breath, collapsing forward on the bench into a suffocating cough. Slowly recovering, he wiped his mouth with the palm of his hand. 'Later that night, Angela and I went to a local bistro for a meal. I sat there, feeling numb, knowing these were the last precious hours for a long time that she would be sitting beside me. I wasn't even listening to anything she was saying as we ate, I was processing in my mind what I was about to do.'

'So, for anyone watching, it was a normal night out for Joe.'

'Right, right,' William said, sucking hard on the cigarette. 'It was past midnight when we got back to the apartment. Angela changed into her favourite Indian silk robe, while I put on the record player, listening to The Gracious Dawn's debut album. I was drinking whiskey and snorting cocaine, to ease my nerves and temper my cough. But uh, I knew I had to be careful, because soon my plan would begin, and I'd need to be in control. Sure enough, at two a.m. there was a knock on the front door. I opened it and in walked three men, acquaintances of Eric Chang. They didn't speak a word as they walked straight past me carrying a black body bag and went into the bedroom. Angela started going crazy, screaming and crying, as I stood at the door and watched them lay the dead body of a man on the bed.'

'Seriously?' Tyler asked, folding his arms. 'Where would these men have found a dead body?'

'Well, the night I overdosed in the toilets at the Jazz Palais, I had one final meeting with Eric. He explained that a recently deceased body would be found in a morgue in one of the outlying areas of Paris, where there was a high mortality rate for drifters, someone without a name who sadly wouldn't be missed. It would be easy for Eric's men to get into a morgue late on a Friday night, when there was only one staff member on shift who could be distracted on a cigarette break. The intense heat in the apartment would fool any medical examiner about the actual time of death. I thought the body looked older than me, perhaps he was in his late thirties, but few people in Paris knew my true identity at that point. We only had to fool the authorities for long enough to get a death certificate and burial permit, then I would be free to escape to a new life.'

'That's crazy,' Tyler said, making no effort to conceal his disbelief at the story he was being told.

William struggled to regulate his breathing before he spoke again, keeping his voice low. 'I locked myself in the spare bedroom and stood behind the door so I could hear every word of the drama about to unfold.' He took out the journal from inside his coat and handed it to Tyler. 'Joe Hawkins, America's most infamous rock star, lay dead in his bed.'

CHAPTER FORTY-FIVE

**The Journal of Joseph Hawkins – June 20th, 1970
(Rue Saint-Paul, Paris)**

Life is an illusion, a trick. You just have to fool the right people.

I must take a moment to write these words while I stay hidden in the spare bedroom of our apartment, a witness and a collaborator to my own death. Soon I will be free to escape to my new life, but only when I have held the official proof in my hands that Joe Hawkins is a dead man. There must be no doubt.

At dawn this morning, I heard Angela telephone Julien Gaston, asking him to come and help her. I wish I could have seen the look of panic and horror on his face when he arrived and saw a beautiful piece of macabre theatre staged for optimum effect: Joe's dead body covered in a bed sheet, with Angela recounting our excesses taking his drugs the previous night. It was a nice touch, a sweet revenge of sorts. With my ear pressed to the door, I heard him say, 'You must not tell the police about the drugs, Angela darling, tell them nothing. Flush away everything I gave you.' Julien could not leave fast enough to save his own skin, with his tail firmly between his aristocratic legs.

Then I heard Angela telephone René asking him to call the emergency services. 'My beautiful Joe is dead, René, please come.' She spoke in this child-like voice, as if she was in a complete state of shock. A fire crew arrived first, as they were the fastest responders in an emergency. One of them tried resuscitation but, as far as they were concerned, the corpse appeared to have been dead for hours.

A police inspector arrived shortly after René, and he was suspicious because a twenty-seven-year-old man does not just die. The inspector questioned René, asking what he knew about the deceased. He said that he knew me as Joseph, an American poet and writer, and I was renting the apartment for the summer. I was grateful that he wanted to protect his friend from a media circus, because if the police discovered too soon that I was Wild Joe Hawkins – the criminal hell-raiser and drug addict rock star – they would have insisted on an investigation and the news of my death would have broken that day.

After the police inspector left, René told Angela that it would be best to hide any documents relating to my criminal problems back in America. Angela was becoming more confused and incoherent. I could hear her crying and saying, 'Oh, my beautiful Joe, this is all a dream.' I do not think she really understood what was going on, and perhaps she began to think it really was her old man dead under the sheet.

Now, as the day of Joe Hawkins' death draws to an end, a medical examiner is on his way to view the body.

My new life – and my future – are balancing on a knife's edge.

CHAPTER FORTY-SIX

An elderly woman, carrying a bunch of pale pink tulips, shuffled past the two men sitting on a bench under the mottled shade of an oak tree. William raised her a kind smile and watched as she continued her lone walk along the path towards a distant corner of the cemetery.

Tyler closed the journal and handed it back, angling his notebook on his lap to avoid his patient's prying eyes. *I need to catch him out. William has disguised the truth in the details. I need to read between the lines. He is turning Joe's fact into William Kendrick's constructed fantasy. This is a conspiracy theorist's idea of what could have happened to Joe Hawkins in 1970, a delusional fallacy, an elaborate hoax. I cannot trust anything William is telling me.*

'William, how could anyone fool a medical examiner that the dead body of some homeless guy was Joe Hawkins?' Tyler asked. 'It's impossible.'

'Well, when the medical examiner arrived,' William replied, 'Angela explained to him how ill I'd been, and he could check my health records with the doctor I'd visited in Paris. She also told him I'd complained of chest pains and shortness of breath that evening. He made a brief examination of the body, found no signs of foul play or track marks on the arms and concluded that death was from heart failure during the night. The medical examiner then agreed to a death certificate being issued and said a mortician would be coming to keep the body cold until the funeral.' William stood and steadied himself, before heading away down the path.

'The police didn't send the body to a morgue?' Tyler asked, resting his hands on his hips.

'Y'see, in France, if the next of kin insisted, then a body could remain at home until the funeral.' William faltered, trying to find his bearings in the warren of paths between the graves. 'It was Saturday evening when Angela and René got back from the Civil Registry with a death certificate and burial permit.'

Tyler stopped at the grave of Marcel Proust. The headstone, adorned with fresh white lilies, lustred in the morning light like a storm-beetle's shell. 'Were you still hiding in the spare bedroom?' he asked, jogging to catch up with William who was continuing his lumbering walk along the path.

'When I finally heard René leave, I unlocked the door and came out. I asked Angela if anyone else was coming back. She told me René had gone and a mortician was coming in the morning. I held the death certificate and burial permit in my hands, the proof that Joe Hawkins was dead, and I was now a free man. I collapsed onto the bed and looked at the body wrapped in the sheet, a witness to my own death. Under my breath I made an apology to this un-named man who would take my place in Joe's coffin, but perhaps the fate of being buried as Joe was kinder than being buried in a nameless pauper's grave. I don't know how long I sat there for, but I had to re-focus, I wasn't out of danger yet.'

William released another violent cough that cracked through the depths of the hushed cemetery. Pausing at the grave of Chopin, he stretched out his fingers to stroke the face of an ageless pre-Raphaelite girl encased in her marble prison.

In the distance, Tyler saw a group of teenagers huddled around an elm tree, pointing up at the trunk before walking off the path and vanishing between the tombs. 'What did you do?' he asked, looking away from where the teenagers had been.

'I, uh, went to the bathroom with a pair of scissors and cut off all my hair until it was cropped close to my head, my infamous golden curls falling into the sink like dead autumn leaves. I took out a bag of clothes from the closet and a new pair of boots – Joe's old boots would stay where I had stepped out of them in the hallway. I filled a canvas bag with my fake passport, my journal, the movie reel of our trip to Italy and a couple of notebooks. Earlier that week, I'd gone to a store near Bastille and purchased another Super 8 camera, my other one would stay in the apartment after my death. As Angela lay asleep, I wept as I whispered in her ear that I loved her … I'd always love her.' Drawing in a laboured breath, William sank his hands into the comfort of his coat pockets. 'Then all I had to do was walk out of the door as a free man.'

While William stopped to compose himself, Tyler walked ahead to the elm tree where he had seen the teenagers. Hacked into the peeling bark was the word *JOE* and an arrow pointing left. He looked away as William reached his side and flashed his eyes up at the mutilated tree.

'How were you going to get out of the apartment building?' Tyler asked, following William down a narrowing path leading into the darkest corner of the cemetery, crowded with the forgotten graves of long-dead souls. 'There would have been police and people outside.'

'The news still hadn't broken that it was Joe Hawkins who'd died, so I hoped there wouldn't be anyone outside after nightfall. I slung my bag across my body, pulled a baseball cap low over my eyes and stepped out of the apartment. I waited for my clouded vision to adjust to the darkness before descending the staircase. Making sure no one was around, I crept over to the front door, knowing it was time to roll the dice.'

'Your plan was to run away into the night?'

'I had hidden a rental car, booked in William Kendrick's name, around the corner on the Rue Charles V. I started the engine and drove south, getting out of Paris as fast as I could. Y'know, it was painful to even drive the car, my legs were shaking so hard I had to turn off the road and vomit. I felt like someone had sprayed bleach through my mind, I had just killed Joe Hawkins and it didn't seem real.'

Gathered around a modest grave stood the teenagers and the two Japanese girls. An empty bottle of Jack Daniels was nestled against the headstone, covered with graffiti in memory of a fallen idol. William walked off the path and hid behind a large family tomb.

'That's his grave, isn't it?' Tyler asked, standing behind William. 'Joe Hawkins' grave.'

'Yeah, man, I think that's it,' William said, peering around the side of the tomb. 'Look what the fans have done to it, look what they've done to my grave. It's so small ... so insignificant.'

'What are you upset about, that there are people still coming here to pay their respects to Joe?'

'Respects!' William's voice rang around the cemetery, causing one of the Japanese girls to look behind her. He glared back at her until she dipped her eyes to the ground and turned away. She resumed her task of placing a single red rose on the grave, giggling with the girl beside her. 'And who exactly is buried over there?'

Tyler sighed. 'Joe Hawkins is buried over there, William, as you well know.'

'Joe Hawkins, huh? And which Joe Hawkins would that be? Which Joe Hawkins are they all falling over themselves to be near? Which Joe Hawkins have they come all this way to pay their *respects* to?'

'What do you mean?'

'Do you think the fans come here to visit the grave of a bloated, alcohol-soaked drug addict? Because that's who is in the cold earth beneath their feet, Tyler, not the young wolf, the twenty-five-year-old beautiful rock star in black leather, their fantasy.'

Tyler's mind raced. He had finally caught William off guard. 'You admit that Joe Hawkins is dead, and he's buried over there. Joe is dead and buried.'

'Yeah, Joe Hawkins died in 1970 and he's buried right over there.'

'At last!' Tyler threw his arms into the air and strode back onto the path. 'Jeez, can we go home now?'

'You haven't let me finish my story yet.' William thrust his hand onto Tyler's chest, stopping him in his tracks. 'On June 23rd, 1970, Joe Hawkins was buried in the grave over there. It was the final part of the trick. While everyone's morbid attention was secured on Joe's death, William could disappear into anonymity to live his new life in peace. A diversion tactic, I guess you could call it.'

The teenagers and two girls scurried away into the depths of the cemetery. Now alone, William's hand slid from Tyler's chest, as he moved across the path with shallow steps towards Joe Hawkins' resting place. In the muted stillness of the morning, William stretched out his hand towards the headstone. Falling to his knees, he caressed his shaking fingers along the length of the stone edging, lifting his tear-filled eyes at Tyler who stood in silence at the foot of the grave.

'I suppose I would have liked a poet's tomb,' William said, wiping his eyes with the sleeve of his coat. 'Maybe an open book resting at my feet so everyone would know I was a writer, a great poet and thinker. But Joe Hawkins was buried in the darkest corner, imprisoned by all the other graves, while William Kendrick flew off unnoticed as a free man into the bright expanse of the world.'

'Tell me more about your funeral, I mean, Joe's funeral.'

'A quick and cheap funeral would be arranged,' William said. 'I was hoping that no one would come over from LA and insist on viewing the body or having an open casket. But I knew the one person who would be suspicious in all of this would be Clark Rivers. I can hear him saying to our manager, "Go to Paris, Tommy, and make sure this isn't some mistake or one of Joe's games." From the reports I've read about my death, it wasn't until the day of Joe's funeral when the news broke. Then the rumours started to circulate, and Tommy Seagram arrived in Paris to witness a sealed coffin being hastily lowered into the ground with Angela weeping at the graveside.' His voice cracked. 'All the radio stations and newspapers exploded with the news that Joe Hawkins was dead and buried. I'd fooled them all.'

Tyler placed his hand on William's back, helping him to his feet and guiding him onto the path. 'Why go to those extreme lengths though, so Joe could vanish into the world as a free man? I mean, why didn't he leave the apartment in Paris one morning and do whatever the hell he liked to satisfy this compulsive search for freedom? Why be so theatrical about the whole thing?' Tyler paused, trying to ease his harshening tone a little. 'All I'm saying, Mr Kendrick, is that it seems a bit far-fetched to have really happened like that, don't you think?'

'Don't you get it? It had to be real. There had to be witnesses to a dead body. I had to do all of the theatrics, so everyone knew with certainty that Joe was dead, there had to be no doubt. Y'see, if I'd walked out of the apartment in Paris and into the world, the fans and the authorities would have hunted me for the rest of my life. They would have pursued me to the ends of the Earth, they would never let me *be*.'

Tyler exhaled a lungful of air, tipping back his head as his patience finally snapped. 'Don't you have any idea that all you're saying, all your perceived memories of Joe, is wholly unbelievable to me?'

'Unbelievable?' William rasped. 'You think I made this all up?'

'There's no evidence,' Tyler said, taking a step back. 'There's no proof that what you're saying about Joe's death is true. This is a fallacy, a contrived conspiracy theory because you couldn't cope with your hero, and your obsession, dying.'

'We'll see about that.' William stalked away towards the entrance of the cemetery.

Tyler Rafferty was left standing alone amid the solitude of the graves.

I'm losing the game, he thought.

CHAPTER FORTY-SEVEN

The Journal of Joseph Hawkins – June 24th, 1970
(Northern Greek Mainland)

My name is William Stanley Kendrick. I am a phoenix rising from the ashes of Joe Hawkins' life.

Last month, when I was planning for my death, I had been studying a map of France and saw a private airfield southwest of Paris. I figured it would be the quickest way for me to get out of France, under the radar. When I found the airfield, I dumped the car and saw a guy who seemed to be in charge. I took out a handful of US dollars from my bag and his face said it all, everyone has their price. There was a freight plane heading to Greece at dawn and I would be on it.

As I boarded the plane, I looked over my shoulder at the world I was leaving behind. There was no time for a long, emotional farewell to Joe Hawkins, only a resigned sensation that as one life had ended, a new one had begun. The pilot ushered me to a fold-down seat and, as my eyes closed, we took off into the glow of a beautiful summer sunrise.

And that was the end of Joe Hawkins.

When the plane landed, at a remote airfield on the northern Greek mainland, all I had to do was let William Kendrick walk off as a free man. The pilot and I were directed to an immigration office, which was no more than a hut, and that was the first time I had to use my fake passport … and my new identity. My heart was thumping so hard I thought I was going to pass out, but the officer merely glanced at my passport and waved in the direction of the exit.

I did not look back.

Feeling tired and disorientated, I had no idea where I was or where I was meant to go. For mile after uneasy mile, I walked until I found myself here in the pastoral beauty of the Greek countryside. After spending months in Paris, with the suffocating dense air, there was a clear sensation filling my lungs, summer's sweet perfume sailing on a temperate breeze.

I had not considered how this sudden liberty would hit me with such violence. I have thrown myself out of the speeding car accelerating towards the cliff edge, hitting the ground with such a brutal force that, as I lay stunned in the dust, all I could do was watch Joe's life crash down into oblivion.

On the first night, when I lay under the protection of an olive tree, a pillow of wild moss cradling my head and the hard ground stiffening into my body, I knew that nothing else mattered. I had the clothes on my back, clean air to breathe and the star-filled skies above me.

I have been walking south, keeping away from the roads, finding refuge at night in abandoned farm buildings. I stop in small villages to buy food, enough to keep me going without having to return to civilisation for another few days.

My life had become so stuck within a glass bowl that I had no idea what it was like for people to live in the real world. Reality was something I thought I knew, but it was a lie. When I walk into these villages, I see how people live day to day … I see what reality is. My old life was an utter sham, a reality I did not understand.

I feel ashamed of it.

There is a rising sense of excitement and trepidation inside me. Joe Hawkins is being re-born as William Kendrick. An open road lies before me and today I am the happiest man alive. This is my long-awaited new dawn.

My old life seeps through the opaque veil of my dreams. I can see Angela standing at my graveside in Paris, crying and confused, unsure if Joe really had died that night. I must stop thinking about her, convince myself that she will find comfort with one of her other boyfriends. All I want is for Angela to be happy until the time comes when we can be together again.

I will never stop loving Angela Jackson, my angel of LA.

CHAPTER FORTY-EIGHT

The gentle warmth of the day had given way to a cool Paris evening.

While William lay napping on the bed, Tyler sat at a table in the hotel room and let his pen sweep across the page of his notebook. *William's delusion has created an entire fabrication of Joe's death in his mind. He could not deal with the loss of his idol nor accept that Joe was a mere mortal. There is no evidence that what William is telling me is true, but he knows I have no evidence to prove that what he is telling me is not true. It is all a mind game, and I am playing on the losing side.*

Tyler stopped writing and threw his pen onto the desk. Scratching his bitten fingernails hard into his scalp, he tried to ease his thoughts as he stared down at his notes, trying to find any coherence or evidence of his patient's true identity. Looking across at the man curled up on the bed, still wrapped in the comfort of his sheepskin coat, Tyler knew he had no option left but to play William Kendrick's game through to the end.

By seven o'clock the two men were sitting in the back of a taxi that took them to the enduring twilight of the Left Bank. 'Ah, this is it,' William said to Tyler when the taxi stopped on the corner of Saint-Germain-des-Prés.

'It's a café.'

'This is Les Deux Magots.' William got out of the car, shifting his weight from hip to hip and pointing up at the deep green awning that framed the café. 'This is where every great poet, writer, artist and thinker came to eat and drink when they were in Paris: Hemingway, Wilde, Picasso …'

'Joe Hawkins.'

William winked at Tyler. 'Yeah, man, him too.'

A gilded light fell from Victorian chandeliers adorning the ceiling of the café. Tyler sat on a maroon leather banquette, under the presiding gaze of two statues of Chinese magicians that hung from the central pillar.

'I always thought they were listening to the thousands of conversations that happened here,' William said, 'presiding in judgement over what they were hearing. Can you imagine eavesdropping on a conversation that Hemingway was having, or uh, listening to Picasso describing the extraordinary new artistic style he was experimenting with?'

'What about your conversations, William?' Tyler asked, drawing his eyes from the statues. 'What do you think they overheard when you came here all those years ago?'

'They probably heard me talking to anyone who would listen, anyone who was drinking with me I suppose. People who could go back home to America and tell their friends that they'd got drunk with good ol' Joe.'

The hum of buoyant conversations intensified around the café, as waiters in floor-skimming white aprons glided with balletic steps between the polished wooden tables. William thanked the waiter who placed a bottle of wine, a steaming bowl of French onion soup and a plate of grilled lamb on their table.

'Did you start to formulate any sort of plan for your new life, where you wanted to go?' Tyler asked.

'I needed to find a place where I could spend a couple of days to process what I'd done in Paris. I thought back to the Greek myths that I devoured as a boy. Y'know, I wanted to breathe the same air as the ancient Gods: Zeus, Poseidon and Apollo, now I had the opportunity to be among them, to reach out across history and touch them. I wanted to go to Mount Olympus, but I was going to have to hitch-hike to get there.'

'Wasn't that dangerous? I mean, Joe's photograph would have been on the front page of every newspaper in the world that week.'

William picked at his lamb, before taking another long drink of wine and topping up both of their glasses. 'Sure, it worried me, and I knew I had to be careful. But who would expect me to be in Greece, when a mortician had banged up Joe Hawkins inside a coffin in Paris? So, I hailed a truck on the highway, and we drove south all the way to the town of Litochoro.'

The café buzzed as animated conversations intensified. William raised his wine glass above his head with the air of an aged gentleman, motioning to the waiter to deliver another bottle of wine to their table. Tyler finished the last of his soup, chasing a macerated strand of onion around the bottom of the bowl with a crust of bread. 'You decided to climb a mountain even though you were still disorientated and only had the clothes on your back?'

The pupils of William's eyes engorged in the mellow light of the café, as he rested his cigarette packet on the table. 'This would be my *Big Sur* adventure which Kerouac had tempted me with as a young man. I figured I'd have to sleep at least one night up there and, even though it was the middle of a scorching summer, the mountain would be cold at night. I found a local store where I bought a blanket and a sweater but, when I went to pay, I saw a bottle of whiskey behind the counter. I could feel my heart race and my hands shook. I had to have that bottle.'

Tyler tore a chunk of bread and put it on William's side plate, trying to persuade him to eat a little more. Taking a piece of crust, William dunked it into the bloody juices on his plate, before forcing it down his throat with a mouthful of wine.

'I thought your new life was meant to be a clean start, a chance for you to change once and for all, to kill Joe and all his addictions.'

William ran his finger around the rim of his wine glass while the muscles across his brow hardened. 'My addictions weren't going to change overnight. The need for alcohol would be the hangover Joe Hawkins had dragged into William Kendrick's brave new world.'

Tyler took a heavy drink from his wine glass.

His stomach twisted with a sudden pang of wariness, as his patient was at last talking as William Kendrick and not Joe

Hawkins. However, Tyler felt neither relief nor victory over the man sitting across the table, only the discomfiting feeling that William was saying exactly what he wanted him to hear.

William offered a receptive grin at the waiter who placed another bottle of red wine on their table. 'The path snaked through a dense pine forest,' he said, 'and, as I started to climb higher and the trees began to thin, I realised that for the first time in my life, I could enjoy the sensation of having nowhere else to be. That was the clearest night I had ever seen. The swollen moon illuminated the valleys below and the barren peaks ahead of me. There was silence in the heavens. The sky was as black as ebony, pooled with stars and planets brighter and more beautiful than I could ever have imagined.'

Tyler pushed away his empty soup bowl and watched William refill both of their wine glasses. 'Did being there fulfil your expectations from when you were a boy?'

'Y'know, I think it exceeded my expectations,' William said, before drinking down the contents of his wine glass in one gulp. 'I could hear the roar of Zeus on the wind. I sat for hours transfixed by the spirals of fir-scented smoke coiling into the cold air from my campfire. It was like watching the bitter embers of Joe's life blowing away. That night, on the hard ground, I slept so heavily that the air drugged my dreams, lulling my mind into a peaceful oblivion. I woke feeling the suffocation of my previous life had cleared and my soul could breathe a new, sweeter air.' Swirling the dregs of wine around the bottom of his glass, he lowered his voice. 'When I came down from the mountain, I'd closed the door on my old life as Joe Hawkins, and it was time for me to step through a new door opening in front of me. And that new life had a name … it was called William Stanley Kendrick.'

Charcoal skies smouldered over the soft illumination of Victorian streetlights standing guard along the bankside of the Seine.

The chill on the night air provided some respite to Tyler from the humid warmth of the Deux Magots café. As they began a listless walk through the tight backstreets towards the river, Tyler felt the red wine drown the food in his stomach, sweeping him into light-headedness. 'Did you ever stop to think about the rest of The Gracious Dawn?' he asked, trying not to slur his words. 'Joe's death destroyed the band.'

'Until that night on the mountain I hadn't even thought about how it would affect the rest of the guys, or anyone else from my old life. I suppose I hoped that if my friends knew what I'd done, they'd be happy for me, knowing I was free from the pain my life had become.'

'What about your parents, your brother and sister, didn't you care they'd lost a son and a brother?'

'No, right then I didn't care,' William said, pausing to light a cigarette before continuing his lumbering walk along the path. 'Although, I did feel some sense of guilt about Patty and Mike losing their brother. I loved those guys and never wanted to hurt them. As for my parents, no, they lost me a long time ago.'

The quiet streets drew the two men to the Pont Neuf, stretching over the river to the tree-lined Right Bank. Tyler buttoned up his denim jacket, gulping the cold night air to try to clear his mind. 'We can get a cab back to the hotel if you like,' he said, seeing William struggling to walk.

'I'm fine, kid. It's the only thing that kept me sane … walking and thinking.'

William paused on the apex of the bridge, bending over to release a violent cough crackling from his lungs. When he stood back up, he drew out an open bottle of Bordeaux wine from inside his coat, swathing his grin around the neck and taking a long drink.

Tyler shook his head. 'You really are in a self-destructive pattern, aren't you?'

'And what's wrong with that, huh?' William laughed. 'Y'know, these past few years I've lived with the reality that there's nothing left of me to destroy. Drinking helped me to pass the time, it always did.'

He twisted the bottle of wine in his hands, offering it to Tyler with a glint in his eyes. Tyler hesitated, before taking the bottle and lifting it to his mouth, tipping back his head until the glittering awning of the night sky filled his vision. William nudged his arm. 'I think you're falling for this place.'

'You're right, there's something about this city,' Tyler said, easing his body against the wall of the bridge. 'I guess I'm starting to wish I'd come somewhere like here to study. Maybe it would have done me good to get away from home, away from America.'

'Away from your father?'

Tyler drank another mouthful of wine and handed back the bottle. 'I suppose so. I don't mean it to sound bad, it's just …'

'You don't need to explain it to me, man.'

Tyler's mind wavered, sensing the evening's wine was breaking down his guard. 'I wanted him to notice me again, that was all.'

'I noticed you. I noticed you before we'd even met.' William slung his arm across Tyler's shoulder. 'I'll tell you this, don't let the problems with your father ruin your life. Look what it did to me, it made me a person who was destroyed by his own past.'

William walked away over the bridge, not waiting for Tyler to catch up with him. 'I won't let that happen to you, my friend,' he said into the still night air.

The next morning, a taxi drove north through the rush hour traffic of central Paris, and twenty minutes later deposited its passengers on the cobbled streets of Montmartre.

The morning light ripped through Tyler's bloodshot eyes and stabbed into the depths of his hangover. He dragged his feet around a tight maze of streets, keeping close behind William. Raised voices punctuated the air from crowded cafés, until the streets opened out into a market square, packed with tourists making their final steps of pilgrimage towards Sacré Coeur.

William positioned himself at a table outside a bistro. 'Now,' he said, waiting for Tyler to sit down. 'I want to tell you about William Kendrick's invasion of Troy.'

Tyler lifted a placatory smile. 'Go on then.'

'I never imagined as a boy, that I'd walk on the same ground, feel the same brackish winds on my face as the greatest men in history … the men who *were* history, Tyler. I was walking on the blood-soaked sands where my greatest heroes once stood, on the shores near Hisarlik in Turkey where Troy fell.'

Tyler thanked the waiter who placed a large glass of beer and a bottle of Coke on the table. 'Now you're some sort of no-mad, wandering through all of young Joey Hawkins' childhood dreams, living out his fantasies as William Kendrick.'

'Something like that, yeah,' William said under his breath. 'At that moment, there was no particular place I needed to be – no interview, no photo-shoot, no recording studio – I felt a complete indifference to space and time. I was at the liberty of my own desires, an anonymous hitch-hiker with no future, no past and no present. I was standing on the distant shores of freedom, and I could command the tides. As I walked across the plains and fields for miles, the sun seared my skin with such ferocity that sweat dripped down my arms. Then I saw the remnants of a long-forgotten citadel. When I got nearer, there was a group of archaeologists excavating at the furthest corner of the site.'

'Weren't you scared of being around people, of being recognised as Joe?' Tyler asked, enjoying the ice-cold cola tempering his hangover and quenching his parched throat.

'Well uh, I thought it was worth the risk to satisfy my curiosity, so I put on my baseball cap and pulled it low over my eyes,' William said, pausing to take a long drink of beer. 'There were ten students and an older guy working across a small area near one of the perimeter walls. The older man stood, shielding his eyes with his hand, so he could get a proper look at me. After a moment he came over, brushing the dust and sand from his clothes and introduced himself as Benjamin Porter, an archaeology professor from Oxford University.'

'And how did you introduce yourself, William?' Tyler asked. 'Whose identity did you use?'

'I shook his hand and said my name was William, hearing the name jar in my mouth as I spoke it. Y'know, Benjamin looked at me with an enthusiasm I hadn't seen before, not in my previous experience of college professors. He took off his wire-rimmed glasses and cleaned them on his T-shirt, studying me through his dry, dusty eyes. I watched as he slipped his hand in his pocket, taking out a silver medallion. It had been in the ground for thousands of years, since someone had treasured it with the vain hope it would protect them while Troy burned to dust. That was when it hit me, man …' William picked up a French centime from the table and turned it between his fingers. 'Holding the medallion in my hand, listening to what Benjamin was saying, finally my place in the world had a sense of perspective and relevance. Everything in my life up to that point became so irrelevant in my mind, compared to the men who fought on the same ground I was standing on.'

'Did you feel at ease speaking to this guy as William Kendrick and not Joe Hawkins?'

'No, it felt unnatural, so I made my excuses and walked away until I found the shade of a cypress tree to sit under for a few hours. The next thing I knew it was dusk and someone was calling my name. "This isn't the best place to spend the night," Benjamin said, smiling down at me. "I'm afraid all I can offer you is a hot meal and some good conversation, if that sounds alright?"'

'Wasn't it a bit soon for you to be spending time with strangers?' Tyler asked. 'Considering you seemed to be unsure who this new version of your personality was. Besides, the students would have recognised the real Joe Hawkins.'

William shifted his body on the metal seat, lowering his eyes away from a group of tourists thronging past. 'No, my heart lifted. I was more than happy to sleep under the stars, but the offer of food and the knowledge that I could talk more with Benjamin thrilled me. You're right though, I didn't want to get too close to the students in case they recognised me, but I figured Benjamin didn't have any clue who I really was.'

'He must have been curious why you were there.'

'Right, right. He asked me if I studied. My mind raced – did William Kendrick study? I had no idea; maybe, probably. I told him I'd read a lot at school, and I always appreciated history and literature. I thought it sounded convincing enough and it wasn't far from the truth.'

'From Joe Hawkins' truth, you mean.'

'Yeah right.' William's eyes flared back at Tyler. 'Joe's truth.'

William swigged the last of his beer and slammed the bottle on the table. Scraping back his chair, he walked away from the bistro, struggling to raise his boots from the ground as he wove through the crowds.

The Basilica of Sacré Coeur rose like an ivory monolith at the pinnacle of Montmartre. Tyler drew himself alongside William, who raised his head at the marbled domes and spires puncturing the cloudless sapphire sky. 'Are we going inside?' Tyler asked, taking off his sunglasses.

'Hmm, we'll see.'

'Why have we come all the way up here if we're not going inside?' Tyler asked, as he walked past. 'Come on, it won't hurt you to take a look.'

Entering the cathedral through carved wooden doors, the chill of the nave was thawed by a glow of candlelight from the private chapels. 'Wow,' Tyler said, tipping up his head to a mural of Jesus that engulfed the domed ceiling. A golden halo rose above his outstretched arms, his eyes boring into the souls of the worshippers who stood in awe beneath him. 'You have to admit, it's impressive.'

'Perhaps,' William said, dropping his voice. 'Although, I always maintained it was acceptance and not religion that was the key to life. To go beyond good or evil you must destroy all your previously established values, invent your own commandments. Then you'll be responsible for your own destiny and create the power to be your own god.' William winked at Tyler, tucked his hands into his coat pockets and walked back outside.

Tyler, now alone, moved down the central aisle and into an alcove adorned with a bank of tapered candles. Putting a centime into a donation box, he picked one out and lit it, holding the flickering light in front of his face. Placing the candle into a holder, he closed his eyes, drawing in a slow breath that he swallowed into the hollows of his stomach.

Emerging back outside, he found William sitting on the cathedral steps, studying the tangled slate rooftops and church spires that spread towards the Eiffel Tower on the western horizon. 'This was the real reason I brought you up here, kid.'

'Seeing Paris from this high, it's like you could disappear down there and be anyone and no one.'

'Exactly,' William said, glancing over his shoulder.

'How long did you spend at the site of Troy?' Tyler asked, helping William to stand.

'Only two days. The next morning, Benjamin took me to the top of the ruined citadel. I imagined that Priam or Paris had maybe touched those same stone walls when they faced the Greek soldiers. I asked Benjamin if those great heroes of history felt fear. He took off his glasses, squinted at me, and said, "I think every great hero felt fear. Anyone who stands out alone in the world knows their destiny is to face death head on. It is how a person deals with the fear that makes them truly great."'

Tyler rested his hand on William's back to aid him down the wide stone stairs descending from the cathedral to the city below. 'Do you think you were feeling the fear of letting Joe go?'

'Y'know, during those days, I hadn't even thought about Joe, let alone feel any fear about letting him go.'

On the lower promenade, a group of French boys were playing Run DMC on a ghetto blaster, shouting and joking with each other. One of the boys turned around, pointing towards William before whispering to his friend. William lowered his head, slamming his eyes to the ground.

'It's alright, they're not looking at us,' Tyler said.

'They're laughing at me, aren't they? I can hear them laughing at me.'

'No one's laughing at you.'

William dipped his head lower, letting his hair curl around his face. 'I suppose you think I'm paranoid.'

'I didn't say that. Besides, what are you afraid of, people recognising you as Joe Hawkins? I thought that was the whole point of this.'

Stroking his hand down the length of his coat sleeve, William paced around the promenade. 'This isn't about me being recognised as Joe, this is about you listening to my memories and believing my truth, that's all. I suppose you think this is all lies, and I wasn't there. You think I've made this all up!'

'Take it easy will you,' Tyler said, trying not to worsen William's agitation. 'I'm listening to you, but I still have to work out whose life you were living. You said there were a triumvirate of personalities: Joey, Joe and Joseph, not to mention your demon JoJo. Joey had grown up, Joe was dead and now there's William Kendrick, so what about Joseph Hawkins? Where does he fit in to all of this?'

William grabbed Tyler's left wrist to check the time on his watch. Muttering to himself, he continued a slow walk down the stairs, past a gang of souvenir sellers keen to part tourists from their cash. 'I think Joseph was there all along,' he said through a deep sigh. 'Joseph was the person who Joey and Joe always wanted to be. He was the complete person who all my other characters, my previous incarnations, were made up from. It was always Joseph who loved poetry, philosophy and history, but it was JoJo who took over and ruined everything, even when I became William. I guess, uh, if you want to analyse the whole William, Joe and Joseph relationship, you need to understand that I simply used William's outer shell, his identity and his appearance, but inside were still my own my interests and passions. Let's just say I know how the Greek warriors felt when they got into the Trojan horse.'

'What do you mean?'

'William Kendrick is my Trojan horse.' He paused on the steps, gazing back up at the cathedral. 'I encased Joe's old life and memories inside William, hiding him away until he was ready to break through the loins of the wooden cage and fight his way back to fame and glory. But when that time came, the wood was impenetrable, rotting away with Joe still trapped inside the body of the beast. There would be no triumph in Troy for me, no moment of eternal glory. I imprisoned my mind within a jail cell of my own making. I didn't know it then, but my life sentence had begun and there would only be one way for me to be free.'

CHAPTER FORTY-NINE

**The Journal of Joseph Hawkins – September 13th, 1970
(Rhodes, Greek Islands)**

For weeks I travelled through Turkey, then sailed from one Greek island to the next, living the simple life of a man with nowhere to be.

When I arrived here on the island of Rhodes, I headed away from the harbour, following the vibrant sound of music in the air and the fragrance of home-cooked food, which led me to a taverna in the old town square. I hid behind a tree and watched the place. It seemed to be only locals eating there and I thought it would be fine for a while, to satisfy my hunger. Sitting under the pergola, I was eating a plate of stuffed vine leaves, when an old Greek man at the next table reached over to shake my hand.

My instant reaction was to recoil. I put on my baseball cap and shook his hand, trying not to draw any more attention to myself. Then the man shouted something in Greek and a moment later, a waiter presented me with a bottle of beer, on the house. That was one of the first times in my adult life that another person had done something good and nice for me … and not because I was Joe Hawkins. He had no idea who I was, he simply wanted to buy a stranger a drink. That was a new and very different feeling for me to understand, but right then I had no choice but to go along with it.

'My name is Yannis,' he said in broken English, beaming with paternal pride as he introduced his son, Nikos, whose right arm was strapped in a sling. We carried on talking while the beers kept coming. 'My family have lived on this island for a thousand years. For generations they have fished the seas, worked on the land and raised their beautiful children.' His smile seemed to fade as he studied the stranger sitting beside him.

I could tell he was curious to know who I was, and I had to stop and think for a moment, trying to remember what false story I had already attempted to construct in my mind about William Kendrick's life. I told him I was an office worker from San Francisco, that I did not know how long I was going to stay, I had no plans. The truth of those words drove the sense of freedom in my blood that this was real, and I could do whatever the hell I wanted with my life.

Yannis offered me a place to stay and explained that his son had broken his arm, so he needed some help on his fishing boat. Then the wariness hit me again; this was all too soon for me to be trusting people, when I had not even got to know and understand myself as William, let alone have any time to mourn the death of Joe Hawkins. The night drew on and we drank more beers until the taverna closed. I knew, with nowhere else to stay, I did not have any other choice but to put my trust in this old man.

We all left the taverna and walked down the winding streets towards a white-washed house on the coast, guided only by the luminous light of a full moon. Yannis opened the front door and welcomed me into a modest living room, decorated with floral wallpaper unchanged for decades. An overwhelming emotion hit me so hard that my legs started to weaken. It was a sensation I had dreamed of experiencing since I was a boy. I had come home.

Positioned in pride of place on a round table, was a framed photograph of Yannis taken on his wedding day. Beside him was a young Greek woman wearing a simple white dress, with a garland of wildflowers tied in her hair with ribbons. The pained silence of the man standing next to me revealed all I needed to know; he was now alone, and his grief was still too raw.

I woke the next morning with Yannis banging on my bedroom door. 'It's time to go, my friend,' he shouted. 'I'll show you my boat, you'll like it I think.' Before we left the house, he took a blue fisherman's hat from a hook on the back of the door and pushed it onto my head. As I adjusted it, a wave of realisation swept through my body; I was becoming my true self.

The guiding light of a lantern led us down the hill towards the cobalt depths of the bay below. A Greek flag billowed out from the stern of a fishing boat, named 'Maria', as Yannis started the engine, and we sailed out to sea.

Every day, since that first idyllic morning, we sail out through comforting scented winds, of cypress and wild rosemary, blowing across the water from the parched land. It is the aroma of coming home and I look forward to it when we return to shore. I watch the sun rise, waiting with a patient expectation for the tides and the fish to play their part. Yannis sits with a cigarette hanging out of the corner of his mouth, fixing his nets in a quiet contentment. I always make sure to stay out of the way, sitting on a crate I have positioned at the front of the boat, lost in the depths of my thoughts.

When we have delivered the fish to the local market, I disappear into the hills, exploring the island with my camera. I have been making a series of films, studying the old men who play chess in the village squares, and mothers herding their children to and from school. Then I spend hours swimming out to sea as far as I dare, floating on an ocean glimmering like a million stars exploding in an azure sky, before my childhood fear of being in the open water draws me back to shore.

For the first time in years, I am living a life of simplistic happiness. I am seeing the world through clearer eyes. I look like a hero erupting off the pages of Homer's imagination. My skin is tanned, the blonde hair of my youth is growing back, and my beard is thick and cropped close to my face. I am wearing the mask of an ancient warrior.

I knew, even before I arrived here, that the Greek Islands would be my new beginning, a place to heal my soul and give me the space and time to work out who William Kendrick is and who he could become.

Joe has been dead for three months, but I feel like I have been alive for an eternity. My frustration and anger about my old life, which had dominated my every thought and word since I was a boy, is slowly beginning to fade. You see, when a person becomes detached from their name and old habits, they start to become an inanimate entity. I have detached Joe Hawkins from my life, he is now inanimate, and I am free to become someone else.

Maybe fate drew me here, to this ancient island in the cradle of civilisation. I must be following a pre-destined path, one on which a greater power is guiding my new journey. Greece changes you, being here has changed my entire thought patterns. I always believed that Los Angeles was the home I loved to death, now I think it was just a place where I once lived.

I am convinced this island has some sort of spiritual or metaphysical properties, the island itself is playing mind games with me. When I sit in the hills and close my eyes it makes me forget my name, forget the world and lose sight of the people who I left behind. Maybe it is the deep-rooted sense of history here, but I feel like the wild hills disguise your past and the sapphire seas reflect your future.

Perhaps more than mourning Joe, this will be a process of reordering my mind so I can learn to understand and live with William Kendrick. I am going through another, even more powerful, metamorphosis.

I now have the freedom to live in a pure existence, to become anything or anyone.

CHAPTER FIFTY

Slim white candles melted down the necks of vintage wine bottles on the tables of La Palette café, brightening the dark-panelled walls which hosted an array of paintings by local artists. William scanned the menu, grumbling at the list of French gastronomic delights, while Tyler raised his hand at the waitress and ordered a bottle of white wine.

'My friendship with Yannis was the closest thing to a paternal relationship I've ever experienced,' William said. 'I spent two years on that blissful island, when the day finally came in July 1972, I had to listen to the voices in my mind telling me to leave.'

'Why didn't you feel you could stay if you were happy?'

'I couldn't risk becoming trapped again, even though for the first time in my life I'd found peace and happiness. The day I left, when we arrived at the harbour, Yannis had tears in his eyes. "Goodbye, my friend, William," he said to me. "I wish you luck, and I hope one day you will come back to my island. You will always be welcome in my home." He embraced me so hard it took the air from my lungs. I couldn't look back as the ferry sailed away, knowing that an old Greek man, a stranger, had shown me the life I could live without Joe Hawkins in it.'

Tyler took out his notebook from his bag. 'Where were you going?'

'*Egypt*,' William whispered, running his fingers across the edge of the polished wooden table. 'I stood on the top deck of a boat to Alexandria, like I was Mark Antony storming away from Rome into the obliging arms of Cleopatra. Then the punctuating sound of car horns, and the stench of city fumes, shook me from my imagination, as the boat docked and the twentieth century screamed back into my mind.'

'Why did you want to go there?'

'Well, in my previous life, as Joe, I wanted to go in search of Alexander the Great and now I could do it on my own terms, as a new person. Joe tried to set the world on fire, but did his flame ever really explode like it did for Alexander? I don't know, but I could feel him there in North Africa, *my* Alexander. I felt so close to him, the man who I'd shaped my life and appearance upon.'

'Joe's life and appearance, you mean.'

'Yeah, Professor Rafferty, Joe's life,' William quietly said. 'Alexander was thirty-two when he died after conquering the world – one of the most powerful men who ever lived. I was now twenty-nine and what had I really achieved in my life?'

Tyler clicked his pen and leaned back into the seat. 'You can't compare Joe Hawkins' or William Kendrick's lives to Alexander the Great. It was a different time, a different world.'

'When Joe was alive, all the authorities kept trying to do was extinguish the small flame I dared to hold up to the world. After Joe's death, maybe they thought they'd succeeded … or maybe, like Alexander, my flame would burn even brighter after my death.'

The waitress deposited a bottle of chilled Pyrenean wine on the table. William lifted it with a trembling hand, pouring a glass for Tyler before filling his own glass to the brim. He drank until his breath ran out and sank his body into the seat. 'I didn't want to spend too much time in that great city. I had to be careful as one look from a teenager, even in Egypt, would hit me like a rush of panic that they'd recognise who I really was. One sweltering afternoon, I purchased a map and found the shade of a date palm. I spread the map on the ground and let my finger move across the top of the African continent, all the way to Morocco in the west.' He paused to take another long drink of wine. 'I was enjoying getting lost in the backstreets of Alexandria when I found a guy selling motorbikes. He had a post-war Triumph Speed Twin, it had deep red paintwork and chrome lines that dazzled under the sun.'

'That was the same bike I saw at your house.'

'Right, right.' William nodded. 'The guy spoke a thousand bartering words that I didn't understand and, before I realised what I'd done, I'd bought the bike. Ten minutes later, my bag was strapped across my body, and I was weaving through the labyrinthine city streets into the suburbs of Alexandria.'

The waitress returned to the table with a wooden board covered in carved rare beef. Tyler lifted a slice with his fork and placed it on William's plate. 'Your plan was to ride a motorbike across the whole of North Africa?'

'Yeah, it seemed like a good plan to me, man,' William said, chasing the food down his throat with more wine. 'I rode west through Egypt, never staying more than a few weeks in each town. The desire to get back out onto the desert roads and sleep under the stars at night like a Bedouin was now my all-consuming passion. The smell of those towns fascinated me, the hot heady aromas of sandalwood and spice, spirals of exotic tobacco, it gave me a strange sense of comfort.'

Tyler tore off a chunk of bread and stuffed it into his mouth, watching William pick at the meat on his plate. 'How was your relationship with alcohol by then?'

'Y'know, after my time with Yannis, I thought I had some self-control back, but riding through Egypt, where it was hard to buy alcohol, was killing me. I forced myself to forget that I would murder a man to have one long drink from a whiskey bottle, and not even because I wanted it, but because I needed it to survive. My bones ached all day, my muscles were in spasm and blistering pain tore into my head, splitting my mind from ear to ear. That was when I had to get off the bike and lie down. I kept looking at my shaking hands thinking it was from the constant vibration of the motorbike, but I knew it was my body's withdrawal from alcohol. I'd spent my entire life at the mercy of a bottle, easing my way towards oblivion with no effort on my part.'

Tyler stopped eating and began to make some notes. 'What about your mental state, William, how were you feeling within your own mind?'

William's eyes half-closed and his head lowered. 'I could hear a pride of lions chasing behind my bike, roaring and clawing at me the harder I rode. Phantom voices on the desert wind haunted my dreams, whispers in the night of a siren's seductive call luring me towards my doom. I'd wake and expect to see someone standing over me, watching me, but as my eyes adjusted to the darkness, I was alone and there was only silence and starlight.'

'What voices were you hearing?'

'Fragmented voices, like uh, when someone walks past you in the street, but you only hear three or four words, and those words aren't in any context. I heard voices telling me I had nothing to live for, telling me to kill myself, that there was no one in the world who cared about William Kendrick, who gave a damn if he lived or died. It was a constant reminder that I was alone … so alone. My mind was a motorbike-riding time-bomb.'

Tyler pushed away his plate, tapping his pen on his notebook. 'If you were riding west, you'd have reached Libya. That wasn't an easy place for an American to be in those days.'

'Libya and Tunisia had interested me since I was a boy. The magnificent settlements of the Phoenicians and the great wars of Carthage sparked my young imagination. I never got a chance to go there when Joe was alive, but now I could as William Kendrick. Riding out on the desert road one crystal clear morning, I knew it would be the day I'd cross the border into Libya.'

'Were you worried about crossing dangerous borders with a forged passport?'

William leaned back in his seat and lit a cigarette. 'Yeah, it was terrifying. I sensed a deep, nauseating fear as I handed over my paperwork. It was at those moments I prayed to pass through unnoticed. But, as I'd feared, the border crossing into Libya wouldn't be easy. I rode up to the security gate and stopped. "What's your business in Libya?" the guard asked, as I handed over my forged passport. "I'm just passing through, man," I said. "Making my way to Morocco."'

'Did he believe you?'

'No.' William chuckled through a large cloud of smoke. '"You work for American government, yes?" The guard's hardening face was now an inch away from mine. I told him I was an office clerk from San Francisco. "You don't look much like an office worker to me Mister … *Kendrick*." He glanced at the name on my passport and spat onto the dusty ground. I said, "Well uh, it's been a long vacation and I've been on the road for weeks, so I guess I don't look much like an office worker right now … *sir*." I added the formality with the same hint of sarcasm I'd enjoyed from previous encounters with military personnel in my youth. That deep-rooted contempt for authority never left my side, Tyler, although authority had never looked me in the eye with a glinting resolution to shoot me in the back of the head.'

For the briefest moment, in their short acquaintance, Tyler laughed. 'Did he let you go?' he asked, thanking the waitress who cleared their table.

'Eventually, yeah.' William peeled his lips into a wide grin and sucked hard on his cigarette, the candlelight in the café shimmering in his widening eyes. 'I revved the throttle and rode away as fast as I could, stopping in villages for a few days at a time, always moving on before I risked becoming a familiar face. I rode the highway west across northern Libya, where citrus trees, olive groves and vast plains of wheat swept across the land. Tripoli was a day's ride away and the place I was excited to see was close: Leptis Magna.'

William paid for their meal, leaving the café and winding through the side streets back towards the river. 'Was going there another of Joe Hawkins' boyhood desires that William Kendrick was fulfilling?' Tyler asked.

'It would fulfil all my own desires to go there. It was the most magical place I'd ever seen, where there was no sense of reality. The remains of ancient streets, lined with honey-coloured ruins, drew me to a vast amphitheatre. The acoustics were still magical, just as they would have been thousands of years ago.' William wavered, seeming to struggle with his breathing as he clenched his hand to his stomach. 'As I stood in the centre of the amphitheatre, I heard a murmur on the coastal winds mutate into a roar of voices. I closed my eyes and in my mind I could hear a distant crowd chanting my name, "Hawkins! Hawkins! Hawkins!"'

William grabbed hold of Tyler's arm as his legs gave way and he fell onto the edge of the narrow path, splaying his feet out into the street. Tyler knelt and placed a hand on his trembling back.

'I closed my eyes as the rush of power engulfed my soul, like a hit of cocaine coursing through my body.' William's eyes widened and his knuckles blanched as he gripped harder onto Tyler's arm. 'From the tips of my toes it grew, like a thunderous current, until it consumed every molecule of my being. I could feel him trying to come back, Tyler, Joe Hawkins was trying to return, stronger and more powerful than ever before. I lay on the sand in the amphitheatre, letting the sun scorch my face, until I screamed at the top of my lungs, helpless as Joe clawed and teared at my soul, being re-born in the dust.'

Tyler kept a steadying hand on William's shoulder, as his body rocked back and forth. 'What did you do?'

'I don't even remember getting back on the bike, man, but after ten minutes of tunnel-vision riding I was thundering along the endless desert highway. My blissful dream had become a wretched nightmare that was now ripping me apart. I kept telling myself Joe was gone, that his old frustrations and feelings of entrapment and depression had all died with him in Paris – but I knew it was a lie. My addiction to being Joe Hawkins was too strong.' William's head crippled down. 'My whole existence was one big lie.'

Tyler Rafferty had not slept.

He lay motionless, tangled in the bed sheets, willing the crisp Paris morning to break through the windows. The crackling snores of the man in the adjoining bed taunted his thoughts; he only had a few hours left before returning to America to face the consequences of his actions.

After a brief and silent breakfast, Tyler followed William's lethargic steps along a tree-lined avenue towards the river, where booksellers and art dealers traded their wares. William paused at a stall stacked with hardbacked books. He craned his head towards a translation of Hermann Hesse's *Der Steppenwolf*, the gilded lettering on the spine radiating in the morning light.

A pale flash of colour on his face drained as he reached to pick up the book, turning it over in his hands to reveal the outline of a snarling wolf on the front cover. As his hands shook, the book fell and landed with a thud on the ground.

'Are you alright?'

'Everything's fine,' William said, straining to return the book to its place on the stall. He clasped his hands behind his back, shook his head and walked away.

Tyler stopped to buy two cups of coffee from a street-side vendor. 'Whose existence did you feel was a lie, Joe's or William's?'

'I don't know, man. I was on an aimless escapist journey across Africa, like the great Arthur Rimbaud, but what was I riding away from, what was I trying to escape?'

'You were escaping from Joe. You were escaping from what you perceived to be his life and your own destructive thought patterns.' Tyler hesitated. 'You couldn't deal with living in a world where Joe Hawkins was dead.'

'Hmm, perhaps.'

Like the prow of a colossal ship, the tip of the Île Saint-Louis jutted out into the murky waters of the Seine. Tyler clutched the coffee cups and followed William through an ornate garden at the crown of the island, finding a hidden set of stairs descending to a promenade on the water's edge. A low stone bench nestled under a budding plane tree, offering Parisiennes a place to rest while watching a stream of boats sail into the heart of the city.

Tyler sat and handed one of the coffee cups to William.

'I used to come here pretty much every day when I first moved to Paris in 1970,' William said, blowing across the surface of his steaming coffee and gazing out at the gardens on the opposite bank of the river. 'I liked that you could look into the dirty water and see what your life had become, see how easy it would be to slide under and never come back up.'

Tyler's focus strayed to an elongated tourist boat, manoeuvring into a wide turn around the curve of the island, before sailing back up the river. 'Why did you want to go to Morocco?' he asked.

'Angela and I had taken a vacation to Casablanca and Marrakech back in '68, at the end of the band's international tour. It was like being in another world and I knew I wanted to go back, but uh, Marrakech was where Julien Gaston owned a large estate, so I had to keep my wits about me.'

After they had finished their coffee, Tyler stood and offered his hand to William, who pulled himself up from the bench. The last traces of morning mist lifted over the bridges that straddled the river, flowing into the eastern suburbs of the city. 'Wasn't it dangerous if Julien could be there?' Tyler asked, resting his back on a set of metal railings overlooking the water at the tip of the island.

'Of course, it was a risk. I was sitting in a quiet café, drinking a sweet peppermint tea, and saw a local newspaper on the table next to me. I couldn't believe it but there was a photograph in the paper of Julien Gaston looking straight back at me. I grabbed the waiter, who I knew spoke a little English, and asked him what the article said. He explained it was a piece about how Julien's estate and all the land was being sold off after his death.'

Tyler stood up straight. 'Julien Gaston was dead?'

'Yeah,' William said, resting his elbows on the railings. 'It turned out he'd died of an overdose, chased Joe into the grave it would seem. All that time I imagined Angela had been with him and my heart sank at the thought of her suffering. It also made me feel some sort of relief that the one man who could blow my identity was dead. Y'see, I'd always feared that Julien would put together the pieces about what I'd done in Paris or Angela would have confided the truth in him.'

The two men left the Île Saint-Louis and entered the dappled side streets that stole away from the river. Reaching the Place de la Bastille, Tyler left William at a bar table and threw his bag onto the opposite chair, before jogging around the corner to check them out of the hotel.

When Tyler returned ten minutes later, William slowly closed the journal and finished the last of his beer. 'I felt both apprehension and excitement leaving Africa and setting sail across the

Atlantic to South America,' he said, glancing up at Tyler. 'My mind was in a perilous place, but I had no comprehension that the next part of my journey could have been the end of both Joe Hawkins and William Kendrick – for good.'

A taxi made its way out of central Paris, through the graffiti-adorned suburbs of high-rise apartment blocks towards Charles de Gaulle Airport. When the car pulled up outside the terminal building, Tyler faltered by the entrance, trying to quell the queasiness rising from his stomach at the thought of returning home to a now uncertain future.

A monotone voice announced the flight to San Francisco was now boarding, affording William the opportunity to give the flight attendant a mischievous grin while she directed him towards the back of the plane. Sinking his body into the seat, every rigid vertebra in Tyler's spine clicked into place. He checked his watch. *Twelve hours is enough time to form my notes and observations into some semblance of a case study proposal,* he thought, lifting his bag from between his feet. *I can make this work. All I have to do is convince Professor Kessler not to kick me out of college and persuade Doctor Marshall to stand down the police. Then there's my father …*

Rummaging his hand deeper into his bag, Tyler's muscles began to constrict around his chest. His notebook was gone.

'Is everything alright there, kid?' William asked, raising his eyebrows at the now pale-faced young man sitting beside him.

Tyler slowly turned his head to his patient. 'What the hell have you done?'

CHAPTER FIFTY-ONE

The Journal of Joseph Hawkins – March 19th, 1973 (Palenque, Mexico)

William Kendrick's life has taken an unexpected turn …

Six months ago, I boarded a boat and sailed from East Africa to South America. I figured going by sea was the safest way for me to travel with my motorbike and remain unnoticed. I shared a room in the bowels of a cargo ship with one of the engineers, who did not speak any English, spending most of my days lying on my bunk or finding a corner on deck where I could sit out of the way. No one knew who I was, or even asked. I must have seemed like another weary traveller, hard out of luck and returning home to whatever meaningless life he had before.

I thought being at sea would blow away this tempest of depression, but as we neared the port of Belize, I watched the ocean churning below the ship and saw how easy it would be to jump overboard and let it drown me. At that moment, I had no choice but to accept that Joe Hawkins was now in control of William Kendrick's fate.

I rode my bike west from Belize City, on sweltering forest roads, when I saw the distant outline of a stone building. I left the bike and walked for what seemed like hours. I probably was not that far from where I had left the road, but the disorientation of the forest made me feel like I was a million miles from the outside world. Then, as the sun broke through the trees, I emerged from the darkness into one of the most magnificent sights I have ever seen.

I had found the ancient city of Palenque.

Two vast temples rose into the sky, and around the periphery were smaller stone buildings, their carved walls seeming to radiate the distant memories of that once great empire. Sweat poured down my face from the crippling humidity as I climbed the temple stairs, an ancient hero ascending to the heights of heaven. I sat up there for hours, filming with my camera, until the light began to fade, and I knew I had to get back to my bike. Reaching the road, I suddenly felt a sharp pain sear into my leg, my vision blurred and then my world fell into darkness.

A day later, I woke in a stranger's bed.

Soft light seeped through muslin drapes at the window, and I had no idea where I was or even who I was. A young woman's voice drifted in and out of my mind. 'Try to rest,' she said. 'I'll bring you a drink.' As my eyesight came into focus, I saw her charcoal hair circling down her back as she left the room. That was when the pain stabbed through my body and my chest burned until I retched. The woman came back to my bedside and mopped the sweat from my forehead. 'My brothers found you yesterday on the road and brought you here, to our home.' She lifted the blanket to reveal a large welt erupting from my ankle. 'Spider,' she said, as my eyes shut once more.

I do not know how long it took me to fall in love with her.

She was the most alluring woman I had ever seen. The ancient Gods had carved her face from a delicate Mayan porcelain. 'My name is Lucia,' she said, smiling down at me. I was fascinated with her simplicity: her hair, her skin, no make-up ... it was just ... her. From that first morning, something stirred in my soul, a longing curiosity to know who this woman was.

I lay there, yielding to her touch as she stroked my head. 'And you are William, I think?' she asked, taking my passport from her skirt pocket. My heart raced as I looked back and saw no recognition of my true identity in her eyes.

I was in bed for what I thought was a lifetime, but by the third day I began to feel a little better. Trying to recover my balance, I walked outside and found Lucia sitting at the back of the house washing clothes by hand. We sat talking for hours, as if we were old friends who had not been together for an eternity.

Then, one morning, a torrid river of sadness swept over me when I realised her family would expect me to leave. Lucia must have seen it written on my face when I found her in the kitchen. She held my hands and squeezed them as if she would never let me go. 'Stay, please, William,' she said. 'I'll find you somewhere to live close by.' The moment she spoke those words to me, a universal connection was created that I know will span both our lifetimes.

For the first time since Joe's death, I could no longer deny my physical desire for a woman. I wanted her more than I have ever wanted another human being, even Angela Jackson. My soul needed to be part of her.

One night, when her family were away and we were finally alone, Lucia turned on the gramophone. The humid, raw tones of a long-forgotten rumba crackled around the living room as she pulled me towards her. She danced and swayed around my body, my hands gripping her rounded hips, drawing each other into a tender seduction. I lay her down on the floor, her mouth gently parting into a whispered moan that slipped from her lips as I lost myself inside her. There was silence between us until the next morning, when we woke still clasped to each other's naked bodies.

I have moved into a small dwelling on the edge of the village, and I do jobs for anyone who wants my help. Every day, Lucia and I jump on my motorbike, and we ride off into the forest to let civilisation fade away. We spend blissful afternoons together. She shows me all the places she has known since she was a girl, and we make love in hidden clearings where no one will ever find us.

I never want to leave, but as each month passes the voices in my mind are getting stronger. There is a constant argument in my head. One voice is saying, 'Stay here forever, William, you are happy. This is the freedom you fought so hard to achieve.' Then another, more powerful voice takes over and says to me,

'Go back to America and clear your name, Joe. Can you hear the roar of the audience? Angela is waiting for you … the fans are chanting your name … they need Joe Hawkins back.'

The day is going to come when I have to decide which voice to acknowledge. You see, either William stays here in South America forever, or one of Joe's triumvirate makes the return to America like Lazarus back from the dead.

I will have to roll the dice and decide who will win the game of life.

CHAPTER FIFTY-TWO

The jet from Paris eased its way over the suburbs of San Francisco, descending through a deepening ochre shroud that enveloped the city. Tyler's leaden legs came to an abrupt halt at the arrivals gate. Three police officers were stationed on the far side of the terminal building, checking a clipboard while one talked into his radio.

'Keep walking, kid,' William said, staying close behind Tyler as they made their way towards the exit, trying not to draw any unwanted attention to themselves.

'If you were happy, and in love with Lucia, then why not stay?'

'I should have married Lucia and spent my old age in a dusty South American village where no one would ever bother me again, but love had doomed my fate.' William turned his reddening eyes to Tyler as they followed the signs to the parking lot. 'Y'see, staying with Lucia was William's fate, it was his destiny, not mine. That was not Joseph Hawkins' destiny.'

Amid the vast expanse of the airport parking lot, a red Mustang had been abandoned across the width of two bays, with a section of the back wing hanging off. 'William!' Tyler let their bags fall to the ground and examined the torn metalwork where one of the brake lights used to be.

'Oh uhm, sorry,' William said, leaning against the side of the car. 'I had a little slip-up on the corner there. It's nothing to worry about, man, just a scratch.'

Tyler drove in silence as a dull ache moved up his spine. However, it was not the result of spending twelve hours in a cramped aircraft seat, furious that his patient had stolen his notebook, nor was it the fact that his car had been damaged, it was the recognition that there was little time left before he would never see William Kendrick again. The numbness drew into his chest as his anger and frustration thawed into an unforeseen sadness.

'How did that make you feel,' he asked, 'knowing Lucia loved William and didn't even know who Joe Hawkins was?'

'That hurt me, and I couldn't tell her why I was getting angry, because I was living a lie,' William said, gripping the journal on his lap while they drove south. 'For the first time in my life I felt guilt, that for all those years Angela was back in LA keeping my secret and I was building a life with another woman. I think deep down Lucia knew she had to let me go if she wanted any peace and happiness back. She deserved that, after all she had rescued me when my life was about to be swept overboard and washed out to sea. I knew I couldn't destroy her by staying. The voices were too strong telling me to go, so in April '76 I left, and I didn't even say goodbye. I got on my bike one morning and rode past her house while she was still asleep. I left with a tropical storm lashing down and didn't look back … not once.'

'You hurt her, the woman who you unconditionally loved,' Tyler said as he drove. 'Why would you do that?'

'Like always, man, I blew my life at the most important moment.' William turned his head away. 'I couldn't bring myself to say goodbye to her, Tyler, and I'll regret it until the day I die. Los Angeles was once again drawing me towards its destructive fire. I rode for weeks, hunted by these killer storms. Thunder crashed around me, and I didn't even feel the rain-soaked clothes sticking to my back or notice how cold I was at night. There was a black fever raging inside me, vicious demons were stripping my soul away. Joe was tearing William Kendrick's world apart, like a wolf who knows he's about to be fed and is being taunted from inside his cage. I was haunted by Lucia's face; it was branded behind my eyes. I could see her in the darkness of my mind, crying, calling me back to her. But Joe was too strong, he was a lost child who wanted to go home. He had once again taken over my world and was crushing the life out of me. It was Joe's hands on the motorbike's throttle, pushing me towards America and back into the arms of Miss Angela Jackson.'

'You could have returned to Lucia if you'd really wanted to.'

A devilish glint flashed in William's eyes, as he turned to face Tyler. 'But for me to return to America as Joe would prove I'd fooled everyone, managing to cheat death itself. I'd rolled the dice and won the game.'

Tyler steered the car off the freeway and onto the Big Basin Highway, relieved that there would be less chance of the traffic police stopping him for the damage to the car. 'What happened when you finally crossed the border?'

'Y'know, the moment I touched American soil, I assumed it would be the death of William Kendrick and the renaissance of Joe Hawkins. I would soon discover those were the thoughts of a naïve fool.' William wound down the passenger window and tilted up his head at the redwoods towering above the road. Closing his eyes, he drew in a lungful of the forest air, before turning his attention back to Tyler. 'Reaching the Arizona border, I stopped at a roadside bar and went to the bathroom, but the man standing before me in the mirror wasn't the man I knew anymore. I no longer looked like Joe Hawkins. I, uh, looked … old. My skin was like leather and my hair was starting to recede, it was thinner and a little greyer, very different from the blonde curls of my youth. My beard was long, and I guess the only traces of Joe were my eyes … yeah, man, those tired blue eyes were ol' Joe's. The face reflected in that filthy mirror held a lost fear I hadn't expected to see. When I walked back through the bar, people looked straight through me, as if I didn't even exist. I'd gone from being a man who people worshipped to a ghost who no one wanted to know. Riding west through Arizona and into California, these confused thoughts filled my mind. Was I still the same man the world wanted? Would I be arrested for being a fugitive from my Texas conviction? Had everyone moved on since Joe died?' William wheezed and tried to temper his quickening breaths. 'Stop, please … stop the car.'

Tyler veered the car off the road and pulled up outside a log cabin at the State Park visitors' centre. William tore at the door handle and threw himself out of the car, his body crippling down as he clasped his hands to his knees and vomited on the ground.

'I'm sorry,' he said as Tyler reached his side, 'but I just needed to stop.' Slowly recovering, he pointed towards a track winding between the trees. 'C'mon, son, let's take a walk.'

Tyler allowed William to guide him away from the safety of the road and into the suffocating gloom of the forest. As the colossal canopy closed in above them, Tyler shivered; like the tribes who sought protection here from the invading settlers, he feared you could disappear in these woods and never be found. 'What happened when you arrived back in Los Angeles?' he asked, listening to the rotting leaves and twigs snapping under his feet.

'On the day I arrived back in LA there was a classic Californian sunrise. The city was alight in a dazzling orange glow, and I knew I was home at last. I don't know what I was expecting, maybe the City of Angels would welcome her prodigal son home from his odyssey with open arms, embrace me with her wings, but there was nothing and no one to greet me that day.'

'Did you try to find anyone from Joe's old life?'

'I knew the first person I had to see was Angela, to tell her I'd kept my promise to come back to her. I wasn't sure where she'd be, so I rode everywhere from Laurel Canyon to the Santa Monica beach house where we'd last lived together. I knocked on the door, but there was no answer. Then a neighbour came out.' William's voice stammered, turning to Tyler walking beside him. 'When I asked about Angela, she told me that the girl who once lived there had died of an accidental overdose two years before.' He released a stabbing sob. 'Angela was dead.'

'I'm sorry.'

William raised his trembling fingers to his lips. 'I was left standing, frozen to the ground, my mind spinning. While I was off finding my freedom in some remote corner of the fuckin' world, Angela was dead.' Tears cascaded down his face, choking on his breath between fierce sobs. 'Man, she must have believed I was never coming back. After Julien died too, she must have believed she'd lost everything.'

The giants of the forest dwarfed the men walking with slow steps along the trail. William brushed the palm of his hand against the ridged bark of a tanoak tree and tried to compose himself. 'What did you do?' Tyler asked.

'I got back on my bike and headed down to Venice Beach, trying to re-focus. When I arrived, I saw a guy selling T-shirts and posters all branded with my infamous young face. The world still only wanted the perfect image of Joe Hawkins, they only wanted the beautiful rock star, their young idol. I stood in the middle of the street, stretched out my arms and at the top of my voice I roared with all my strength, "My name is Joe Hawkins and I'm back from the dead!" I opened my eyes and a few people stopped, then they pointed and laughed at me ... they laughed at me, Tyler.'

The calm trickle of a stream, meandering through the ancient woodland, quietened the intermittent hum of passing cars from the road. The forest opened into a circular clearing, sheltering the remains of a long-abandoned encampment. A wooden plank-house lay collapsed under its own weight and the ground still bore the charred scars from where a fire once burned. William sat on the low-hanging branch of a fallen tree and motioned for Tyler to sit beside him.

'What did you expect though?' Tyler asked, listening to the last chimes of birdsong carried along on a light breeze before dusk sank through the forest. 'Like you said, you didn't look like Joe anymore.'

'They laughed at me. They laughed at a tired, broken man claiming to be the great Joe Hawkins they still craved after all those years. Standing there I could feel the blood running dry in my veins, as I realised the only person who could prove I'd faked my death, and that I really was Joe Hawkins, was dead. I wrestled my hands into my pockets, wondering if I had anything to prove my identity. Of course, everything I owned in the world had only one name on it: William Stanley Kendrick. I sat back on my bike, my brain becoming engulfed in a dark cloud of grief and despair that I couldn't see through.'

'What about your friends, or the other members of the band, surely any one of them would have recognised the real Joe?'

'I waited until night had fallen and I made my way to Walt Wilson's house in the Hollywood Hills. I saw the look of suspicion on his face when he opened the front door and saw a homeless guy standing there. I didn't say anything for another minute until he tried to slam the door. "You really don't know who I am, Walt?" I asked him. "You don't recognise your favourite old client, Joe Hawkins?"'

'Did he believe you were Joe?'

'Uhm, not at first. I reminded him about the situation with the guy from my past who tried to blackmail me, because only Joe Hawkins knew the truth about that. I saw all the life drain out of Walt's face when he realised who I was. He fell back into the hallway, letting the door swing open for me to walk back through it again. "You miss me, Walt?" I asked him. He drew me into such a hard embrace I could barely breathe. "The world mourned you, Joe," he said at last, before he released his grip, his tone suddenly changing. "Why did you do it, putting us through hell for all these years? Since you died, do you have any idea what happened to the band? Did you ever think about that, or think about your friends?"'

'I guess he was right about that.' Tyler said under his breath. 'Did you ask him what had happened to Angela?'

'Walt told me that soon after Joe died, Angela returned to LA, when a legal battle broke out over my will. All that time I was away, I thought she'd be in the arms of one her boyfriends, happy with my money until we could be together again. But when Angela died, she was a penniless addict. I would never have done that to her, man, never. I would never have left her to end up like that.' William let out a gasp and tore into his coat pockets to get his cigarettes. 'I'm sorry, Tyler ... she was my girl ... I'm so sorry.' He exhaled a spiral of smoke that seemed to soothe his sharp breaths. 'My world was falling apart as if the air had been sucked out of my lungs. I broke down and told Walt I was sorry for everything I'd done, and it would be best if he never mentioned that he'd seen me. He tried to stop me from leaving, begged me to stay, but I couldn't get out of his house fast enough, the shame of what I'd done to Angela was burning inside me. That night, I rode my bike all over LA, stopping at my old friends' houses. My hand was stuck on the throttle as I hid in the shadows and watched Clark Rivers playing with his young kids, watched Joel Arden taking out the trash, waiting for the right moment to crash back into their lives … but I couldn't do it. I'd caused so much pain and destruction with my death that I had no right to bring Joe back. How would they ever forgive me for what I'd done? No, Joe Hawkins was gone.'

William pushed himself off the tree branch and paced around the encampment, kicking the bed of dry vegetation. 'I knew the game was over. I'd rolled the dice and lost.' Crushing the dead cigarette under his boot, he tightened his arms around his torso against the chill on the dampening air. 'That evening I rode out of Los Angeles for the last time. I didn't know where I was going, all I knew was that I had to get away.'

'Why didn't you turn around and head south, to Lucia?' Tyler asked, standing up.

'Because I left her, I abandoned her. I broke her heart and there was no way her family would ever let me come back.'

'You gave up?'

'Yeah, I gave up. I gave up and said to the world that I'd had enough. If this was how my life would end up, then so be it.'

'You gave up on Joe Hawkins, on William Kendrick so easily?'

William stopped moving and craned his face towards Tyler. 'Like you gave up on your father, huh?'

'What?'

'You blame your father for shutting you out, Tyler, but I think it was the other way around. I think it was you who abandoned your father after your mother died. You couldn't handle the death of one parent, so to protect yourself you shut out your father as a defence mechanism. And then what happens, man?' William stalked around to face his prey. 'He gets disappointed and angry with you because he loves you, but you had abandoned him. That's why you're still a frightened little boy who's scared of his father.'

'That's not true.' Tyler turned his back, slamming his eyes to the ground. 'He's the one who abandoned me, he shut me out and left me alone when I needed him the most. I'll never live up to his expectations. I'll never be good enough no matter what I do.'

William sharpened his voice. 'Alright, if it isn't your father then what is it you're so scared to death of?'

'I'm not scared!' Tyler shouted, his voice ripping through the trees as he turned around and thrust his hands onto William's chest, pushing him to the ground. 'I'm sorry, Mr Kendrick, I didn't mean to …'

William flailed on his back like a wounded beast. Slowly he got to his knees and pushed himself up from the forest floor, brushing dead leaves from his coat while keeping his stare riveted on Tyler. 'Ah, now we're seeing the real Mr Rafferty,' he said in a low voice as he caught his breath. 'I think you need to tell me what it really is you're scared of.'

'I'm sorry,' Tyler said, tugging his hands through his hair. 'I … I don't want to let my mom down. One of the last things she said to me was that I should never accept having an ordinary life. That's why I wanted to study psychology. I wanted to understand people so I could find ways to make their lives more bearable, to do the right thing and try to make some sort of difference in this screwed-up world. I couldn't save my mom, but maybe one day I can help someone else. You're right, though, I'm scared. I'm scared that because of you, Mr Kendrick, I'm going to fail college and let her down. That's all.'

'You won't let your mother down.' William lit a cigarette and exhaled the smoke from the corner of his mouth. 'But the time has come for you to let go of the past and take responsibility for your life. Your destiny is in your own hands, only if you're brave enough to hold it. I think one day your father will see the man you truly are.' He pulled out Joe Hawkins' journal from inside his coat and handed it to Tyler. 'You're so close now, my friend, so close to understanding why you've ended up here. The light is fading on my story, the final chapters of my life are now ready for you to read.'

CHAPTER FIFTY-THREE

The Journal of Joseph Hawkins – May 29th, 1980
(Baton Rouge, Louisiana)

It has taken me years to even look at this journal, let alone write in it. It has remained a closed book, the pain inside me has been too much to bear.

Joe has been dead for ten years. I wanted to hide his life away, neither look at it, nor acknowledge it even existed. If I could not see it or acknowledge it, then it could not hurt me anymore. I can still feel Joe screaming to be released from inside William's prison, but there is nothing I can do. I can never bring him back to a world that still does not understand the person who I was and yearned to be.

I have trapped myself inside the mind and body of William Kendrick until the day I die.

As one year drags into the next, I still cannot bear the guilt of what I allowed my life to become and what I did to Angela. I still cannot live with the guilt that she died without me … she died because of me. I should have been there to protect her. In the stillness and silence of the night, I can hear Angela's childish laugh like an everlasting echo in my mind. I wake to the sweet scent of a temperate English garden on my pillow, my nose buried into the nape of her neck, intoxicated by her floral perfume of roses and hyacinths.

One day we will fly high together on angel's wings. Until that day, my grief remains a breathless sorrow.

You see, the man who is brave enough to walk through the door to freedom will be changed, damaged but maybe a little wiser and more humble in acknowledging his mistakes. I wanted to see it all, feel it all and explore what it means to be ALIVE. I wanted the freedom to push existence to the limits, to see what would happen if I looked into the void and reached absolute zero. But I did not foresee there would be such terrible consequences.

I only discovered when it was too late that William Kendrick would be punished for Joe Hawkins' reckless actions. The folly of an impetuous youth would return to sour my spirit.

I have rolled the dice for the last time and have chosen to live a lukewarm life ... the life of a normal man.

CHAPTER FIFTY-FOUR

At a secluded house in the Redwoods Forest, a single lamp shone from behind the weightlessness of a thin lace drape. A figure moved with hesitant steps in front of the window before opening the front door. 'Billy, is that you?' Adeline Parker's voice called down the path.

'Yeah, it's me, Miss Parker,' William hollered, getting out of the car and approaching the house.

'Oh, I was so worried. I thought I'd lost you.'

He drew her into a tight embrace and kissed her forehead. 'You haven't lost me yet, Adie.'

'The police came here yesterday, knocked on my door looking for you and Tyler.' Adeline gripped William's hands. 'They said you'd escaped from a hospital in San Francisco and that I was to telephone them if I saw you. They said such terrible things, Billy, that you were a dangerous man, but I didn't believe a word of it.'

'And what did you tell them?'

'I told the police the truth, that I hadn't seen either of you.'

'Good,' William said, along with a slow wink. 'Very good.'

Adeline stole herself away into the kitchen, followed by the sound of pots and pans rattling as she prepared dinner. Tyler paced across rough patches of grass at the front of the house. 'I know you stole my notebook in Paris. Are you going to tell me why?'

William sat down on a bench on the veranda and let the hint of a smile flick up at the corner of his mouth. Resting back his head, he closed his eyes. 'I did you a favour, man.'

'How is stealing my notebook doing me a favour? Don't you see that without it I can't write my case study.' Tyler kicked a stone by his foot that landed away into the trees. 'Why don't you understand? You asked me to help you, I broke the law for you, and this is how you repay me.'

'Oh, you can't see it yet, but you will.' William's face softened, as the glow of a blood-red sunset rippled across his closed eyes. 'Before this is all over, you'll see it, my friend.' He drew one eye open. 'I'll tell you this, Tyler Rafferty, you'll thank me for it.'

Adeline reappeared on the veranda wearing a creased white apron. 'It's so good to have you back with me, Billy.' She handed William a bottle of beer and stroked the top of his head. Smiling, she turned to Tyler and gave him a glass of chilled milk. 'And it's lovely to see you again. I do hope the two of you have had a nice time getting to know each other.'

Tyler sat on the bench beside William, leaning his aching body against the splintering timber-framed house. He listened to the trees that creaked and moaned as the forest succumbed to the cooling solitude of the evening. 'Where did you go after you left Los Angeles in '76?'

'I rode,' William said, taking a long drink and watching Adeline go back inside her house. 'I rode north until I ended up in Seattle. I was cold inside. I felt nothing, Tyler, nothing. I needed to keep moving until I could work out what I wanted to do with my life and whose identity I was going to exist in.'

'And whose identity did you choose?'

'I guess I'd run out of choices, fate decreed I had to exist as Mr William Stanley Kendrick. I saw it was time for me to live the life I was unwittingly born to live. I chose to live a normal life as a normal guy. I spent years riding all over America, moving on every so often, taking jobs to keep me entertained, keep me amused.'

'What sort of jobs?'

'Well, I worked at a gas station out in Idaho, stripped down cars in Cincinnati, worked as a janitor at a girls' college in Pittsburgh – got fired pretty quick from that one, hee hee. I even worked as an office clerk for a while.'

'You worked in an office?' Tyler asked, smelling the warming scent of fried pork chops drifting from the kitchen. 'That was

William Kendrick's occupation before he left America, you said he was an office clerk from San Francisco.'

'Right, right. It was time to bring William's life back to where it started … to close the circle.'

'If you really were Joe Hawkins, the famous rock star, how could you walk into a regular office job and fit in? It's impossible.'

'Oh, that was the easy part. I already had a fake identity, fake passport, and fake birth certificate. Faking a résumé wasn't too hard. Bill Kendrick, the office clerk, would prove to be my greatest theatrical creation, he was my masterpiece.'

Adeline opened the front door, wiping her hands on her apron. 'I hope you boys are hungry. Come on in, Tyler, make yourself at home, my dear.'

Tyler followed her inside the house, holding open the front door for William to walk through. A modest meal was set on the wooden kitchen table; an embroidered tablecloth, riddled with moth holes, took pride of place.

'I'm afraid I don't entertain much these days, not since my younger years,' Adeline said, looking around at her ramshackle kitchen. She took a pitcher of milk from the refrigerator and refilled Tyler's glass. 'It's so lovely having a young man to dinner.'

William lowered his hands into his lap. 'God bless this food,' he said, clamping his eyes shut. 'God bless this house. God bless friends who walk into the darkness beside me without judgement, because they have proven to be my true friends.' William flashed one eye open at the elderly woman sitting opposite him, slurring his voice into a deep southern drawl. '*An' gawd bluss Muss Adeline Parker.*'

'Oh, Mr Kendrick, you behave,' Adeline said, giggling into her napkin while keeping her attention secured on her younger dinner guest.

'Are you telling me that after living as the world's most famous rock star, followed by years of aimless nomadic wandering, you were happy to take a normal office job?' Tyler asked.

'It was a performance, I suppose. I put on a suit and tie every day and I grew a moustache, cut my hair short. I was working for a company that insured cars and trucks. Y'know, I enjoyed the numb simplicity of moving pieces of paper from here to there. I studied everyone around me to see how they did their jobs and how they behaved, so it only took a couple of weeks for Bill Kendrick to fit right in. Don't forget, Tyler, I'd seen how a business was run at the band's office back in Los Angeles. I always took an interest in how things worked, and I, uh, always paid attention.'

'What did people think of Bill, the office clerk?'

'I guess people liked him. I made it easy for people to like him. He was quiet, kind, funny, generous and y'know that's all I ever wanted people to see in Joe Hawkins ... those were all Joe's traits. The world couldn't see through the veil of the rock star to understand what I was really like underneath, the real Joe Hawkins who people would never know.'

Tyler flashed a cautious glance at Adeline, who dipped her head back at him. This was not the first time Joe Hawkins' name had been spoken in her house. His eyes widened, turning his attention across the table to William, whose mouth had peeled into a beaming grin. 'Were you ever worried that people might discover your previous life?'

'No one knew my dirty little secret, Tyler. Why would anyone suspect good ol' Bill Kendrick of having a previous life? I created this new character and that meant I could control him. It gave me the power to construct his past, exist in his present and conceive his future. I created stories and memories about friends I'd met and places I'd lived, hiding my tracks as I went. I enjoyed fooling people every day, so no one had the first clue of my previous incarnation as Joe Hawkins. I was just playing the game. I was, uh, always playing the game.'

Tyler looked across at Adeline, who now seemed to be ignoring the conversation, running her fingertips over the worn silk embroidery of a bird of paradise on the tablecloth. 'What about women?' he asked.

William stopped eating and rested down his fork. 'I decided I couldn't have another serious relationship, not after what I'd done to Angela and Lucia. I met women, but I always walked away if things got too serious. Maybe I was destined never to be settled in that way. I knew by then I was going to be a lone wolf.'

'Don't say that,' Adeline said, looking up from the tablecloth. 'Love can come along when you least expect it. I'm sure you'll meet a nice girl, there's always time.'

William reached his arm across the table and squeezed Adeline's hand. 'There's no time left for William Kendrick, Adie.'

'It didn't have to end up like Lucia and Angela,' Tyler said. 'Do you think you chose to isolate yourself, like when you were a boy?'

'I knew that as soon as I got close to anyone it would end in heartbreak for us both, so ending it sooner was purely a preventative measure. It would start again whenever I met a woman I cared about, it was those same feelings I had with Lucia, when I got angry because she loved William and not me ... not Joe.'

Tyler finished his food and thanked Adeline, who busied herself clearing the table. 'If you'd found some sort of structure and happiness in your life at last, why wasn't that enough?'

'It was those same destructive feelings, they kept coming back. No matter how happy I became, it was the old overpowering feeling that I couldn't stay. After a while I was getting a little bored of my life as an office clerk.'

'What do you think had changed?'

William stood and took a log from a pile beside the back door and slipped it inside the rusted iron stove. 'I think Joseph Hawkins longed to get away again, he was getting frustrated having to live in Bill Kendrick's mundane world. Joseph wanted to have the time to think, to write and draw. My passion for poetry was also returning, stronger than when Joe was alive. It was finally time for me to accept my true fate, the fate I now understood I was born to live ... Joseph Hawkins, poet.'

The moon rose into the tranquil depths of the night sky.

Strands of stove smoke coiled away from the crumpled chimney and danced between the trees, the sharp scent of burning redwood tingeing the sweet forest air. On the veranda Adeline took Tyler's hand. 'Goodbye, my dear. I'm sure I'll be seeing you again very soon.'

'Thank you, Adeline – I mean, Miss Parker.'

William nudged Tyler's arm and pointed towards the car. 'Wait for me over there, would you, son?'

Tyler sat on the hood of his car and squinted through the darkness, watching William take a folded piece of paper from the back pocket of his jeans and press it into Adeline's hand. She clasped it to her chest, closing her eyes while William whispered in her ear and placed a delicate kiss on her cheek.

'It's time to go home, Tyler,' he said, ambling down the path before sinking into the passenger seat of the car. 'It's time to close the circle.'

CHAPTER FIFTY-FIVE

**The Journal of Joseph Hawkins – August 2nd, 1985
(Redwoods State Park, California)**

All my life, since I can remember, I have had a recurring dream …

There is a beautiful moon-lit beach. Free spirited young men and women are running along the shoreline with garlands of flowers in their hair, in a state of pure, unbridled joy. During my Joe Hawkins years, the dream waned in my mind, it became lost in a labyrinth of nightmares … perhaps I had locked it away in a dark corner of my troubled imagination to keep it safe. These past few years though, almost every night, I see that beach in the forefront of my dreams. An opulent moon radiates off the opaque waters like a sacred mirror reflecting my subconscious mind. Every night when I dream, the moonlight becomes more clear and bright, as if the heavenly beach is luring me towards it.

I spent so many years trying to recreate myself. I kept ripping off each mask expecting to see my true self hidden underneath, but the more masks I ripped off, the more disfigured I became. When I look inside myself, all I can see are my distorted, fragmented personalities laughing back at me, as if I am lost in a hall of mirrors and my reflections are tarnished and warped. I am like a Russian doll, stacked one inside another, but inside me one of the dolls is missing. Joe is missing, and I feel empty.

I have learned to forget about my past, it serves me no purpose anymore.

In the Sixties, Joe's fame and notoriety cast a long and impenetrable shadow into which Joseph was forced to live. Then the tables turned, and Joe Hawkins had no choice but to exist in the lonely shadow of William Kendrick.

To silence my mind, I had to allow William and Joseph to coexist in some sort of harmony. It became a marriage of convenience where two enemies had to learn to become brothers. I settled on simplicity and maybe that is what my soul had really been craving since I was a child.

At least I have Adeline who takes care of me. She spends hours typing my poetry and she loves me unconditionally, like a mother should love her child. I enjoy sitting out on my veranda at the end of the day, with my dog beside me, having the time to write and to think. I have made friends with the other strangers who exist around here in this lost paradise. We drink together, play cards and talk. Some nights we get a fire going and I sing like an old blues master, tell wild stories from distant lands, always keeping everyone entertained. The shaman has learned, at long last, that he can impart his universal knowledge through a calm contemplation with his other lost souls.

Since Joe died, I have achieved my dream of living in a state of pure awareness. But it has become my fate to endure the life of a normal man and I am still curious to see how much of it I can bear … you see, the game is pointless when there is only one player.

I fear that I will have drink the bitter wine down to its sordid dregs, however and whenever that day will come.

CHAPTER FIFTY-SIX

Threads of moonlight cascaded through the trees along the winding forest road. The overhanging branches seemed to reach out like a mother's embrace to cradle William's solitary house and protect it from the outside world.

William drew out his key from behind the log pile and hurled it at Tyler, gesturing for him to unlock the front door. A contented smile melted across his face as he settled into his armchair, greeting his dog who had scampered into the living room and settled at his master's feet.

Tyler went into the kitchen and grabbed two bottles of beer from the refrigerator.

'Thank you, son, thank you for everything,' William said, drinking hard from the bottle.

Reaching over to a lamp on the writing desk, Tyler switched it on, filling the living room with a subdued jade light. 'For what?'

'For listening, for holding open the doors to freedom for me.'

William took out his cigarette lighter from his coat pocket and motioned to Tyler to take it, waving his hand at a row of red candles that had melted into waxy stubs on the coffee table. 'Do you ever think about Joe's family, about what his death did to them?' Tyler asked, lighting each of the candles.

'That was when the guilt about what I'd done to my family hit me. It was when I stopped moving that I tried to understand how my death would have hurt them.'

Tyler roamed around the living room, twisting his head to look at the dog-eared novels stuffed on the creaking bookshelves. He pulled out a copy of *City of Night* by John Rechy and leafed through it, pausing to read William's pencil-scrawled annotations in the margins of each page. 'Joe's parents lost their child,' he said, closing the book and slotting it back on the shelf.

'I'm sorry for what I did to them, Tyler. I never meant to hurt anyone.' William turned his head away, biting his bottom lip. 'I couldn't walk back into their lives; it was better for everyone concerned that I should stay dead. How could I ever explain to my parents that I'd let them grieve for their dead son all those years? I worked out too late that they had loved me all along, I just couldn't see it. I rang their house a couple of times, listening to my father's voice echo down the line, but I could never let him get past, "Hello". Even now there's a part of me that hopes they would have been proud of what I achieved in my life, proud that deep down I was a decent human being.'

Tyler secured the windows open, allowing a cooling night breeze to billow through the drapes which hung down to the wooden floorboards. 'When did you decide to settle here?' he asked, sitting down on the couch.

'Six years ago. I suppose by then I'd grown tired. I knew I needed to be back in California, it was my home, but uhm, I couldn't live back in Los Angeles again, so I found myself here.'

'You decided to shut out the world?'

'No, man, that's not what I've done. I decided to withdraw from my own reality, to allow chaos to become comfort and to turn crisis into clarity.' William's brow furrowed, leaning forward in his armchair. 'You don't get it, do you? I've found peace. I've lived the life I now understand I was born to live.' He stood and reached over to the bookshelves. Pulling out a stack of bound folios, crammed with hundreds of typed pages, he handed each of them to Tyler.

'I've achieved every one of my dreams, all of Joseph Hawkins' dreams. Like I told you when we first met, the greatest reward is granted to those who have suffered the most. I suffered for a hundred lifetimes and my reward was the renaissance of creativity in my mind. I've written five movie scripts, two novels and a whole collection of new poetry. It's all there, Tyler, my life's work is finally completed. I've created something worthwhile, works of importance which *mean* something. Y'see, that's all Joe ever wanted to achieve, to give meaning and form to the reality he found himself living in.'

Tyler flicked through each of the folios containing the typed novels, *The Wolf of Los Angeles*, and *Dawn's Early Light* by W.S. Kendrick. 'You must have had some sort of anger left over from feeling unable to live your life as Joe Hawkins though? That anger can't just disappear.' He closed the last of the folios and handed them back.

'Right, it never disappeared.' William shuffled his feet across the living room towards the comfort of his armchair. 'I always felt, even to this day, that I was cheated out of being able to claim back my life as Joe. It wasn't fair, it was an injustice I could never avenge. I miss my old friends, y'know, Joe's old friends. I would give anything for one last crazy road trip with Joel Arden or to spend a lazy day walking through Paris with René Moreau. As for the rest of the world, even if people believed my identity, then I'd have to give them back the wild rock star and not the simple poet. That was something I wasn't prepared to do.' William took an elongated breath, gently stroking the edge of his thumb on the cuff of his sheepskin coat. 'Can I ask you something, Tyler?'

'Sure, of course.'

'Do you think the world still wants Joe Hawkins, the man I am now?'

'You want the truth I suppose?' Tyler asked with a slight caution, leaning forward to rest his elbows onto his knees. 'Alright, I think the world still craves Joe Hawkins. Like you said, the legend of Joe's life hasn't diminished. But his legend is that of a twenty-five-year-old rock star, dressed in leather, his words blowing the minds of his audience. If Joe returned from the dead now, the world would be curious … curious to hear how he claims to have faked his death and how he lived his life, curious to hear what he thinks of the 1980s. No doubt The Gracious Dawn would once again sell a million records and play every arena in the world. In all honesty though, I think they'd want to see the old Joe perform, still crave the circus master, the Joe who the world loved.'

'That's just it though, we've all grown up, we've all changed. Those kids smoking dope with flowers in their hair in the Summer of Love are working in an office now, raising a family. I grew up too. I'm not the same stoned rock star who the world wanted back then and still wants now.'

Picking up his beer bottle from the floor, Tyler took a long drink. 'Do you think, after Joe's death, that you ever found the freedom you were searching for all your life?'

'Y'see, the mistake I made was thinking that freedom was somehow geographical. I didn't know it at the time, but I'd been free all along, ever since I was a boy. I started to see that my childhood, which I was so determined to leave behind, was a perfect simplistic freedom. I alone locked myself in a jail cell by creating Joe Hawkins. I am solely to blame for it.' William pressed his fingertip into the middle of his forehead. 'Freedom existed in here all along, man, but I was too blind to see it. All I had to do was let Joe go to become free. I understood, all too late, that the only person responsible for my happiness was my true self.'

Tyler's watch bleeped as the evening swept past midnight. 'Do you feel any regret when you look back over your life, how you thought and behaved?'

'It's taken me years to understand the consequences my actions had on the other guys in The Gracious Dawn, and I wish I could say sorry to them. I'll tell you the truth though, Tyler, I had a good time, and met some interesting people. We played over two hundred shows, and they were a blast. So no, I don't regret anything in that narrow window of my life, it was an extraordinary experience. Looking back now, if I had known what would happen to Angela, I would have cleaned up my act, faced my imprisonment, then married the girl I loved.'

'Have your feelings towards Joe changed now?' Tyler asked, drinking the last of his beer.

William drew in a long, pained breath. 'What you have to understand, Tyler, is that I'm no longer the frightened boy trapped at the bottom of a well. It was Joe Hawkins who reached into the darkness, took my tiny hand and pulled out a broken, fragile child and let me stand in the light.' His weakening voice fractured. 'And I'll always be grateful to Joe for that.'

'I'd like to ask you one last question,' Tyler said, watching William's head sink. 'I want you to concentrate and imagine a world without Joe Hawkins in it. How do you see yourself in that world?'

William closed his eyes for a moment before opening them, wiping away a tear with the sleeve of his coat. '*Hollow*,' he whispered. '*Alone.*'

Tyler stood and draped a blanket across his patient's trembling body. He picked up the journal and sat back down. In the morning, he would at last return William Kendrick into the care of Doctor Marshall and a locked hospital room.

The game was at an end.

CHAPTER FIFTY-SEVEN

The Journal of Joseph Hawkins – March 31st, 1987
(Redwoods State Park, California)

I started to feel unwell fast, and I guess it took me by surprise, but I did not need a doctor to tell me I was going to die. As Alexander the Great prophesied when he faced his own mortality, 'Even the greatest doctors cannot save you from death.'

I knew the lifestyle I led as Joe would catch up with me one day; my recklessness, the over-indulgence, the times I pushed my mind and body to the edge of the abyss. I always thought I would die as an old man, peacefully slip away in my bed one night, but that is now a distant dream.

Sitting here on Adeline's veranda, as the light of another day dies, I see that my behaviour and actions during those years in the Sixties made me immortal, a mythical icon who will never fade. The tragic irony is that an innocent dream of success born between me and Clark Rivers on Santa Monica Pier one perfect summer's day, became a wretched nightmare that would destroy me as soon as the dream was achieved.

I gave people a fantasy they craved, a beautiful, dangerous rock star to idolise, a poet whose words wanted to challenge and change society. I gave the world the best of me to consume for their pleasure and entertainment.

What a terrible price I had to pay to satisfy other people's fantasies.

Tyler does not know why it had to be him, why I chose to tell my life story to a student. It had to be someone with a clear mind, someone who could question me, but not judge me until he knew all the facts. Someone who I could control … a little. Someone who was pliable and who had something to lose in order to agree to come along for the ride.

Make no mistake, I only ever had his best interests at heart. Tyler Rafferty was Joe Hawkins' last chance to do something right and good. I hope he understands that.

My soul feels old, it has lived a hundred lifetimes. To set my spirit free, I must metamorphose again, to transcend space and time, to break through this mortal life to reach the divine. I spent so many years trying to be Joe, trying to create an iconic character, a person who I thought I wanted to be. Letting him go, letting the idea of Joe go, was what I needed to do from the start.

If Joe Hawkins had not existed in my mind, so many people would not have been hurt.

I am sorry for that.

Forgive me.

CHAPTER FIFTY-EIGHT

The air was heavy with the damp scent of a spring dawn when the forest awoke. There was no sunshine this morning, only dense clouds blanketing the trees in a morose gloom. William wrapped his shivering body in his sheepskin coat and was staring through the passenger window of the car when it exited the State Park. 'Take a left here, man.'

'That's not the way to the hospital,' Tyler said.

'No, it isn't. I have to tell you the last of my tale and then you'll be free of me for good. I just need a little more time, that's all I've ever needed.'

Following William's hushed directions, Tyler drove along a deserted coastal road and swung the car into a parking bay overlooking the ocean. A steep path took them down through the dunes and onto a beach that curved around to a headland, shrouded in mist.

'When you became sick, you decided not to fight it, you ignored it?' Tyler asked, standing on the beach and watching a lone group of surfers paddling out to sea on their boards.

William collapsed onto the sand and splayed out his legs in front of him. 'I didn't ignore it. I saw it as a blessing that I was given a free ticket out of this life. I always knew death was an experience I didn't want to miss and here was my opportunity to face it head on. I had no intention whatsoever of fighting it.'

'You didn't even bother to try?' Tyler threw himself onto the sand beside William, trying to calm his temper. 'It makes me angry when I see people giving up on their life.'

'I'm sorry, son.' William placed a hand on Tyler's shoulder. 'I don't want you to be angry with me. I simply need you to understand that this was the only control I had left, to give in to the disease and let it take me away before I lose my mind in a locked hospital room. I want to rest in peace with a cleansed soul, is that too much to ask considering the life I've led?' He looked out towards the surfers who rose and swayed across the crest of the rough water, before turning and narrowing his eyes at Tyler. 'Now, I want to hear something from you.'

'What?'

'I want to hear your deductions about the life of Mr William Stanley Kendrick. And tell me the truth, not some chickenshit you think I want to hear.'

'The truth?' Tyler asked. 'You really want to hear what I think about all of this, all the stories you've told me?'

'Yeah, I think I do. The truth is what a dying man deserves.'

'Alright.' Tyler stood and took a deep breath of the sharp saline air. 'Mr Kendrick, you are a schizophrenic. Your illness has manifested into a grandiose delusion where you believe that you are Joe Hawkins. You've replaced your own life and memories with those of the infamous rock star of the 1960s.'

'Go on.'

'Joe Hawkins died in Paris in 1970 and is buried in Père Lachaise Cemetery. It's his body in the ground that people still go to pay their respects to.'

'So far so good.'

'In your early twenties you discovered that you bore a strong physical resemblance to Joe. That was the destructive seed planted in your mind. Why did William Kendrick have to live the provincial life of an office clerk, when a man who was your doppelgänger was living the life of a great rock star, the life any man would dream of living?' Tyler paused. 'I think you saw Joe Hawkins in the Sixties and you were jealous.'

'Jealous?' William gripped his knees with his hands and rocked his body. 'You think I was *jealous* of Joe?'

'You've suffered from depression since you were a child and that allowed the delusion to fester and grow. At some point you watched The Gracious Dawn play, you saw yourself in Joe

Hawkins, and became obsessed. Your thoughts about him were your coping mechanism, a way of dealing with your troubled childhood and the distance from your parents. The fantasies became so powerful, they were like an addictive drug, masking your pain and giving you a daily high. You moved to LA to live at the heart of Joe's world, following him, watching every aspect of his life – a voyeur, a faceless stranger, watching Joe Hawkins from the darkness of anonymity.' Tyler hesitated. 'And I think you followed him to Paris.'

William dropped his head away. He tugged at his coat pocket to get his pack of cigarettes, forcing one between his lips and cupping his hand around the lighter against the biting wind. 'Oh, don't stop now,' he said, exhaling the smoke. 'Let it roll.'

'Then Joe died and that was your trigger,' Tyler said, striding around William, who remained sitting on the sand. 'Maybe you even had something to do with Joe's death. Perhaps you saw an opportunity to kill the man who you could never hope to be, to put Joe out of his turmoil so you didn't have to watch him suffer anymore – slit the wounded young wolf's throat, drown the helpless spider trapped in the bath. You thought destroying Joe would destroy the fantasy that had engulfed your life, but you were wrong. After Joe's death, you had to start a new life, as a new incarnation of William Kendrick. You had to resurrect yourself in another place, as another person, without Joe Hawkins in your life.'

William released a long stream of smoke out of his mouth. 'You don't believe that I travelled the world after Joe died, you think I made it all up?'

'After you fled Paris, you could live as a man who had at last found freedom from his obsession with Joe. Joseph wanted to discover the wonders of ancient history, to follow the path of Alexander the Great, but that was his dream, not yours. I'm sure William did find love in South America, in the strangest of circumstances, but it was William who Lucia loved, not Joe Hawkins.'

'She fell in love with *me*.'

Tyler pressed his hands onto his hips. 'After all those years away, you had an overwhelming yearning to return to your perceived old life as Joe, because you missed the structure and comfort he gave you. When you returned to America in '76, you didn't know it, but you'd changed. Somehow, the delusion in your mind had become so powerful again that it was out of your control. People laughed at you on Venice Beach, when you shouted that you were back from the dead, because it wasn't Joe Hawkins standing there was it? It was William Stanley Kendrick.'

William smirked at Tyler and flicked the cigarette away. 'Oh, this is getting *real* good now.'

'Walt Wilson did close his front door on a homeless guy because you were a stranger to him. That night you rode all over LA, you didn't approach Clark Rivers and Joel Arden to confirm your identity, because you never knew them. Angela Jackson wasn't your girlfriend, and she played no role in a conspiracy for Joe to fake his death. There was no part of Joe Hawkins' life left for you to live, which is why you rode out of LA and never returned. It can't be a coincidence that Joe never made a spectacular return from the dead. Can you imagine if he came back to take his place, centre stage with the band again? People around the world would pay fortunes to see that for the next twenty years, but there's no sign of Joe coming back, is there? The reason Joe Hawkins hasn't reappeared after all these years is that he's dead and buried. I think Joe was an addiction for you, like the drugs and alcohol that have consumed your life. It wasn't Joe who wrote the journal you so desperately cling to. You wrote every line, a fabrication of a truth only you want to believe in. Everything you've told me is a conspiracy theorist's idea of what could have happened to Joe Hawkins if he'd faked his death. It's the great *what if*, isn't it?'

William skimmed a smile out of the corner of his mouth. 'Are you done?'

'Yeah, that's it.'

'Alright, alright, Professor Rafferty, pretty fuckin' good, man!' He roared with laughter, clapping his hands. 'I said you didn't need that notebook holding you back, I said you'd thank me for it. Y'see, I needed you to learn how to listen, Tyler, and only when you'd listened to my truth could you judge me.'

'I didn't mean it to sound so brutal. Like you said, I can't lie to a dying man.'

'Yeah right.' William sniggered and looked out across the ocean. 'William Kendrick is already dead.'

'What do you mean?'

'He never existed. William Stanley Kendrick was a baby who died in San Francisco in 1942. It was his identity that was given to me by Eric Chang in Paris. William Kendrick is dead because he never even had a chance to live.'

'That's impossible.'

'Anything is possible, you just have to trust me. Haven't you realised that by now?' William extended his hand to Tyler to help him stand. 'You've listened to my truth, and you've given me your understanding of that truth: quid pro quo. That makes us equal in this little … game.'

'A game! This was all a game to you? This is my life. My career is over before it's begun. I've ruined everything for you, and for what?'

'It made you feel alive, didn't it?' William drew close to Tyler's cheek and whispered deep into his ear. '*Alive.*' He took a step back, letting his head tilt to one side. 'Besides, uh, you'd never have stayed interested in me if I hadn't played one or two games with you.'

'Oh, I don't think there was any danger of you not retaining my interest, William.'

'Now, you've had your say, I think it's my turn. Do you want to know what my deductions are about you? What I think about Mr Tyler Rafferty?'

'Alright then. What are your deductions about me?'

William lowered his voice. 'Tyler Rafferty is a master manipulator.'

A sanguineous chill fell from Tyler's scalp all the way down to his feet. 'What?'

'It's you who has manipulated me from the moment we first met. You played along with my memories, making me think you believed I was Joe, screwing around inside my head to pacify me so I'd be compliant with your case study. Oh, man, you kept the beers coming to keep my tongue loose, to keep me talking. You played the mind games and you wanted to win. You are the master manipulator, Tyler, not me.'

'I … I was trying to help you, to do the right thing.'

William smiled, dipping his head into a slow nod. 'I get it, and you've helped me more than you'll ever know. Now you're going to do one last favour for me then we're done. I need something to uhm … quench my thirst.'

'You want a drink?' Tyler looked over his shoulder towards his car parked high above the dunes.

'Yes.'

The strained lines on William's face sank into a soft pallor as he stood alone on the beach, watching Tyler walk back through the dunes and up to the cliff top. When Tyler was out of sight, William reached his hand into his coat pocket and took out the withered hyacinth floret. Cupping it around his nose, he inhaled the light trace of its sweet scent, before gently blowing it away. He turned and walked towards the shoreline, taking off his sheepskin coat and letting it fall into the foaming sea.

Silence welled in the air.

Grey mists hung like the memory of ghosts over the ocean, as the sun struggled to penetrate a thick layer of cloud. William lifted his head, inhaled a slow breath and closed his eyes. When he opened them again, they burned with a fierce determination, the eyes of an eagle hunting down its prey. He strode forward, his face transfixed on the crashing waves ahead of him.

'William, no!' Tyler's scream was lost on the wind, as he dropped the beer cans and ran back through the dunes.

William strode deeper into the water.

Tyler sprinted across the beach and slammed his body through the sea until he reached his patient's side, the frigid water lapped up his legs to his hips and snatched his breath away. He grabbed William's shoulders and tried to pull him back to the shore.

'Take your hands off me, man.' William's stare remained fixed on the ocean's horizon. 'Let me go.'

'You don't have to do this.' Tyler forced himself around to create a barricade between William and the encroaching waves. The water splashed up onto their faces as the current pulled stronger around their bodies. 'I'm sorry. I had to tell you the truth as I see it.'

'Let me go, Tyler.' Tears drowned William's eyes and it became harder for him to keep his balance. 'It's the last thing I'll ask of you. Please, you have to let me go. It's my time, he's coming for me, I can hear him coming for me.'

'Who's coming for you?'

William pushed forward again until the water was high over his waist. '*The shaman*,' he whispered. 'I always knew he'd come for me. I can hear him riding his horse, coming for me across the water.' He fought to stay standing as the onslaught of waves destroyed his energy. 'I will not die in a locked hospital room. My mind is all I've ever possessed, and I won't let the doctors take it away from me.'

'They won't do that, I promise.'

'I don't fear death, Tyler. I'll fall into its open arms, die in the dark water like I nearly did as a child.'

Tyler fought to keep his footing. 'William, please.'

'Everything I told you was the truth. All I asked was for you to listen to my memories … *my* memories.' William clamped his hands around Tyler's terrified face. 'You're right; Joe died in 1970, but Joseph Hawkins lived on for years afterwards. When you look into my eyes, I know you can see the shadow of Joe in there. I had to be true to my own spirit, but the tragedy was that Joseph Hawkins had to live as William Kendrick in order to survive. I was just interested in finding my freedom, that was all.'

'Come back to the beach,' Tyler begged. 'Please let me help you, I have to help you.'

'I was the greatest for a time there, wasn't I?' William said, forcing a fragile smile. 'Everyone looked up at me in wonderment. I was a shooting star, burning in the darkness and exploding in a wave of enlightenment.' Slivers of sunlight broke through the grey cloud and melted onto William's skin, banishing the lines of pain from his face. 'The world should have wept for me, Tyler, the world should have wept for me until the oceans turned to dust.'

'I can save you, William, please.'

'There's nothing left of me to save. You asked me whether I believed in fate and destiny. Well, it was destiny that you and I should meet, and fate that only one of us would survive.'

Staring into the crumbling eyes of his patient, Tyler felt the last traces of energy tremble through his arms. 'Mr Kendrick–'

'It's time for you to do the right thing, to help me.' William gently kissed the top of Tyler's head. 'The time has come to let go.'

Tyler's mind slowly cleared into a calm decision to release his hands from William's body. Fighting against the current, he swung himself around and struggled back to the shore. Breathless, he collapsed onto the sand, clutching his saturated T-shirt to his aching chest.

William turned his head to look over his shoulder at Tyler, his wet curls gripping to his face, as a gentle smile broke at the corner of his mouth. '*Thank you*,' he whispered.

Closing his eyes, William extended his arms out to his sides with his palms raised to the heavens. He fell forward for the ocean to capture him, tossing and wringing his flesh at its mercy, until his limp body floated on the water and was worshipped by a single sunbeam in all its brilliance.

Time stood still.

Death smiled and drew William Kendrick into its welcoming embrace.

CHAPTER FIFTY-NINE

An early summer rain shower fell from overcast skies above the chapel of remembrance, secreted in a peaceful corner of the cemetery. Adeline Parker buttoned up her woollen coat and wept into her handkerchief. 'Thank you, my dear,' she said to Tyler who stood beside her, resting his hand on her arm.

'I'm sorry, Miss Parker. I didn't mean for it to end this way. I tried to save him.'

'You did everything you needed to do for him,' Adeline said, drying her eyes. She opened her purse and took out a piece of paper, handing it to Tyler. 'Billy wanted you to have this when the time came.'

Tyler unfolded the paper and read it. Staring up from his hands, his eyes met the knowing smile of the old woman, who patted him on the shoulder and walked away.

Doctor Wesley Marshall, the only other mourner, offered his thanks to the priest who hurried away from the chapel towards the dry haven of his car. 'Mr Rafferty,' the doctor said, approaching Tyler and shielding him with his umbrella, 'this was not your fault.' He waved his hand towards a path winding through the cemetery. 'Shall we take a walk?'

'I can't sleep,' Tyler said, gripping the damp piece of paper between his fingers. 'I lie awake at night trying to think how I could have handled the situation differently. Maybe if I'd listened to you, he'd still be alive.'

'I think William formulated a plan to die from the moment his illness was diagnosed. He had no intention of dying on someone else's terms.'

'There's something else. Adeline gave me this.' Tyler handed the piece of paper to the doctor. 'That's the death certificate of

William Stanley Kendrick, from San Francisco, who died aged two months in December 1942. William was telling me the truth.'

Doctor Marshall folded the paper and handed it back to Tyler. 'To be honest, I don't think we'll ever know who William really was. He could have had multiple identities during the course of his lifetime.'

Tyler lowered his voice. 'What if he wasn't lying about Joe? What if he really was Joe Hawkins and I didn't believe him? All he asked me to do was listen to his stories and believe his identity and I couldn't do it.'

'Whoever William Kendrick was, he's at peace now. As you said, Tyler, he wanted to cleanse his soul before he died, and you tried to give him what he wanted. Now, there was something else I wanted to talk to you about. Do you remember when we first met, I mentioned a doctor called Fabien Gerard who supervised me during my training?'

'Sure, I remember.'

'Well, he moved back to France to run a private clinic in Paris. It would be your choice, of course, but I hear he has an opening for a summer intern. It could be a useful few months before starting your master's degree in the fall.'

'Really? That would be incredible.' Tyler frowned. 'But after everything I've done, Doctor, why the hell would you want to help me?'

'I can't condone your actions, but when I heard you giving evidence at the Coroner's Court last week, I understood that what you said when we first met was the truth; you wanted to do the right thing for William. You had his best interests at heart, and you were prepared to put your career on the line for it. That's why I arranged for the police to drop the charges against you. I think there are more than enough people in our profession who think it best to play the game with straight dice.' Doctor Marshall shook Tyler's hand and turned to walk away. 'I have a feeling you and Doctor Gerard will get on very well indeed.'

At his Westwood apartment, Tyler packed up the last of his student life. Standing at his desk, he picked up a typed copy of his case study, which he had bound into a hard leather cover.

THE CREATION AND CONFLICT OF TRUE AND IMAGINED IDENTITIES – A COGNITIVE BEHAVIOURAL STUDY OF GRANDIOSE DELUSION

A study of William Kendrick, a patient of Saint Cecilia's Hospital, San Francisco

by Tyler D. Rafferty

He ran his fingertips over William's embossed name and closed his eyes. Lost in his thoughts, the afternoon peace was soon obliterated by the sound of a car's wheels screeching up to the apartment entrance. Tyler did not have to look out of the window to know who it was. *Consequences*, he thought.

'Hello, Dad,' he said, stepping outside to find his father leaning against the side of a pristine convertible Mercedes, his arms folded.

Daniel Rafferty took off his aviator sunglasses and hooked them into the top pocket of his grey suit. 'You know I had to pull a lot of strings to persuade Kessler to let you graduate.'

'I know,' Tyler said, lowering his head. 'Thanks.'

'Can we now draw a line under this unfortunate charade?'

'Unfortunate charade? Don't talk about William like that, you didn't know him. I admit what I did was wrong, I should never have agreed to help him. But do you know what, Dad? William was interested in me, he noticed me, and yeah to everyone else he may have seemed crazy, but not to me.' His voice broke. 'Not to me.'

'Alright, calm down.' Daniel reached out his hand towards his son, before drawing it back and allowing his tone to soften.

'Look, I know things haven't been easy. I know I can't always be there for you because some days …' he paused as his words caught in the back of his throat '… some days the only way I can get through life is to bury myself in work. You need to understand that losing the only woman I ever loved, my wife, is still too much to bear. So when I heard you'd disappeared with this guy, I was–'

'Angry.'

'Yes, I was angry because I don't want you throwing your life away. I don't want to lose you. Why can't you understand that? You're all I have left.'

Tyler released a slow breath. 'You haven't lost me.'

'Why don't you come back home for the summer?' Daniel placed his hand on Tyler's shoulder. 'I can find a job for you at the firm. You'd have to start in the mail room, but it wouldn't be so bad.'

'No.' Tyler stepped back from his father's touch. 'I need some time away from here. I've been offered an internship in Paris, and they want me to start next week. This is my chance to be the person who I truly want to be, Dad, and one day I want you to be proud of me.'

'I've always tried to be proud of you, son, you just couldn't see it.' Daniel began to walk away, but the troubled thoughts that had kept him awake at night for the past week made him turn back. 'There's something else I need to ask you.' Stepping closer, he lowered his voice. 'Please tell me the report you gave the police was the truth. Do you swear on your mother's grave that you weren't responsible for this guy's death?'

Tyler's body stiffened and he folded his arms. 'What do you mean?'

'When I read the coroner's report, there were some inconsistencies about what you told me happened on the beach that day, all of those bruises on Kendrick's chest and arms.'

'Dad, I swear what I told the police was the truth. William took his own life. I did everything I could to stop him.'

Daniel Rafferty inched closer to his son. 'This wouldn't be the first time a patient you were studying ended up trying to take their own life; the incident last year with the patient who was depressed after her husband died. She took an overdose of painkillers while you were with her.'

'I told the truth back then too. I had nothing to do with her attempted suicide, I was only trying to help her. It was the same with William. I tried to save him, and he took his own life. I did nothing wrong.' A shadow sank across Tyler's face as he turned and walked away. 'You just have to trust me.'

Tyler stood at the window of his apartment, his head low, his eyes fixed and unblinking as he watched his father's car speed away towards the exit of the campus grounds.

There was a brisk knock on the front door.

'Rafferty?' a delivery man asked, checking his clipboard, and pointing to a trolley in the hallway which held six large packing boxes. 'Sign here.' He handed over the clipboard and a sealed white envelope.

'There must be some mistake.' Tyler signed his name and held open the apartment door for the boxes to be deposited in his living room. He looked at his name scrawled in large spider-like writing across the front of the envelope, before sliding his finger under the seal and opening it.

Tyler,

Our time together has been short, time passing like winds and waters through the ancient lands, flowing, unstoppable by God or man. Have you found the answers to your questions? Do you have the courage to accept the answers, or the strength to change the questions? Are you brave enough to be true to your own spirit and hold your destiny in your hands?

You have set me free, Tyler, opened the door to the ultimate freedom that I have been searching for all my life. In death, I will find peace, so my soul can live on forever. Flights of angels will sing me to my rest.

Go on your own journey of discovery. Always speak your truth and never let anyone tell you what to do or what person to be. Never be afraid of who you truly are.

Let the world remember Joe Hawkins. On a clear night, when you look up to the heavens, I am a shining star burning bright in the black seas of the universe and in the blink of an eye I am gone again. Close your eyes and my light will still burn in your mind.

I was not crazy. I was just interested in finding freedom. Good luck, kid ... and keep out of trouble.

Joe

Tyler ripped off the tape from one of the packing boxes and peered inside.

A tattered San Francisco Giants baseball cap was nestled between dozens of books from William Kendrick's house. Reaching inside, he took out a copy of *Twilight of the Idols* by Friedrich Nietzsche and flicked through the pages of scribbled marginal notes. He tore open the next box to find a collection of Super 8 home movie reels with a hand-written note resting on top: *The angel has flown on golden wings. His truth lies beyond the grave.*

Clutching the reels, he ran out of his apartment block, not stopping until he reached the college Film Department. Finding a vacant projection room, he spooled the first reel, switching off the lights and watching the white screen fill with a flickering home movie. A dusty archaeological dig zoomed into focus. A spectacle-wearing man, wearing an Oxford University T-shirt, squinted up and smiled at the camera, pointing with his trowel to an excavated trench.

Tyler watched the footage cut to a weather-worn fisherman sitting in silent contentment on a boat, a rolled cigarette hanging out of his mouth while he repaired his nets. The film cut again to a rural Greek village, where two elderly men played chess under the shade of a cypress tree.

Loading the next reel, a beautiful South American girl came into focus, her ageless skin glowing in the afternoon light. She sat on the steps of a village house with her white skirt pulled up to her knees, washing a pile of clothes by hand. Glancing up from her work, she blushed while the camera remained transfixed on her. The footage cut once more, pursuing the young woman deep into a lush forest. Tyler began to feel like a voyeur, spying on her while she danced and twirled through the trees, hiding and reappearing, much to the cameraman's delight. She swept forward and took the camera in her hands, turning it around as a man came in and out of focus. Waves of blonde hair skimmed his shoulders, his cropped beard was thick, and his skin tanned. He turned his face away from the lens, as if taken by a sudden shyness.

Tyler loaded the final film reel.

A young brunette woman, with jewelled green eyes and draped in an ethereal dress, walked through a palatial garden above an Italian lake. She leaned down and picked a pink rose and tucked the bloom behind her ear. The film juddered to reveal a man standing by an ornate fountain, his effortless weight held on his left hip. Turning around with a languid ease, he walked forward and looked straight into the camera lens.

Tyler Rafferty sat in silence as the infamous face of Joe Hawkins stared back at him.

The end of the film reel spurred and clattered through the projector. Tyler stood, enthralled by the frozen image of the man's face engulfing the screen. Stepping closer, he looked deep into Joe Hawkins' eyes.

'Who are you?'

*

A full moon climbed high in the midnight sky.

In the nocturnal silence, Tyler left his student apartment for the last time, and rested a wooden urn and a leather-bound journal on the passenger seat of his car. Driving north, he pressed The Gracious Dawn's debut album into the radio's cassette player and turned up the volume, releasing Joe Hawkins' resonant voice out of the car and onto the desolate streets of Los Angeles. *"Farewell, fragile child. My angel soul who sighed to die. Your time has come to live to fly. Farewell, fragile child."*

A thick dawn mist clung to the forested hillsides of the Big Sur State Park, when Tyler turned the car off the highway and into a parking bay overlooking the ocean. Standing on the cliff's edge, with the urn on the grass by his feet, he closed his eyes and listened to the crashing waves against the rocks below. Taking a final deep breath of the salty air, he opened his eyes and pulled out the journal from inside his denim jacket.

He turned to the last page.

The Journal of Joseph Hawkins – April 1st, 1987 (Redwoods State Park, California)

One more thing …

<u>Do what is right for me</u>. When the time comes and my strength is gone, help me to open the door so I can reach the other side.

It is the last request of a good friend.

With a calm calculation, Tyler tore the page from the journal and twisted it into a tight stick. He took a cigarette lighter from the back pocket of his jeans and held the flame to the tip, feeling the encroaching heat of the burning paper as it turned to ash and danced away.

Tucking Joe Hawkins' journal back inside his jacket, he lifted the urn to greet a tender breeze that carried William Kendrick away into the western sky.

'I see myself as a poet first, a thinker second and a member of the human race third. I hope that my abiding legacy will be a simple philosophy of standing up for what you believe in, finding your soul's freedom and being true to your own spirit. When all this is done, I want people to know who I really am, that I am an honest and decent man. I hope that during this short period of my life I will achieve enough for my name to be remembered … forever.'

Joe Hawkins, *Music Hits* magazine interview, January 1969